The Weiser Book of

THE FANTASTIC
AND FORGOTTEN

TALES OF THE SUPERNATURAL,
STRANGE, AND BIZARRE

The Weiser Book of

THE FANTASTIC
AND FORGOTTEN

Edited and Introduced by JUDIKA ILLES

WEISER BOOKS

This edition first published in 2016 by Weiser Books, an imprint of
Red Wheel/Weiser, llc
With offices at:
65 Parker Street, Suite 7
Newburyport, MA 01950
www.redwheelweiser.com

ISBN: 978-1-57863-606-8

Library of Congress Cataloging-in-Publication Data available upon request.

Cover design by Jim Warner
Cover image: hand-drawn set of old school tattoos © Symonenko Viktoriia/
    Shutterstock
Interior by Maureen Forys, Happenstance Type-O-Rama
Typeset in Mrs. Eaves and Futura

Printed in the United States of America
M&G
10 9 8 7 6 5 4 3 2 1

For Zoltan Illés, who taught me to love a good short story.

ACKNOWLEDGMENTS

With heartfelt thanks to Michael Kerber, Bonni Hamilton, Jane Hagaman, and the wonderful staff of Weiser Books; to Rachel Nagengast, typist extraordinaire; and, especially, to the authors of the fabulous stories in this compilation for the many hours of reading pleasure they have given me

CONTENTS

INTRODUCTION

It is pleasant to be afraid when we are conscious that we are in no kind of danger . . .

—Virginia Woolf

Welcome to *The Weiser Book of the Fantastic and Forgotten*. In these pages, you will find a host of supernatural and weird tales featuring ghosts, witches, vampires, ominous crossroads, houses with secrets, haunted paintings, and more. The stories in this book are old—vintage and classic. They are written in the language of their time, but language has a way of evolving, shapeshifting into new meanings that may obscure previous ones. For that reason, let's define some words to make sure we're all on the same page.

This book contains "fantastic and forgotten tales." "Forgotten" is straightforward: it means no longer remembered; an accurate assessment of some of the stories and their authors; for example, the works of H. D. Everett and Marie Corelli. How many readers are now familiar with the massive literary output of Lord Dunsany, among the primary masters of the weird tale genre? Even something like "The Monkey's Paw"—sure, people are familiar with the title and the basic plot outline, but how many have actually read the original tale or, in fact, realize that there *is* an original tale, that the monkey's paw is not some kind of ancient folklore?

These collected stories are each powerfully evocative; forgotten in the manner of long-buried treasure. I hope *The Weiser Book of the Fantastic and Forgotten* will help remedy this situation, transforming the status of these tales from forgotten to favorite. I confess: there is not a single story in this collection that I do not enjoy, even after repeated readings.

Not all the tales in this book are forgotten, although each one is fantastic.

Exactly what does that mean? Am I telling you that these are all "good" stories? Well, yes, as a matter of fact, they are, but also no: "fantastic" is among those words whose archaic meanings are now frequently overlooked.

Let's look at the dictionary. Three definitions are offered for "fantastic":

☞ extremely good

☞ extremely high or great

☞ very strange, unusual, unlikely

The first definition is not inaccurate, but it's that last one that truly describes the content of this book: the concept of the "fantastic" as something beyond belief or, at least, beyond conventional thought. Conventional wisdom would suggest that many of the events in these stories could *not* occur. And yet . . .

(So as not to keep mentioning it, let's be clear: all stories mentioned in this introduction are to be found within *The Weiser Book of the Fantastic and Forgotten.*)

Should the execution of a witch have any impact on the lives of the descendants of the man whose testimony convicted her? You'll find out in "The Ash Tree," by M. R. James. What is the likelihood that three people, with absolutely nothing in common and nothing to connect them, should commit suicide in precisely the same manner in the very same room on three successive Fridays? That is the puzzle at the heart of "The Spider," by Hanns Heinz Ewers.

H. P. Lovecraft writes in his story "Dagon": *"Once I sought out a celebrated ethnologist, and amused him with peculiar questions regarding the ancient Philistine legend of Dagon, the Fish-God; but soon perceiving that he was hopelessly conventional, I did not press my inquiries."* Recognizing that the "celebrated ethnologist" will resist the fantastic, not even considering the possibility that it *might* be true, the narrator of "Dagon" does not share his tale with him. (That said, many of the stories in this volume, including "Dagon," offer the reader a choice of a conventional or a fantastic solution. Are his the ramblings of a drug-addled mind, or have strange experiences, unbelievable to others, including many readers, sent him around the bend?)

I have had my own share of odd experiences: things that occurred that, by all conventional logic, should not have; experiences that many others might find hard to believe; *incredible* in the most traditional sense of that word. It is for this reason that I do not automatically scoff when people tell me of their own strange experiences.

I am haunted by something said by Betty Hill. It's a simple statement, but it shocked me when I first read it. I've never forgotten it, and it's something I find myself pondering from time to time. Betty Hill, you may recall, along with her husband Barney Hill, are considered to be the first documented case of alien abduction. Theirs was the first case to be taken seriously by a broad audience.

According to their account, on the night of September 19–20, 1961, the couple, together with their dachshund, were abducted by extraterrestrial beings near Indian Hill, New Hampshire. The Hills appeared credible to many people, because they seemed so *normal:* they were a middle-aged, middle-class couple; he was a postal worker; she was a social worker; they were involved with local politics. Their story had to be pried out of them; they clearly weren't publicity seekers. The Hills seemed as if they would be nice neighbors. They didn't seem *weird.* Because they couldn't be simply dismissed as crackpots, neither could their story be automatically dismissed.

Perhaps to enhance their aura of normalcy, to further bolster their credibility, Betty Hill wrote that—and this is the part that haunts me—she and Barney did not believe in ghosts but did believe in extraterrestrial life and travel. Well I've seen ghosts all my life, and that is precisely why I'm willing to believe that the Hills were abducted by something not of this planet.[1] Having experienced something

---

1. This quote and more information about the Hills may be found in *The Weiser Field Guide to the Paranormal,* by Judith Joyce; Weiser Books, San Francisco, 2010.

completely out of this world, how does one automatically reject someone else's strange story?

The stories in this book are among the best weird tales, which means they make us *think*. They introduce and explore *possibilities:* things that perhaps *could* happen. They encourage our minds to venture beyond the mundane into the realm of the fantastic, to question and redefine reality. In an interview for *Weird Fiction Review*, author Neil Gaiman describes weird fiction as "like a visit to a strange place . . . a holiday in unearthly beauty and oddness, from which you may not always safely return."[2]

Many of the stories in our collection have to do with death, the greatest mystery of all; not necessarily dying or even what to expect in the afterlife, rather these tales explore the relationship between the dead and the living, although whether this relationship is contentious, friendly, or mutually beneficial varies. In Oscar Wilde's story "The Canterville Ghost," the heroine says that the eponymous ghost made her "see what Life is, and what Death signifies, and why Love is stronger than both."

But the genre of the weird isn't limited to ghost stories. Other great mysteries of our universe are also explored: ancient civilizations and what they've left behind and how this impacts us, the realm of spirits, as well as experiences that we may currently be unable to accurately categorize. Weird tales reflect the reality that we live in a world of wonders: weird and wonderful, as the old saying goes.

Some of these stories explore the potential supernatural power inherent in words and objects; for example, a book that, if read, shatters the very sanity of its readers (R. W. Chambers's "The Yellow Sign"). Artists and portraits feature in several stories, including "The Yellow Sign." When the art of photography first emerged in the 19th century, many people feared being photographed, afraid that bits of their soul or their vital essence would be stolen in the process, leaving

---

2 "Exclusive Interview: Neil Gaiman on The Weird," *Weird Fiction Review*, November 1, 2011 *http://weirdfictionreview.com/2011/11/exclusive-interview-neil-gaiman-on-the-weird/*.

them debilitated, devitalized, and endangered. Was Edgar Allan Poe cognizant of this fear while writing "The Oval Portrait"?

It's not only portraits that potentially cause anxiety. Sellers on eBay and similar auction sites frequently advertise objects like rings, boxes, talismans, and dolls purporting to contain genies or the trapped souls of powerful magicians who will allegedly do your bidding. Consider the implications. If a powerful magician or a supernatural entity can be enslaved in this manner, what about the rest of us? Is it even possible for one's essence to somehow be captured and contained in an object, trapped and at the mercy of another? That's among the themes of Arthur Machen's complex story, "The Inmost Light." Many of these tales leave us with mysteries that will keep us pondering long after the story has been read.

Fantastic tales are frequently referred to as weird tales. Technically, they fall into the literary genre of weird fiction. Academia has now further classified weird fiction as a subgenre of speculative fiction, defined as any literary fiction containing elements, characters, plots, or settings deriving from speculative sources, as in the human imagination, as opposed to being based on everyday life or "reality." Science fiction, horror, and fantasy are all categorized under the speculative fiction umbrella. To me, there is an inherent flaw in this particular system of literary classification. Whose reality sets the standard? Whose everyday life? I suspect that my reality and your reality and Betty Hill's reality may not all be precisely the same, although clearly we share commonalities. I prefer calling it weird fiction, especially because of the complexity and history of the word "weird."

Like "fantastic," "weird" is a word with both modern and archaic connotations. Should you survey a group of random people and ask them to define the word "weird" for you, most will likely suggest that "weird" means strange or odd. This now most common interpretation of the word "weird" is fairly modern. It is only since the early 20th century that "weird" has been applied to everyday situations. ("He sounded weird when he spoke to me," for example, or "What a weird ring tone!") Previously, the word intimated something supernatural in nature or portentous. In fact, the word "weird" has a long, complex, and *weird* history!

The word has its roots in Norse mythology among the Norns, a trio of fate goddesses. According to Norse myth, the Norns, three wise women, are the most powerful of all beings: they determine the destiny of everything that lives. The Norns are the repository of all knowledge: past, present, and future. They are three sisters who operate together as a unit.

- Urd, the eldest sister, is the Norn of the past.

- Verdandi, the middle sister, is the Norn of the present.

- Skuld, the youngest sister, is the Norn of what shall be.

The Norns live together in a beautiful hall beside the Well of Urd, essentially the Well of Destiny, which is situated beside Yggdrasil, the world tree—a giant, eternally green ash tree. (Coincidentally, M. R. James's story "The Ash Tree" explores the influence of past events upon the present and how fate can be changed.) The Well of Urd waters the roots of the world tree; rain that drips from its leaves falls back into the Well of Urd. As the name indicates, the Well of Urd is most closely associated with the Norn of the Past. One could interpret this as indicating how much the actions and events of the past nourish the present and future, determining what sort of fruit will be borne, a theme implicit in so many weird stories.

Our fantastic tales are intended as entertainment; rarely heavy handed, they are instead fun or suspenseful or pleasantly scary— thrillers and chillers. Keep the implications of the Well of Urd in mind, however, and you may recognize a subtle current that runs thematically through these tales.

In Norse cosmology, Yggdrasil is the *axis mundi* that unites all worlds. The world of living humanity, the world of the dead, and the worlds of the deities and other spiritual entities may all be accessed via the trunk and branches of this world tree. (Norse cosmology recognizes nine such worlds.) In other words, all these realms, even though distinct, are also all interconnected. Anything that happens to one part of the tree, whether accidentally or intentionally, potentially affects another. The Norns are the caretakers of the well and the tree, hence the world.

The Norns are spinning goddesses. They weave the Web of Urd, the matrix of fate. The Old English variant of the word "urd" is *wyrd,* which eventually evolved into our modern spelling, *weird.* The Anglo-Saxon variant of the Norns, known as the Weird Sisters, spin the Web of Wyrd. This web is the reminder that the actions of the past and present impact the future and perhaps vice versa.

By the 16th century, the word *weird* was extinct in the English language, although it survived in Scots. When William Shakespeare wrote *Macbeth,* his Scottish play, he reintroduced the word with his trio of witches, named after the Weird Sisters. (Coincidentally, *norn* is an Old Norse word meaning "a witch or a practitioner of the magical arts.") Shakespeare used "weird" as an atmospheric, ambient word. The modern connotation of *weird* as something uncanny derives from Shakespeare's era and after.

Let's take another look at that dictionary to make sure we understand the true and complete concept of weird. Here are some meanings:

1. connected with fate or destiny; able to influence fate

2. of or pertaining to witches or witchcraft; supernatural; unearthly; suggestive of witches, witchcraft, or unearthliness; wild; uncanny

3. having supernatural or preternatural power

4. having an unusually strange character or behavior

5. deviating from the normal; bizarre

6. (archaic) of or pertaining to the Fates

Unless they are already metaphysically minded, most random modern people asked to define "weird" would probably think of the fourth and fifth definitions, but what of the authors of classic weird fiction? Which definitions did they have in mind as they wrote? These are other mysteries to ponder rather than answer definitively or, at least, not in this brief space. The subject of the orientation of the finest writers of weird fiction—the world views of the masters—has been the subject of bitter, contentious debate for decades and will probably remain so. This is especially true for author H. P. Lovecraft, whose many devotees argue about the nature of his fictional creations. Just how fictional are they, in other words?

Although he didn't invent it—the term was used previously—H. P. Lovecraft is credited with popularizing the name "weird fiction." Lovecraft was not only a spinner of weird tales; he was a lover, scholar, and *definer* of the genre. In this, he was a member of a very small minority. Even now, the weird fiction and fantastic tale genres receive little critical respect, although this is changing. Slowly, more and more university conferences and symposia are dedicated to weird tales and supernatural fiction, but this was not always so—quite the contrary.

In Lovecraft's day, weird fiction was relegated to pulp magazines, like *Weird Tales* or *Uncanny Stories.* If you think comic books get little respect, the pulps received even less. The entire genre of weird fiction was considered disreputable, disposable, rubbish, trash. H. P. Lovecraft, along with a few others, disagreed.

Lovecraft, who had been raised on *The Arabian Nights,* which he loved, recognized the inherent power of the best weird stories. He devoted the same kind of attention to them that others give to what are conventionally considered more scholarly subjects. Lovecraft laid the groundwork for the appreciation and reappraisal of weird fiction. He believed it to be worthy of respect, analysis, and study.

In his lengthy essay, "Supernatural Horror in Literature," which was written and revised over a period of several years, Lovecraft named the four authors he deemed to be the "modern masters" of supernatural horror: Lord Dunsany, Algernon Blackwood, M. R. James, and Arthur Machen. All four are represented by stories in *The Weiser Book of the Fantastic and Forgotten,* as is Lovecraft himself, both on his own and in collaboration with his wife, Sonia Greene. Lovecraft is the only author represented in this book by more than one title, but general Lovecraftian scholarship suggests that Greene wrote the bulk of "The Horror at Martin's Beach," while Lovecraft revised and enhanced the initial tale. There are those who disagree with that assessment, however, and it may never be possible for this to be definitively determined.

Paradoxically, because stories intended to serve as popular entertainment have historically garnered so little respect, they have served as repositories for otherwise hidden wisdom. If information is important, we wish to share it or at least preserve it. What if by doing so, however, we put ourselves and others in jeopardy? For centuries, millennia perhaps, bits of suppressed spiritual, magical, and shamanic knowledge has hidden in plain sight within folklore and fairy tales. Instead of being presented directly, the information has been passed on in an oblique fashion via storytelling.

It is not even necessary to travel that far back in history to consider this practice. Until 1951, when the last law against witchcraft was repealed in the United Kingdom, it was illegal to publish books that in any way advocated the practice of witchcraft. Gerald Gardner, founder of modern Wicca, is credited with authoring the first factual book in English about the practice of witchcraft, written by a self-professed practitioner. His *Witchcraft Today* was published in 1954.

Before the repeal of the Witchcraft Act of 1604, should an author wish to share magical wisdom—or anything that could potentially be interpreted as promoting witchcraft—the way to get around the law was to present the information as fiction, typically in the form of a novel. Gardner himself wrote such a novel, publishing *High Magic's Aid* in 1949. Dion Fortune, author of "Blood Lust," is best known for her six romantic novels, including *The Sea Priestess* and *The Goat Foot God*. These may be enjoyed merely as fiction; however, Fortune, a true adept, sidestepped the witchcraft laws by presenting esoteric instructional material in the form of these novels. Material in her novels have since been incorporated into Wiccan and Neo-Pagan rituals.

Essentially, stories, whether folktales or popular novels, were not considered worthy of surveillance, so the information contained within them could slip beneath the radar. Exceptions exist, of course. Medieval Russian church leaders, recognizing the subversive potential of stories, especially those told within women's spinning circles, included injunctions against storytelling amid various antiwitchcraft and anti-Paganism laws.

A good story is the perfect hiding place for information that one may, for one reason or another, be otherwise unable to share more overtly. Popular stories tend to be static, repeated the same way over and over again. This may just be human nature. Consider the ability of small children to detect the tiniest deviation in the telling of a favorite bedtime story. Likewise, consider W. W. Jacobs's story, "The Monkey's Paw"—even those who haven't read the story, who may have only seen parody versions, know the rough outline of the tale and its message to be careful of what you wish for.

The prime example of this phenomenon lies in fairy tales. Many, although not all, fairy tales are loaded with references to ancient and once-forbidden Pagan practices. There are clues to this content, if only one knows where to look or rather what to listen for, as these stories were originally not read but told out loud. Look for references to spinning, for instance, as with the spindle in the story "Sleeping Beauty." These are often oblique references to the ancient veneration of fairies and the goddesses of fate from whom they derive. (The word *fairy* derives from the same linguistic roots as *fate*. This is more obvious in Italian, where the word for fairy is *fata*, as in Fata Morgana: Fairy Morgan.) In the Brothers Grimm fairy tale "Mother Holle," a girl sent to sit beside a well and spin inadvertently discovers that dropping her spindle into the well opens a portal to another dimension. Those of an esoteric bent would suggest that that story, named for a Germanic goddess, contains vestigial shamanic lore.

All this said, however, after several generations of the telling of a tale, these hidden gems are easily distorted or forgotten. Information not presented explicitly is easily lost, so even if the hidden references survive, listeners may lack the ability to recognize or interpret them.

It is appropriate for stories to serve as repositories for arcane knowledge. In many cultures, storytelling is considered a sacred art, potentially as mystical as divination. Spiritual traditions are taught through storytelling—consider mythology or Bible stories. In some traditions, storytelling is a healer's art. Ghosts and restless spirits are reputedly soothed by stories in the manner of tired children. A method of allaying temperamental djinn, for example, is to catch their interest by telling exciting or suspenseful stories. Lured by the narrative, they will become at least temporarily peaceful and distracted from the trouble they had intended to cause.

Winter, in northern climates, is the time when ghosts roam. Ancestors return to visit their families, sometimes happily, sometimes not. It is also the season of storytelling: the repetition of certain stories is said to attract these ghosts, who will cease any harmful hauntings to listen instead. In some cultures, both European and Native American, certain stories are reserved for certain seasons, told only at that time.

How does this apply to modern weird tales? Do these potent and often mystical tales serve a similar purpose, or are they merely good stories? That question provokes incendiary arguments among devotees of weird fiction. We all carry our own experiences and orientation. Lovers of weird fiction may have little in common beyond that love. Some are convinced that at least some of these stories contain deep metaphysical secrets, while others are appalled at that suggestion. Either way, these tales are easily enjoyed, but let's consider for a moment.

Do these weird tales knowingly or unknowingly preserve esoteric information or serve as portals to other dimensions? We know what the most vocal scholars of weird fiction think, but what about the authors, especially the masters? Are they spinning the web of weird or just spinning a good yarn? In some cases, these authors were genuine occultists—Dion Fortune, William Butler Yeats, Hanns Heinz Ewers, and possibly others. Bram Stoker knew Yeats, as well as several other prominent members of the Golden Dawn, but there is no proof that he ever joined that mystical organization himself.

Other authors, particularly Lovecraft, claimed to be materialists, believing in nothing that wasn't tangible or visible. Some devotees are offended at the suggestion that his stories may be anything more than great fiction, the product of his inventive mind. Others argue that Lovecraft, like his creation the narrator of "Dagon," hid esoteric leanings beneath the mask of fiction, as have so many other authors over the years. Still others claim, even if Lovecraft himself didn't realize it, that he was a portal or channel for spirits and wisdom seeking to emerge from the shadows into the light.

Lovecraft often received inspiration for his tales in dreams. During his childhood, he experienced night terrors, figures that terrorized him that he named "Night Gaunts." As an adult, he would incorporate these creatures into his fiction. Some point to this as proof that Lovecraft was in touch with genuine mystical phenomena, while others vociferously deny the possibility. No definitive answer to these mysteries exists. Neither side can be convinced by the other. What is known for sure is that Lovecraft spent his childhood immersed in classic tales, especially *The Arabian Nights,* and that he was a man who understood the power of a good story. I leave this as a mystery for you to ponder.

Here's another point to ponder. Many fantastic tales, especially, although not exclusively, those of Charles Dickens and M. R. James, were written specifically as Christmas entertainment. Consider Dickens's famous novella, *A Christmas Carol,* in which three ghosts take Scrooge on a wild ride through his past, present, and future, behaving like chain-clanking Norns. Dickens wrote many ghost stories for Christmas and presented them aloud as well. He was among the first celebrity authors—a showman, he loved telling a good story to an appreciative audience, especially at Christmastime. Many of M. R. James's ghost stories were written specifically to be read aloud to select gatherings of his friends as Christmas Eve entertainment.

Christmas is the weird season of ghosts. The BBC has a history of presenting a televised supernatural story as Christmas entertainment, many written by the stars of the weird fiction firmament. This echoes that ancient Northern tradition of stories reserved for the dead of winter. The old Pagan Germanic calendar was divided into *tides*. Each tide was roughly the equivalent of two of our modern months. The peak of this season of storytelling fell within Yuletide, the time corresponding to the months December and January. The winter solstice falls within this period, as do the twelve days of Christmas. The word Yule has evolved, for many people, into a synonym for Christmas—when some say *Yule log*, they really mean *Christmas log*. Yule also names the modern Wiccan sabbat that corresponds to the winter solstice. And so, one wonders, were Dickens, James, and other authors conscious of carrying on an ancient tradition of winter storytelling, or is it just that the time itself is conducive to the practice?

I hope you enjoy these stories as much as I do. I hope they encourage you to delve further into the treasure trove that is weird, supernatural, and fantastic fiction. A word of advice: these old stories were carefully wrought by meticulous authors. To leave them as intact as possible, their spellings and sentence structure have been preserved as written. In many cases, these are no longer technically grammatically correct, but, as we've seen, language evolves, and it's best to be conscious of that evolution. Some authors used standard British English spelling, while others used standard American English spelling. These have been left as written, so for those readers with sharp eyes who recognize inconsistencies, this is why.

May I also make a suggestion? Transcending anything else, these stories were intended to provide entertainment. Many were written with the expectation that they would be read aloud. With the advent of radio, television, and the Internet, with the exception of reading to young children, the practice of reading aloud to others has fallen by the wayside. Studies indicate that information processed through oral transmission affects brain chemistry differently from information processed through reading. (Those interested in this topic may find Leonard Shlain's 1999 study, *The Alphabet and the Goddess* [Penguin Books], to be insightful.) The tales within *The Weiser Book of the Fantastic and Forgotten*, while wonderful if read silently, reveal their nuances, humor, and suspense with even more potency if read aloud. Their flavor is, essentially, better savored. Even if you do not normally read out loud, try it. You will be following in ancient footsteps. During the dark, eerie hours, when the wind is blowing and the ghosts are roaming outside, the night can be filled with pleasant terror.

JUDIKA ILLES

The Weiser Book of

THE FANTASTIC
AND FORGOTTEN

THE STORIES

DRACULA'S GUEST

Bram Stoker

Abraham "Bram" Stoker (1847–1912) has earned worldwide renown as the author of Dracula, the pivotally influential 1897 novel. Dracula is not the earliest English-language vampire tale to be published: *Varney the Vampire, or the Feast of Blood* appeared in book form in the year of Stoker's birth, having first been serialized in penny dreadfuls two years earlier. It was *Dracula,* however, that would define the literary vampire genre, transforming the loathsome vampire of Central and Eastern European folklore into a suave and charismatic bloodsucker.

During his lifetime, Stoker was best known as the personal assistant of the great actor Henry Irving and the business manager of Irving's Lyceum Theatre. Stoker ran in the same circles as the artist Pamela Colman Smith, now most famous for illustrating the Rider-Waite-Smith tarot deck. She also did illustrations for Stoker, including those for his 1911 horror novel, *The Lair of the White Worm,* published by William Rider and Son. Stoker's friends included his fellow Irishmen, William Butler Yeats and Oscar Wilde. All three are represented by stories in *The Weiser Book of the Fantastic and Forgotten.*

"Dracula's Guest" was first published in 1914, two years after Stoker's death, in the book *Dracula's Guest and Other Weird Stories.* The unnamed narrator is generally assumed to be Jonathan Harker, on his way to see the Count. In the preface to the original edition, Florence, Stoker's widow, wrote: "To his original list of stories in this book, I have added an hitherto unpublished episode from Dracula. It was originally excised owing to the length of the book, and may prove of interest to the many readers of what is considered my husband's most remarkable work." That said, "Dracula's Guest" stands alone as an excellent tale of mystical suspense. It is not necessary to have read

Stoker's novel nor have seen any of the over two hundred films inspired by it to enjoy it.

Dracula's Guest

When we started for our drive the sun was shining brightly on Munich, and the air was full of the joyousness of early summer. Just as we were about to depart, Herr Delbrück (the maître d'hôtel of the Quatre Saisons, where I was staying) came down, bareheaded, to the carriage and, after wishing me a pleasant drive, said to the coachman, still holding his hand on the handle of the carriage door: 'Remember you are back by nightfall. The sky looks bright but there is a shiver in the north wind that says there may be a sudden storm. But I am sure you will not be late.' Here he smiled, and added, 'for you know what night it is.'

Johann answered with an emphatic, 'Ja, mein Herr,' and, touching his hat, drove off quickly. When we had cleared the town, I said, after signalling to him to stop: 'Tell me, Johann, what is tonight?'

He crossed himself, as he answered laconically: 'Walpurgis nacht.' then he took out his watch, a great, old-fashioned German silver thing as big as a turnip, and looked at it, with his eyebrows gathered together and a little impatient shrug of his shoulders. I realised that this was his way of respectfully protesting against the unnecessary delay, and sank back in the carriage, merely motioning him to proceed. He started off rapidly, as if to make up for lost time. Every now and then the horses seemed to throw up their heads and sniffed the air suspiciously. On such occasions I often looked round in alarm. The road was pretty bleak, for we were traversing a sort of high, wind-swept plateau. As we drove, I saw a road that looked but little used, and which seemed to dip through a little, winding valley. It looked so inviting that, even at the risk of offending him, I called Johann to stop—and when he had pulled up, I told him I would like to drive down that road. He made all sorts of excuses, and frequently crossed himself as he spoke. This somewhat piqued my curiosity, so I asked him various questions. He answered fencingly, and repeatedly looked at his watch in protest. Finally I said:

'Well, Johann, I want to go down this road. I shall not ask you to come unless you like; but tell me why you do not like to go, that is all I ask.' For answer he seemed to throw himself off the box, so quickly did he reach the ground. Then he stretched out his hands appealingly to me, and implored me not to go. There was just enough of English mixed with the German for me to understand the drift of his talk. He seemed always just about to tell me something—the very idea of which evidently frightened him; but each time he pulled himself up, saying, as he crossed himself: 'Walpurgis-Nacht!'

I tried to argue with him, but it was difficult to argue with a man when I did not know his language. The advantage certainly rested with him, for although he began to speak in English, of a very crude and broken kind, he always got excited and broke into his native tongue—and every time he did so, he looked at his watch. Then the horses became restless and sniffed the air. At this he grew very pale, and, looking around in a frightened way, he suddenly jumped forward, took them by the bridles and led them on some twenty feet. I followed, and asked why he had done this. For answer he crossed himself, pointed to the spot we had left and drew his carriage in the direction of the other road, indicating a cross, and said, first in German, then in English: 'Buried him—him what killed themselves.'

I remembered the old custom of burying suicides at cross-roads: 'Ah! I see, a suicide. How interesting!' but for the life of me I could not make out why the horses were frightened.

Whilst we were talking, we heard a sort of sound between a yelp and a bark. It was far away; but the horses got very restless, and it took Johann all his time to quiet them. He was pale, and said, 'It sounds like a wolf—but yet there are no wolves here now.'

'No?' I said, questioning him; 'isn't it long since the wolves were so near the city?'

'Long, long,' he answered, 'in the spring and summer; but with the snow the wolves have been here not so long.'

Whilst he was petting the horses and trying to quiet them, dark clouds drifted rapidly across the sky. The sunshine passed away, and a breath of cold wind seemed to drift past us. It was only a breath, however, and more in the nature of a warning than a fact, for the sun came out brightly again. Johann looked under his lifted hand at the horizon and said: 'The storm of snow, he comes before long time.' Then he looked at his watch again, and, straightway holding his reins firmly—for the horses were still pawing the ground restlessly and shaking their heads—he climbed to his box as though the time had come for proceeding on our journey.

I felt a little obstinate and did not at once get into the carriage.

'Tell me,' I said, 'about this place where the road leads,' and I pointed down.

Again he crossed himself and mumbled a prayer, before he answered, 'It is unholy.'

'What is unholy?' I enquired.

'The village.'

'Then there is a village?'

'No, no. No one lives there hundreds of years.' My curiosity was piqued, 'But you said there was a village.'

'There was.'

'Where is it now?'

Whereupon he burst out into a long story in German and English, so mixed up that I could not quite understand exactly what he said, but roughly I gathered that long ago, hundreds of years, men had died there and been buried in their graves; and sounds were heard under the clay, and when the graves were opened, men and women were found rosy with life, and their mouths red with blood. And so, in haste to save their lives (aye, and their souls!—and here he crossed himself) those who were left fled away to other places, where the living lived, and the dead were dead and not—not something. He was evidently afraid to speak the last words. As he proceeded with his narration, he grew more and more excited. It seemed as if his imagination had got hold of him, and he ended in a perfect paroxysm of fear—white-faced, perspiring, trembling and looking round him, as if expecting that some dreadful presence would manifest itself there in the bright sunshine on the open plain. Finally, in an agony of desperation, he cried:

'Walpurgis nacht!' and pointed to the carriage for me to get in. All my English blood rose at this, and, standing back, I said:

'You are afraid, Johann—you are afraid. Go home; I shall return alone; the walk will do me good.' The carriage door was open. I took from the seat my oak walking-stick—which I always carry on my holiday excursions—and closed the door, pointing back to Munich, and said, 'Go home, Johann—Walpurgis-nacht doesn't concern Englishmen.'

The horses were now more restive than ever, and Johann was trying to hold them in, while excitedly imploring me not to do anything so foolish. I pitied the poor fellow, he was deeply in earnest; but all the same I could not help laughing. His English was quite gone now. In his anxiety he had forgotten that his only means of making me understand was to talk my language, so he jabbered away in his native German. It began to be a little tedious. After giving the direction, 'Home!' I turned to go down the cross-road into the valley.

With a despairing gesture, Johann turned his horses towards Munich. I leaned on my stick and looked after him. He went slowly along the road for a while: then there came over the crest of the hill a man tall and thin. I could see so much in the distance. When he drew near the horses, they began to jump and kick about, then to scream with terror. Johann could not hold them in; they bolted down the road, running away madly. I watched them out of sight, then looked for the stranger, but I found that he, too, was gone.

With a light heart I turned down the side road through the deepening valley to which Johann had objected. There was not the slightest reason, that I could see, for his objection; and I daresay I tramped for a couple of hours without thinking of time or distance, and certainly without seeing a person or a house. So far as the place was concerned, it was desolation, itself. But I did not notice this particularly till, on turning a bend in the road, I came upon a scattered fringe of wood; then I recognised that I had been impressed unconsciously by the desolation of the region through which I had passed.

I sat down to rest myself, and began to look around. It struck me that it was considerably colder than it had been at the commencement of my walk—a sort of sighing sound seemed to be around me, with, now and then, high overhead, a sort of muffled roar. Looking upwards I noticed that great thick clouds were drifting rapidly across the sky from North to South at a great height. There were signs of coming storm in some lofty stratum of the air. I was a little chilly, and, thinking that it was the sitting still after the exercise of walking, I resumed my journey.

The ground I passed over was now much more picturesque. There were no striking objects that the eye might single out; but in all there was a charm of beauty. I took little heed of time and it was only when the deepening twilight forced itself upon me that I began to think of how I should find my way home. The brightness of the day had gone. The air was cold, and the drifting of clouds high overhead was more marked. They were accompanied by a sort of far-away rushing sound, through which seemed to come at intervals that mysterious cry which the driver had said came from a wolf. For a while I hesitated. I had said I would see the deserted village, so on I went, and presently came on a wide stretch of open country, shut in by hills all around. Their sides were covered with trees which spread down to the plain, dotting, in clumps, the gentler slopes and hollows which showed here and there. I followed with my eye the winding of the road, and saw that it curved close to one of the densest of these clumps and was lost behind it.

As I looked there came a cold shiver in the air, and the snow began to fall. I thought of the miles and miles of bleak country I had passed, and then hurried on to seek the shelter of the wood in front. Darker and darker grew the sky, and faster and heavier fell the snow, till the earth before and around me was a glistening white carpet the further edge of which was lost in misty vagueness. The road was here but crude, and when on the level its boundaries were not so marked, as when it passed through the cuttings; and in a little while I found that I must have strayed from it, for I missed underfoot the hard surface, and my feet sank deeper in the grass and moss. Then the wind grew stronger and blew with ever increasing force, till I was fain to run before it. The air became icy-cold, and in spite of my exercise I began to suffer. The snow was now falling so thickly and whirling around me in such rapid eddies that I could hardly keep my eyes open. Every now and then the heavens were torn asunder by vivid lightning, and in the flashes I could see ahead of me a great mass of trees, chiefly yew and cypress all heavily coated with snow.

I was soon amongst the shelter of the trees, and there, in comparative silence, I could hear the rush of the wind high overhead. Presently the blackness of the storm had become merged in the darkness of the night. By-and-by the storm seemed to be passing away: it now only came in fierce puffs or blasts. At such moments the weird sound of the wolf appeared to be echoed by many similar sounds around me.

Now and again, through the black mass of drifting cloud, came a straggling ray of moonlight, which lit up the expanse, and showed me that I was at the edge of a dense mass of cypress and yew trees. As the snow had ceased to fall, I walked out from the shelter and began to investigate more closely. It appeared to me that, amongst so many old foundations as I had passed, there might be still standing a house in which, though in ruins, I could find some sort of shelter for a while. As I skirted the edge of the copse, I found that a low wall encircled it, and following this I presently found an opening. Here the cypresses formed an alley leading up to a square mass of some kind of building. Just as I caught sight of this, however, the drifting clouds obscured the moon, and I passed up the path in darkness. The wind must have grown colder, for I felt myself shiver as I walked; but there was hope of shelter, and I groped my way blindly on.

I stopped, for there was a sudden stillness. The storm had passed; and, perhaps in sympathy with nature's silence, my heart seemed to cease to beat. But this was only momentarily; for suddenly the moonlight broke through the clouds, showing me that I was in a graveyard, and that the square object before me was a great massive tomb of marble, as white as the snow that lay on and all around it. With the moonlight there came a fierce sigh of the storm, which appeared to resume its course with a long, low howl, as of many dogs or wolves. I was awed and shocked, and felt the cold perceptibly grow upon me till it seemed to grip me by the heart. Then while the flood of moonlight still fell on the marble tomb, the storm gave further evidence of renewing, as though it was returning on its track. Impelled by some sort of fascination, I approached the sepulchre to see what it was, and why such a thing stood alone in such a place. I walked around it, and read, over the Doric door, in German:

COUNTESS DOLINGEN OF GRATZ IN STYRIA
SOUGHT AND FOUND DEATH 1801

On the top of the tomb, seemingly driven through the solid marble—for the structure was composed of a few vast blocks of stone—was a great iron spike or stake. On going to the back I saw, graven in great Russian letters:
'The dead travel fast.'
There was something so weird and uncanny about the whole thing that it gave me a turn and made me feel quite faint. I began to wish, for the first time, that I had taken Johann's advice. Here a thought struck me, which came under almost mysterious circumstances and with a terrible shock. This was Walpurgis Night!
Walpurgis Night, when, according to the belief of millions of people, the devil was abroad—when the graves were opened and the dead came forth and walked. When all evil things of earth and air and water held revel. This very place the driver had specially shunned. This was the depopulated village of centuries ago. This was where the suicide lay; and this was the place where I was alone—unmanned, shivering with cold in a shroud of snow with a wild storm gathering again upon me! It took all my philosophy, all the religion I had been taught, all my courage, not to collapse in a paroxysm of fright.

And now a perfect tornado burst upon me. The ground shook as though thousands of horses thundered across it; and this time the storm bore on its icy wings, not snow, but great hailstones which drove with such violence that they might have come from the thongs of Balearic slingers—hailstones that beat down leaf and branch and made the shelter of the cypresses of no more avail than though their stems were standing-corn. At the first I had rushed to the nearest tree; but I was soon fain to leave it and seek the only spot that seemed to afford refuge, the deep Doric doorway of the marble tomb. There, crouching against the massive bronze door, I gained a certain amount of protection from the beating of the hailstones, for now they only drove against me as they ricocheted from the ground and the side of the marble.

As I leaned against the door, it moved slightly and opened inwards. The shelter of even a tomb was welcome in that pitiless tempest, and I was about to enter it when there came a flash of forked-lightning that lit up the whole expanse of the heavens. In the instant, as I am a living man, I saw, as my eyes were turned into the darkness of the tomb, a beautiful woman, with rounded cheeks and red lips, seemingly sleeping on a bier. As the thunder broke overhead, I was grasped as by the hand of a giant and hurled out into the storm. The whole thing was so sudden that, before I could realise the shock, moral as well as physical, I found the hailstones beating me down. At the same time I had a strange, dominating feeling that I was not alone. I looked towards the tomb. Just then there came another blinding flash, which seemed to strike the iron stake that surmounted the tomb and to pour through to the earth, blasting and crumbling the marble, as in a burst of flame. The dead woman rose for a moment of agony, while she was lapped in the flame, and her bitter scream of pain was drowned in the thundercrash. The last thing I heard was this mingling of dreadful sound, as again I was seized in the giant-grasp and dragged away, while the hailstones beat on me, and the air around seemed reverberant with the howling of wolves. The last sight that I remembered was a vague, white, moving mass, as if all the graves around me had sent out the phantoms of their sheeted-dead, and that they were closing in on me through the white cloudiness of the driving hail.

Gradually there came a sort of vague beginning of consciousness; then a sense of weariness that was dreadful. For a time I remembered nothing; but slowly my senses returned. My feet seemed positively racked with pain, yet I could not move them. They seemed to be numbed. There was an icy feeling at the back of my neck and all down my spine, and my ears, like my feet, were dead, yet in torment; but there was in my breast a sense of warmth which was, by comparison, delicious. It was as a nightmare—a physical nightmare, if one may use such an expression; for some heavy weight on my chest made it difficult for me to breathe.

This period of semi-lethargy seemed to remain a long time, and as it faded away I must have slept or swooned. Then came a sort of loathing, like the first stage of sea-sickness, and a wild desire to be free from something—I knew not what. A vast stillness enveloped me, as though all the world were asleep or dead—only broken by the low panting as of some animal close to me. I felt a warm rasping at my throat, then came a consciousness of the awful truth, which chilled me to the heart and sent the blood surging up through my brain. Some great animal was lying on me and now licking my throat. I feared to stir, for some instinct of prudence bade me lie still; but the brute seemed to realise that there was now some change in me, for it raised its head. Through my eyelashes I saw above me the two great flaming eyes of a gigantic wolf. Its sharp white teeth gleamed in the gaping red mouth, and I could feel its hot breath fierce and acrid upon me.

For another spell of time I remembered no more. Then I became conscious of a low growl, followed by a yelp, renewed again and again. Then, seemingly very far away, I heard a 'Holloa! holloa!' as of many voices calling in unison. Cautiously I raised my head and looked in the direction whence the sound came; but the cemetery blocked my view. The wolf still continued to yelp in a strange way, and a red glare began to move round the grove of cypresses, as though following the sound. As the voices drew closer, the wolf yelped faster and louder. I feared to make either sound or motion. Nearer came the red glow, over the white pall which stretched into the darkness around me. Then all at once from beyond the trees there came at a trot a troop of horsemen bearing torches. The wolf rose from my breast and made for the cemetery. I saw one of the horsemen (soldiers by their caps and their long military cloaks) raise his carbine and take aim. A companion knocked up his arm, and I heard the ball whizz over my head. He had evidently taken my body for that of the wolf. Another sighted the animal as it slunk away, and a shot followed. Then, at a gallop, the troop rode forward—some towards me, others following the wolf as it disappeared amongst the snow-clad cypresses.

As they drew nearer I tried to move, but was powerless, although I could see and hear all that went on around me. Two or three of the soldiers jumped from their horses and knelt beside me. One of them raised my head, and placed his hand over my heart.

'Good news, comrades!' he cried. 'His heart still beats!'

Then some brandy was poured down my throat; it put vigour into me, and I was able to open my eyes fully and look around. Lights and shadows were moving among the trees, and I heard men call to one another. They drew together, uttering frightened exclamations; and the lights flashed as the others came pouring out of the cemetery pell-mell, like men possessed.

When the further ones came close to us, those who were around me asked them eagerly:

'Well, have you found him?'

The reply rang out hurriedly:

'No! no! Come away quick—quick! This is no place to stay, and on this of all nights!'

'What was it?' was the question, asked in all manner of keys. The answer came variously and all indefinitely as though the men were moved by some common impulse to speak, yet were restrained by some common fear from giving their thoughts.

'It—it—indeed!' gibbered one, whose wits had plainly given out for the moment.

'A wolf—and yet not a wolf!' another put in shudderingly.

'No use trying for him without the sacred bullet,' a third remarked in a more ordinary manner.

'Serve us right for coming out on this night! Truly we have earned our thousand marks!' were the ejaculations of a fourth.

'There was blood on the broken marble,' another said after a pause—'the lightning never brought that there. And for him—is he safe? Look at his throat! See, comrades, the wolf has been lying on him and keeping his blood warm.'

The officer looked at my throat and replied:

'He is all right; the skin is not pierced. What does it all mean? We should never have found him but for the yelping of the wolf.'

'What became of it?' asked the man who was holding up my head, and who seemed the least panic-stricken of the party, for his hands were steady and without tremor. On his sleeve was the chevron of a petty officer.

'It went to its home,' answered the man, whose long face was pallid, and who actually shook with terror as he glanced around him fearfully. 'There are graves enough there in which it may lie. Come, comrades—come quickly! Let us leave this cursed spot.'

The officer raised me to a sitting posture, as he uttered a word of command; then several men placed me upon a horse. He sprang to the saddle behind me, took me in his arms, gave the word to advance; and, turning our faces away from the cypresses, we rode away in swift, military order.

As yet my tongue refused its office, and I was perforce silent. I must have fallen asleep; for the next thing I remembered was finding myself standing up, supported by a soldier on each side of me. It was almost broad daylight, and to the north a red streak of sunlight was reflected, like a path of blood, over the waste of snow. The officer was telling the men to say nothing of what they had seen, except that they found an English stranger, guarded by a large dog.

'Dog! that was no dog,' cut in the man who had exhibited such fear. 'I think I know a wolf when I see one.'

The young officer answered calmly: 'I said a dog.'

'Dog!' reiterated the other ironically. It was evident that his courage was rising with the sun; and, pointing to me, he said, 'Look at his throat. Is that the work of a dog, master?'

Instinctively I raised my hand to my throat, and as I touched it I cried out in pain. The men crowded round to look, some stooping down from their saddles; and again there came the calm voice of the young officer:

'A dog, as I said. If aught else were said we should only be laughed at.'

I was then mounted behind a trooper, and we rode on into the suburbs of Munich. Here we came across a stray carriage, into which I was lifted, and it was driven off to the Quatre Saisons—the young officer accompanying me, whilst a trooper followed with his horse, and the others rode off to their barracks.

When we arrived, Herr Delbrück rushed so quickly down the steps to meet me that it was apparent he had been watching within. Taking me by both hands he solicitously led me in. The officer saluted me and was turning to withdraw, when I recognised his purpose, and insisted that he should come to my rooms. Over a glass of wine I warmly thanked him and his brave comrades for saving me. He replied simply that he was more than glad, and that Herr Delbrück had at the first taken steps to make all the searching party pleased; at which ambiguous utterance the maître d'hôtel smiled, while the officer pleaded duty and withdrew.

'But Herr Delbrück,' I enquired, 'how and why was it that the soldiers searched for me?'

He shrugged his shoulders, as if in depreciation of his own deed, as he replied: 'I was so fortunate as to obtain leave from the commander of the regiment in which I served, to ask for volunteers.'

'But how did you know I was lost?' I asked.

'The driver came hither with the remains of his carriage, which had been upset when the horses ran away.'

'But surely you would not send a search-party of soldiers merely on this account?'

'Oh, no!' he answered; 'but even before the coachman arrived, I had this telegram from the Boyar whose guest you are,' and he took from his pocket a telegram which he handed to me, and I read:

Bistritz.

Be careful of my guest—his safety is most precious to me. Should aught happen to him, or if he be missed, spare nothing to find him and ensure his safety. He is English and therefore adventurous. There are often dangers from snow and wolves and night. Lose not a moment if you suspect harm to him. I answer your zeal with my fortune. —Dracula.

As I held the telegram in my hand, the room seemed to whirl around me; and, if the attentive maître d'hôtel had not caught me, I think I should have fallen. There was something so strange in all this, something so weird and impossible to imagine, that there grew on me a sense of my being in some way the sport of opposite forces—the mere vague idea of which seemed in a way to paralyse me. I was certainly under some form of mysterious protection. From a distant country had come, in the very nick of time, a message that took me out of the danger of the snow-sleep and the jaws of the wolf.

A WATER WITCH

H. D. Everett

Henrietta Dorothea Everett, née Huskisson (1851–1923), a prolific and once popular British author, is now virtually forgotten. Little is known of her life. As was not uncommon for women writers of her era, most of her literary output was published under a man's name. Between 1896 and 1920, Everett published twenty-two books, using the pen name Theo Douglas.

"A Water Witch" first appeared in 1920 as part of *The Death Mask and Other Ghosts,* a collection of fourteen fantastic tales. It was Everett's last book to be published, as well as the first and only one published under her own name. Although Everett writes gently, "A Water Witch" is an eerie tale.

Some thoughts to keep in mind, as you read this story and ponder the nature of its title character:

> ☞ A folkloric attempt to reconcile pre-Christian Pagan spirits with the Bible suggests that fairies dwell on Earth because they are too wicked for Heaven but too innocent for Hell.

> ☞ The "white woman" who haunts this story may be a type of ghost, now more commonly known as a White Lady, deemed by some schools of folklore to be a harbinger of doom.

> ☞ The term "white woman" or "White Lady" may also refer to several species of dangerous European water spirits, such as Russia's Rusalka.

NOTE: "Freda" is an affectionate pet-name for "Frederica."

A Water Witch

We were disappointed when Robert married. We had for long wanted him to marry, as he is our only brother and head of the family since my father died, as well as of the business firm; but we should have liked his wife to be a different sort of person. We, his sisters, could have chosen much better for him than he did for himself. Indeed we had our eye on just the right girl—bright-tempered and sensibly brought up, who would not have said 'No': of that I am assured, had Robert on his side shown signs of liking. But he took a holiday abroad the spring of 1912, and the next thing we heard was that he had made up his mind to marry Frederica. Frederica, indeed! We Larcombs have been plain Susans and Annes and Marys and Elizabeths for generations (I am Mary), and the fantastic name was an annoyance. The wedding took place at Mentone in a great hurry, because the stepmother was marrying again, and Freda was unhappy. Was that not weak of Robert?—he did not give himself time to think. We may perhaps take that as some excuse for a departure from the Larcomb traditions: on consideration, the match would very likely have been broken off. Freda had some money of her own, though not much; all the Larcomb brides have had money up to now. And her dead father was a General and a K.C.B., which did not look amiss in the announcement; but there our satisfaction ended. He brought her to make our acquaintance three weeks after the marriage, a delicate little shrinking thing well matched to her fanciful name, and desperately afraid of mother and of us girls, so the introductory visit was hardly a success. Then Robert took her off to London, and when the baby was born—a son, but too weakly to live beyond a day or two—she had a severe illness, and was slow in recovering strength. And there is no doubt that by this time he was conscious of having made a mistake.

I used to be his favourite sister, being next to him in age, and when he found himself in a difficulty at Roscawen he appealed to me. Roscawen was a moor Robert had lately rented on the Scotch side of the Border, and we were given to understand that a bracing air, and the complete change of scene, were expected to benefit Freda, who was pleased by the arrangement. So his letter took me by surprise.

> DEAR MARY (*he wrote, and characteristically, he did not beat about the bush.*)— Pack up your things as soon as you get this, and come off here the day after tomorrow. You will have to travel via York, and I will meet you at Draycott Halt, where the afternoon train stops by signal. Freda is a bit nervous, and doesn't like staying alone here, so I am in a fix. I want you to keep her company the weeks I am at Shepstow. I know you'll do as much as this for—
>
> YOUR AFFECTIONATE BROTHER,
> ROBERT LARCOMB

This abrupt call upon me, making sure of response and help, recalled bygone times when we were much to each other, and Freda still in the unknown. A bit nervous, was she, and Robert in a fix because of it: here again was evidence of the mistake. It was not very easy then to break off from work, and for an indefinite time; but I resolved to satisfy the family curiosity, to say nothing of my own, by doing as I was bid. When I got out of the train at Draycott Halt, Robert was waiting for me with his car. My luggage was put in at the back, and I mounted to the seat beside him; and again it reminded me of old times, for he seemed genuinely pleased to see me.

'Good girl,' he said, 'to make no fuss, and come at once.'

'We Larcombs are not apt to fuss, are we?'—and as I said this, it occurred to me that probably he was in these days well acquainted with fuss—Freda's fuss. Then I asked: 'What is the matter?'

I only had a sideways glimpse of him as he answered, for he was busy with the driving-gear.

'Why, I told you, didn't I, that it was arranged for me to be here and at Shepstow week and week about, Falkner and I together, for it is better than taking either moor with a single gun. And I can't take Freda there, for the Shepstow cottage has not accommodation for a lady—only the one room Falkner and I share. Freda is nervous, poor girl, since her illness, and somehow she has taken a dislike to Roscawen. It is nothing but a fancy, of course, but something had to be done.'

'Why, you wrote to mother that you had both fallen in love with the place, and thought it quite ideal.'

'Oh, the place is right enough, it is just my poor girl's fancy. She'll tell you I dare say, but don't let her dwell on it more than you can help. You will have Falkner's room, and the week he is over here I've arranged for Vickers to put him up, though I dare say he will come in to meals. Vickers? Oh, he's a neighbour on the opposite side of the water, Roscawen Water, the stream that overflows from the lake in the hills. He's a doctor of science as well as medicine, and has written some awfully clever books. I understand he's at work on another, and comes here for the sake of quiet. But he's a very good sort though not a sportsman, does not mind taking in Falkner, and he is by way of being a friend of Freda's—they read Italian together. No, he isn't married, neither is the parson, worse luck; and there isn't another woman of her own sort within miles. It's desperately lonely for her, I allow, when I'm not here. So there was no help for it. I was bound to send for you or for the mater, and I thought you would be best!'

We were passing through wild scenery of barren broken hills, following the course of the river upstream. It came racing down a rocky course, full and turbulent from recent rains. Presently the road divided, crossing a narrow bridge; and there we came in sight of the leap the water makes over a shelf of rock, plunging into a deep pool below with a swirl of foam and spray. I would have liked to linger and look, but the car carried us forward quickly, allowing only a glimpse in passing. And, directly after, Robert called my attention to a stone-built small house high up on the hillside—a bare place it looked, flanked by a clump of firs, but with no surrounding garden-ground; the wild moor and the heather came close under the windows.

'That's Roscawen,' he said. 'Just a shooting-box, you see. A new-built place, raw, with no history behind it later than yesterday. I was in treaty for Corby, seventeenth century that was, with a ghost in the gallery, but the arrangement fell through. And I'm jolly glad it did'—and here he laughed; an uncomfortable laugh, not of the Larcomb sort, or like himself. And in another minute we were at the door.

Freda welcomed me, and I thought her improved; she was indeed pretty—as pretty as such a frail little thing could be, who looked as if a puff of wind would blow her away. She was very well dressed—of course Robert would take care of that—and her one thought appeared to be of him. She was constantly turning to him with appeal of one sort or another, and seemed nervous and ill of ease when he was out of her sight. 'Must you really go tomorrow?' I caught her whisper later, and heard his answer: 'Needs must, but you will not mind now you have Mary.' I could plainly see that she did mind, and that my companionship was no fair exchange for the loss of his. But was not all this exaction the very way to tire out love?

The ground-floor of the house was divided into a sitting-hall, upon which the front door opened without division, and to the right you entered a fair-sized dining-room. Each of these apartments had the offshoot of a smaller room, one being Freda's snuggery, and the other the gun-room where the gentlemen smoked. Above there were two good bedrooms, a dressing-room and a bathroom, but no higher floor: the gable-space was not utilised, and the servants slept over the kitchen at the back. The room allotted to me, from which Captain Falkner had been ejected, had a wide window and a pleasant aspect. As I was hurriedly dressing for dinner, I could hear the murmur of the river close at hand, but the actual water was not visible, as it flowed too far below the over-hanging bank.

I could not see the flowing water, but as I glanced from the window, a wreath of white mist or spray floated up from it, stretched itself out before the wind, and disappeared after the fashion of a puff of steam. Probably there was at that point another fall (so I thought) churning the river into foam. But I had no time to waste in speculation, for we Larcombs adhere to the good ways of punctuality. I fastened a final hook and eye, and ran downstairs.

Captain Falkner came to dinner and made a fourth at the table, but the fifth place which had been laid remained vacant. The two men were full of plans for the morrow, and there was to be an early setting out: Shepstow, the other moor, was some thirty miles away.

'I'm afraid you will be dull, Mary,' Robert said to me in a sort of apology. 'I am forced to keep the car at Shepstow, as I am my own chauffeur. But you and Freda will have her cart to jog about in, so you will be able to look round the nearer country while I am away. You will have to put up with the old mare. I know you like spirit in a horse, but this quiet gee suits Freda, as she can drive her going alone. Then Vickers will look in on you most days. I do not know what is keeping him away tonight.'

Freda was in low spirits next morning, and she hung about Robert up to the time of his departure, in a way I should have found supremely irritating had I been her husband. And I will not be sure that she did not beg him again not to leave her—to my tender mercies I supposed—though I did not hear the request. When the two men had set out with the guns and baggage, the cart was ordered round, and my sister-in-law took me for a drive. Robert had done well to prepare me for the 'quiet gee': a meek old creature named Grey Madam, that had whitened in the snows of many winters, and expected to progress at a walk whenever the road inclined uphill. And all the roads inclined uphill or down about Roscawen; I do not remember anywhere a level quarter of a mile. It was truly a dull progress, and Freda did not find much to say; perhaps she was still fretting after Robert. But the moors and the swelling hills were beautiful to look at in their crimson flush of heather. 'I think Roscawen is lovely,' I was prompted to exclaim; and when she agreed in my admiration I added: 'You liked it when you first came here, did you not?'

'Yes, I liked it when I first came,' she assented, repeating my words, but did not go on to say why she disliked Roscawen now.

She had an errand to discharge at one of the upland farms which supplied them with milk and butter. She drew rein at the gate, and was about to alight, but the woman of the house came forward, and so I heard what passed. Freda gave her order, and then an enquiry. 'I hope you have found your young cow, Mrs Elliot? I was sorry to hear it had strayed.'

'We've found her, ma'am, but she was dead in the river, and a sad loss it has been to us. A fine young beast as ever we reared, and coming on with her second calf. My husband has been rarely put about, and I'll own I was fit to cry over her myself. This is the fifth loss we have had within the year—a sheep and two lambs in March, and the cart-foal in July.'

Freda expressed sympathy. 'You need better fences, is that it, to keep your cattle from the river?'

Mrs Elliot pursed up her lips and shook her head. 'I won't say, ma'am, but that our fences might be bettered if the landlord would give us material; as it is, we do our best. But when the creatures take that madness for the water, nought but deer-palings would keep them in. I've seen enough in my time here to be sure of that. What makes it come over them I don't take upon myself to say. They make up fine tales in the district about the white woman, but I know nothing of any white women. I only know that when the madness takes them they make for the river, and then they get swept into the deeps.'

When we were driving away, I asked Freda what the farmer's wife meant about a white woman and the drowning of her stock.

'I believe there is some story about a woman who was drowned, whose spirit calls the creatures to the river. If you ask Dr Vickers he will tell you. He makes a study of folklore and local superstitions, and—and that sort of thing. Robert thinks it is all nonsense, and no doubt you will think it nonsense too.'

What her own opinion was, Freda did not say. She had a transparent complexion, and a trifling matter made her change colour; a blush rose unaccountably as she answered me, and for a full minute her cheek burned. Why should she blush about Roscawen superstitions and a drowned cow? Then the attention of both of us was suddenly diverted, because Grey Madam took it into her head to shy.

She had mended her pace appreciably since Freda turned her head towards home, trotting now without needing to be urged. We were close upon a crossroads where three ways met, a triangular green centred by a finger-post. There was in our direction a bank and hedge (hedges here and there replaced the stone walls of the district) and the right wheel went up that bank giving the cart a dangerous tilt; it covered balance, however, and went on. Freda, a timid driver, was holding on desperately to the reins.

'Does she often do this sort of thing?' I asked. 'I thought Robert said she was quiet.'

'So she is—so we thought her. I never knew her to do it before,' gasped my sister-in-law, still out of breath with her fright.

'And I cannot think what made her shy. There was nothing—absolutely nothing; not even a heap of stones.'

Freda did not answer, but I was to hear more about that crossroads in the course of the day.

2

After lunch Freda did not seem willing to go out again, so, as I was there to companion her, we both settled down to needlework and a book for alternate reading aloud. The reading, however, was languished; when it came to Freda's turn she tired quickly, lost her place twice and again, and seemed unable to fix her attention on the printed page. Was she listening, I wondered later. When silence fell between us, I became aware of a sound recurring at irregular intervals, the sound of water dripping. I looked up at the ceiling expecting to see a stain of wet, for the drip seemed to fall within the room, and close beside me

'Do you hear that?' I asked. 'Has anything gone wrong in the bathroom, do you think?' For we were in Freda's snuggery, and the bathroom was overhead.

But my suggestion of overflowing taps and broken water-pipes left her cold.

'I don't think it is from the bathroom,' she replied. 'I hear it often. We cannot find out what it is.'

Directly she ceased speaking the drip fell again, apparently between us as we sat, and plump upon the carpet. I looked up at the ceiling again, but Freda did not raise her eyes from her embroidery.

'It is very odd,' I remarked, and this time she assented, repeating my words, and I saw a shiver pass over her. 'I shall go upstairs to the bathroom,' I said decidedly, putting down my work. 'I am sure those taps must be wrong.'

She did not object, or offer to accompany me, she only shivered again.

'Don't be long away, Mary,' she said, and I noticed she had grown pale.

There was nothing wrong with the bathroom, or with any part of the water supply; and when I returned to the snuggery the drip had ceased. The next event was a ring at the door bell, and again Freda changed colour, much as she had done when we were driving. In that quiet place, where comers and goers are few, a visitor is an event. But I think this visitor must have been expected. The servant announced Dr Vickers.

Freda gave him her hand, and made the necessary introduction. This was the friend Robert said would come often to see us, but he was not at all the stuffy old scientist my fancy had pictured. He was old certainly, if it is a sign of age to be grey-haired, and I dare say there were crows' feet about those piercing eyes of his; but when you met the eyes, the wrinkles were forgotten. They, at least, were full of youth and fire, and his figure was still upright and flat-shouldered.

We exchanged a few remarks; he asked me if I was familiar with that part of Scotland; and when I answered that I was making its acquaintance for the first time, he praised Roscawen and its neighbourhood. It suited him well, he said, when his object was to seek quiet; and I should find, as he did, that it possessed many attractions. Then he asked me if I was an Italian scholar, and showed a book in his hand, the *Vita Nuova*. Mrs. Larcomb was forgetting her Italian, and he had promised to brush it up for her. So, if I did not find it too great a bore to sit by, he proposed to read aloud. And, should I not know the book, he would give me a sketch of its purport, so that I could follow.

I had, of course, heard of the *Vita Nuova* (who has not?), but my knowledge of the language in which it was written went no further than a few modern phrases, of use to a traveller. I disclaimed my ability to follow, and I imagine Dr Vickers was not ill-pleased to find me ignorant. He took his seat at one end of the Chesterfield sofa, Freda occupying the other, still with that flush on her cheek; and after an observation or two in Italian, he opened his book and began to read.

I imagine he read well. The crisp, flowing syllables sounded very foreign to my ear, and he gave his author the advantage of dramatic expression and emphasis. Now and then he remarked in English on some difficulty in the text, or slipped in a question in Italian which Freda answered, usually by a monosyllable. She kept her eyes fixed upon her work. It was as if she would not look at him, even when he was most impassioned; but I was watching them both, although I never thought—but of course I never thought!

Presently I remembered how time was passing, and the place where letters should be laid ready for the post-bag going out. I had left an unfinished one upstairs, so I slipped away to complete and seal. This done, I re-entered softly (the entrance was behind a screen) and found the Italian lesson over, and a conversation going on in English. Freda was speaking with some animation. 'It cannot any more be called my fancy, for Mary heard it too.'

'And you had not told her beforehand? There was no suggestion?'

'I had not said a word to her. Had I, Mary?'—appealing to me as I advanced into sight.

'About what?' I asked, for I had forgotten the water incident.

'About the drops falling. You remarked on them first: I had told you nothing. And you went to look at the taps.'

'No, certainly you had not told me. What is the matter? Is there any mystery?'

Dr Vickers answered: 'The mystery is that Mrs Larcomb heard these drippings when everyone else was deaf to them. It was supposed to be auto-suggestion on her part. You have disproved that, Miss Larcomb, as your ears are open to them too. That will go far to convince your brother; and now we must seriously seek for cause. The

Roscawen district has many legends of strange happenings. We do not want to add one more to the list, and give this modern shooting-box the reputation of a haunted house.'

'And it would be an odd sort of ghost, would it not—the sound of dripping water! But—you speak of legends of the district; do you know anything of a white woman who is said to drown cattle? Mrs Elliott mentioned her this morning at the farm, when she told us she had lost her cow in the river.'

'Ay, I heard a cow had been found floating dead in the Pool. I am sorry it belonged to the Elliotts. Nobody lives here for long without hearing that story, and, though the wrath of Roscawen is roused against her, I cannot help being sorry for the white woman. She was young and beautiful once, and well-to-do, for she owned land in her own right, and flocks and herds. But she became very unhappy—'

He was speaking to me, but he looked at Freda. She had taken up her work again, but with inexpert hands, dropping first cotton, and then her thimble.

'She was unhappy, because her husband neglected her. He had—other things to attend to, and the charm she once possessed for him was lost and gone. He left her too much alone. She lost her health, they say, through fretting, and so fell into a melancholy way, spending her time in weeping, and in wandering up and down on the banks of Roscawen Water. She may have fallen in by accident, it was not exactly known; but her death was thought to be suicide, and she was buried at the crossroads.'

'That was where Grey Madam shied this morning,' Freda put in.

'And—people suppose—that on the other side of death, finding herself lonely (too guilty, perhaps, for Heaven, but at the same time too innocent for Hell) she wants companions to join her; wants sheep and cows and horses such as used to stock her farms. So she puts madness upon the creatures, and also upon some humans, so that they go down to the river. They see her, so it is said, or they receive a sign which in some way points to the manner of her death. If they see her, she comes for them once, twice, thrice, and the third time they are bound to follow.'

This was a gruesome story, I thought as I listened, though not of the sort I could believe. I hoped Freda did not believe it, but of this I was not sure.

'What does she look like?' I asked. 'If human beings see her as you say, do they give any account?'

'The story goes that they see foam rising from the water, floating away and dissolving, vaguely in form at first, but afterwards more like the woman she was once; and some say there is a hand that beckons. But I have never seen her, Miss Larcomb, nor spoken to one who has: first-hand evidence of this sort is rare, as I dare say you know. So I can tell you no more.'

And I was glad there was no more for me to hear, for the story was too tragic for my liking. The happenings of that afternoon left me discomforted—annoyed with Dr Vickers, which perhaps was unreasonable—with poor Freda, whose fancies had thus proved contagious—annoyed, and here more justly, with myself. Somehow, with such tales going about, Roscawen seemed a far from desirable residence for a nervous invalid; and I was also vaguely conscious of an undercurrent which I did not understand. It gave me the feeling you have when you stumble against something unexpected blindfold, or in the dark, and cannot define its shape.

Dr Vickers accepted a cup of tea when the tray was brought to us, and then he took his departure, which was as well seeing we had no gentleman at home to entertain him.

'So Larcomb is away again for the whole week? Is that so?' he said to Freda as he made his adieux.

There was no need for the question, I thought impatiently, as he must very well have known when he was required again to put up Captain Falkner.

'Yes, for a whole week,' Freda answered, again with that flush on her cheek; and as soon as we were alone she put up her hand, as if the color burned.

3

I did not like Dr Vickers and his Italian lessons, and I had the impression Freda would have been better pleased by their intermission. On the third day she had a headache and charged me to make her excuses, so it fell on me to receive this friend of Robert's, who seemed quite unruffled by her absence. He took advantage of the opportunity to cross-examine me about the water-dripping: had I heard it again since that first occasion, and what explanation of the sounds appeared satisfactory to myself?

The fact was, I had heard it again, twice when I was alone in my room, and once more when sitting with Freda. Then we both sat listening—listening, such small nothings as we had to say to each other dying away, waiting to see which of us would first admit it to the other, and this went on for more than an hour. At last Freda broke out into hysterical crying, the result of over-strained nerves, and with her outburst the sounds ceased. I had been inclined to entertain a notion of the spiritualist order, that they might be connected with her presence as medium; but I suppose that must be held disproved, as I also heard them when alone in my own room.

I admitted as little as possible to Dr Vickers, and was stout in asserting that natural causes would and must be found, if the explanation were diligently sought for. But I confess I was posed when confronted with the fact that these sounds heard by Freda were inaudible to her husband, also present—to Robert, who has excellent hearing, in common with all our family. Until I came, and was also an auditor, no-one in the house but Freda had noticed the dripping, so there was reason for assuming it to be hallucination. Yes, I was sorry for her trouble (answering a question pressed on me), but I maintained that, pending discovery, the best course was to take no notice of drops that wet nothing and left no stain, and did not proceed from overflowing cisterns or faulty pipes.

'They will leave off doing it if not noticed; is that what you think, Miss Larcomb?' And when I rashly assented—'Now perhaps you will define for me what you mean by *they*? Is it the "natural cause"?'

Here again was a poser: I had formulated no idea that I cared to define. Probably the visitor divined the subject was unwelcome, for he turned to others, conversing agreeably enough for another quarter of an hour. Then he departed, leaving a message of concern for Freda's headache. He hoped it would have amended by next day, when he would call to enquire.

He did call on the following day, when the Italian lesson was mainly conversational, and I had again a feeling Freda was distressed by what was said, though I could only guess at what passed between them under the disguise of a foreign tongue. But at the end I recognized the words 'not tomorrow' as spoken by her, and when some protest appeared to follow, she dumbly shook her head.

Dr Vickers did not stay on for tea as before. Did Freda think she had offended him, for some time later I noticed she had been crying?

That night I had an odd dream that the Roscawen house was sliding down from its foundations into the river at the call of the white woman, and I woke suddenly with the fright.

The next day was the last of Robert's stay at Shepstow. In the evening he and Captain Falkner returned, and at once a different atmosphere seemed to pervade the house. Freda recovered her cheerfulness, I heard no more dripping water, and except at dinner on the second evening we saw nothing of Dr Vickers. But he sent an Italian book with many scored passages, and a note in it, also in Italian, which I saw her open and read, and then immediately tear up into the minutest pieces. I supposed he wished her to keep up her studies, though the lessons were for a while suspended; I heard him say at dinner that he was busy correcting proofs.

So passed four days out of the seven Robert should have spent at Roscawen. But on the fourth evening came a telegraphic summons: his presence was needed in London, at the office, and he was bound to go up to town by the early express the next day. And the arrangement was that in returning he should go straight to Shepstow and join Captain Falkner there; this distant moor was to be reached from a station on another line.

Freda must have known that Robert could not help himself, but it was easy to see how her temporary restored spirits fell again to zero. I hope I shall never be so dependent on another person's society as she seemed to be on Robert's. I got up to give him his early breakfast, but Freda did not appear; she had a headache, he said, and had passed a restless night. She would not rise till later: perhaps I would go up and see her by-and-by.

I did go later in the morning, to find her lying like a child that had sobbed itself to sleep, her eyelashes still wet, and a tear sliding down her cheek. So I took a book, and drew a chair to the bedside, waiting for her to wake.

It was a long waiting; she slept on, and slept heavily. And as I sat and watched, there began again the dripping of water, and, for the first time in my experience of them, the drips were wet.

I could find traces now on the carpet of where they fell, and on the spread linen of the sheet; were they made, I wondered fantastically, out of Freda's tears? But they had ceased before she woke, and I did not remark on them to her. Yes, she had a headache, she said, answering my question: it was better, but not gone: she would lie quietly where she was for the present. The servants might bring her a cup of tea when I had luncheon, and she would get up later in the afternoon.

So, as I was not needed, I went out after lunch for a solitary walk. Not being governed by Freda's choice of direction, I determined to explore the course of the river, and especially how it flowed under the steep bank below the house, where I saw the wreath of foam rise in the air on my first evening at Roscawen. I expected to find a fall at this spot, but there was only broken water and rapids, alternating with smoother reaches and deep pools, one of which, I concluded, had been the death-trap of the Elliotts' cow. It was a still, perfect autumn day, warm, but not with the oppression of summer heat, and I walked with enjoyment, following the stream upward to where it issued from the miniature lake among the hills, in which it slept for a while in mid-course. Then I turned homewards, and was within sight of our dwelling when I again beheld the phenomenon of the pillar of foam.

It rose above the rapids, as nearly as I could guess in the same spot as before; and as there was now little or no wind, it did not so quickly spread out and dissipate. I could imagine that at early morning, or in the dimness of evening, it might be taken for a figure of the ghostly sort, especially as, in dissolving, it seemed to move and beckon. I smiled to myself to think that, according to local superstition, I too had seen the white woman; but I felt no least inclination to rush to the river and precipitate myself into its depths. Nor would I gratify Dr Vickers by telling him what had been my experience, or confide in Freda lest she should tell again.

On reaching home, I turned into the snuggery to see if Freda was downstairs. It must, I thought, be nearly tea-time. She was there; and, as I pushed the door open and was still behind the screen, I heard Dr Vickers' voice. 'Mind,' he was saying in English, 'I do not press you to decide at once. Wait till you are convinced he does not care. To my thinking he has already made it plain.'

I stood arrested, not intending to play eavesdropper, but stricken with surprise. As I moved into sight, the two were standing face to face, and the doctor's figure hid Freda from me. I think his hands were on her shoulders, holding her before him, but of this I am not sure. He was quick of hearing as a cat, and he turned on me at once.

'Ah, how do you do, Miss Larcomb? I was just bidding adieu to your sister-in-law, for I do not think she is well enough today to take her lesson. In fact, I think she is very far from well. These headaches spell slow progress with our study, but we must put up with delay.'

He took up the slim book from the table and bestowed it in his pocket, bowed over my hand and was gone.

If Freda had been agitated she concealed any disturbance, and we talked as usual over tea, of my walk, and even of Robert's journey. But she surprised me later in the evening by an unexpected proposition.

'Do you think Mrs Larcomb would have me to stay at Aston Bury? It would be very kind of her if she would take me in while Robert has these shootings. I do not like Roscawen, and I am not well here. Will you ask her, Mary?'

I answered that I was sure mother would have her if she wished to come to us; but what would Robert say when he had asked me to companion her here? If Robert was willing, I would write—of course. Did he know what she proposed?

No, she said, and there would be no time to consult him. She would like to go as soon as tomorrow. Could we send a telegram, and set out in the morning, staying the night in York, to receive an answer there? That she was very much in earnest about this wish of hers there could be no doubt. She was trembling visibly, and a red fever-spot burned on her cheek.

I wish I had done as she asked. But my Larcomb commonsense was up in arms, and I required to know the reason why. Mother would think it strange if we rushed off to her so, and Robert would not like it; but, given time to make the arrangement, she could certainly pay the visit, and would be received as a welcome guest. I would write to mother on the morrow, and she could write to Robert and send the letter by Captain Falkner. Then I said: 'Are you nervous here, Freda? Is it because these water drippings are unexplained?' And when she made a sort of dumb assent, I went on: 'You ought not to dwell on anything so trivial; it isn't fair to Robert. It cannot be only this. Surely there is something more?'

The question seemed to increase her distress.

'I want to be a good wife to Robert; oh, I want that, Mary. I can do my duty if I go away; if you will keep me safe at Aston Bury for only a little while. Robert does not understand; he thinks me crazed with delusions. I tried to tell him—I did indeed; hard as it was to tell.' While this was spoken she was torn with sobs. 'I am terrified to be alone. What is compelling me is too strong. Oh Mary, take me away.'

I could get no fuller explanation than this of what was at the root of the trouble. We agreed at last that the two letters should be written and sent on the morrow, and we would hold ourselves in readiness to set out as soon as answers were received. It might be no more than an hysterical fantasy on Freda's part, but I was not without suspicion of another sort. But she never mentioned their neighbour's name, and I could not insult her by the suggestion.

The letters were written early on that Thursday morrow, and then Grey Madam was brought round for Freda's drive. The direction chosen took us past the crossroads in the outward going, and also in return. I remember Freda talked more cheerfully and freely than usual, asking questions about Aston Bury, as if relieved at the prospect of taking refuge there with us. As we went, Grey Madam shied badly at the same spot as before, though there was no visible cause for her terror. I suggested we had better go home a different way; but this appeared impracticable, as the other direction involved an added distance of several miles, and the crossing of a bridge which was thought to be unsafe. In returning, the mare went unwillingly, and, though our pace had been a sober one and the day was not warm, I could see she had broken out into a lather of sweat. As we came to the crossroads for the second time, the poor creature again shied away from the invisible object which terrified her, and then, seizing the bit between her teeth, she set off at a furious gallop.

Freda was tugging at the reins, but it was beyond her power to stop that mad career, or even guide it; but the mare kept by instinct to the middle of the road. The home gate was open, and I expected she would turn in stablewards; but instead she dashed on to the open moor, making for the river.

We might possibly have jumped out, but there was no time even for thought before we were swaying on the edge of the steep bank. The next moment there was a plunge, a crash, and I remember no more.

The accident was witnessed from the further side—so I heard later. A man left his digging and ran, and it was he who dragged me out, stunned, but not suffocated by the immersion. I came to myself quickly on the bank, and my instant thought was of Freda, but she, entangled with the reins, had been swept down with the mare into the deeper pool. When I staggered up, dizzy and half-blind, begging she might be sought for, he ran on downstream, and there he and Dr Vickers and another man drew her from the water—lifeless it seemed at first, and it was long before any spark of animation repaid their utmost efforts.

That was a strange return to Roscawen house, she tenderly carried, I able to walk thither; both of us dripping water, real drops, of which the ghostly ones may have been some mysterious forecast, if that is not too fantastic for belief!

It was impossible to shut Dr Vickers out, and of course he accompanied us; for all my doubt of him, I welcomed the service of his skill when Freda's life was hanging in the balance, and she herself was too remote from this world to recognise who was beside her. But I would have preferred to owe that debt of service to any other; and the feeling I had against him deepened as I witnessed his anguished concern, and caught some unguarded expressions he let fall.

I wired to Robert to acquaint him with what had happened, and he replied 'I am coming.' And upon that I resolved to speak out, and tell what I had guessed of the true cause of Freda's trouble, and why she must be removed, not so much from a haunted house, as from an overmastering influence which she dreaded.

Did the risk of loss—the peril barely surmounted, restore the old tenderness between these two? I think it did, at any rate for the time, when Robert found her lying white as a broken lily, and when her weak hands clung about his neck. Perhaps this made him more patient than he would have been otherwise with what I had to say.

He could hardly tax me with being fancy-ridden, but he was aghast—angry—incredulous, all in one. Vickers, of all people in the world; and Freda so worked upon as to be afraid to tell him—afraid to claim the protection that was hers by right. And now the situation was complicated by the fact that Vickers had saved her life, so that thanks were due to him as well as a kicking out of doors. And there was dignity to be thought of too; Freda's dignity as well as his own. Any open scandal must be avoided; she must neither be shamed nor pained.

I do not know what passed between him and Dr Vickers when they met, but the latter came no more to Roscawen, and after a while I heard incidentally that he had gone abroad. As soon as Freda could be moved, her wish was fulfilled, and I took her to Aston Bury. Mother was very gentle with her, and I think before the end a genuine affection grew up between the two.

The end was not long delayed; a few months passed, and then she faded out of life in a sort of decline; the shock to the system, so they said, had been greater than her vitality can repair. Robert was a free man again, war had been declared, and he was one of the earliest volunteers for service.

That service won distinction, as everybody knows; and now he is convalescent from his second wound, and here at Aston Bury on leave. And I think the wiser choice his sisters made for him in the first place is now likely to be his own. A much more suitable person than Frederica, and her name is quite a plain one—a real Larcomb name: it is Mary, like my own. I am glad; but in spite of all, poor Freda has a soft place in my memory and my heart. Whatever were her faults and failings, I believe she strove hard to be loyal. And I am sure that she loved Robert well.

THE ASH TREE

M. R. James

English author, academic, medievalist scholar, and paleographer, Montague Rhodes James (1862–1936) ranks among the foremost masters of the weird. Monty, as he was known to friends, is credited with redefining the entire genre of ghost stories, jettisoning old clichés in favor of bringing them into the modern era. H. P. Lovecraft was a fan. In his essay, "Supernatural Horror in Literature," Lovecraft described James as being "gifted with an almost diabolic power of calling horror by gentle steps from the midst of prosaic daily life." Many of James's works have been adapted for film, stage, and radio, particularly "Casting the Runes" and "Whistle and I'll Come to You."

"The Ash Tree," which was initially published in James's first collection of supernatural stories, *Ghost Stories of an Old Antiquary* (1904), is the tale of what happens in the aftermath of a witch trial.

The Ash Tree

Everyone who has travelled over Eastern England knows the smaller country-houses with which it is studded—the rather dank little buildings, usually in the Italian style, surrounded with parks of some eighty to a hundred acres. For me they have always had a very strong attraction: with the grey paling of split oak, the noble trees, the meres with their reed-beds, and the line of distant woods. Then, I like the pillared portico—perhaps stuck on to a red-brick Queen Anne house which has been faced with stucco to bring it into line with the 'Grecian' taste of the end of the eighteenth century; the hall inside, going up to the roof, which hall ought always to be provided with a gallery and a small organ. I like the library, too, where you may find anything from a Psalter of the thirteenth century to a Shakespeare quarto. I like the pictures, of course; and perhaps most of all I like fancying what life in such a house was when it was first built, and in the piping times of landlords' prosperity, and not least now, when, if money is not so plentiful, taste is more varied and life quite as interesting. I wish to have one of these houses, and enough money to keep it together and entertain my friends in it modestly.

But this is a digression. I have to tell you of a curious series of events which happened in such a house as I have tried to describe. It is Castringham Hall in Suffolk. I think a good deal has been done to the building since the period of my story, but the essential features I have sketched are still there—Italian portico, square block of white house, older inside than out, park with fringe of woods, and mere. The one feature that marked out the house from a score of others is gone. As you looked at it from the park, you saw on the right a great old ash-tree growing within half a dozen yards of the wall, and almost or quite touching the building with its branches. I suppose it had stood there ever since Castringham ceased to be a fortified place, and since the moat was filled in and the Elizabethan dwelling-house built. At any rate, it had well-nigh attained its full dimensions in the year 1690.

In that year the district in which the Hall is situated was the scene of a number of witch-trials. It will be long, I think, before we arrive at a just estimate of the amount of solid reason—if there was any—which lay at the root of the universal fear of witches in old times. Whether the persons accused of this offence really did imagine that they were possessed of unusual powers of any kind; or whether they had the will at least, if not the power, of doing mischief to their neighbours; or whether all the confessions, of which there are so many, were extorted by the mere cruelty of the witch-finders—these are questions which are not, I fancy, yet solved. And the present narrative gives me pause. I cannot altogether sweep it away as mere invention. The reader must judge for himself.

Castringham contributed a victim to the auto-da-fé. Mrs Mother-sole was her name, and she differed from the ordinary run of village

witches only in being rather better off and in a more influential position. Efforts were made to save her by several reputable farmers of
the parish. They did their best to testify to her character, and showed
considerable anxiety as to the verdict of the jury.

But what seems to have been fatal to the woman was the evidence
of the then proprietor of Castringham Hall—Sir Matthew Fell. He
deposed to having watched her on three different occasions from his
window, at the full of the moon, gathering sprigs 'from the ash-tree
near my house'. She had climbed into the branches, clad only in her
shift, and was cutting off small twigs with a peculiarly curved knife,
and as she did so she seemed to be talking to herself. On each occasion Sir Matthew had done his best to capture the woman, but she had
always taken alarm at some accidental noise he had made, and all he
could see when he got down to the garden was a hare running across
the park in the direction of the village.

On the third night he had been at the pains to follow at his best
speed, and had gone straight to Mrs Mothersole's house; but he had
had to wait a quarter of an hour battering at her door, and then she
had come out very cross, and apparently very sleepy, as if just out of
bed; and he had no good explanation to offer of his visit.

Mainly on this evidence, though there was much more of a less
striking and unusual kind from other parishioners, Mrs Mothersole was found guilty and condemned to die. She was hanged a week
after the trial, with five or six more unhappy creatures, at Bury St
Edmunds. Sir Matthew Fell, then Deputy-Sheriff, was present at the
execution. It was a damp, drizzly March morning when the cart made
its way up the rough grass hill outside Northgate, where the gallows
stood. The other victims were apathetic or broken down with misery; but Mrs Mothersole was, as in life so in death, of a very different
temper. Her 'poysonous Rage', as a reporter of the time puts it, 'did
so work upon the Bystanders—yea, even upon the Hangman—that it
was constantly affirmed of all that saw her that she presented the living
Aspect of a mad Divell. Yet she offer'd no Resistance to the Officers of
the Law; only she looked upon those that laid Hands upon her with

so direfull and venomous an Aspect that—as one of them afterwards assured me—the meer Thought of it preyed inwardly upon his Mind for six Months after.'

However, all that she is reported to have said was the seemingly meaningless words: 'There will be guests at the Hall.' Which she repeated more than once in an undertone.

Sir Matthew Fell was not unimpressed by the bearing of the woman. He had some talk upon the matter with the Vicar of his parish, with whom he travelled home after the assize business was over. His evidence at the trial had not been very willingly given; he was not specially infected with the witch-finding mania, but he declared, then and afterwards, that he could not give any other account of the matter than that he had given, and that he could not possibly have been mistaken as to what he saw. The whole transaction had been repugnant to him, for he was a man who liked to be on pleasant terms with those about him; but he saw a duty to be done in this business, and he had done it. That seems to have been the gist of his sentiments, and the Vicar applauded it, as any reasonable man must have done.

A few weeks after, when the moon of May was at the full, Vicar and Squire met again in the park, and walked to the Hall together. Lady Fell was with her mother, who was dangerously ill, and Sir Matthew was alone at home; so the Vicar, Mr Crome, was easily persuaded to take a late supper at the Hall.

Sir Matthew was not very good company this evening. The talk ran chiefly on family and parish matters, and, as luck would have it, Sir Matthew made a memorandum in writing of certain wishes or intentions of his regarding his estates, which afterwards proved exceedingly useful.

When Mr Crome thought of starting for home, about half-past nine o'clock, Sir Matthew and he took a preliminary turn on the gravelled walk at the back of the house. The only incident that struck Mr Crome was this: they were in sight of the ash-tree which I described as growing near the windows of the building, when Sir Matthew stopped and said:

'What is that that runs up and down the stem of the ash? It is never a squirrel? They will all be in their nests by now.'

The Vicar looked and saw the moving creature, but he could make nothing of its colour in the moonlight. The sharp outline, however, seen for an instant, was imprinted on his brain, and he could have sworn, he said, though it sounded foolish, that, squirrel or not, it had more than four legs.

Still, not much was to be made of the momentary vision, and the two men parted. They may have met since then, but it was not for a score of years.

Next day Sir Matthew Fell was not downstairs at six in the morning, as was his custom, nor at seven, nor yet at eight. Hereupon the servants went and knocked at his chamber door. I need not prolong the description of their anxious listenings and renewed batterings on the panels. The door was opened at last from the outside, and they found their master dead and black. So much you have guessed. That there were any marks of violence did not at the moment appear; but the window was open.

One of the men went to fetch the parson, and then by his directions rode on to give notice to the coroner. Mr Crome himself went as quick as he might to the Hall, and was shown to the room where the dead man lay. He has left some notes among his papers which show how genuine a respect and sorrow was felt for Sir Matthew, and there is also this passage, which I transcribe for the sake of the light it throws upon the course of events, and also upon the common beliefs of the time:

'There was not any the least Trace of an Entrance having been forc'd to the Chamber: but the Casement stood open, as my poor Friend would always have it in this Season. He had his Evening Drink of small Ale in a silver vessel of about a pint measure, and tonight had not drunk it out. This Drink was examined by the Physician from

Bury, a Mr Hodgkins, who could not, however, as he afterwards declar'd upon his Oath, before the Coroner's quest, discover that any matter of a venomous kind was present in it. For, as was natural, in the great Swelling and Blackness of the Corpse, there was talk made among the Neighbours of Poyson. The Body was very much Disorder'd as it laid in the Bed, being twisted after so extream a sort as gave too probable Conjecture that my worthy Friend and Patron had expir'd in great Pain and Agony. And what is as yet unexplain'd, and to myself the Argument of some Horrid and Artfull Designe in the Perpetrators of this Barbarous Murther, was this, that the Women which were entrusted with the laying-out of the Corpse and washing it, being both sad Persons and very well Respected in their Mournfull Profession, came to me in a great Pain and Distress both of Mind and Body, saying, what was indeed confirmed upon the first View, that they had no sooner touch'd the Breast of the Corpse with their naked Hands than they were sensible of a more than ordinary violent Smart and Acheing in their Palms, which, with their whole Forearms, in no long time swell'd so immoderately, the Pain still continuing, that, as afterwards proved, during many weeks they were forc'd to lay by the exercise of their Calling; and yet no mark seen on the Skin.

'Upon hearing this, I sent for the Physician, who was still in the House, and we made as carefull a Proof as we were able by the Help of a small Magnifying Lens of Crystal of the condition of the Skinn on this Part of the Body: but could not detect with the Instrument we had any Matter of Importance beyond a couple of small Punctures or Pricks, which we then concluded were the Spotts by which the Poyson might be introduced, remembering that Ring of Pope Borgia, with other known Specimens of the Horrid Art of the Italian Poysoners of the last age.

'So much is to be said of the Symptoms seen on the Corpse. As to what I am to add, it is meerly my own Experiment, and to be left to Posterity to judge whether there be anything of Value therein. There was on the Table by the Beddside a Bible of the small size, in which my Friend—punctuall as in Matters of less Moment, so in this more weighty one—used nightly, and upon his First Rising, to read a sett Portion. And I taking it up—not without a Tear duly paid to him which from the Study of this poorer Adumbration was now pass'd to the contemplation of its great Originall—it came into my Thoughts, as at such moments of Helplessness we are prone to catch at any the least Glimmer that makes promise of Light, to make trial of that old and by many accounted Superstitious Practice of drawing the Sortes: of which a Principall Instance, in the case of his late Sacred Majesty the Blessed Martyr King Charles and my Lord Falkland, was now much talked of. I must needs admit that by my Trial not much Assistance was afforded me: yet, as the Cause and Origin of these Dreadful Events may hereafter be search'd out, I set down the Results, in the case it may be found that they pointed the true Quarter of the Mischief to a quicker Intelligence than my own. 'I made, then, three trials, opening the Book and placing my Finger upon certain Words: which gave in the first these words, from Luke xiii 7, Cut it down; in the second, Isaiah xiii 20, It shall never be inhabited; and upon the third Experiment, Job xxxix 30, Her young ones also suck up blood.'

This is all that need be quoted from Mr Crome's papers. Sir Matthew Fell was duly coffined and laid into the earth, and his funeral sermon, preached by Mr Crome on the following Sunday, has been printed under the title of 'The Unsearchable Way; or, England's Danger and the Malicious Dealings of Anti-christ', it being the Vicar's view, as well as that most commonly held in the neighbourhood, that the Squire was the victim of a recrudescence of the Popish Plot.

His son, Sir Matthew the second, succeeded to the title and estates. And so ends the first act of the Castringham tragedy. It is to be mentioned, though the fact is not surprising, that the new Baronet did not occupy the room in which his father had died. Nor, indeed, was it slept in by anyone but an occasional visitor during the whole of his occupation. He died in 1735, and I do not find that anything particular marked his reign, save a curiously constant mortality among his cattle and livestock in general, which showed a tendency to increase slightly as time went on.

Those who are interested in the details will find a statistical account in a letter to the Gentleman's Magazine of 1772, which draws the facts from the Baronet's own papers. He put an end to it at last by a very simple expedient that of shutting up all his beasts in sheds at night, and keeping no sheep in his park. For he had noticed that nothing was ever attacked that spent the night indoors. After that the disorder confined itself to wild birds, and beasts of chase. But as we have no good account of the symptoms, and as all-night watching was quite unproductive of any clue, I do not dwell on what the Suffolk farmers called the 'Castringham sickness'.

The second Sir Matthew died in 1735, as I said, and was duly succeeded by his son, Sir Richard. It was in his time that the great family pew was built out on the north side of the parish church. So large were the Squire's ideas that several of the graves on that unhallowed side of the building had to be disturbed to satisfy his requirements. Among them was that of Mrs Mothersole, the position of which was accurately known, thanks to a note on a plan of the church and yard, both made by Mr Crome.

A certain amount of interest was excited in the village when it was known that the famous witch, who was still remembered by a few, was to be exhumed. And the feeling of surprise, and indeed disquiet, was very strong when it was found that, though her coffin was fairly sound and unbroken, there was no trace whatever inside it of body, bones, or dust. Indeed, it is a curious phenomenon, for at the time of her burying no such things were dreamt of as resurrection-men, and it is difficult to conceive any rational motive for stealing a body otherwise than for the uses of the dissecting-room.

The incident revived for a time all the stories of witch-trials and of the exploits of the witches, dormant for forty years, and Sir Richard's orders that the coffin should be burnt were thought by a good many to be rather foolhardy, though they were duly carried out.

Sir Richard was a pestilent innovator, it is certain. Before his time the Hall had been a fine block of the mellowest red brick; but Sir Richard had travelled in Italy and become infected with the Italian taste, and, having more money than his predecessors, he determined to leave an Italian palace where he had found an English house. So stucco and ashlar masked the brick; some indifferent Roman marbles were planted about in the entrance-hall and gardens; a reproduction of the Sibyl's temple at Tivoli was erected on the opposite bank of the mere; and Castringham took on an entirely new, and, I must say, a less engaging, aspect. But it was much admired, and served as a model to a good many of the neighbouring gentry in after years.

One morning (it was in 1754) Sir Richard woke after a night of discomfort. It had been windy, and his chimney had smoked persistently, and yet it was so cold that he must keep up a fire. Also something had so rattled about the window that no man could get a moment's peace. Further, there was the prospect of several guests of position arriving in the course of the day, who would expect sport of some kind, and the inroads of the distemper (which continued among his game) had been lately so serious that he was afraid for his reputation as a game-preserver. But what really touched him most nearly was the other matter of his sleepless night. He could certainly not sleep in that room again.

That was the chief subject of his meditations at breakfast, and after it he began a systematic examination of the rooms to see which would suit his notions best. It was long before he found one. This had a window with an eastern aspect and that with a northern; this door the servants would be always passing, and he did not like the bedstead in that. No, he must have a room with a western look-out, so that the sun could not wake him early, and it must be out of the way of the business of the house. The housekeeper was at the end of her resources. 'Well, Sir Richard,' she said, 'you know that there is but one room like that in the house.' 'Which may that be?' said Sir Richard. 'And that is Sir Matthew's—the West Chamber.' 'Well, put me in there, for there I'll lie tonight,' said her master. 'Which way is it? Here, to be sure'; and he hurried off.

'Oh, Sir Richard, but no one has slept there these forty years. The air has hardly been changed since Sir Matthew died there.' Thus she spoke, and rustled after him. 'Come, open the door, Mrs Chiddock. I'll see the chamber, at least.'

So it was opened, and, indeed, the smell was very close and earthy. Sir Richard crossed to the window, and, impatiently, as was his wont, threw the shutters back, and flung open the casement. For this end of the house was one which the alterations had barely touched, grown up as it was with the great ash-tree, and being otherwise concealed from view.

'Air it, Mrs Chiddock, all today, and move my bed-furniture in in the afternoon. Put the Bishop of Kilmore in my old room.'

'Pray, Sir Richard,' said a new voice, breaking in on this speech, 'might I have the favour of a moment's interview?'

Sir Richard turned round and saw a man in black in the doorway, who bowed. 'I must ask your indulgence for this intrusion, Sir Richard. You will, perhaps, hardly remember me. My name is William Crome, and my grandfather was Vicar here in your grandfather's time.'

'Well, sir,' said Sir Richard, 'the name of Crome is always a passport to Castringham. I am glad to renew a friendship of two generations' standing. In what can I serve you? for your hour of calling—and, if I do not mistake you, your bearing—shows you to be in some haste.'

'That is no more than the truth, sir. I am riding from Norwich to Bury St Edmunds with what haste I can make, and I have called in on my way to leave with you some papers which we have but just come upon in looking over what my grandfather left at his death. It is thought you may find some matters of family interest in them.'

'You are mighty obliging, Mr Crome, and, if you will be so good as to follow me to the parlour, and drink a glass of wine, we will take a first look at these same papers together. And you, Mrs Chiddock, as I said, be about airing this chamber . . . Yes, it is here my grandfather died . . . Yes, the tree, perhaps, does make the place a little dampish . . . No; I do not wish to listen to any more. Make no difficulties, I beg. You have your orders—go. Will you follow me, sir?'

They went to the study. The packet which young Mr Crome had brought—he was then just become a Fellow of Clare Hall in Cambridge, I may say, and subsequently brought out a respectable edition of Polyaenus—contained among other things the notes which the old Vicar had made upon the occasion of Sir Matthew Fell's death. And for the first time Sir Richard was confronted with the enigmatical Sortes Biblicae which you have heard. They amused him a good deal.

'Well,' he said, 'my grandfather's Bible gave one prudent piece of advice—Cut it down. If that stands for the ash-tree, he may rest assured I shall not neglect it. Such a nest of catarrhs and agues was never seen.'

The parlour contained the family books, which, pending the arrival of a collection which Sir Richard had made in Italy, and the building of a proper room to receive them, were not many in number.

Sir Richard looked up from the paper to the bookcase.

'I wonder,' says he, 'whether the old prophet is there yet? I fancy I see him.'

Crossing the room, he took out a dumpy Bible, which, sure enough, bore on the flyleaf the inscription: 'To Matthew Fell, from his Loving Godmother, Anne Aldous, 2 September, 1659.'

'It would be no bad plan to test him again, Mr Crome. I will wager we get a couple of names in the Chronicles. H'm! what have we here? "Thou shalt seek me in the morning, and I shall not be." Well, well! Your grandfather would have made a fine omen of that, hey? No more prophets for me! They are all in a tale. And now, Mr Crome, I am infinitely obliged to you for your packet. You will, I fear, be impatient to get on. Pray allow me—another glass.' So with offers of hospitality, which were genuinely meant (for Sir Richard thought well of the young man's address and manner), they parted.

In the afternoon came the guests—the Bishop of Kilmore, Lady Mary Hervey, Sir William Kentfield, etc. Dinner at five, wine, cards, supper, and dispersal to bed.

Next morning Sir Richard is disinclined to take his gun with the rest. He talks with the Bishop of Kilmore. This prelate, unlike a good many of the Irish Bishops of his day, had visited his see, and, indeed, resided there for some considerable time. This morning, as the two were walking along the terrace and talking over the alterations and improvements in the house, the Bishop said, pointing to the window of the West Room:

'You could never get one of my Irish flock to occupy that room, Sir Richard.'

'Why is that, my lord? It is, in fact, my own.'

'Well, our Irish peasantry will always have it that it brings the worst of luck to sleep near an ash-tree, and you have a fine growth of ash not two yards from your chamber window. Perhaps,' the Bishop went on, with a smile, 'it has given you a touch of its quality already, for you do not seem, if I may say it, so much the fresher for your night's rest as your friends would like to see you.'

'That, or something else, it is true, cost me my sleep from twelve to four, my lord. But the tree is to come down tomorrow, so I shall not hear much more from it.'

'I applaud your determination. It can hardly be wholesome to have the air you breathe strained, as it were, through all that leafage.'

'Your lordship is right there, I think. But I had not my window open last night. It was rather the noise that went on—no doubt from the twigs sweeping the glass—that kept me open-eyed.'

'I think that can hardly be. Sir Richard. Here—you see it from this point. None of these nearest branches even can touch your casement unless there were a gale, and there was none of that last night. They miss the panes by a foot.'

'No, sir, true. What, then, will it be, I wonder, that scratched and rustled so—ay, and covered the dust on my sill with lines and marks?'

At last they agreed that the rats must have come up through the ivy. That was the Bishop's idea, and Sir Richard jumped at it.

So the day passed quietly, and night came, and the party dispersed to their rooms, and wished Sir Richard a better night.

And now we are in his bedroom, with the light out and the Squire in bed. The room is over the kitchen, and the night outside still and warm, so the window stands open.

There is very little light about the bedstead, but there is a strange movement there; it seems as if Sir Richard were moving his head rapidly to and fro with only the slightest possible sound. And now you would guess, so deceptive is the half-darkness, that he had several heads, round and brownish, which move back and forward, even as low as his chest. It is a horrible illusion. Is it nothing more? There! something drops off the bed with a soft plump, like a kitten, and is out of the window in a flash; another—four—and after that there is quiet again.

'Thou shalt seek me in the morning, and I shall not be.'

As with Sir Matthew, so with Sir Richard—dead and black in his bed! A pale and silent party of guests and servants gathered under the window when the news was known. Italian poisoners, Popish emissaries, infected air—all these and more guesses were hazarded, and the Bishop of Kilmore looked at the tree, in the fork of whose lower boughs a white tom-cat was crouching, looking down the hollow which years had gnawed in the trunk. It was watching something inside the tree with great interest.

Suddenly it got up and craned over the hole. Then a bit of the edge on which it stood gave way, and it went slithering in. Everyone looked up at the noise of the fall.

It is known to most of us that a cat can cry; but few of us have heard, I hope, such a yell as came out of the trunk of the great ash. Two or three screams there were—the witnesses are not sure which—and then a slight and muffled noise of some commotion or struggling was all that came. But Lady Mary Hervey fainted outright, and the housekeeper stopped her ears and fled till she fell on the terrace.

The Bishop of Kilmore and Sir William Kentfield stayed. Yet even they were daunted, though it was only at the cry of a cat; and Sir William swallowed once or twice before he could say:

'There is something more than we know of in that tree, my lord. I am for an instant search.' And this was agreed upon. A ladder was brought, and one of the gardeners went up, and, looking down the hollow, could detect nothing but a few dim indications of something moving. They got a lantern, and let it down by a rope.

'We must get at the bottom of this. My life upon it, my lord, but the secret of these terrible deaths is there.'

Up went the gardener again with the lantern, and let it down the hole cautiously. They saw the yellow light upon his face as he bent over, and saw his face struck with an incredulous terror and loathing before he cried out in a dreadful voice and fell back from the ladder—where, happily, he was caught by two of the men—letting the lantern fall inside the tree. He was in a dead faint, and it was some time before any word could be got from him. By then they had something else to look at. The lantern must have broken at the bottom, and the light in it caught upon dry leaves and rubbish that lay there, for in a few minutes a dense smoke began to come up, and then flame; and, to be short, the tree was in a blaze. The bystanders made a ring at some yards' distance, and Sir William and the Bishop sent men to get what weapons and tools they could; for, clearly, whatever might be using the tree as its lair would be forced out by the fire.

So it was. First, at the fork, they saw a round body covered with fire—the size of a man's head—appear very suddenly, then seem to collapse and fall back. This, five or six times; then a similar ball leapt into the air and fell on the grass, where after a moment it lay still. The Bishop went as near as he dared to it, and saw—what but the remains of an enormous spider, veinous and seared! And, as the fire burned lower down, more terrible bodies like this began to break out from the trunk, and it was seen that these were covered with greyish hair.

All that day the ash burned, and until it fell to pieces the men stood about it, and from time to time killed the brutes as they darted out. At last there was a long interval when none appeared, and they cautiously closed in and examined the roots of the tree. 'They found,' says the Bishop of Kilmore, 'below it a rounded hollow place in the earth, wherein were two or three bodies of these creatures that had plainly been smothered by the smoke; and, what is to me more curious, at the side of this den, against the wall, was crouching the anatomy or skeleton of a human being, with the skin dried upon the bones, having some remains of black hair, which was pronounced by those that examined it to be undoubtedly the body of a woman, and clearly dead for a period of fifty years.'

THE CANTERVILLE GHOST

Oscar Wilde

In his own words, Oscar Wilde (1854–1900) "wanted to eat of the fruit of all the trees in the garden of the world. . . . And so, indeed, I went out, and so I lived." Wilde, author of the novel *The Picture of Dorian Gray*, wrote and produced nine plays, including *Salomé, Lady Windermere's Fan,* and *The Importance of Being Earnest.* Considered among the greatest playwrights of the Victorian Era, he has also been described as the first modern celebrity.

Wilde's brilliance and numerous accomplishments are often overshadowed by the scandals and persecution that drove him to his tragic denouement. Ensnared in the vicious antihomosexuality laws then current in Britain, Wilde was convicted of gross indecency in 1895 and sentenced to two years' hard labor. Wilde, a lover of luxury, was not suited for a life of "hard labor, hard fare, and a hard bed." Suffering from severe depression, his health declined sharply. Following his release from prison, having served his term, Wilde spent his last three years in impoverished exile on the European continent, dying destitute in Paris at age forty-six.

"The Canterville Ghost" was the first of Wilde's stories to be published, appearing in February 1887 in the magazine *The Court and Society Review.* In 1891, the story was included in *Lord Arthur Savile's Crime and Other Stories*, a collection of Wilde's short mystery stories. Like so much of Wilde's work, "The Canterville Ghost" is fun: a wickedly sly haunted house tale that juxtaposes comedy with horror motifs. There have been numerous film and theatrical adaptations, including the 1944 film starring Charles Laughton (who was the real life husband of actress Elsa Lanchester, famous for playing the Bride of Frankenstein and the witch, Aunt Queenie, in the film *Bell, Book, and Candle*), as well as a Bollywood movie and an animated version featuring the long-awaited reunion of Hugh Laurie and Stephen Fry.

The Canterville Ghost

An amusing chronicle of the tribulations of the Ghost of Canterville Chase when his ancestral halls became the home of the American Minister to the Court of St. James.

I

When Mr. Hiram B. Otis, the American Minister, bought Canterville Chase, every one told him he was doing a very foolish thing, as there was no doubt at all that the place was haunted. Indeed, Lord Canterville himself, who was a man of the most punctilious honour, had felt it his duty to mention the fact to Mr. Otis when they came to discuss terms.

"We have not cared to live in the place ourselves," said Lord Canterville, "since my grandaunt, the Dowager Duchess of Bolton, was frightened into a fit, from which she never really recovered, by two skeleton hands being placed on her shoulders as she was dressing for dinner, and I feel bound to tell you, Mr. Otis, that the ghost has been seen by several living members of my family, as well as by the rector of the parish, the Rev. Augustus Dampier, who is a Fellow of King's College, Cambridge. After the unfortunate accident to the Duchess, none of our younger servants would stay with us, and Lady Canterville often got very little sleep at night, in consequence of the mysterious noises that came from the corridor and the library."

"My Lord," answered the Minister, "I will take the furniture and the ghost at a valuation. I have come from a modern country, where we have everything that money can buy; and with all our spry young fellows painting the Old World red, and carrying off your best actors and prima-donnas, I reckon that if there were such a thing as a ghost in Europe, we'd have it at home in a very short time in one of our public museums, or on the road as a show."

"I fear that the ghost exists," said Lord Canterville, smiling, "though it may have resisted the overtures of your enterprising impresarios. It has been well known for three centuries, since 1584 in fact, and always makes its appearance before the death of any member of our family."

"Well, so does the family doctor for that matter, Lord Canterville. But there is no such thing, sir, as a ghost, and I guess the laws of Nature are not going to be suspended for the British aristocracy."

"You are certainly very natural in America," answered Lord Canterville, who did not quite understand Mr. Otis's last observation, "and if you don't mind a ghost in the house, it is all right. Only you must remember I warned you."

A few weeks after this, the purchase was concluded, and at the close of the season the Minister and his family went down to Canterville Chase. Mrs. Otis, who, as Miss Lucretia R. Tappan, of West 53rd Street, had been a celebrated New York belle, was now a very handsome, middle-aged woman, with fine eyes, and a superb profile. Many American ladies on leaving their native land adopt an appearance of chronic ill-health, under the impression that it is a form of European refinement, but Mrs. Otis had never fallen into this error. She had a magnificent constitution, and a really wonderful amount of animal spirits. Indeed, in many respects, she was quite English, and was an excellent example of the fact that we have really everything in common with America nowadays, except, of course, language. Her eldest son, christened Washington by his parents in a moment of patriotism, which he never ceased to regret, was a fair-haired, rather good-looking young man, who had qualified himself for American diplomacy by leading the German at the Newport Casino for three successive seasons, and even in London was well known as an excellent dancer. Gardenias and the peerage were his only weaknesses. Otherwise he was extremely sensible. Miss Virginia E. Otis was a little girl of fifteen, lithe and lovely as a fawn, and with a fine freedom in her large blue eyes. She was a wonderful Amazon, and had once raced old Lord Bilton on her pony twice round the park, winning by a length and a half, just in front of the Achilles statue, to the huge delight of the young Duke of Cheshire, who proposed for her on the spot, and was sent back to Eton that very night by his guardians, in floods of tears. After Virginia came the twins, who were usually called "The Star and Stripes," as they were always getting swished. They were delightful boys, and, with the exception of the worthy Minister, the only true republicans of the family.

As Canterville Chase is seven miles from Ascot, the nearest railway station, Mr. Otis had telegraphed for a waggonette to meet them, and they started on their drive in high spirits. It was a lovely July evening, and the air was delicate with the scent of the pinewoods. Now and then they heard a wood-pigeon brooding over its own sweet voice, or saw, deep in the rustling fern, the burnished breast of the pheasant. Little squirrels peered at them from the beech-trees as they went by, and the rabbits scudded away through the brushwood and over the mossy knolls, with their white tails in the air. As they entered the avenue of Canterville Chase, however, the sky became suddenly overcast with clouds, a curious stillness seemed to hold the atmosphere, a great flight of rooks passed silently over their heads, and, before they reached the house, some big drops of rain had fallen.

Standing on the steps to receive them was an old woman, neatly dressed in black silk, with a white cap and apron. This was Mrs. Umney, the housekeeper, whom Mrs. Otis, at Lady Canterville's earnest request, had consented to keep in her former position. She made them each a low curtsey as they alighted, and said in a quaint, old-fashioned manner, "I bid you welcome to Canterville Chase." Following her, they passed through the fine Tudor hall into the library, a long, low room, panelled in black oak, at the end of which was a large stained glass window. Here they found tea laid out for them, and, after taking off their wraps, they sat down and began to look round, while Mrs. Umney waited on them.

Suddenly Mrs. Otis caught sight of a dull red stain on the floor just by the fireplace, and, quite unconscious of what it really signified, said to Mrs. Umney, "I am afraid something has been spilt there."

"Yes, madam," replied the old housekeeper in a low voice, "blood has been spilt on that spot."

"How horrid!" cried Mrs. Otis; "I don't at all care for blood-stains in a sitting-room. It must be removed at once."

The old woman smiled, and answered in the same low, mysterious voice, "It is the blood of Lady Eleanore de Canterville, who was murdered on that very spot by her own husband, Sir Simon de Canterville, in 1575. Sir Simon survived her nine years, and disappeared suddenly under very mysterious circumstances. His body has never been discovered, but his guilty spirit still haunts the Chase. The blood-stain has been much admired by tourists and others, and cannot be removed."

"That is all nonsense," cried Washington Otis; "Pinkerton's Champion Stain Remover and Paragon Detergent will clean it up in no time," and before the terrified housekeeper could interfere, he had fallen upon his knees, and was rapidly scouring the floor with a small stick of what looked like a black cosmetic. In a few moments no trace of the blood-stain could be seen.

"I knew Pinkerton would do it," he exclaimed, triumphantly, as he looked round at his admiring family; but no sooner had he said these words than a terrible flash of lightning lit up the sombre room, a fearful peal of thunder made them all start to their feet, and Mrs. Umney fainted.

"What a monstrous climate!" said the American Minister, calmly, as he lit a long cheroot. "I guess the old country is so overpopulated that they have not enough decent weather for everybody. I have always been of opinion that emigration is the only thing for England."

"My dear Hiram," cried Mrs. Otis, "what can we do with a woman who faints?"

"Charge it to her like breakages," answered the Minister; "she won't faint after that;" and in a few moments Mrs. Umney certainly came to. There was no doubt, however, that she was extremely upset, and she sternly warned Mr. Otis to beware of some trouble coming to the house.

"I have seen things with my own eyes, sir," she said, "that would make any Christian's hair stand on end, and many and many a night I have not closed my eyes in sleep for the awful things that are done here." Mr. Otis, however, and his wife warmly assured the honest soul that they were not afraid of ghosts, and, after invoking the blessings of Providence on her new master and mistress, and making arrangements for an increase of salary, the old housekeeper tottered off to her own room.

II

The storm raged fiercely all that night, but nothing of particular note occurred. The next morning, however, when they came down to breakfast, they found the terrible stain of blood once again on the floor. "I don't think it can be the fault of the Paragon Detergent," said Washington, "for I have tried it with everything. It must be the ghost." He accordingly rubbed out the stain a second time, but the second morning it appeared again. The third morning also it was there, though the library had been locked up at night by Mr. Otis himself, and the key carried up-stairs. The whole family were now quite interested; Mr. Otis began to suspect that he had been too dogmatic in his denial of the existence of ghosts, Mrs. Otis expressed her intention of joining the Psychical Society, and Washington prepared a long letter to Messrs. Myers and Podmore on the subject of the Permanence of Sanguineous Stains when connected with Crime. That night all doubts about the objective existence of phantasmata were removed for ever.

The day had been warm and sunny; and, in the cool of the evening, the whole family went out to drive. They did not return home till nine o'clock, when they had a light supper. The conversation in no way turned upon ghosts, so there were not even those primary conditions of receptive expectations which so often precede the presentation of psychical phenomena. The subjects discussed, as I have since learned from Mr. Otis, were merely such as form the ordinary conversation of cultured Americans of the better class, such as the immense superiority of Miss Fanny Devonport over Sarah Bernhardt as an actress; the difficulty of obtaining green corn, buckwheat cakes, and hominy, even in the best English houses; the importance of Boston in the development of the world-soul; the advantages of the baggage-check system in railway travelling; and the sweetness of the New York accent as compared to the London drawl. No mention at all was made of the supernatural, nor was Sir Simon de Canterville alluded to in any way. At eleven o'clock the family retired, and by half-past all the lights were out. Some time after, Mr. Otis was awakened by a curious noise in the corridor, outside his room. It sounded like the clank of metal, and seemed to be coming nearer every moment. He got up at once, struck a match, and looked at the time. It was exactly one o'clock. He was quite calm, and felt his pulse, which was not at all feverish. The strange noise still continued, and with it he heard distinctly the sound of footsteps. He put on his slippers, took a small oblong phial out of his dressing-case, and opened the door. Right in front of him he saw, in the wan moonlight, an old man of terrible aspect. His eyes were as red burning coals; long grey hair fell over his shoulders in matted coils; his garments, which were of antique cut, were soiled and ragged, and from his wrists and ankles hung heavy manacles and rusty gyves.

"My dear sir," said Mr. Otis, "I really must insist on your oiling those chains, and have brought you for that purpose a small bottle of the Tammany Rising Sun Lubricator. It is said to be completely efficacious upon one application, and there are several testimonials to that effect on the wrapper from some of our most eminent native divines. I shall leave it here for you by the bedroom candles, and will be happy to supply you with more, should you require it." With these words the United States Minister laid the bottle down on a marble table, and, closing his door, retired to rest.

For a moment the Canterville ghost stood quite motionless in natural indignation; then, dashing the bottle violently upon the polished floor, he fled down the corridor, uttering hollow groans, and emitting a ghastly green light. Just, however, as he reached the top of the great oak staircase, a door was flung open, two little white-robed figures appeared, and a large pillow whizzed past his head! There was evidently no time to be lost, so, hastily adopting the Fourth dimension of Space as a means of escape, he vanished through the wainscoting, and the house became quite quiet.

On reaching a small secret chamber in the left wing, he leaned up against a moonbeam to recover his breath, and began to try and realize his position. Never, in a brilliant and uninterrupted career of three hundred years, had he been so grossly insulted. He thought of the Dowager Duchess, whom he had frightened into a fit as she stood before the glass in her lace and diamonds; of the four housemaids, who had gone into hysterics when he merely grinned at them through the curtains on one of the spare bedrooms; of the rector of the parish, whose candle he had blown out as he was coming late one night from the library, and who had been under the care of Sir William Gull ever since, a perfect martyr to nervous disorders; and of old Madame de Tremouillac, who, having wakened up one morning early and seen a skeleton seated in an armchair by the fire reading her diary, had been confined to her bed for six weeks with an attack of brain fever, and, on her recovery, had become reconciled to the Church, and broken off her connection with that notorious sceptic, Monsieur de Voltaire. He remembered the terrible night when the wicked Lord Canterville was found choking in his dressing-room, with the knave of diamonds half-way down his throat, and confessed, just before he died, that he had cheated Charles James Fox out of £50,000 at Crockford's by means of that very card, and swore that the ghost had made him swallow it. All his great achievements came back to him again, from the butler who had shot himself in the pantry because he had seen a green hand tapping at the window-pane, to the beautiful Lady Stutfield, who was always obliged to wear a black velvet band round her throat to hide the mark of five fingers burnt upon her white skin, and who drowned herself at last in the carp-pond at the end of the King's Walk. With the enthusiastic egotism of the true artist, he went over his most celebrated performances, and smiled bitterly to himself as he recalled to mind his last appearance as "Red Reuben, or the Strangled Babe," his *début* as "Guant Gibeon, the Blood-sucker of Bexley Moor," and the *furore* he had excited one lovely June evening by merely playing ninepins with his own bones upon the lawn-tennis ground. And after all this some wretched modern Americans were to come and offer him the Rising Sun Lubricator, and throw pillows at his head! It was quite unbearable. Besides, no ghost in history had ever been treated in this manner. Accordingly, he determined to have vengeance, and remained till daylight in an attitude of deep thought.

III

The next morning, when the Otis family met at breakfast, they discussed the ghost at some length. The United States Minister was naturally a little annoyed to find that his present had not been accepted. "I have no wish," he said, "to do the ghost any personal injury, and I must say that, considering the length of time he has been in the house, I don't think it is at all polite to throw pillows at him,"—a very just remark, at which, I am sorry to say, the twins burst into shouts of laughter. "Upon the other hand," he continued, "if he really declines to use the Rising Sun Lubricator, we shall have to take his chains from him. It would be quite impossible to sleep, with such a noise going on outside the bedrooms."

For the rest of the week, however, they were undisturbed, the only thing that excited any attention being the continual renewal of the blood-stain on the library floor. This certainly was very strange, as the door was always locked at night by Mr. Otis, and the windows kept closely barred. The chameleon-like colour, also, of the stain excited a good deal of comment. Some mornings it was a dull (almost Indian) red, then it would be vermilion, then a rich purple, and once when they came down for family prayers, according to the simple rites of the Free American Reformed Episcopalian Church, they found it a bright emerald-green. These kaleidoscopic changes naturally amused the party very much, and bets on the subject were freely made every evening. The only person who did not enter into the joke was little

Virginia, who, for some unexplained reason, was always a good deal distressed at the sight of the blood-stain, and very nearly cried the morning it was emerald-green.

The second appearance of the ghost was on Sunday night. Shortly after they had gone to bed they were suddenly alarmed by a fearful crash in the hall. Rushing down-stairs, they found that a large suit of old armour had become detached from its stand, and had fallen on the stone floor, while seated in a high-backed chair was the Canterville ghost, rubbing his knees with an expression of acute agony on his face. The twins, having brought their pea-shooters with them, at once discharged two pellets on him, with that accuracy of aim which can only be attained by long and careful practice on a writing-master, while the United States Minister covered him with his revolver, and called upon him, in accordance with Californian etiquette, to hold up his hands! The ghost started up with a wild shriek of rage, and swept through them like a mist, extinguishing Washington Otis's candle as he passed, and so leaving them all in total darkness. On reaching the top of the staircase he recovered himself, and determined to give his celebrated peal of demoniac laughter. This he had on more than one occasion found extremely useful. It was said to have turned Lord Raker's wig grey in a single night, and had certainly made three of Lady Canterville's French governesses give warning before their month was up. He accordingly laughed his most horrible laugh, till the old vaulted roof rang and rang again, but hardly had the fearful echo died away when a door opened, and Mrs. Otis came out in a light blue dressing-gown. "I am afraid you are far from well," she said, "and have brought you a bottle of Doctor Dobell's tincture. If it is indigestion, you will find it a most excellent remedy." The ghost glared at her in fury, and began at once to make preparations for turning himself into a large black dog, an accomplishment for which he was justly renowned, and to which the family doctor always attributed the permanent idiocy of Lord Canterville's uncle, the Hon. Thomas Horton. The sound of approaching footsteps, however, made him hesitate in his fell purpose, so he contented himself with becoming faintly phosphorescent, and vanished with a deep churchyard groan, just as the twins had come up to him.

On reaching his room he entirely broke down, and became a prey to the most violent agitation. The vulgarity of the twins, and the gross materialism of Mrs. Otis, were naturally extremely annoying, but what really distressed him most was that he had been unable to wear the suit of mail. He had hoped that even modern Americans would be thrilled by the sight of a Spectre in armour, if for no more sensible reason, at least out of respect for their natural poet Longfellow, over whose graceful and attractive poetry he himself had whiled away many a weary hour when the Cantervilles were up in town. Besides it was his own suit. He had worn it with great success at the Kenilworth tournament, and had been highly complimented on it by no less a person than the Virgin Queen herself. Yet when he had put it on, he had been completely overpowered by the weight of the huge breastplate and steel casque, and had fallen heavily on the stone pavement, barking both his knees severely, and bruising the knuckles of his right hand.

For some days after this he was extremely ill, and hardly stirred out of his room at all, except to keep the blood-stain in proper repair. However, by taking great care of himself, he recovered, and resolved to make a third attempt to frighten the United States Minister and his family. He selected Friday, August 17th, for his appearance, and spent most of that day in looking over his wardrobe, ultimately deciding in favour of a large slouched hat with a red feather, a winding-sheet frilled at the wrists and neck, and a rusty dagger. Towards evening a violent storm of rain came on, and the wind was so high that all the windows and doors in the old house shook and rattled. In fact, it was just such weather as he loved. His plan of action was this. He was to make his way quietly to Washington Otis's room, gibber at him from the foot of the bed, and stab himself three times in the throat to the sound of low music. He bore Washington a special grudge, being quite aware that it was he who was in the habit of removing the famous Canterville blood-stain by means of Pinkerton's Paragon Detergent. Having reduced the reckless and foolhardy youth to a condition of abject terror, he was then to proceed to the room occupied by the United States Minister and his wife, and there to place a clammy hand on Mrs. Otis's forehead, while he hissed into her trembling husband's ear the awful secrets of the charnel-house. With regard to little Virginia, he had not quite made up his mind. She had never insulted him in any way, and was pretty and gentle. A few hollow groans from the wardrobe, he thought, would be more than sufficient, or, if that failed to wake her, he might grabble at the counterpane with palsy-twitching fingers. As for the twins, he was quite determined to teach them a lesson. The first thing to be done was, of course, to sit upon their chests, so as to produce the stifling sensation of nightmare. Then, as their beds were quite close to each other, to stand between them in the form of a green, icy-cold corpse, till they became paralyzed with fear, and finally, to throw off the winding-sheet, and crawl round the room, with white, bleached bones and one rolling eyeball, in the character of "Dumb Daniel, or the Suicide's Skeleton," a rôle in which he had on more than one occasion produced a great effect, and which he considered quite equal to his famous part of "Martin the Maniac, or the Masked Mystery."

At half-past ten he heard the family going to bed. For some time he was disturbed by wild shrieks of laughter from the twins, who, with the light-hearted gaiety of schoolboys, were evidently amusing themselves before they retired to rest, but at a quarter-past eleven all was still, and, as midnight sounded, he sallied forth. The owl beat against the window-panes, the raven croaked from the old yew-tree, and the wind wandered moaning round the house like a lost soul; but the Otis family slept unconscious of their doom, and high above the rain and storm he could hear the steady snoring of the Minister for the United States. He stepped stealthily out of the wainscoting, with an evil smile on his cruel, wrinkled mouth, and the moon hid her face in a cloud as he stole past the great oriel window, where his own arms and those of his murdered wife were blazoned in azure and gold. On and on he glided, like an evil shadow, the very darkness seeming to loathe him as he passed. Once he thought he heard something call, and stopped;

but it was only the baying of a dog from the Red Farm, and he went on, muttering strange sixteenth-century curses, and ever and anon brandishing the rusty dagger in the midnight air. Finally he reached the corner of the passage that led to luckless Washington's room. For a moment he paused there, the wind blowing his long grey locks about his head, and twisting into grotesque and fantastic folds the nameless horror of the dead man's shroud. Then the clock struck the quarter, and he felt the time was come. He chuckled to himself, and turned the corner; but no sooner had he done so than, with a piteous wail of terror, he fell back, and hid his blanched face in his long, bony hands. Right in front of him was standing a horrible spectre, motionless as a carven image, and monstrous as a madman's dream! Its head was bald and burnished; its face round, and fat, and white; and hideous laughter seemed to have writhed its features into an eternal grin. From the eyes streamed rays of scarlet light, the mouth was a wide well of fire, and a hideous garment, like to his own, swathed with its silent snows the Titan form. On its breast was a placard with strange writing in antique characters, some scroll of shame it seemed, some record of wild sins, some awful calendar of crime, and, with its right hand, it bore aloft a falchion of gleaming steel.

Never having seen a ghost before, he naturally was terribly frightened, and, after a second hasty glance at the awful phantom, he fled back to his room, tripping up in his long winding-sheet as he sped down the corridor, and finally dropping the rusty dagger into the Minister's jack-boots, where it was found in the morning by the butler. Once in the privacy of his own apartment, he flung himself down on a small pallet-bed, and hid his face under the clothes. After a time, however, the brave old Canterville spirit asserted itself, and he determined to go and speak to the other ghost as soon as it was daylight. Accordingly, just as the dawn was touching the hills with silver, he returned towards the spot where he had first laid eyes on the grisly phantom, feeling that, after all, two ghosts were better than one, and that, by the aid of his new friend, he might safely grapple with the twins. On reaching the spot, however, a terrible sight met his gaze.

Something had evidently happened to the spectre, for the light had entirely faded from its hollow eyes, the gleaming falchion had fallen from its hand, and it was leaning up against the wall in a strained and uncomfortable attitude. He rushed forward and seized it in his arms, when, to his horror, the head slipped off and rolled on the floor, the body assumed a recumbent posture, and he found himself clasping a white dimity bed-curtain, with a sweeping-brush, a kitchen cleaver, and a hollow turnip lying at his feet! Unable to understand this curious transformation, he clutched the placard with feverish haste, and there, in the grey morning light, he read these fearful words:—

YE OTIS GHOSTE

Ye Onlie True and Originale Spook,
Beware of Ye Imitationes.
All others are counterfeite.

The whole thing flashed across him. He had been tricked, foiled, and out-witted! The old Canterville look came into his eyes; he ground his toothless gums together; and, raising his withered hands high above his head, swore according to the picturesque phraseology of the antique school, that, when Chanticleer had sounded twice his merry horn, deeds of blood would be wrought, and murder walk abroad with silent feet.

Hardly had he finished this awful oath when, from the red-tiled roof of a distant homestead, a cock crew. He laughed a long, low, bitter laugh, and waited. Hour after hour he waited, but the cock, for some strange reason, did not crow again. Finally, at half-past seven, the arrival of the housemaids made him give up his fearful vigil, and he stalked back to his room, thinking of his vain oath and baffled purpose. There he consulted several books of ancient chivalry, of which he was exceedingly fond, and found that, on every occasion on which this oath had been used, Chanticleer had always crowed a second time. "Perdition seize the naughty fowl," he muttered, "I have seen the day when, with my stout spear, I would have run him through the gorge, and made him crow for me as 'twere in death!" He then retired to a comfortable lead coffin, and stayed there till evening.

IV

The next day the ghost was very weak and tired. The terrible excitement of the last four weeks was beginning to have its effect. His nerves were completely shattered, and he started at the slightest noise. For five days he kept his room, and at last made up his mind to give up the point of the blood-stain on the library floor. If the Otis family did not want it, they clearly did not deserve it. They were evidently people on a low, material plane of existence, and quite incapable of appreciating the symbolic value of sensuous phenomena. The question of phantasmic apparitions, and the development of astral bodies, was of course quite a different matter, and really not under his control. It was his solemn duty to appear in the corridor once a week, and to gibber from the large oriel window on the first and third Wednesdays in every month, and he did not see how he could honourably escape from his obligations. It is quite true that his life had been very evil, but, upon the other hand, he was most conscientious in all things connected with the supernatural. For the next three Saturdays, accordingly, he traversed the corridor as usual between midnight and three o'clock, taking every possible precaution against being either heard or seen. He removed his boots, trod as lightly as possible on the old worm-eaten boards, wore a large black velvet cloak, and was careful to use the Rising Sun Lubricator for oiling his chains. I am bound to acknowledge that it was with a good deal of difficulty that he brought himself to adopt this last mode of protection. However, one night, while the family were at dinner, he slipped into Mr. Otis's bedroom and carried off the bottle. He felt a little humiliated at first, but afterwards was sensible enough to see that there was a great deal to be said for the invention, and, to a certain degree, it served his purpose. Still in spite of everything he was not left unmolested. Strings were continually being stretched across the corridor, over which he tripped in the dark, and on one occasion, while dressed for the part of "Black Isaac, or the Huntsman of Hogley Woods," he met with a severe fall, through treading on a butter-slide, which the twins had constructed from the entrance of the Tapestry Chamber to the top of the oak staircase. This last insult so enraged him, that he resolved to make one final effort to assert his dignity and social position, and determined to visit the insolent young Etonians the next night in his celebrated character of "Reckless Rupert, or the Headless Earl."

He had not appeared in this disguise for more than seventy years; in fact, not since he had so frightened pretty Lady Barbara Modish by means of it, that she suddenly broke off her engagement with the present Lord Canterville's grandfather, and ran away to Gretna Green with handsome Jack Castletown, declaring that nothing in the world would induce her to marry into a family that allowed such a horrible phantom to walk up and down the terrace at twilight. Poor Jack was afterwards shot in a duel by Lord Canterville on Wandsworth Common, and Lady Barbara died of a broken heart at Tunbridge Wells before the year was out, so, in every way, it had been a great success. It was, however an extremely difficult "make-up," if I may use such a theatrical expression in connection with one of the greatest mysteries of the supernatural, or, to employ a more scientific term, the higher-natural world, and it took him fully three hours to make his preparations. At last everything was ready, and he was very pleased with his appearance. The big leather riding-boots that went with the dress were just a little too large for him, and he could only find one of the two horse-pistols, but, on the whole, he was quite satisfied, and at a quarter-past one he glided out of the wainscoting and crept down the corridor. On reaching the room occupied by the twins, which I should mention was called the Blue Bed Chamber, on account of the colour of its hangings, he found the door just ajar. Wishing to make an effective entrance, he flung it wide open, when a heavy jug of water fell right down on him, wetting him to the skin, and just missing his left shoulder by a couple of inches. At the same moment he heard stifled shrieks of laughter proceeding from the four-post bed. The shock to his nervous system was so great that he fled back to his room as hard as he could go, and the next day he was laid up with a severe cold. The only thing that at all consoled him in the whole affair was the fact that he had not brought his head with him, for, had he done so, the consequences might have been very serious.

He now gave up all hope of ever frightening this rude American family, and contented himself, as a rule, with creeping about the passages in list slippers, with a thick red muffler round his throat for fear of draughts, and a small arquebuse, in case he should be attacked by the twins. The final blow he received occurred on the 19th of September. He had gone down-stairs to the great entrance-hall, feeling sure that there, at any rate, he would be quite unmolested, and was amusing himself by making satirical remarks on the large Saroni photographs of the United States Minister and his wife which had now taken the place of the Canterville family pictures. He was simply but neatly clad in a long shroud, spotted with churchyard mould, had tied up his jaw with a strip of yellow linen, and carried a small lantern and a sexton's spade. In fact, he was dressed for the character of "Jonas the Graveless, or the Corpse-Snatcher of Chertsey Barn," one of his most remarkable impersonations, and one which the Cantervilles had every reason to remember, as it was the real origin of their quarrel with their neighbour, Lord Rufford. It was about a quarter-past two o'clock in the morning, and, as far as he could ascertain, no one was stirring. As he was strolling towards the library, however, to see if there were any traces left of the blood-stain, suddenly there leaped out on him from a dark corner two figures, who waved their arms wildly above their heads, and shrieked out "BOO!" in his ear.

Seized with a panic, which, under the circumstances, was only natural, he rushed for the staircase, but found Washington Otis waiting for him there with the big garden-syringe, and being thus hemmed in by his enemies on every side, and driven almost to bay, he vanished into the great iron stove, which, fortunately for him, was not lit, and had to make his way home through the flues and chimneys, arriving at his own room in a terrible state of dirt, disorder, and despair.

After this he was not seen again on any nocturnal expedition. The twins lay in wait for him on several occasions, and strewed the passages with nutshells every night to the great annoyance of their parents and the servants, but it was of no avail. It was quite evident that his feelings were so wounded that he would not appear. Mr. Otis consequently resumed his great work on the history of the Democratic Party, on which he had been engaged for some years; Mrs. Otis organized a wonderful clam-bake, which amazed the whole county; the boys took to lacrosse euchre, poker, and other American national games, and Virginia rode about the lanes on her pony, accompanied by the young Duke of Cheshire, who had come to spend the last week of his holidays at Canterville Chase. It was generally assumed that the ghost had gone away, and, in fact, Mr. Otis wrote a letter to that effect to Lord Canterville, who, in reply, expressed his great pleasure at the news, and sent his best congratulations to the Minister's worthy wife.

The Otises, however, were deceived, for the ghost was still in the house, and though now almost an invalid, was by no means ready to let matters rest, particularly as he heard that among the guests was the young Duke of Cheshire, whose grand-uncle, Lord Francis Stilton, had once bet a hundred guineas with Colonel Carbury that he would play dice with the Canterville ghost, and was found the next morning lying on the floor of the card-room in such a helpless paralytic state that, though he lived on to a great age, he was never able to say anything again but "Double Sixes." The story was well known at the time, though, of course, out of respect to the feelings of the two noble families, every attempt was made to hush it up, and a full account of all the circumstances connected with it will be found in the third volume of Lord Tattle's *Recollections of the Prince Regent and His Friends.* The ghost, then, was naturally very anxious to show that he had not lost his influence over the Stiltons, with whom, indeed, he was distantly connected, his own first cousin having been married *en secondes noces* to the Sieur de Bulkeley, from whom, as every one knows, the Dukes of Cheshire are lineally descended. Accordingly, he made arrangements for appearing to Virginia's little lover in his celebrated impersonation of "The Vampire Monk, or the Bloodless Benedictine," a performance so horrible that when old Lady Startup saw it, which she did on one fatal New Year's Eve, in the year 1764, she went off into the most piercing shrieks, which culminated in violent apoplexy, and died in three days, after disinheriting the Cantervilles, who were her nearest relations, and leaving all her money to her London apothecary. At the last moment, however, his terror of the twins prevented his leaving his room, and the little Duke slept in peace under the great feathered canopy in the Royal Bedchamber, and dreamed of Virginia.

V

A few days after this, Virginia and her curly-haired cavalier went out riding on Brockley meadows, where she tore her habit so badly in getting through a hedge that, on their return home, she made up her mind to go up by the back staircase so as not to be seen. As she was running past the Tapestry Chamber, the door of which happened to be open, she fancied she saw some one inside, and thinking it was her mother's maid, who sometimes used to bring her work there, looked in to ask her to mend her habit. To her immense surprise, however, it was the Canterville Ghost himself! He was sitting by the window, watching the ruined gold of the yellowing trees fly through the air, and the red leaves dancing madly down the long avenue. His head was leaning on his hand, and his whole attitude was one of extreme depression. Indeed, so forlorn, and so much out of repair did he look, that little Virginia, whose first idea had been to run away and lock herself in her room, was filled with pity, and determined to try and comfort him. So light was her footfall, and so deep his melancholy, that he was not aware of her presence till she spoke to him.

"I am so sorry for you," she said, "but my brothers are going back to Eton to-morrow, and then, if you behave yourself, no one will annoy you."

"It is absurd asking me to behave myself," he answered, looking round in astonishment at the pretty little girl who had ventured to address him, "quite absurd. I must rattle my chains, and groan through keyholes, and walk about at night, if that is what you mean. It is my only reason for existing."

"It is no reason at all for existing, and you know you have been very wicked. Mrs. Umney told us, the first day we arrived here, that you had killed your wife."

"Well, I quite admit it," said the Ghost, petulantly, "but it was a purely family matter, and concerned no one else."

"It is very wrong to kill any one," said Virginia, who at times had a sweet puritan gravity, caught from some old New England ancestor.

"Oh, I hate the cheap severity of abstract ethics! My wife was very plain, never had my ruffs properly starched, and knew nothing about cookery. Why, there was a buck I had shot in Hogley Woods, a magnificent pricket, and do you know how she had it sent to table? However, it is no matter now, for it is all over, and I don't think it was very nice of her brothers to starve me to death, though I did kill her."

"Starve you to death? Oh, Mr. Ghost—I mean Sir Simon, are you hungry? I have a sandwich in my case. Would you like it?"

"No, thank you, I never eat anything now; but it is very kind of you, all the same, and you are much nicer than the rest of your horrid, rude, vulgar, dishonest family."

"Stop!" cried Virginia, stamping her foot, "it is you who are rude, and horrid, and vulgar, and as for dishonesty, you know you stole the paints out of my box to try and furbish up that ridiculous blood-stain in the library. First you took all my reds, including the vermilion, and I couldn't do any more sunsets, then you took the emerald-green and the chrome-yellow, and finally I had nothing left but indigo and Chinese white, and could only do moonlight scenes, which are always depressing to look at, and not at all easy to paint. I never told on you, though I was very much annoyed, and it was most ridiculous, the whole thing; for who ever heard of emerald-green blood?"

"Well, really," said the Ghost, rather meekly, "what was I to do? It is a very difficult thing to get real blood nowadays, and, as your brother began it all with his Paragon Detergent, I certainly saw no reason why I should not have your paints. As for colour, that is always a matter of taste: the Cantervilles have blue blood, for instance, the very bluest in England; but I know you Americans don't care for things of this kind."

"You know nothing about it, and the best thing you can do is to emigrate and improve your mind. My father will be only too happy to give you a free passage, and though there is a heavy duty on spirits of every kind, there will be no difficulty about the Custom House, as the officers are all Democrats. Once in New York, you are sure to be a great success. I know lots of people there who would give a hundred thousand dollars to have a grandfather, and much more than that to have a family ghost."

"I don't think I should like America."

"I suppose because we have no ruins and no curiosities," said Virginia, satirically.

"No ruins! no curiosities!" answered the Ghost; "you have your navy and your manners."

"Good evening; I will go and ask papa to get the twins an extra week's holiday."

"Please don't go, Miss Virginia," he cried; "I am so lonely and so unhappy, and I really don't know what to do. I want to go to sleep and I cannot."

"That's quite absurd! You have merely to go to bed and blow out the candle. It is very difficult sometimes to keep awake, especially at church, but there is no difficulty at all about sleeping. Why, even babies know how to do that, and they are not very clever."

"I have not slept for three hundred years," he said sadly, and Virginia's beautiful blue eyes opened in wonder; "for three hundred years I have not slept, and I am so tired."

Virginia grew quite grave, and her little lips trembled like rose-leaves. She came towards him, and kneeling down at his side, looked up into his old withered face.

"Poor, poor Ghost," she murmured; "have you no place where you can sleep?"

"Far away beyond the pine-woods," he answered, in a low, dreamy voice, "there is a little garden. There the grass grows long and deep, there are the great white stars of the hemlock flower, there the night-ingale sings all night long. All night long he sings, and the cold crystal moon looks down, and the yew-tree spreads out its giant arms over the sleepers."

Virginia's eyes grew dim with tears, and she hid her face in her hands.

"You mean the Garden of Death," she whispered.

"Yes, death. Death must be so beautiful. To lie in the soft brown earth, with the grasses waving above one's head, and listen to silence. To have no yesterday, and no to-morrow. To forget time, to forget life, to be at peace. You can help me. You can open for me the portals of death's house, for love is always with you, and love is stronger than death is."

Virginia trembled, a cold shudder ran through her, and for a few moments there was silence. She felt as if she was in a terrible dream.

Then the ghost spoke again, and his voice sounded like the sighing of the wind.

"Have you ever read the old prophecy on the library window?"

"Oh, often," cried the little girl, looking up; "I know it quite well. It is painted in curious black letters, and is difficult to read. There are only six lines:

> "'When a golden girl can win
> Prayer from out the lips of sin,
> When the barren almond bears,
> And a little child gives away its tears,
> Then shall all the house be still
> And peace come to Canterville.'

But I don't know what they mean."

"They mean," he said, sadly, "that you must weep with me for my sins, because I have no tears, and pray with me for my soul, because I have no faith, and then, if you have always been sweet, and good, and gentle, the angel of death will have mercy on me. You will see fearful shapes in darkness, and wicked voices will whisper in your ear, but they will not harm you, for against the purity of a little child the powers of Hell cannot prevail."

Virginia made no answer, and the ghost wrung his hands in wild despair as he looked down at her bowed golden head. Suddenly she stood up, very pale, and with a strange light in her eyes. "I am not afraid," she said firmly, "and I will ask the angel to have mercy on you."

He rose from his seat with a faint cry of joy, and taking her hand bent over it with old-fashioned grace and kissed it. His fingers were as cold as ice, and his lips burned like fire, but Virginia did not falter, as he led her across the dusky room. On the faded green tapestry were broidered little huntsmen. They blew their tasselled horns and with their tiny hands waved to her to go back. "Go back! little Virginia," they cried, "go back!" but the ghost clutched her hand more tightly, and she shut her eyes against them. Horrible animals with lizard tails and goggle eyes blinked at her from the carven chimneypiece, and murmured, "Beware! little Virginia, beware! we may never see you again," but the Ghost glided on more swiftly, and Virginia did not listen. When they reached the end of the room he stopped, and muttered some words she could not understand. She opened her eyes, and saw the wall slowly fading away like a mist, and a great black cavern in front of her. A bitter cold wind swept round them, and she felt something pulling at her dress. "Quick, quick," cried the Ghost, "or it will be too late," and in a moment the wainscoting had closed behind them, and the Tapestry Chamber was empty.

VI

About ten minutes later, the bell rang for tea, and, as Virginia did not come down, Mrs. Otis sent up one of the footmen to tell her. After a little time he returned and said that he could not find Miss Virginia anywhere. As she was in the habit of going out to the garden every evening to get flowers for the dinner-table, Mrs. Otis was not at all alarmed at first, but when six o'clock struck, and Virginia did not appear, she became really agitated, and sent the boys out to look for her, while she herself and Mr. Otis searched every room in the house. At half-past six the boys came back and said that they could find no trace of their sister anywhere. They were all now in the greatest state of excitement, and did not know what to do, when Mr. Otis suddenly remembered that, some few days before, he had given a band of gipsies permission to camp in the park. He accordingly at once set off for Blackfell Hollow, where he knew they were, accompanied by his eldest son and two of the farm-servants. The little Duke of Cheshire, who was perfectly frantic with anxiety, begged hard to be allowed to go too, but Mr. Otis would not allow him, as he was afraid there might be a scuffle. On arriving at the spot, however, he found that the gipsies had gone, and it was evident that their departure had been rather sudden, as the fire was still burning, and some plates were lying on the grass. Having sent off Washington and the two men to scour the district, he ran home, and despatched telegrams to all the police inspectors in the county, telling them to look out for a little girl who had been kidnapped by tramps or gipsies. He then ordered his horse to be brought round, and, after insisting on his wife and the three boys sitting down to dinner, rode off down the Ascot road with a groom. He had hardly, however, gone a couple of miles, when he heard somebody galloping after him, and, looking round, saw the little Duke coming up on his pony, with his face very flushed, and no hat. "I'm awfully sorry, Mr. Otis," gasped out the boy, "but I can't eat any dinner as long as Virginia is lost. Please don't be angry with me; if you had let us be engaged last year, there would never have been all this trouble. You won't send me back, will you? I can't go! I won't go!"

The Minister could not help smiling at the handsome young scapegrace, and was a good deal touched at his devotion to Virginia, so leaning down from his horse, he patted him kindly on the shoulders, and said, "Well, Cecil, if you won't go back, I suppose you must come with me, but I must get you a hat at Ascot."

"Oh, bother my hat! I want Virginia!" cried the little Duke, laughing, and they galloped on to the railway station. There Mr. Otis inquired of the station-master if any one answering to the description of Virginia had been seen on the platform, but could get no news of her. The station-master, however, wired up and down the line, and assured him that a strict watch would be kept for her, and, after having bought a hat for the little Duke from a linen-draper, who was just putting up his shutters, Mr. Otis rode off to Bexley, a village about four miles away, which he was told was a well-known haunt of the gipsies, as there was a large common next to it. Here they roused up the rural policeman, but could get no information from him, and, after riding all over the common, they turned their horses' heads homewards, and reached the Chase about eleven o'clock, dead-tired and almost heart-broken. They found Washington and the twins waiting for them at the gate-house with lanterns, as the avenue was very dark. Not the slightest trace of Virginia had been discovered. The gipsies had been caught on Brockley meadows, but she was not with them, and they had explained their sudden departure by saying that they had mistaken the date of Chorton Fair, and had gone off in a hurry for fear they should be late. Indeed, they had been quite distressed at hearing of Virginia's disappearance, as they were very grateful to Mr. Otis for having allowed them to camp in his park, and four of their number had stayed behind to help in the search. The carp-pond had been dragged, and the whole Chase thoroughly gone over, but without any result. It was evident that, for that night at any rate, Virginia was lost to them; and it was in a state of the deepest depression that Mr. Otis and the boys walked up to the house, the groom following behind with the two horses and the pony. In the hall they found a group of frightened servants, and lying on a sofa in the library was poor Mrs. Otis, almost out of her mind with terror and anxiety, and having her forehead bathed with eau de cologne by the old housekeeper. Mr. Otis at once insisted on her having something to eat, and ordered up supper for the whole party. It was a melancholy meal, as hardly any one spoke, and even the twins were awestruck and subdued, as they were very fond of their sister. When they had finished, Mr. Otis, in spite of the entreaties of the little Duke, ordered them all to bed, saying that nothing more could be done that night, and that he would telegraph

THE CANTERVILLE GHOST **77**

in the morning to Scotland Yard for some detectives to be sent down immediately. Just as they were passing out of the dining-room, midnight began to boom from the clock tower, and when the last stroke sounded they heard a crash and a sudden shrill cry; a dreadful peal of thunder shook the house, a strain of unearthly music floated through the air, a panel at the top of the staircase flew back with a loud noise, and out on the landing, looking very pale and white, with a little casket in her hand, stepped Virginia. In a moment they had all rushed up to her. Mrs. Otis clasped her passionately in her arms, the Duke smothered her with violent kisses, and the twins executed a wild war-dance round the group.

"Good heavens! child, where have you been?" said Mr. Otis, rather angrily, thinking that she had been playing some foolish trick on them. "Cecil and I have been riding all over the country looking for you, and your mother has been frightened to death. You must never play these practical jokes any more."

"Except on the Ghost! except on the Ghost!" shrieked the twins, as they capered about.

"My own darling, thank God you are found; you must never leave my side again," murmured Mrs. Otis, as she kissed the trembling child, and smoothed the tangled gold of her hair.

"Papa," said Virginia, quietly, "I have been with the Ghost. He is dead, and you must come and see him. He had been very wicked, but he was really sorry for all that he had done, and he gave me this box of beautiful jewels before he died."

The whole family gazed at her in mute amazement, but she was quite grave and serious; and, turning round, she led them through the opening in the wainscoting down a narrow secret corridor, Washington following with a lighted candle, which he had caught up from the table. Finally, they came to a great oak door, studded with rusty nails. When Virginia touched it, it swung back on its heavy hinges, and they found themselves in a little low room, with a vaulted ceiling, and one tiny grated window. Imbedded in the wall was a huge iron ring, and chained to it was a gaunt skeleton, that was stretched out at full length on the stone floor, and seemed to be trying to grasp with its long fleshless fingers an old-fashioned trencher and ewer, that were placed just out of its reach. The jug had evidently been once filled with water, as it was covered inside with green mould. There was nothing on the trencher but a pile of dust. Virginia knelt down beside the skeleton, and, folding her little hands together, began to pray silently, while the rest of the party looked on in wonder at the terrible tragedy whose secret was now disclosed to them.

"Hallo!" suddenly exclaimed one of the twins, who had been looking out of the window to try and discover in what wing of the house the room was situated. "Hallo! the old withered almond-tree has blossomed. I can see the flowers quite plainly in the moonlight."

"God has forgiven him," said Virginia, gravely, as she rose to her feet, and a beautiful light seemed to illumine her face.

"What an angel you are!" cried the young Duke, and he put his arm round her neck, and kissed her.

VII

Four days after these curious incidents, a funeral started from Canterville Chase at about eleven o'clock at night. The hearse was drawn by eight black horses, each of which carried on its head a great tuft of nodding ostrich-plumes, and the leaden coffin was covered by a rich purple pall, on which was embroidered in gold the Canterville coat-of-arms. By the side of the hearse and the coaches walked the servants with lighted torches, and the whole procession was wonderfully impressive. Lord Canterville was the chief mourner, having come up specially from Wales to attend the funeral, and sat in the first carriage along with little Virginia. Then came the United States Minister and his wife, then Washington and the three boys, and in the last carriage was Mrs. Umney. It was generally felt that, as she had been frightened by the ghost for more than fifty years of her life, she had a right to see the last of him. A deep grave had been dug in the corner of the churchyard, just under the old yew-tree, and the service was read in the most impressive manner by the Rev. Augustus Dampier. When the ceremony was over, the servants, according to an old custom observed in the Canterville family, extinguished their torches, and, as the coffin was being lowered into the grave, Virginia stepped forward, and laid on it a large cross made of white and pink almond-blossoms. As she did so, the moon came out from behind a cloud, and flooded with its silent silver the little churchyard, and from a distant copse a nightingale began to sing. She thought of the ghost's description of the Garden of Death, her eyes became dim with tears, and she hardly spoke a word during the drive home.

The next morning, before Lord Canterville went up to town, Mr. Otis had an interview with him on the subject of the jewels the ghost had given to Virginia. They were perfectly magnificent, especially a certain ruby necklace with old Venetian setting, which was really a superb specimen of sixteenth-century work, and their value was so great that Mr. Otis felt considerable scruples about allowing his daughter to accept them.

"My lord," he said, "I know that in this country mortmain is held to apply to trinkets as well as to land, and it is quite clear to me that these jewels are, or should be, heirlooms in your family. I must beg you, accordingly, to take them to London with you, and to regard them simply as a portion of your property which has been restored to you under certain strange conditions. As for my daughter, she is merely a child, and has as yet, I am glad to say, but little interest in such appurtenances of idle luxury. I am also informed by Mrs. Otis, who, I may say, is no mean authority upon Art,—having had the privilege of spending several winters in Boston when she was a girl,—that these gems are of great monetary worth, and if offered for sale would fetch a tall price. Under these circumstances, Lord Canterville, I feel sure that you will recognize how impossible it would be for me to allow them to remain in the possession of any member of my family; and, indeed, all such vain gauds and toys, however suitable or necessary to the dignity of the British aristocracy, would be completely out of place among those who have been brought up on the severe, and I believe immortal, principles of Republican simplicity. Perhaps I should mention that Virginia is very anxious that you should allow her to retain the box, as a memento of your unfortunate but misguided ancestor. As it is extremely old, and consequently a good deal out of repair, you may perhaps think fit to comply with her request. For my own part, I confess I am a good deal surprised to find a child of mine expressing sympathy with mediævalism in any form, and can only account for it by the fact that Virginia was born in one of your London suburbs shortly after Mrs. Otis had returned from a trip to Athens."

Lord Canterville listened very gravely to the worthy Minister's speech, pulling his grey moustache now and then to hide an involuntary smile, and when Mr. Otis had ended, he shook him cordially by the hand, and said: "My dear sir, your charming little daughter rendered my unlucky ancestor, Sir Simon, a very important service, and I and my family are much indebted to her for her marvellous courage and pluck. The jewels are clearly hers, and, egad, I believe that if I were heartless enough to take them from her, the wicked old fellow would be out of his grave in a fortnight, leading me the devil of a life. As for their being heirlooms, nothing is an heirloom that is not so mentioned in a will or legal document, and the existence of these jewels has been quite unknown. I assure you I have no more claim on them than your butler, and when Miss Virginia grows up, I dare say she will be pleased to have pretty things to wear. Besides, you forget, Mr. Otis, that you took the furniture and the ghost at a valuation, and anything that belonged to the ghost passed at once into your possession, as, whatever activity Sir Simon may have shown in the corridor at night, in point of law he was really dead, and you acquired his property by purchase."

Mr. Otis was a good deal distressed at Lord Canterville's refusal, and begged him to reconsider his decision, but the good-natured peer was quite firm, and finally induced the Minister to allow his daughter to retain the present the ghost had given her, and when, in the spring of 1890, the young Duchess of Cheshire was presented at the Queen's first drawing-room on the occasion of her marriage, her jewels were the universal theme of admiration. For Virginia received the coronet, which is the reward of all good little American girls, and was married to her boy-lover as soon as he came of age. They were both so charming, and they loved each other so much, that every one was delighted at the match, except the old Marchioness of Dumbleton, who had tried to catch the Duke for one of her seven unmarried daughters, and had given no less than three expensive dinner-parties for that purpose, and, strange to say, Mr. Otis himself. Mr. Otis was extremely fond of the young Duke personally, but, theoretically, he objected to titles, and, to use his own words, "was not without apprehension lest, amid the enervating influences of a pleasure-loving aristocracy, the true principles of Republican simplicity should be forgotten." His objections, however, were completely overruled, and I believe that when he walked up the aisle of St. George's, Hanover Square, with his daughter leaning on his arm, there was not a prouder man in the whole length and breadth of England.

The Duke and Duchess, after the honeymoon was over, went down to Canterville Chase, and on the day after their arrival they walked over in the afternoon to the lonely churchyard by the pine-woods. There had been a great deal of difficulty at first about the inscription on Sir Simon's tombstone, but finally it had been decided to engrave on it simply the initials of the old gentleman's name, and the verse from the library window. The Duchess had brought with her some lovely roses, which she strewed upon the grave, and after they had stood by it for some time they strolled into the ruined chancel of the old abbey. There the Duchess sat down on a fallen pillar, while her husband lay at her feet smoking a cigarette and looking up at her beautiful eyes. Suddenly he threw his cigarette away, took hold of her hand, and said to her, "Virginia, a wife should have no secrets from her husband."

"Dear Cecil! I have no secrets from you."

"Yes, you have," he answered, smiling, "you have never told me what happened to you when you were locked up with the ghost."

"I have never told any one, Cecil," said Virginia, gravely.

"I know that, but you might tell me."

"Please don't ask me, Cecil, I cannot tell you. Poor Sir Simon! I owe him a great deal. Yes, don't laugh, Cecil, I really do. He made me see what Life is, and what Death signifies, and why Love is stronger than both."

The Duke rose and kissed his wife lovingly.

"You can have your secret as long as I have your heart," he murmured.

"You have always had that, Cecil."

"And you will tell our children some day, won't you?"

Virginia blushed.

THE HAUNTED ORCHARD

Richard Le Gallienne

Richard Le Gallienne (1866–1947) was an English author, journalist, and poet, now most likely to be remembered as the father of American actress Eva Le Gallienne. In his own era, however, Le Gallienne, a prolific writer, was quite popular, especially his verse translation of the *Rubáiyát of Omar Khayyám*.

Le Gallienne lived for a time in the United States. In "The Haunted Orchard," he describes landscapes that were familiar to him. First published in *Harper's Magazine* in January 1912, "The Haunted Orchard" is an evocative tale of the communication between the deceased and those among the living who have the capacity to hear them.

The Haunted Orchard

Spring was once more in the world. As she sang to herself in the far-away woodlands her voice reached even the ears of the city, weary with the long winter. Daffodils flowered at the entrances to the Subway, furniture removing vans blocked the side streets, children clustered like blossoms on the doorsteps, the open cars were running, and the cry of the "cash clo'" man was once more heard in the land.

Yes, it was the spring, and the city dreamed wistfully of lilacs and the dewy piping of birds in gnarled old apple-trees, of dogwood lighting up with sudden silver the thickening woods, of water-plants unfolding their glossy scrolls in pools of morning freshness.

On Sunday mornings, the outbound trains were thronged with eager pilgrims, hastening out of the city, to behold once more the ancient marvel of the spring; and, on Sunday evenings, the railway termini were aflower with banners of blossom from rifled woodland and orchard carried in the hands of the returning pilgrims, whose eyes still shone with the spring magic, in whose ears still sang the fairy music.

And as I beheld these signs of the vernal equinox I knew that I, too, must follow the music, forsake awhile the beautiful siren we call the city, and in the green silences meet once more my sweetheart Solitude.

As the train drew out of the Grand Central, I hummed to myself, "I've a neater, sweeter maiden, in a greener, cleaner land," and so I said good-by to the city, and went forth with beating heart to meet the spring.

I had been told of an almost forgotten corner on the south coast of Connecticut, where the spring and I could live in an inviolate loneliness—a place uninhabited save by birds and blossoms, woods and thick grass, and an occasional silent farmer, and pervaded by the breath and shimmer of the Sound.

Nor had rumor lied, for when the train set me down at my destination I stepped out into the most wonderful green hush, a leafy Sabbath silence through which the very train, as it went farther on its way, seemed to steal as noiselessly as possible for fear of breaking the spell.

2

After a winter in the town, to be dropped thus suddenly into the intense quiet of the country-side makes an almost ghostly impression upon one, as of an enchanted silence, a silence that listens and watches but never speaks, finger on lip. There is a spectral quality about everything upon which the eye falls: the woods, like great green clouds, the wayside flowers, the still farm-houses half lost in orchard bloom—all seem to exist in a dream. Everything is so still, everything so supernaturally green. Nothing moves or talks, except the gentle susurrus of the spring wind swaying the young buds high up in the quiet sky, or a bird now and again, or a little brook singing softly to itself among the crowding rushes.

Though, from the houses one notes here and there, there are evidently human inhabitants of this green silence, none are to be seen. I have often wondered where the countryfolk hide themselves, as I have walked hour after hour, past farm and croft and lonely door-yards, and never caught sight of a human face. If you should want to ask the way, a farmer is as shy as a squirrel, and if you knock at a farm-house door, all is as silent as a rabbit-warren.

As I walked along in the enchanted stillness, I came at length to a quaint old farm-house—"old Colonial" in its architecture—embowered in white lilacs, and surrounded by an orchard of ancient apple-trees which cast a rich shade on the deep spring grass. The orchard had the impressiveness of those old religious groves, dedicated to the strange worship of sylvan gods, gods to be found now only in Horace or Catullus, and in the hearts of young poets to whom the beautiful antique Latin is still dear.

The old house seemed already the abode of Solitude. As I lifted the latch of the white gate and walked across the forgotten grass, and up on to the veranda already festooned with wistaria, and looked into the window, I saw Solitude sitting by an old piano, on which no composer later than Bach had ever been played.

In other words, the house was empty; and going round to the back, where old barns and stables leaned together as if falling asleep, I found a broken pane, and so climbed in and walked through the echoing rooms. The house was very lonely. Evidently no one had lived in it for a long time. Yet it was all ready for some occupant, for whom it seemed to be waiting. Quaint old four-poster bedsteads stood in three rooms—dimity curtains and spotless linen—old oak chests and mahogany presses; and, opening drawers in Chippendale sideboards, I came upon beautiful frail old silver and exquisite china that set me thinking of a beautiful grandmother of mine, made out of old lace and laughing wrinkles and mischievous old blue eyes.

3

There was one little room that particularly interested me, a tiny bedroom all white, and at the window the red roses were already in bud. But what caught my eye with peculiar sympathy was a small bookcase, in which were some twenty or thirty volumes, wearing the same forgotten expression—forgotten and yet cared for—which lay like a kind of memorial charm upon everything in the old house. Yes, everything seemed forgotten and yet everything, curiously— even religiously—remembered. I took out book after book from the shelves, once or twice flowers fell out from the pages—and I caught sight of a delicate handwriting here and there and frail markings. It was evidently the little intimate library of a young girl. What surprised me most was to find that quite half the books were in French— French poets and French romancers: a charming, very rare edition of Ronsard, a beautifully printed edition of Alfred de Musset, and a copy of Théophile Gautier's *Mademoiselle de Maupin.* How did these exotic books come to be there alone in a deserted New England farm-house?

This question was to be answered later in a strange way. Meanwhile I had fallen in love with the sad, old, silent place, and as I closed the white gate and was once more on the road, I looked about for someone who could tell me whether or not this house of ghosts might be rented for the summer by a comparatively living man.

I was referred to a fine old New England farm-house shining white through the trees a quarter of a mile away. There I met an ancient couple, a typical New England farmer and his wife; the old man, lean, chin-bearded, with keen gray eyes flickering occasionally with a shrewd humor, the old lady with a kindly old face of the withered-apple type and ruddy. They were evidently prosperous people, but their minds—for some reason I could not at the moment divine—seemed to be divided between their New England desire to drive a hard bargain and their disinclination to let the house at all.

Over and over again they spoke of the loneliness of the place. They feared I would find it very lonely. No one had lived in it for a long time, and so on. It seemed to me that afterwards I understood their curious hesitation, but at the moment only regarded it as a part of the circuitous New England method of bargaining. At all events, the rent I offered finally overcame their disinclination, whatever its cause, and so I came into possession—for four months—of that silent old house, with the white lilacs, and the drowsy barns, and the old piano, and the strange orchard; and, as the summer came on, and the year changed its name from May to June, I used to lie under the apple-trees in the afternoons, dreamily reading some old book, and through half-sleepy eyelids watching the silken shimmer of the Sound.

4

I had lived in the old house for about a month, when one afternoon a strange thing happened to me. I remember the date well. It was the afternoon of Tuesday, June 13th. I was reading, or rather dipping here and there, in Burton's *Anatomy of Melancholy*. As I read, I remember that a little unripe apple, with a petal or two of blossom still clinging to it, fell upon the old yellow page. Then I suppose I must have fallen into a dream, though it seemed to me that both my eyes and my ears were wide open, for I suddenly became aware of a beautiful young voice singing very softly somewhere among the leaves. The singing was very frail, almost imperceptible, as though it came out of the air. It came and went fitfully, like the elusive fragrance of sweetbrier—as though a girl was walking to and fro, dreamily humming to herself in the still afternoon. Yet there was no one to be seen. The orchard had never seemed more lonely. And another fact that struck me as strange was that the words that floated to me out of the aerial music were French, half sad, half gay snatches of some long-dead singer of old France, I looked about for the origin of the sweet sounds, but in vain. Could it be the birds that were singing in French in this strange orchard? Presently the voice seemed to come quite close to me, so near that it might have been the voice of a dryad singing to me out of the tree against which I was leaning. And this time I distinctly caught the words of the sad little song:

> "*Chante, rossignol, chante,*
> *Toi qui as le cœur gai;*
> *Tu as le cœur à rire,*
> *Moi, je l'ai-t-à pleurer.*"

But, though the voice was at my shoulder, I could see no one, and then the singing stopped with what sounded like a sob; and a moment or two later I seemed to hear a sound of sobbing far down the orchard. Then there followed silence, and I was left to ponder on the strange occurrence. Naturally, I decided that it was just a day-dream between sleeping and waking over the pages of an old book; yet when next day and the day after the invisible singer was in the orchard again, I could not be satisfied with such mere matter-of-fact explanation.

5

"*A la claire fontaine,*"

went the voice to and fro through the thick orchard boughs,

> "*M'en allant promener,*
> *J'ai trouvé l'eau si belle*
> *Que je m'y suis baigné,*
> *Lui y a longtemps que je t'aime,*
> *Jamais je ne t'oubliai.*"

It was certainly uncanny to hear that voice going to and fro the orchard, there somewhere amid the bright sun-dazzled boughs—yet not a human creature to be seen—not another house even within half a mile. The most materialistic mind could hardly but conclude that here was something "not dreamed of in our philosophy." It seemed to me that the only reasonable explanation was the entirely irrational one—that my orchard was haunted: haunted by some beautiful young spirit, with some sorrow of lost joy that would not let her sleep quietly in her grave.

And next day I had a curious confirmation of my theory. Once more I was lying under my favorite apple-tree, half reading and half watching the Sound, lulled into a dream by the whir of insects and the spices called up from the earth by the hot sun. As I bent over the page, I suddenly had the startling impression that someone was leaning over my shoulder and reading with me, and that a girl's long hair was falling over me down on to the page. The book was the Ronsard I had found in the little bedroom. I turned, but again there was nothing there. Yet this time I knew that I had not been dreaming, and I cried out:

"Poor child! tell me of your grief—that I may help your sorrowing heart to rest."

But, of course, there was no answer; yet that night I dreamed a strange dream. I thought I was in the orchard again in the afternoon and once again heard the strange singing—but this time, as I looked up, the singer was no longer invisible. Coming toward me was a young girl with wonderful blue eyes filled with tears and gold hair that fell to her waist. She wore a straight, white robe that might have been a shroud or a bridal dress. She appeared not to see me, though she came directly to the tree where I was sitting. And there she knelt and buried her face in the grass and sobbed as if her heart would break. Her long hair fell over her like a mantle, and in my dream I stroked it pityingly and murmured words of comfort for a sorrow I did not understand. . . . Then I woke suddenly as one does from dreams. The moon was shining brightly into the room. Rising from my bed, I looked out into the orchard. It was almost as bright as day. I could plainly see the tree of which I had been dreaming, and then a fantastic notion possessed me. Slipping on my clothes, I went out into one of the old barns and found a spade. Then I went to the tree where I had seen the girl weeping in my dream and dug down at its foot.

6

I had dug little more than a foot when my spade struck upon some hard substance, and in a few more moments I had uncovered and exhumed a small box, which, on examination, proved to be one of those pretty old-fashioned Chippendale work-boxes used by our grandmothers to keep their thimbles and needles in, their reels of cotton and skeins of silk. After smoothing down the little grave in which I had found it, I carried the box into the house, and under the lamplight examined its contents.

Then at once I understood why that sad young spirit went to and fro the orchard singing those little French songs—for the treasure-trove I had found under the apple-tree, the buried treasure of an unquiet, suffering soul, proved to be a number of love-letters written mostly in French in a very picturesque hand—letters, too, written but some five or six years before. Perhaps I should not have read them—yet I read them with such reverence for the beautiful, impassioned love that animated them, and lit-erally made them "smell sweet and blossom in the dust," that I felt I had the sanction of the dead to make myself the confidant of their story. Among the letters were little songs, two of which I had heard the strange young voice singing in the orchard, and, of course, there were many withered flowers and such like remem-brances of bygone rapture.

Not that night could I make out all the story, though it was not dif-ficult to define its essential tragedy, and later on a gossip in the neigh-borhood and a headstone in the churchyard told me the rest. The unquiet young soul that had sung so wistfully to and fro the orchard was my landlord's daughter. She was the only child of her parents, a beautiful, willful girl, exotically unlike those from whom she was sprung and among whom she lived with a disdainful air of exile. She was, as a child, a little creature of fairy fancies, and as she grew up it was plain to her father and mother that she had come from another world than theirs. To them she seemed like a child in an old fairy-tale strangely found on his hearth by some shepherd as he returns from the fields at evening—a little fairy girl swaddled in fine linen, and dowered with a mysterious bag of gold.

7

Soon she developed delicate spiritual needs to which her simple parents were strangers. From long truancies in the woods she would come home laden with mysterious flowers, and soon she came to ask for books and pictures and music, of which the poor souls that had given her birth had never heard. Finally she had her way, and went to study at a certain fashionable college; and there the brief romance of her life began. There she met a romantic young Frenchman who had read Ronsard to her and written her those picturesque letters I had found in the old mahogany work-box. And after a while the young Frenchman had gone back to France, and the letters had ceased. Month by month went by, and at length one day, as she sat wistful at the window, looking out at the foolish sunlit road, a message came. He was dead. That headstone in the village churchyard tells the rest. She was very young to die—scarcely nineteen years; and the dead who have died young, with all their hopes and dreams still like unfolded buds within their hearts, do not rest so quietly in the grave as those who have gone through the long day from morning until evening and are only too glad to sleep.

Next day I took the little box to a quiet corner of the orchard, and made a little pyre of fragrant boughs—for so I interpreted the wish of that young, unquiet spirit—and the beautiful words are now safe, taken up again into the aerial spaces from which they came.

But since then the birds sing no more little French songs in my old orchard.

THE YELLOW SIGN

Robert W. Chambers

American author and artist, Robert William Chambers (1865–1933) was born in Brooklyn; a descendant of Roger Williams, founder of the Providence Plantation, which provided sanctuary for religious minorities in England's North American colonies. A prolific author, Chambers wrote in various genres. He achieved success during his lifetime; his romantic and historical fiction was wildly popular. He is now best known, however, for his 1895 book of short stories, *The King in Yellow,* frequently described as among the most influential works of supernatural fiction.

Some of the stories in the book, including "The Yellow Sign," share a loose thematic connection via scattered references to a fictional play, also named *The King in Yellow.* This play possesses the power to drive those who read it hopelessly insane, although no explanation is given as to how or why this is so. This lack of explanation is a common element of Chambers's supernatural fiction. Loose ends are not tied up neatly; the stories are vague and have gaps in the narrative: this mysterious quality, however, only enhances their aura of horror.

The King in Yellow's renown and influence has only increased with time. Popular entertainment and media are punctuated with frequent references. For example, the detective narrator of Raymond Chandler's 1938 short story, also titled "The King in Yellow," has clearly read Chambers's book. The King in Yellow is also the name of the "head shop" in Stephen King's 1984 horror novel, *Thinner* (published under his alias, Richard Bachman). Most prominently, the mysterious and popular 2014 television series, *True Detective,* season 1, is peppered with references to Carcosa and the yellow king.

The Yellow Sign

Let the red dawn surmise
What we shall do,
When this blue starlight dies
And all is through.

I

There are so many things which are impossible to explain! Why should certain chords in music make me think of the brown and golden tints of autumn foliage? Why should the Mass of Sainte Cecile send my thoughts wandering among caverns whose walls blaze with ragged masses of virgin silver? What was it in the roar and turmoil of Broadway at six o'clock that flashed before my eyes the picture of a still Breton forest where sunlight filtered through spring foliage and Sylvia bent, half curiously, half tenderly, over a small green lizard, murmuring: "To think that this is also a little ward of God!"

When I first saw the watchman his back was toward me. I looked at him indifferently until he went into the church. I paid no more attention to him than I had to any other man who lounged through Washington Square that morning, and when I shut my window and turned back into my studio I had forgotten him. Late in the afternoon, the day being warm, I raised the window again and leaned out to get a sniff of the air. A man was standing in the courtyard of the church, and I noticed him again with as little interest as I had that morning. I looked across the square to where the fountain was playing and then, with my mind filled with vague impressions of trees, asphalt drives, and the moving groups of nursemaids and holidaymakers, I started to walk back to my easel. As I turned, my listless glance included the man below in the churchyard. His face was toward me now, and with a perfectly involuntary movement I bent to see it. At the same moment he raised his head and looked at me. Instantly I thought of a coffin-worm. Whatever it was about the man that repelled me I did not know, but the impression of a plump white grave-worm was so intense and nauseating that I must have shown it in my expression, for he turned his puffy face away with a movement which made me think of a disturbed grub in a chestnut.

I went back to my easel and motioned the model to resume her pose. After working awhile I was satisfied that I was spoiling what I had done as rapidly as possible, and I took up a palette knife and scraped the color out again. The flesh tones were sallow and unhealthy, and I did not understand how I could have painted such sickly color into a study which before that had glowed with healthy tones.

I looked at Tessie. She had not changed, and the clear flush of health dyed her neck and cheeks as I frowned.

"Is it something I've done?" she said.

"No—I've made a mess of this arm, and for the life of me I can't see how I came to paint such mud as that into the canvas," I replied.

"Don't I pose well?" she insisted.

"Of course, perfectly."

"Then it's not my fault?"

"No. It's my own."

"I'm very sorry," she said.

I told her she could rest while I applied rag and turpentine to the plague spot on my canvas, and she went off to smoke a cigarette and look over the illustrations in the *Courier Français*.

I did not know whether it was something in the turpentine or a defect in the canvas, but the more I scrubbed the more that gangrene seemed to spread. I worked like a beaver to get it out, and yet the disease appeared to creep from limb to limb of the study before me. Alarmed I strove to arrest it, but now the color on the breast changed and the whole figure seemed to absorb the infection as a sponge soaks up water. Vigorously I plied palette knife, turpentine, and scraper, thinking all the time what a séance I should hold with Duval who had sold me the canvas; but soon I noticed that it was not the canvas which was defective nor yet the colors of Edward. "It must be the turpentine," I thought angrily, "or else my eyes have become so blurred and confused by the afternoon light that I can't see straight." I called

Tessie, the model. She came and leaned over my chair blowing rings of smoke into the air.

"What have you been doing to it?" she exclaimed.

"Nothing," I growled, "it must be this turpentine!"

"What a horrible color it is now," she continued. "Do you think my flesh resembles green cheese?"

"No, I don't," I said angrily, "did you ever know me to paint like that before?"

"No, indeed!"

"Well, then!"

"It must be the turpentine, or something," she admitted.

She slipped on a Japanese robe and walked to the window. I scraped and rubbed until I was tired and finally picked up my brushes and hurled them through the canvas with a forcible expression, the tone alone of which reached Tessie's ears.

Nevertheless she promptly began: "That's it! Swear and act silly and ruin your brushes! You have been three weeks on that study, and now look! What's the good of ripping the canvas? What creatures artists are!"

I felt about as much ashamed as I usually did after such an outbreak, and I turned the ruined canvas to the wall. Tessie helped me clean my brushes, and then danced away to dress. From the screen she regaled me with bits of advice concerning whole or partial loss of temper, until, thinking, perhaps, I had been tormented sufficiently, she came out to implore me to button her waist where she could not reach it on the shoulder.

"Everything went wrong from the time you came back from the window and talked about that horrid-looking man you saw in the churchyard," she announced.

"Yes, he probably bewitched the picture," I said, yawning. I looked at my watch.

"It's after six, I know," said Tessie, adjusting her hat before the mirror.

"Yes," I replied, "I didn't mean to keep you so long." I leaned out the window but recoiled with disgust, for the young man with the pasty face stood below in the churchyard. Tessie saw my gesture of disapproval and leaned from the window.

"Is that the man you don't like?" she whispered.

I nodded.

"I can't see his face, but he does look fat and soft. Someway or other," she continued, looking at me, "he reminds me of a dream,—and awful dream I once had. Or," she mused looking down at her shapely shoes, "was it a dream after all?"

"How should I know?" I smiled.

Tessie smiled in reply.

"You were in it," she said, "so perhaps you might know something about it."

"Tessie! Tessie!" I protested, "don't you dare flatter by saying you dream about me!"

"But I did," she insisted; "shall I tell you about it?"

"Go ahead," I replied, lighting a cigarette.

Tessie leaned back on the open window-sill and began very seriously.

"One night last winter I was lying in bed thinking about nothing at all in particular. I had been posing for you and I was tired out, yet it seemed impossible for me to sleep. I heard the bells in the city ring ten, eleven, and midnight. I must have fallen asleep about midnight because I don't remember hearing the bells after that. It seemed to me that I had scarcely closed my eyes when I dreamed that something impelled me to go to the window. I rose, and raising the sash, leaned out. Twenty-fifth Street was deserted as far as I could see. I began to be afraid; everything outside seemed so—so black and uncomfortable. Then the sound of wheels in the distance came to my ears, and it seemed to me as though that was what I must wait for. Very slowly the wheels approached, and, finally, I could make out a vehicle moving along the street. It came nearer and nearer, and when it passed beneath my window I saw it was a hearse. Then, as I trembled with fear, the driver turned and looked straight at me. When I awoke I was standing by the open window shivering with cold, but the black-plumed hearse and the driver were gone. I dreamed this dream again in March last, and again awoke beside the open window. Last night the dream came again. You remember how it was raining; when I awoke, standing at the open window, my nightdress was soaked."

"But where did I come into the dream?" I asked.

"You—you were in the coffin; but you were not dead."

"In the coffin?"

"Yes."

"How did you know? Could you see me?"

"No; I only knew you were there."

"Had you been eating Welsh rarebits, or lobster salad?" I began laughing, but the girl interrupted me with a frightened cry.

"Hello! What's up?" I said, as she shrank into the embrasure by the window.

"The—the man below in the churchyard;—he drove the hearse."

"Nonsense," I said, but Tessie's eyes were wide with terror. I went to the window and looked out. The man was gone. "Come, Tessie," I urged, "don't be foolish. You have posed too long; you are nervous."

"Do you think I could forget that face?" she murmured. "Three times I saw that hearse pass below my window, and every time the driver turned and looked up at me. Oh, his face was so white and—and soft? It looked dead—it looked as if it had been dead a long time."

I induced the girl to sit down and swallow a glass of Marsala. Then I sat down beside her and tried to give her some advice.

"Look here, Tessie," I said, "you go to the country for a week or two, and you'll have no more dreams about hearses. You pose all day, and when night comes your nerves are upset. You can't keep this up. Then again, instead of going to bed when your day's work is done, you run off to picnics at Sulzer's Park, or go to the Eldorado or Coney Island, and when you come down here in the morning you are fagged out. There was no real hearse. That was a soft-shell crab dream."

She smiled faintly.

"What about the man in the churchyard?"

"Oh, he's an ordinary unhealthy, everyday creature."

"As true as my name is Tessie Reardon, I swear to you, Mr. Scott, that the face of the man below in the churchyard is the face of the man who drove the hearse!"

"What of it?" I said. "It's an honest trade."

"Then you think I did see a hearse?"

"Oh," I said diplomatically, "if you really did, it might not be unlikely that the man below drove it. There is nothing in that."

Tessie rose, unrolled her scented handkerchief, and taking a bit of gum from a knot in the hem, placed it in her mouth. Then drawing on her gloves she offered me her hand, with a frank, "Good-night, Mr. Scott," and walked out.

II

The next morning, Thomas, the bellboy, brought me the *Herald* and a bit of news. The church next door had been sold. I thanked Heaven for it, not that being a Catholic I had any repugnance for the congregation next door, but because my nerves were shattered by a blatant exhorter, whose every word echoed through the aisle of the church as if it had been my own rooms, and who insisted on his r's with a nasal persistence which revolted my every instinct. Then, too, there as a fiend in human shape, an organist, who reeled off some of the grand old hymns with an interpretation of his own, and I longed for the blood of a creature who could play the doxology with an amendment of minor chords which one hears only in a quartet of very young undergraduates. I believe the minister was a good man, but when he bellowed: "And the Lorrrrd said unto Moses, the Lorrrrd is a man of war; the Lorrrrd is his name. My wrath shall wax hot and I will kill you with the sworrrrd!" I wondered how many centuries of purgatory it would take to atone for such a sin.

"Who bought the property?" I asked Thomas.

"Nobody that I knows, sir. They do say the gent wot owns this 'ere 'Amilton flats was lookin' at it. 'E might be a bildin' more studios."

I walked to the window. The young man with the unhealthy face stood by the churchyard gate, and at the mere sight of him the same overwhelming repugnance took possession of me.

"By the way, Thomas," I said, "who is that fellow down there?"

Thomas sniffed. "That there worm, sir? 'E's night-watchman of the church, sir. 'E maikes me tired a-sittin' out all night on them steps and lookin' at you insultin' like. I'd a punched 'is 'ed, sir—beg pardon sir—"

"Go on, Thomas."

"One night a comin' 'ome with 'Arry, the other English boy, I sees 'im a sittin' there on them steps. We 'ad Molly and Jen with us, sir, the two girls on the tray service, an' 'e looks so insultin' at us that I up and sez: 'Wat you looking hat, you fat slug?'—beg pardon, sir, but that's 'ow I sez, sir. Then 'e don't say nothin' and I sez; 'Come out and I'll punch that puddin' 'ed.' Then I hopens the gate an' goes in, but 'e don't say nothin', only looks insultin' like. Then I 'its 'im one, but ugh! 'is 'ed was that cold and mushy it ud sicken you to touch 'im."

"What did he do then?" I asked, curiously.

"'Im? Nawthin'."

"And you, Thomas?"

The young fellow flushed in embarrassment and smiled uneasily.

"Mr. Scott, sir, I ain't no coward an' I can't make it out at all why I run. I was with the 5th Lawncers, sir, bugler at Tel-el-Kebir, an' was shot by the wells."

"You don't mean to say you ran away?"

"Yes, sir; I run."

"Why?"

"That's just what I want to know, sir. I grabbed Molly an' run, an' the rest of us just as frightened as I."

"But what were they frightened at?"

Thomas refused to answer for a while, but now my curiosity was aroused about the repulsive young man below and I pressed him. Three years' sojourn in America had not only modified Thomas' cockney dialect but had given him the American's fear of ridicule.

"You won't believe me, Mr. Scott, sir?"

"Yes, I will."

"You will lawf at me, sir?"

"Nonsense!"

He hesitated. "Well, sir, it's God's truth that when I 'it 'im 'e grabbed me wrists, sir, and when I twisted 'is soft, mushy fist one of 'is fingers come off in me 'and."

The utter loathing and horror of Thomas' face must have been reflected in my own for he added:

"It's orful, an' now when I see 'im I just go away. 'E maikes me hill."

When Thomas had gone I went to the window. The man stood beside the church-railing with both hands on the gate, but I hastily retreated to my easel again, sickened and horrified, for I saw that the middle finger of his right hand was missing.

At nine o'clock Tessie appeared and vanished behind the screen with a merry "Good-morning, Mr. Scott." While she had reappeared and taken her pose upon the model-stand I started a new canvas much to her delight. She remained silent as long as I was on the drawing, but as soon as the scrape of the charcoal ceased and I took up my fixative she began to chatter.

"Oh, I had such a lovely time last night. We went to Tony Pastor's."

"Who are 'we'?" I demanded.

"Oh, Maggie, you know, Mr. Whyte's model, and Pinkie McCormick—we call her Pinkie because she's got that beautiful red hair you artists like so much—and Lizzie Burke."

I sent a shower of fixative over the canvas and said: "Well, go on."

"We saw Kelly and Baby Barnes the skirt-dancer and—and all the rest. I made a mash."

"Then you have gone back on me, Tessie?"

She laughed and shook her head.

"He's Lizzie Burke's brother, Ed. He's a perfect gen'l'man."

I felt constrained to give her some parental advice concerning mashing, which she took with a bright smile.

"Oh, I can take care of a strange mash," she said, examining her chewing gum, "but Ed is different. Lizzie is my best friend."

Then she related how Ed had come back from the stocking mill in Lowell, Massachusetts, to find her and Lizzie grown up, and what an accomplished young man he was, and how he thought nothing of squandering half a dollar for ice-cream and oysters to celebrate his entry as clerk into the woolen department of Macy's. Before she finished I began to paint, and she resumed the pose, smiling and chattering like a sparrow. By noon I had the study fairly well rubbed in and Tessie came to look at it.

"That's better," she said.

I thought so too, and ate my lunch with a satisfied feeling that all was going well. Tessie spread her lunch on a drawing table opposite me and we drank our claret from the same bottle and lighted our cigarettes from the same match. I was very much attached to Tessie. I had watched her shoot up into a slender but exquisitely formed woman from a frail, awkward child. She had posed for me during the last three years, and among all my models she was my favorite. It would have troubled me very much indeed had she become "tough" or "fly," as the phrase goes, but I had never noticed any deterioration of her manner, and felt at heart that she was all right. She and I never discussed morals at all, and I had no intention of doing so, partly because I had none myself, and partly because I knew she would do what she liked in spite of me. Still I did hope she would steer clear of complications, because I wished her well, and then also I had a selfish desire to retain the best model I had. I knew that mashing, as she termed it, had no significance with girls like Tessie, and that such things in America did not resemble in the least the same things in Paris. Yet, having lived with my eyes open, I also knew that somebody would take Tessie away some day in one manner or another, and though I professed to myself that marriage was nonsense, I sincerely hoped that, in this case, there would be a priest at the end of the vista. I am a Catholic. When I listen to high mass, when I sign myself, I feel that everything, including myself, is more cheerful, and when I confess, it does me good. A man who lives as much alone as I do, must confess to somebody. Then, again, Sylvia was Catholic, and it was reason enough for me. But I was speaking of Tessie, which is very different. Tessie also was Catholic and much more devout than I, so, taking it all in all, I had little fear for my pretty model until she should fall in love. But then I knew that fate alone would decide her future for her, and I prayed inwardly that fate would keep her away from men like me and throw into her path nothing but Ed Burkes and Jimmy McCormicks, bless her sweet face!

Tessie sat blowing smoke up to the ceiling and tinkling the ice in her tumbler.

"Do you know, Kid, that I also had a dream last night?" I observed. I sometimes called her "the Kid."

"Not about that man," she laughed.

"Exactly. A dream similar to yours, only much worse."

It was foolish and thoughtless of me to say this, but you know how little tact the average painter has.

"I must have fallen asleep about 10 o'clock," I continued, "and after a while I dreamt that I awoke. So plainly did I hear the midnight bells, the wind in the tree-branches, and the whistle of steamers from the bay, that even now I can scarcely believe that I was not awake. I seemed to be lying in a box which had a glass cover. Dimly I saw the street lamps as I passed, for I must tell you, Tessie, the box in which I reclined appeared to lie in a cushioned wagon which jolted me over a stony pavement. After a while I became impatient and tried to move but the box was too narrow. My hands were crossed on my breast so I could not raise them to help myself. I listened and then tried to call. My voice was gone. I could hear the trample of the horses attached to the wagon and even the breathing of the driver. Then another sound broke upon my ears like the raising of a window sash. I managed to turn my head a little, and found I could look, not only through the glass cover of my box, but also through the glass panes in the side of the covered vehicle. I saw houses, empty and silent, with neither light nor life about any of them excepting one. In that house a window was open on the first floor and a figure all in white stood looking down into the street. It was you."

Tessie had turned her face away from me and leaned on the table with her elbow.

"I could see your face," I resumed, "and it seemed to me to be very sorrowful. Then we passed on and turned into a narrow black lane. Presently the horses stopped. I waited and waited, closing my eyes with fear and impatience, but all was silent as the grave. After what seemed to me hours, I began to feel uncomfortable. A sense that somebody was close to me made me unclose my eyes. Then I saw the white face of the hearse-driver looking at me through the coffin-lid—"

A sob from Tessie interrupted me. She was trembling like a leaf. I saw I had made an ass of myself and attempted to repair the damage.

"Why, Tess," I said, "I only told you this to show you what influence your story might have on another person's dreams. You don't suppose I really lay in a coffin, do you? What are you trembling for? Don't you see that your dream and my unreasonable dislike for that inoffensive watchman of the church simply set my brain working as soon as I fell asleep?"

She laid her head between her arms and sobbed as if her heart would break. What a precious triple donkey I had made of myself! But I was about to break my record. I went over and put my arm about her.

"Tessie, dear, forgive me," I said; "I had no business to frighten you with such nonsense. You are too sensible a girl, too good a Catholic to believe in dreams."

Her hand tightened on mine and her head fell back upon my shoulder, but she still trembled and I petted her and comforted her.

"Come, Tess, open your eyes and smile."

Her eyes opened with a slow languid movement and met mine, but their expression was so queer that I hastened to reassure her again.

"It's all humbug, Tessie, you surely are not afraid that any harm will come to you because of that."

"No," she said, but her scarlet lips quivered.

"Then what's the matter? Are you afraid?"

"Yes. Not for myself."

"For me, then?" I demanded gaily.

"For you," she murmured in a voice almost inaudible, "I—I care— for you."

At first I started to laugh, but when I understood her, a shock passed through me and I sat like one turned to stone. This was the crowning bit of idiocy I had committed. During the moment which elapsed between her reply and my answer I thought of a thousand responses to that innocent confession. I could pass it by with a laugh, I could misunderstand her and reassure her as to my health, I could simply point out that it was impossible she could love me. But my reply was quicker than my thoughts and I might think and think now when it was too late, for I had kissed her on the mouth.

That evening I took my usual walk in Washington Park, pondering over the occurrences of the day. I was thoroughly committed. There was no back out now, and I stared the future straight in the face. I was not good, not even scrupulous, but I had no idea of deceiving either myself or Tessie. The one passion of my life lay buried in the sunlit forests of Brittany. Was it buried forever? Hope cried "No!" For three years I had been listening to the voice of Hope, and for three years I had waited for a footstep on my threshold. Had Sylvia forgotten? "No!" cried Hope.

I said that I was not good. That is true, but still I was not exactly a comic opera villain. I had led an easy-going reckless life, taking what invited me of pleasure, deploring and sometimes bitterly regretting consequences. In one thing alone, except my painting, I was serious, and that was something which lay hidden if not lost in the Breton forests.

It was too late now for me to regret what had occurred during the day. Whatever it had been, pity, a sudden tenderness for sorrow, of the more brutal instinct of gratified vanity, it was all the same now, and unless I wished to bruise an innocent heart my path lay marked before me. The fire and strength, the depth of passion of a love which I had never even suspected, with all my imagined experience in the world, left me no alternative but to respond or send her away. Whether because I am so cowardly about giving pain to others, or whether it was that I have little of the gloomy Puritan in me, I do not know, but I shrank from disclaiming responsibility for that thoughtless kiss, and in fact had no time to do so before the gates of her heart opened and the flood poured forth. Others who habitually do their duty and find a sullen satisfaction in making themselves and everybody else unhappy, might have withstood it. I did not. I dared not. After the storm had abated I did tell her that she might better have loved Ed Burke and worn a plain gold ring, but she would not hear of it, and I thought perhaps that as long as she had decided to love somebody she could not marry, it had better be me. I, at least, could treat her with an intelligent affection, and whenever she became tired of her infatuation she could go none the worse for it. For I was decided on that point although I knew how hard it would be. I remembered the usual termination of Platonic liaisons and thought how disgusted I had been whenever I heard of one. I knew I was undertaking a great deal for so unscrupulous a man as I was, and I dreaded the future, but never for one moment did I doubt that she was safe with me. Had it been anybody but Tessie I should not have bothered my head about scruples. For it did not occur to me to sacrifice Tessie as I would have sacrificed a woman of the world. I looked the future squarely in the face and saw the several probable endings to the affair. She would either tire of the whole thing, or become so unhappy that I should have either to marry her or go away. If I married her we would be unhappy. I with a wife unsuited to me, and she with a husband unsuitable for any woman. For my past life could scarcely entitle me to marry. If I went away she might either fall ill, recover, and marry some Eddie Burke, or she might recklessly or deliberately go and do something foolish. On the other hand if she tired of me, then her whole life would be before her with beautiful vistas of Eddie Burkes and marriage rings and twins and Harlem flats and Heaven knows what. As I strolled along through the trees by Washington Arch, I decided that she should find a substantial friend in me anyway and the future could take care of itself. Then I went into the house and put on my evening dress for the little faintly perfumed note on my dresser said, "Have a cab at the stage door at eleven," and the note was signed "Edith Carmichael, Metropolitan Theater, June 19th, 189-."

I took supper that night, or rather we took supper, Miss Carmichael and I, at Solari's and the dawn was just beginning to gild the cross on the Memorial Church as I entered Washington Square after leaving Edith at the Brunswick. There was not a soul in the park as I passed among the trees and took the walk which leads from the Garibaldi statue to the Hamilton Apartment House, but as I passed the churchyard I saw a figure sitting on the stone steps. In spite of myself a chill crept over me at the sight of the white puffy face, and I hastened to pass. Then he said something which might have been addressed to me or might merely have been a mutter to himself, but a sudden furious anger flamed up within me that such a creature should address me. For an instant I felt like wheeling about and smashing my stick over his head, but I walked on, and entering the Hamilton went to my apartment. For some time I tossed about the bed trying to get the sound of his voice out of my ears, but could not. It filled my head, that muttering sound, like thick oily smoke from a fat-rendering vat or an odor of noisome decay. And as I lay and tossed about, the voice in my ears seemed more distinct, and I began to understand the words he had muttered. They came to me slowly as if I had forgotten them, and at last I could make some sense out of the sounds. It was this:

"Have you found the Yellow Sign?"

"Have you found the Yellow Sign?"

"Have you found the Yellow Sign?"

I was furious. What did he mean by that? Then with a curse upon him and his I rolled over and went to sleep, but when I awoke later I looked pale and haggard, for I had dreamed the dream of the night before and it troubled me more than I cared to think.

I dressed and went down into my studio. Tessie sat by the window, but as I came in she rose and put both arms around my neck for an innocent kiss. She looked so sweet and dainty that I kissed her again and then sat down before the easel.

"Hello! Where's the study I began yesterday?" I asked.

Tessie looked conscious, but did not answer. I began to hunt among the piles of canvases, saying, "Hurry up, Tess, and get ready; we must take advantage of the morning light."

When at last I gave up the search among the other canvases and turned to look around the room for the missing study I noticed Tessie standing by the screen with her clothing still on.

"What's the matter," I asked, "don't you feel well?"

"Yes."

"Then hurry."

"Do you want me to pose as—as I have always posed?"

Then I understood. Here was a new complication. I had lost, of course, the best nude model I had ever seen. I looked at Tessie. Her face was scarlet. Alas! Alas! We had eaten of the tree of knowledge, and Eden and native innocence were dreams of the past—I mean—for her.

I suppose she noticed the disappointment on my face, for she said: "I will pose if you wish. The study is behind the screen here where I put it."

"No," I said, "we will begin something new"; and I went to my wardrobe and picked out a Moorish costume which fairly blazed with tinsel. It was a genuine costume, and Tessie retired to the screen with it enchanted. When she came forth again I was astonished. Her long black hair was bound above her forehead with a circlet of turquoises, and the ends curled about her glittering girdle. Her feet were encased in the embroidered pointed slippers and the skirt of her costume, curiously wrought with arabesques in silver, fell to her ankles. The deep metallic blue vest embroidered with silver and the short Mauresque jacket spangled and sewn with turquoises became her wonderfully. She came up to me and held up her face smiling. I slipped my hand into my pocket and drawing out a gold chain with a cross attached, dropped it over her head.

"It's yours, Tessie."

"Mine?" she faltered.

"Yours. Now go and pose." Then with a radiant smile she ran behind the screen and presently reappeared with a little box on which was written my name.

"I had intended to give it to you when I went home tonight," she said, "but I can't wait now."

I opened the box. On the pink cotton inside lay a clasp of black onyx, on which was inlaid a curious symbol or letter in gold. It was neither Arabic nor Chinese, nor as I found afterwards did it belong to any human script.

"It's all I had to give you for a keepsake," she said, timidly.

I was annoyed, but I told her how much I should prize it, and promised to wear it always. She fastened it on my coat beneath the lapel.

"How foolish, Tess, to go and buy me such a beautiful thing as this," I said.

"I did not buy it," she laughed.

"Where did you get it?"

Then she told me how she had found it one day while coming from the Aquarium in the Battery, how she had advertised it and watched the papers, but at last gave up all hopes of finding the owner.

"That was last winter," she said, "the very day I had the first horrid dream about the hearse."

I remembered my dream of the previous night but said nothing, and presently my charcoal was flying over a new canvas, and Tessie stood motionless on the model-stand.

III

The day following was a disastrous one for me. While moving a framed canvas from one easel to another my foot slipped on the polished floor and I fell heavily on both wrists. They were so badly sprained that it was useless to attempt to hold a brush, and I was obliged to wander about the studio, glaring at unfinished drawings and sketches until despair seized me and I sat down to smoke and twiddle my thumbs with rage. The rain blew against the windows and rattled on the roof of the church, driving me into a nervous fit with its interminable patter. Tessie sat sewing by the window, and every now and then raised her head and looked at me with such innocent compassion that I began to feel ashamed of my irritation and looked about for something to occupy me. I had read all the papers and all the books in the library, but for the sake of something to do I went to the bookcases and shoved them open with my elbow. I knew every volume by its color and examined them all, passing slowly around the library and whistling to keep up my spirits. I was turning to go into the dining-room when my eye fell upon a book bound in yellow, standing in a corner of the top shelf of the last bookcase. I did not remember it and from the floor could not decipher the pale lettering on the back, so I went to the smoking-room and called Tessie. She came in from the studio and climbed to reach the book.

"What is it?" I asked.

"*The King in Yellow*."

I was dumbfounded. Who had placed it there? How came it to my rooms? I had long ago decided that I should never open that book, and nothing on earth could have persuaded me to buy it. Fearful lest curiosity might tempt me to open it, I had never even looked at it in book-stores. If I ever had had any curiosity to read it, the awful tragedy of young Castaigne, whom I knew, prevented me from exploring its wicked pages. I had always refused to listen to any description of it, and indeed, nobody ever ventured to discuss the second part aloud, so I had absolutely no knowledge of what those leaves might reveal. I stared at the poisonous yellow binding as I would at a snake.

"Don't touch it, Tessie," I said, "come down."

Of course my admonition was enough to arouse her curiosity, and before I could prevent it she took the book and, laughing, danced away into the studio with it. I called to her but she slipped away with a tormenting smile at my helpless hands, and I followed her with some impatience.

"Tessie!" I cried, entering the library, "listen, I am serious. Put that book away. I do not wish you to open it!" The library was empty. I went into both drawing-rooms, then into the bedrooms, laundry, kitchen, and finally returned to the library and began a systematic search. She had hidden herself so well that it was half an hour later when I discovered her crouching white and silent by the latticed window in the store-room above. At the first glance I saw she had been punished for her foolishness. *The King in Yellow* lay at her feet, but the book was open to the second part. I looked at Tessie and saw it was too late. She had opened *The King in Yellow*. Then I took her by the hand and led her into the studio. She seemed dazed, and when I told her to lie down on the sofa she obeyed me without a word. After a while she closed her eyes and her breathing became regular and deep, but I could not determine whether or not she slept. For a long while I sat silently beside her, but she neither stirred nor spoke, and at last I rose and entering the unused store-room took the yellow book in my least injured hand. It seemed heavy as lead, but I carried it into the studio again, and sitting down on the rug beside the sofa, opened it and read it through from beginning to end.

When, faint with the excess of my emotions, I dropped the volume and leaned wearily back against the sofa, Tessie opened her eyes and looked at me.

We had been speaking for some time in a dull and monotonous strain before I realized that we were discussing *The King in Yellow*. Oh the sin of writing such words,—words which are clear as crystal, limpid and musical as bubbling springs, words which sparkle and glow like the poisoned diamonds of the Medicis! Oh the wickedness, the hopeless damnation of a soul who could fascinate and paralyze human creatures with such words,—words understood by the ignorant and wise alike, words which are more precious than jewels, more soothing than Heavenly music, more awful than death itself.

We talked on, unmindful of the gathering shadows, and she was begging me to throw away the clasp of black onyx quaintly inlaid with what we now knew to be the Yellow Sign. I never shall know why I refused, though even at this hour, here in my bedroom as I write this confession, I should be glad to know what it was that prevented me from tearing the Yellow Sign from my breast and casting it into the fire. I am sure I wished to do so, but Tessie pleaded with me in vain. Night fell and the hours dragged on, but still we murmured to each other of the King and the Pallid Mask, and midnight sounded from the misty spires in the fog-wrapped city. We spoke of Hastur and of Cassilda, while outside the fog rolled against the blank window-panes as the cloud waves roll and break on the shores of Hali.

The house was very silent now and not a sound from the misty streets broke the silence. Tessie lay among the cushions, her face a gray blot in the gloom, but her hands were clasped in mine and I knew that she knew and read my thoughts as I read hers, for we had understood the mystery of the Hyades and the Phantom of Truth was laid. Then as we answered each other, swiftly, silently, thought on thought, the shadows stirred in the gloom about us, and far in the distant streets we heard a sound. Nearer and nearer it came, the dull crunching of wheels, nearer, nearer and yet nearer, and now, outside the door it ceased, and I dragged myself to the window and saw a black-plumed hearse. The gate below opened and shut, and I crept shaking to my door and bolted it, but I knew no bolts, no locks, could keep that creature out who was coming for the Yellow Sign. And now I heard him moving very softly along the hall. Now he was at the door, and the bolts rotted at his touch. Now he had entered. With eyes starting from my head I peered into the darkness, but when he came into the room I did not see him. It was only when I felt him envelop me in his cold soft grasp that I cried out and struggled with deadly fury, but my hands were useless and he tore the onyx clasp from my coat and struck me full in the face. Then, as I fell, I heard Tessie's soft cry and her spirit fled to God, and even while falling I longed to follow her, for I knew that the King in Yellow had opened his tattered mantle and there was only Christ to cry to now.

I could tell more, but I cannot see what help it will be to the world. As for me I am past human help or hope. As I lie here, writing, careless even whether or not I die before I finish, I can see the doctor gathering up his powders and phials with a vague gesture to the good priest beside me, which I understand.

They will be very curious to know the tragedy—they of the outside world who write books and print millions of newspapers, but I will write no more, and the father confessor will seal my last words with the seal of sanctity when his holy office is done. They of the outside world may send their creatures into wrecked homes and death-smitten firesides, and their newspapers will batten on blood and tears, but with me their spies must halt before the confessional. They know that Tessie is dead and that I am dying. They know how the people in the house, aroused by an infernal scream, rushed into my room and found one living and two dead, but they do not know that the doctor said as he pointed to a horrible decomposed heap on the floor—the livid corpse of the watchman from the church: "I have no theory, no explanation. That man must have been dead for months!"

I think I am dying. I wish the priest would—

DAGON

H. P. Lovecraft

Howard Phillips Lovecraft (1890–1937), author, scholar, and connoisseur of weird fiction is renowned now, but his fame is entirely posthumous. During his lifetime, he languished in obscurity, only published in pulp magazines such as *Weird Tales* and *Astounding Stories*.

Of course, that's all different now: H. P. Lovecraft is acclaimed as one of the most significant and influential authors of supernatural fiction. His literary creations such as Cthulhu and the Necronomicon have entered the very lexicon and taken on lives of their own. Stephen King, another master of horror, has described Lovecraft as "the twentieth century's greatest practitioner of the classic horror tale."[3]

Born and brought up in Providence, Rhode Island, Lovecraft was a sickly child who was mostly educated at home. Shy, reclusive, and socially awkward, he was also a brilliant autodidact. He loved weird fiction, studied and analyzed it. Commercial success eluded him, however, and he lived much of his life in poverty. Lovecraft was thirty-one when he was first published in a professional magazine.

Written in July 1917, "Dagon" was one of the first stories Lovecraft produced as an adult, and it was first published in the November 1919 edition of the amateur press journal, *The Vagrant* (issue #11). The story is an early precursor of themes that would appear in Lovecraft's later work, including what is now known as the Cthulhu Mythos. According to Lovecraft, the story was inspired by a dream.

---

3. H. P. Lovecraft, *The Best of H. P. Lovecraft: Bloodcurdling Tales of Horror and the Macabre* (Ballantine Books, 1982).

The title refers to the ancient Semitic deity Dagon, who, although he seems to have first emerged in Mesopotamia, is best known from his appearance in the Old Testament as one of the leading gods of the Philistine pantheon. NOTE: "Dagon" was written before Piltdown Man was exposed as a hoax.

Dagon

I am writing this under an appreciable mental strain, since by tonight I shall be no more. Penniless, and at the end of my supply of the drug which alone makes life endurable, I can bear the torture no longer; and shall cast myself from this garret window into the squalid street below. Do not think from my slavery to morphine that I am a weakling or a degenerate. When you have read these hastily scrawled pages you may guess, though never fully realise, why it is that I must have forgetfulness or death.

It was in one of the most open and least frequented parts of the broad Pacific that the packet of which I was supercargo fell a victim to the German sea-raider. The great war was then at its very beginning, and the ocean forces of the Hun had not completely sunk to their later degradation; so that our vessel was made a legitimate prize, whilst we of her crew were treated with all the fairness and consideration due us as naval prisoners. So liberal, indeed, was the discipline of our captors that five days after we were taken I managed to escape alone in a small boat with water and provisions for a good length of time.

When I finally found myself adrift and free, I had but little idea of my surroundings. Never a competent navigator, I could only guess vaguely by the sun and stars that I was somewhat south of the equator. Of the longitude I knew nothing, and no island or coast-line was in sight. The weather kept fair, and for uncounted days I drifted aimlessly beneath the scorching sun; waiting either for some passing ship, or to be cast on the shores of some habitable land. But neither ship nor land appeared, and I began to despair in my solitude upon the heaving vastnesses of unbroken blue.

The change happened whilst I slept. Its details I shall never know; for my slumber, though troubled and dream-infested, was continuous. When at last I awaked, it was to discover myself half sucked into a slimy expanse of hellish black mire which extended about me in monotonous undulations as far as I could see, and in which my boat lay grounded some distance away.

Though one might well imagine that my first sensation would be of wonder at so prodigious and unexpected a transformation of scenery, I was in reality more horrified than astonished; for there was in the air and in the rotting soil a sinister quality which chilled me to the very core. The region was putrid with the carcasses of decaying fish, and of other less describable things which I saw protruding from the nasty mud of the unending plain. Perhaps I should not hope to convey in mere words the unutterable hideousness that can dwell in absolute silence and barren immensity. There was nothing within hearing, and nothing in sight save a vast reach of black slime; yet the very completeness of the stillness and the homogeneity of the landscape oppressed me with a nauseating fear.

The sun was blazing down from a sky which seemed to me almost black in its cloudless cruelty; as though reflecting the inky marsh beneath my feet. As I crawled into the stranded boat I realised that only one theory could explain my position. Through some unprecedented volcanic upheaval, a portion of the ocean floor must have been thrown to the surface, exposing regions which for innumerable millions of years had lain hidden under unfathomable watery depths. So great was the extent of the new land which had risen beneath me, that I could not detect the faintest noise of the surging ocean, strain my ears as I might. Nor were there any sea-fowl to prey upon the dead things.

For several hours I sat thinking or brooding in the boat, which lay upon its side and afforded a slight shade as the sun moved across the heavens. As the day progressed, the ground lost some of its stickiness, and seemed likely to dry sufficiently for travelling purposes in a short time. That night I slept but little, and the next day I made for myself a pack containing food and water, preparatory to an overland journey in search of the vanished sea and possible rescue.

On the third morning I found the soil dry enough to walk upon with ease. The odour of the fish was maddening; but I was too much concerned with graver things to mind so slight an evil, and set out boldly for an unknown goal. All day I forged steadily westward, guided by a far-away hummock which rose higher than any other elevation on the rolling desert. That night I encamped, and on the following day still travelled toward the hummock, though that object seemed scarcely nearer than when I had first espied it. By the fourth evening I attained the base of the mound, which turned out to be much higher than it had appeared from a distance; an intervening valley setting it out in sharper relief from the general surface. Too weary to ascend, I slept in the shadow of the hill.

I know not why my dreams were so wild that night; but ere the waning and fantastically gibbous moon had risen far above the eastern plain, I was awake in a cold perspiration, determined to sleep no more. Such visions as I had experienced were too much for me to endure again. And in the glow of the moon I saw how unwise I had been to travel by day. Without the glare of the parching sun, my journey would have cost me less energy; indeed, I now felt quite able to perform the ascent which had deterred me at sunset. Picking up my pack, I started for the crest of the eminence.

I have said that the unbroken monotony of the rolling plain was a source of vague horror to me; but I think my horror was greater when I gained the summit of the mound and looked down the other side into an immeasurable pit or canyon, whose black recesses the moon had not yet soared high enough to illumine. I felt myself on the edge of the world; peering over the rim into a fathomless chaos of eternal night. Through my terror ran curious reminiscences of *Paradise Lost,* and of Satan's hideous climb through the unfashioned realms of darkness.

As the moon climbed higher in the sky, I began to see that the slopes of the valley were not quite so perpendicular as I had imagined. Ledges and outcroppings of rock afforded fairly easy foot-holds for a descent, whilst after a drop of a few hundred feet, the declivity became very gradual. Urged on by an impulse which I cannot definitely analyse, I scrambled with difficulty down the rocks and stood on the gentler slope beneath, gazing into the Stygian deeps where no light had yet penetrated.

All at once my attention was captured by a vast and singular object on the opposite slope, which rose steeply about an hundred yards ahead of me; an object that gleamed whitely in the newly bestowed rays of the ascending moon. That it was merely a gigantic piece of stone, I soon assured myself; but I was conscious of a distinct impression that its contour and position were not altogether the work of Nature. A closer scrutiny filled me with sensations I cannot express; for despite its enormous magnitude, and its position in an abyss which had yawned at the bottom of the sea since the world was young, I perceived beyond a doubt that the strange object was a well-shaped monolith whose massive bulk had known the workmanship and perhaps the worship of living and thinking creatures.

Dazed and frightened, yet not without a certain thrill of the scientist's or archaeologist's delight, I examined my surroundings more closely. The moon, now near the zenith, shone weirdly and vividly above the towering steeps that hemmed in the chasm, and revealed the fact that a far-flung body of water flowed at the bottom, winding out of sight in both directions, and almost lapping my feet as I stood on the slope. Across the chasm, the wavelets washed the base of the Cyclopean monolith; on whose surface I could now trace both inscriptions and crude sculptures. The writing was in a system of hieroglyphics unknown to me, and unlike anything I had ever seen in books; consisting for the most part of conventionalised aquatic symbols such as fishes, eels, octopi, crustaceans, molluscs, whales, and the like. Several characters obviously represented marine things which are unknown to the modern world, but whose decomposing forms I had observed on the ocean-risen plain.

It was the pictorial carving, however, that did most to hold me spellbound. Plainly visible across the intervening water on account of their enormous size, were an array of bas-reliefs whose subjects would have excited the envy of a Doré. I think that these things were supposed to depict men—at least, a certain sort of men; though the creatures were shewn disporting like fishes in the waters of some marine grotto, or paying homage at some monolithic shrine which appeared to be under the waves as well. Of their faces and forms I dare not speak in detail; for the mere remembrance makes me grow faint. Grotesque beyond the imagination of a Poe or a Bulwer, they were damnably human in general outline despite webbed hands and feet, shockingly wide and flabby lips, glassy, bulging eyes, and other features less pleasant to recall. Curiously enough, they seemed to have been chiselled badly out of proportion with their scenic background; for one of the creatures was shewn in the act of killing a whale represented as but little larger than himself. I remarked, as I say, their grotesqueness and strange size; but in a moment decided that they were merely the imaginary gods of some primitive fishing or seafaring tribe; some tribe whose last descendant had perished eras before the first ancestor of the Piltdown or Neanderthal Man was born. Awestruck at this unexpected glimpse into a past beyond the conception of the most daring anthropologist, I stood musing whilst the moon cast queer reflections on the silent channel before me.

Then suddenly I saw it. With only a slight churning to mark its rise to the surface, the thing slid into view above the dark waters. Vast, Polyphemus-like, and loathsome, it darted like a stupendous monster of nightmares to the monolith, about which it flung its gigantic scaly arms, the while it bowed its hideous head and gave vent to certain measured sounds. I think I went mad then.

Of my frantic ascent of the slope and cliff, and of my delirious journey back to the stranded boat, I remember little. I believe I sang a great deal, and laughed oddly when I was unable to sing. I have indistinct recollections of a great storm some time after I reached the boat; at any rate, I know that I heard peals of thunder and other tones which Nature utters only in her wildest moods.

When I came out of the shadows I was in a San Francisco hospital; brought thither by the captain of the American ship which had picked up my boat in mid-ocean. In my delirium I had said much, but found that my words had been given scant attention. Of any land upheaval in the Pacific, my rescuers knew nothing; nor did I deem it necessary to insist upon a thing which I knew they could not believe. Once I sought out a celebrated ethnologist, and amused him with peculiar questions regarding the ancient Philistine legend of Dagon, the Fish-God; but soon perceiving that he was hopelessly conventional, I did not press my inquiries.

It is at night, especially when the moon is gibbous and waning, that I see the thing. I tried morphine; but the drug has given only transient surcease, and has drawn me into its clutches as a hopeless slave. So now I am to end it all, having written a full account for the information or the contemptuous amusement of my fellow-men. Often I ask myself if it could not all have been a pure phantasm—a mere freak of fever as I lay sun-stricken and raving in the open boat after my escape from the German man-of-war. This I ask myself, but ever does there come before me a hideously vivid vision in reply. I cannot think of the deep sea without shuddering at the nameless things that may at this very moment be crawling and floundering on its slimy bed, worshipping their ancient stone idols and carving their own detestable likenesses on submarine obelisks of water-soaked granite. I dream of a day when they may rise above the billows to drag down in their reeking talons the remnants of puny, war-exhausted mankind—of a day when the land shall sink, and the dark ocean floor shall ascend amidst universal pandemonium.

The end is near. I hear a noise at the door, as of some immense slippery body lumbering against it. It shall not find me. God, *that hand!* The window! The window!

THE HORROR AT MARTIN'S BEACH

H. P. Lovecraft and Sonia H. Greene

Although H. P. Lovecraft lived most of his adult life reclusively, there was a brief period, after the death of his mother, when he ventured from his Rhode Island home. During this time, he married and moved to Brooklyn, New York. Lovecraft and Sonia Greene (1883–1972), the woman he married, were are an unlikely couple. He feared and disliked immigrants, African Americans, and Jews. Sonia fit two out of three of those categories.

Sonia's origins are somewhat mysterious. Her maiden name is sometimes given as Haft Shafirkin and sometimes as Shafirkin Haft. She is believed to have been born in Ichnya in what is now Ukraine; however, the year before she was reputedly born, a tsarist edict expelled local Jews from the village. They were not permitted to return before 1903.[4] Sonia arrived in the United States in 1892.

Unlike the isolated, inexperienced Lovecraft, Greene had done a lot of living by the time they met. Following her father's death, her mother had traveled to America alone, leaving Sonia and her brother behind until she could afford to send for them. Sonia then learned to navigate a new country and become fluent in a new language. At age sixteen, she married an older and allegedly abusive husband, from whom she inherited the name Greene. When he died, Sonia was left to support their daughter as a single mother. She became a successful milliner. Her interest in weird fiction predates

---

4 *http://www.yadvashem.org/untoldstories/database/index.asp?cid=510.*

her association with Lovecraft: they met at an amateur press convention in Boston. They married in New York on March 3, 1924, and resided together in Brooklyn. Sonia supported his writing, but eventually beset by financial and perhaps other problems, the marriage fell apart, although their divorce was never finalized.

"The Horror at Martin's Beach" was written in June 1922 and first published in November 1923 as "The Invisible Monster" in *Weird Tales* (vol. 2, no. 4, 75–76, 83). The story is generally believed to have been written by Greene and revised by Lovecraft. If, upon reading it, you are reminded of Beowulf, you would not be the first.

The Horror at Martin's Beach

I have never heard an even approximately adequate explanation of the horror at Martin's Beach. Despite the large number of witnesses, no two accounts agree; and the testimony taken by local authorities contains the most amazing discrepancies.

Perhaps this haziness is natural in view of the unheard-of character of the horror itself, the almost paralytic terror of all who saw it, and the efforts made by the fashionable Wavecrest Inn to hush it up after the publicity created by Prof. Alton's article "Are Hypnotic Powers Confined to Recognized Humanity?"

Against all these obstacles I am striving to present a coherent version; for I beheld the hideous occurrence, and believe it should be known in view of the appalling possibilities it suggests. Martin's Beach is once more popular as a watering-place, but I shudder when I think of it. Indeed, I cannot look at the ocean at all now without shuddering.

Fate is not always without a sense of drama and climax, hence the terrible happening of August 8, 1922, swiftly followed a period of minor and agreeably wonder-fraught excitement at Martin's Beach. On May 17 the crew of the fishing smack *Alma* of Gloucester, under Capt. James P. Orne, killed, after a battle of nearly forty hours, a marine monster whose size and aspect produced the greatest possible stir in scientific circles and caused certain Boston naturalists to take every precaution for its taxidermic preservation.

The object was some fifty feet in length, of roughly cylindrical shape, and about ten feet in diameter. It was unmistakably a gilled fish in its major affiliations; but with certain curious modifications, such as rudimentary forelegs and six-toed feet in place of pectoral fins, which prompted the widest speculation. Its extraordinary mouth, its thick and scaly hide, and its single, deep-set eye were wonders scarcely less remarkable than its colossal dimensions; and when the naturalists pronounced it an infant organism, which could not have been hatched more than a few days, public interest mounted to extraordinary heights.

Capt. Orne, with typical Yankee shrewdness, obtained a vessel large enough to hold the object in its hull, and arranged for the exhibition of his prize. With judicious carpentry he prepared what amounted to an excellent marine museum, and, sailing south to the wealthy resort district of Martin's Beach, anchored at the hotel wharf and reaped a harvest of admission fees.

The intrinsic marvelousness of the object, and the importance which it clearly bore in the minds of many scientific visitors from near and far, combined to make it the season's sensation. That it was absolutely unique—unique to a scientifically revolutionary degree—was well understood. The naturalists had shown plainly that it radically differed from the similarly immense fish caught off the Florida coast; that, while it was obviously an inhabitant of almost incredible depths, perhaps thousands of feet, its brain and principal organs indicated a development startlingly vast, and out of all proportion to anything hitherto associated with the fish tribe.

On the morning of July 20 the sensation was increased by the loss of the vessel and its strange treasure. In the storm of the preceding night it had broken from its moorings and vanished forever from the sight of man, carrying with it the guard who had slept aboard despite the threatening weather. Capt. Orne, backed by extensive scientific interests and aided by large numbers of fishing boats from Gloucester, made a thorough and exhaustive searching cruise, but with no result other than the prompting of interest and conversation. By August 7 hope was abandoned, and Capt. Orne had returned to the Wavecrest Inn to wind up his business affairs at Martin's Beach and confer with certain of the scientific men who remained there. The horror came on August 8.

It was in the twilight, when grey sea-birds hovered low near the shore and a rising moon began to make a glittering path across the waters. The scene is important to remember, for every impression counts. On the beach were several strollers and a few late bathers; stragglers from the distant cottage colony that rose modestly on a green hill to the north, or from the adjacent cliff-perched Inn whose imposing towers proclaimed its allegiance to wealth and grandeur.

Well within viewing distance was another set of spectators, the loungers on the Inn's high-ceiled and lantern-lighted veranda, who appeared to be enjoying the dance music from the sumptuous ballroom inside. These spectators, who included Capt. Orne and his group of scientific confreres, joined the beach group before the horror progressed far; as did many more from the Inn. Certainly there was no lack of witnesses, confused though their stories be with fear and doubt of what they saw.

There is no exact record of the time the thing began, although a majority say that the fairly round moon was "about a foot" above the low-lying vapors of the horizon. They mention the moon because what they saw seemed subtly connected with it—a sort of stealthy, deliberate, menacing ripple which rolled in from the far skyline along the shimmering lane of reflected moonbeams, yet which seemed to subside before it reached the shore.

Many did not notice this ripple until reminded by later events; but it seems to have been very marked, differing in height and motion from the normal waves around it. Some called it *cunning* and *calculating*. And as it died away craftily by the black reefs afar out, there suddenly came belching up out of the glitter-streaked brine a cry of death; a scream of anguish and despair that moved pity even while it mocked it.

First to respond to the cry were the two life guards then on duty; sturdy fellows in white bathing attire, with their calling proclaimed in large red letters across their chests. Accustomed as they were to rescue work, and to the screams of the drowning, they could find nothing familiar in the unearthly ululation; yet with a trained sense of duty they ignored the strangeness and proceeded to follow their usual course.

Hastily seizing an air-cushion, which with its attached coil of rope lay always at hand, one of them ran swiftly along the shore to the scene of the gathering crowd; whence, after whirling it about to gain momentum, he flung the hollow disc far out in the direction from which the sound had come. As the cushion disappeared in the waves, the crowd curiously awaited a sight of the hapless being whose distress had been so great; eager to see the rescue made by the massive rope.

But that rescue was soon acknowledged to be no swift and easy matter; for, pull as they might on the rope, the two muscular guards could not move the object at the other end. Instead, they found that object pulling with equal or even greater force in the very opposite direction, till in a few seconds they were dragged off their feet and into the water by the strange power which had seized on the proffered life-preserver.

One of them, recovering himself, called immediately for help from the crowd on the shore, to whom he flung the remaining coil of rope; and in a moment the guards were seconded by all the hardier men, among whom Capt. Orne was foremost. More than a dozen strong hands were now tugging desperately at the stout line, yet wholly without avail.

Hard as they tugged, the strange force at the other end tugged harder; and since neither side relaxed for an instant, the rope became rigid as steel with the enormous strain. The struggling participants, as well as the spectators, were by this time consumed with curiosity as to the nature of the force in the sea. The idea of a drowning man had long been dismissed; and hints of whales, submarines, monsters, and demons now passed freely around. Where humanity had first led the rescuers, wonder kept them at their task; and they hauled with a grim determination to uncover the mystery.

It being decided at last that a whale must have swallowed the air-cushion, Capt. Orne, as a natural leader, shouted to those on the shore that a boat must be obtained in order to approach, harpoon, and land the unseen leviathan. Several men at once prepared to scatter in quest of a suitable craft, while others came to supplant the captain at the straining rope, since his place was logically with whatever boat party might be formed. His own idea of the situation was very broad, and by no means limited to whales, since he had to do with a monster so much stranger. He wondered what might be the acts and manifestations of an adult of the species of which the fifty-foot creature had been the merest infant.

And now there developed with appalling suddenness the crucial fact which changed the entire scene from one of wonder to one of horror, and dazed with fright the assembled band of toilers and onlookers. Capt. Orne, turning to leave his post at the rope, found his hands held in their place with unaccountable strength; and in a moment he realized that he was unable to let go of the rope. His plight was instantly divined, and as each companion tested his own situation the same condition was encountered. The fact could not be denied— every struggler was irresistibly held in some mysterious bondage to the hempen line which was slowly, hideously, and relentlessly pulling them out to sea.

Speechless horror ensued; a horror in which the spectators were petrified to utter inaction and mental chaos. Their complete demoralization is reflected in the conflicting accounts they give, and the sheepish excuses they offer for their seemingly callous inertia. I was one of them, and know.

Even the strugglers, after a few frantic screams and futile groans, succumbed to the paralyzing influence and kept silent and fatalistic in the face of unknown powers. There they stood in the pallid moonlight, blindly pulling against a spectral doom and swaying monotonously backward and forward as the water rose first to their knees, then to their hips. The moon went partly under a cloud, and in the half-light the line of swaying men resembled some sinister and gigantic centipede, writhing in the clutch of a terrible creeping death.

Harder and harder grew the rope, as the tug in both directions increased, and the strands swelled with the undisturbed soaking of the rising waves. Slowly the tide advanced, till the sands so lately peopled by laughing children and whispering lovers were now swallowed by the inexorable flow. The herd of panic-stricken watchers surged blindly backward as the water crept above their feet, while the frightful line of strugglers swayed hideously on, half submerged, and now at a substantial distance from their audience. Silence was complete.

The crowd, having gained a huddling-place beyond reach of the tide, stared in mute fascination; without offering a word of advice or encouragement, or attempting any kind of assistance. There was in the air a nightmare fear of impending evils such as the world had never before known.

Minutes seemed lengthened into hours, and still that human snake of swaying torsos was seen above the fast rising tide. Rhythmically it undulated; slowly, horribly, with the seal of doom upon it. Thicker clouds now passed over the ascending moon, and the glittering path on the waters faded nearly out.

Very dimly writhed the serpentine line of nodding heads, with now and then the livid face of a backward-glancing victim gleaming pale in the darkness. Faster and faster gathered the clouds, till at length their angry rifts shot down sharp tongues of febrile flame. Thunders rolled, softly at first, yet soon increasing to a deafening, maddening intensity. Then came a culminating crash—a shock whose reverberations seemed to shake land and sea alike—and on its heels a cloudburst whose drenching violence overpowered the darkened world as if the heavens themselves had opened to pour forth a vindictive torrent.

The spectators, instinctively acting despite the absence of conscious and coherent thought, now retreated up the cliff steps to the hotel veranda. Rumors had reached the guests inside, so that the refugees found a state of terror nearly equal to their own. I think a few frightened words were uttered, but cannot be sure.

Some, who were staying at the Inn, retired in terror to their rooms; while others remained to watch the fast sinking victims as the line of bobbing heads showed above the mounting waves in the fitful lightning flashes. I recall thinking of those heads, and the bulging eyes they must contain; eyes that might well reflect all the fright, panic, and delirium of a malignant universe—all the sorrow, sin, and misery, blasted hopes and unfulfilled desires, fear, loathing and anguish of the ages since time's beginning; eyes alight with all the soul-racking pain of eternally blazing infernos.

And as I gazed out beyond the heads, my fancy conjured up still another eye; a single eye, equally alight, yet with a purpose so revolting to my brain that the vision soon passed. Held in the clutches of an unknown vise, the line of the damned dragged on; their silent screams and unuttered prayers known only to the demons of the black waves and the night-wind.

There now burst from the infuriate sky such a mad cataclysm of satanic sound that even the former crash seemed dwarfed. Amidst a blinding glare of descending fire the voice of heaven resounded with the blasphemies of hell, and the mingled agony of all the lost reverberated in one apocalyptic, planet-rending peal of Cyclopean din. It was the end of the storm, for with uncanny suddenness the rain ceased and the moon once more cast her pallid beams on a strangely quieted sea.

There was no line of bobbing heads now. The waters were calm and deserted, and broken only by the fading ripples of what seemed to be a whirlpool far out in the path of the moonlight whence the strange cry had first come. But as I looked along that treacherous lane of silvery sheen, with fancy fevered and senses overwrought, there trickled upon my ears from some abysmal sunken waste the faint and sinister echoes of a laugh.

THE TRIAL FOR MURDER

Charles Dickens

Charles Dickens (1812–1870) is among the most successful, popular, and renowned of all authors. His books are classics: *A Tale of Two Cities, Oliver Twist, David Copperfield, Great Expectations.* Charles Dickens loved a good ghost story. He had been introduced to them in earliest childhood by his nanny, who told him terrifying tales. His most famous ghost story—perhaps the most famous ghost story of all—is "A Christmas Carol," with its iconic characters Scrooge, Tiny Tim, and the Ghosts of Christmas Past, Present, and Future.

What is less well known is that Dickens wrote numerous ghost stories. A lover of the genre, he encouraged other authors to do so as well. Dickens traveled widely, offering readings of his works. It is perhaps not surprising that Dickens himself has become the subject of ghost stories: allegedly, within days of his death, Dickens's own ghost began turning up in English séance parlors, offering strange tales from beyond the grave.

In "The Trial for Murder," first published in November 1865, a ghost does his best to ensure that a jury renders the correct verdict.

The Trial for Murder

I have always noticed a prevalent want of courage, even among persons of superior intelligence and culture, as to imparting their own psychological experiences when those have been of a strange sort. Almost all men are afraid that what they could relate in such wise would find no parallel or response in a listener's internal life, and might be suspected or laughed at. A truthful traveller, who should have seen some extraordinary creature in the likeness of a sea-serpent, would have no fear of mentioning it; but the same traveller, having had some singular presentiment, impulse, vagary of thought, vision (so-called), dream, or other remarkable mental impression, would hesitate considerably before he would own to it. To this reticence I attribute much of the obscurity in which such subjects are involved. We do not habitually communicate our experiences of these subjective things as we do our experiences of objective creation. The consequence is, that the general stock of experience in this regard appears exceptional, and really is so, in respect of being miserably imperfect.

In what I am going to relate, I have no intention of setting up, opposing, or supporting, any theory whatever. I know the history of the Bookseller of Berlin, I have studied the case of the wife of a late Astronomer Royal as related by Sir David Brewster, and I have followed the minutest details of a much more remarkable case of Spectral Illusion occurring within my private circle of friends. It may be necessary to state as to this last, that the sufferer (a lady) was in no degree, however distant, related to me. A mistaken assumption on that head might suggest an explanation of a part of my own case,—but only a part,—which would be wholly without foundation. It cannot be referred to my inheritance of any developed peculiarity, nor had I ever before any at all similar experience, nor have I ever had any at all similar experience since.

It does not signify how many years ago, or how few, a certain murder was committed in England, which attracted great attention. We hear more than enough of murderers as they rise in succession to their atrocious eminence, and I would bury the memory of this particular brute, if I could, as his body was buried, in Newgate Jail. I purposely abstain from giving any direct clue to the criminal's individuality.

When the murder was first discovered, no suspicion fell—or I ought rather to say, for I cannot be too precise in my facts, it was nowhere publicly hinted that any suspicion fell—on the man who was afterwards brought to trial. As no reference was at that time made to him in the newspapers, it is obviously impossible that any description of him can at that time have been given in the newspapers. It is essential that this fact be remembered.

Unfolding at breakfast my morning paper, containing the account of that first discovery, I found it to be deeply interesting, and I read it with close attention. I read it twice, if not three times. The discovery had been made in a bedroom, and, when I laid down the paper, I was aware of a flash—rush—flow—I do not know what to call it,—no word I can find is satisfactorily descriptive,—in which I seemed to see that bedroom passing through my room, like a picture impossibly painted on a running river. Though almost instantaneous in its passing, it was perfectly clear; so clear that I distinctly, and with a sense of relief, observed the absence of the dead body from the bed.

It was in no romantic place that I had this curious sensation, but in chambers in Piccadilly, very near to the corner of St. James's Street. It was entirely new to me. I was in my easy-chair at the moment, and the sensation was accompanied with a peculiar shiver which started the chair from its position. (But it is to be noted that the chair ran easily on castors.) I went to one of the windows (there are two in the room, and the room is on the second floor) to refresh my eyes with the moving objects down in Piccadilly. It was a bright autumn morning, and the street was sparkling and cheerful. The wind was high. As I looked out, it brought down from the Park a quantity of fallen leaves, which a gust took, and whirled into a spiral pillar. As the pillar fell and the leaves dispersed, I saw two men on the opposite side of the way, going from West to East. They were one behind the other. The foremost man often looked back over his shoulder. The second man followed him, at a distance of some thirty paces, with his right hand menacingly raised. First, the singularity and steadiness of this threatening gesture in so public a thoroughfare attracted my attention; and next, the more remarkable circumstance that nobody heeded it. Both men threaded their way among the other passengers with a smoothness hardly consistent even with the action of walking on a pavement; and no single creature, that I could see, gave them place, touched them, or looked after them. In passing before my windows, they both stared up at me. I saw their two faces very distinctly, and I knew that I could recognise them anywhere. Not that I had consciously noticed anything very remarkable in either face, except that the man who went first had an unusually lowering appearance, and that the face of the man who followed him was of the colour of impure wax.

I am a bachelor, and my valet and his wife constitute my whole establishment. My occupation is in a certain Branch Bank, and I wish that my duties as head of a Department were as light as they are popularly supposed to be. They kept me in town that autumn, when I stood in need of change. I was not ill, but I was not well. My reader is to make the most that can be reasonably made of my feeling jaded, having a depressing sense upon me of a monotonous life, and being "slightly dyspeptic." I am assured by my renowned doctor that my real state of health at that time justifies no stronger description, and I quote his own from his written answer to my request for it.

As the circumstances of the murder, gradually unravelling, took stronger and stronger possession of the public mind, I kept them away from mine by knowing as little about them as was possible in the midst of the universal excitement. But I knew that a verdict of Wilful Murder had been found against the suspected murderer, and that he had been committed to Newgate for trial. I also knew that his trial had been postponed over one Sessions of the Central Criminal Court, on the ground of general prejudice and want of time for the preparation of the defence. I may further have known, but I believe I did not, when, or about when, the Sessions to which his trial stood postponed would come on.

My sitting-room, bedroom, and dressing-room, are all on one floor. With the last there is no communication but through the bedroom. True, there is a door in it, once communicating with the staircase; but a part of the fitting of my bath has been—and had then been for some years—fixed across it. At the same period, and as a part of the same arrangement,—the door had been nailed up and canvased over.

I was standing in my bedroom late one night, giving some directions to my servant before he went to bed. My face was towards the only available door of communication with the dressing-room, and it was closed. My servant's back was towards that door. While I was speaking to him, I saw it open, and a man look in, who very earnestly and mysteriously beckoned to me. That man was the man who had gone second of the two along Piccadilly, and whose face was of the colour of impure wax.

The figure, having beckoned, drew back, and closed the door. With no longer pause than was made by my crossing the bedroom, I opened the dressing-room door, and looked in. I had a lighted candle already in my hand. I felt no inward expectation of seeing the figure in the dressing-room, and I did not see it there.

Conscious that my servant stood amazed, I turned round to him, and said: "Derrick, could you believe that in my cool senses I fancied I saw a—" As I there laid my hand upon his breast, with a sudden start he trembled violently, and said, "O Lord, yes, sir! A dead man beckoning!"

Now I do not believe that this John Derrick, my trusty and attached servant for more than twenty years, had any impression whatever of having seen any such figure, until I touched him. The change in him was so startling, when I touched him, that I fully believe he derived his impression in some occult manner from me at that instant.

I bade John Derrick bring some brandy, and I gave him a dram, and was glad to take one myself. Of what had preceded that night's phenomenon, I told him not a single word. Reflecting on it, I was absolutely certain that I had never seen that face before, except on the one occasion in Piccadilly. Comparing its expression when beckoning at the door with its expression when it had stared up at me as I stood at my window, I came to the conclusion that on the first occasion it had sought to fasten itself upon my memory, and that on the second occasion it had made sure of being immediately remembered.

I was not very comfortable that night, though I felt a certainty, difficult to explain, that the figure would not return. At daylight I fell into a heavy sleep, from which I was awakened by John Derrick's coming to my bedside with a paper in his hand.

This paper, it appeared, had been the subject of an altercation at the door between its bearer and my servant. It was a summons to me to serve upon a Jury at the forthcoming Sessions of the Central Criminal Court at the Old Bailey. I had never before been summoned on such a Jury, as John Derrick well knew. He believed—I am not certain at this hour whether with reason or otherwise—that that class of Jurors were customarily chosen on a lower qualification than mine, and he had at first refused to accept the summons. The man who served it had taken the matter very coolly. He had said that my attendance or non-attendance was nothing to him; there the summons was; and I should deal with it at my own peril, and not at his.

For a day or two I was undecided whether to respond to this call, or take no notice of it. I was not conscious of the slightest mysterious bias, influence, or attraction, one way or other. Of that I am as strictly sure as of every other statement that I make here. Ultimately I decided, as a break in the monotony of my life, that I would go.

The appointed morning was a raw morning in the month of November. There was a dense brown fog in Piccadilly, and it became positively black and in the last degree oppressive East of Temple Bar. I found the passages and staircases of the Court-House flaringly lighted with gas, and the Court itself similarly illuminated. I THINK that, until I was conducted by officers into the Old Court and saw its crowded state, I did not know that the Murderer was to be tried that day. I THINK that, until I was so helped into the Old Court with considerable difficulty, I did not know into which of the two Courts sitting my summons would take me. But this must not be received as a positive assertion, for I am not completely satisfied in my mind on either point.

I took my seat in the place appropriated to Jurors in waiting, and I looked about the Court as well as I could through the cloud of fog and breath that was heavy in it. I noticed the black vapour hanging like a murky curtain outside the great windows, and I noticed the stifled sound of wheels on the straw or tan that was littered in the street;

also, the hum of the people gathered there, which a shrill whistle, or a louder song or hail than the rest, occasionally pierced. Soon afterwards the Judges, two in number, entered, and took their seats. The buzz in the Court was awfully hushed. The direction was given to put the Murderer to the bar. He appeared there. And in that same instant I recognised in him the first of the two men who had gone down Piccadilly.

If my name had been called then, I doubt if I could have answered to it audibly. But it was called about sixth or eighth in the panel, and I was by that time able to say, "Here!" Now, observe. As I stepped into the box, the prisoner, who had been looking on attentively, but with no sign of concern, became violently agitated, and beckoned to his attorney. The prisoner's wish to challenge me was so manifest, that it occasioned a pause, during which the attorney, with his hand upon the dock, whispered with his client, and shook his head. I afterwards had it from that gentleman, that the prisoner's first affrighted words to him were, "AT ALL HAZARDS, CHALLENGE THAT MAN!" But that, as he would give no reason for it, and admitted that he had not even known my name until he heard it called and I appeared, it was not done.

Both on the ground already explained, that I wish to avoid reviving the unwholesome memory of that Murderer, and also because a detailed account of his long trial is by no means indispensable to my narrative, I shall confine myself closely to such incidents in the ten days and nights during which we, the Jury, were kept together, as directly bear on my own curious personal experience. It is in that, and not in the Murderer, that I seek to interest my reader. It is to that, and not to a page of the Newgate Calendar, that I beg attention.

I was chosen Foreman of the Jury. On the second morning of the trial, after evidence had been taken for two hours (I heard the church clocks strike), happening to cast my eyes over my brother jurymen, I found an inexplicable difficulty in counting them. I counted them several times, yet always with the same difficulty. In short, I made them one too many.

I touched the brother jurymen whose place was next me, and I whispered to him, "Oblige me by counting us." He looked surprised by the request, but turned his head and counted. "Why," says he, suddenly, "we are Thirt—; but no, it's not possible. No. We are twelve."

According to my counting that day, we were always right in detail, but in the gross we were always one too many. There was no appearance—no figure—to account for it; but I had now an inward foreshadowing of the figure that was surely coming.

The Jury were housed at the London Tavern. We all slept in one large room on separate tables, and we were constantly in the charge and under the eye of the officer sworn to hold us in safe-keeping. I see no reason for suppressing the real name of that officer. He was intelligent, highly polite, and obliging, and (I was glad to hear) much respected in the City. He had an agreeable presence, good eyes, enviable black whiskers, and a fine sonorous voice. His name was Mr. Harker.

When we turned into our twelve beds at night, Mr. Harker's bed was drawn across the door. On the night of the second day, not being disposed to lie down, and seeing Mr. Harker sitting on his bed, I went and sat beside him, and offered him a pinch of snuff. As Mr. Harker's hand touched mine in taking it from my box, a peculiar shiver crossed him, and he said, "Who is this?"

Following Mr. Harker's eyes, and looking along the room, I saw again the figure I expected,—the second of the two men who had gone down Piccadilly. I rose, and advanced a few steps; then stopped, and looked round at Mr. Harker. He was quite unconcerned, laughed, and said in a pleasant way, "I thought for a moment we had a thirteenth juryman, without a bed. But I see it is the moonlight."

Making no revelation to Mr. Harker, but inviting him to take a walk with me to the end of the room, I watched what the figure did. It stood for a few moments by the bedside of each of my eleven brother jurymen, close to the pillow. It always went to the right-hand side of the bed, and always passed out crossing the foot of the next bed. It seemed, from the action of the head, merely to look down pensively at each recumbent figure. It took no notice of me, or of my bed, which was that nearest to Mr. Harker's. It seemed to go out where the moonlight came in, through a high window, as by an aerial flight of stairs.

Next morning at breakfast, it appeared that everybody present had dreamed of the murdered man last night, except myself and Mr. Harker.

I now felt as convinced that the second man who had gone down Piccadilly was the murdered man (so to speak), as if it had been borne into my comprehension by his immediate testimony. But even this took place, and in a manner for which I was not at all prepared.

On the fifth day of the trial, when the case for the prosecution was drawing to a close, a miniature of the murdered man, missing from his bedroom upon the discovery of the deed, and afterwards found in a hiding-place where the Murderer had been seen digging, was put in evidence. Having been identified by the witness under examination, it was handed up to the Bench, and thence handed down to be inspected by the Jury. As an officer in a black gown was making his way with it across to me, the figure of the second man who had gone down Piccadilly impetuously started from the crowd, caught the miniature from the officer, and gave it to me with his own hands, at the same time saying, in a low and hollow tone,—before I saw the miniature, which was in a locket,—"I WAS YOUNGER THEN, AND MY FACE WAS NOT THEN DRAINED OF BLOOD." It also came between me and the brother juryman to whom I would have given the miniature, and between him and the brother juryman to whom he would have given it, and so passed it on through the whole of our number, and back into my possession. Not one of them, however, detected this.

At table, and generally when we were shut up together in Mr. Harker's custody, we had from the first naturally discussed the day's proceedings a good deal. On that fifth day, the case for the prosecution being closed, and we having that side of the question in a completed shape before us, our discussion was more animated and serious. Among our number was a vestryman,—the densest idiot I have ever seen at large,—who met the plainest evidence with the most preposterous objections, and who was sided with by two flabby parochial parasites; all the three impanelled from a district so delivered over to Fever that they ought to have been upon their own trial for five hundred Murders. When these mischievous blockheads were at their loudest, which was towards midnight, while some of us were already preparing for bed, I again saw the murdered man. He stood grimly behind them, beckoning to me. On my going towards them, and striking into the conversation, he immediately retired. This was the beginning of a separate series of appearances, confined to that long room in which we were confined. Whenever a knot of my brother jurymen laid their heads together, I saw the head of the murdered man among theirs. Whenever their comparison of notes was going against him, he would solemnly and irresistibly beckon to me.

It will be borne in mind that down to the production of the miniature, on the fifth day of the trial, I had never seen the Appearance in Court. Three changes occurred now that we entered on the case for the defence. Two of them I will mention together, first. The figure was now in Court continually, and it never there addressed itself to me, but always to the person who was speaking at the time. For instance: the throat of the murdered man had been cut straight across. In the opening speech for the defence, it was suggested that the deceased might have cut his own throat. At that very moment, the figure, with its throat in the dreadful condition referred to (this it had concealed before), stood at the speaker's elbow, motioning across and across its windpipe, now with the right hand, now with the left, vigorously suggesting to the speaker himself the impossibility of such a wound having been self-inflicted by either hand. For another instance: a witness to character, a woman, deposed to the prisoner's being the most amiable of mankind. The figure at that instant stood on the floor before her, looking her full in the face, and pointing out the prisoner's evil countenance with an extended arm and an outstretched finger.

The third change now to be added impressed me strongly as the most marked and striking of all. I do not theorise upon it; I accurately state it, and there leave it. Although the Appearance was not itself perceived by those whom it addressed, its coming close to such persons was invariably attended by some trepidation or disturbance on their part. It seemed to me as if it were prevented, by laws to which I was not amenable, from fully revealing itself to others, and yet as if it could invisibly, dumbly, and darkly overshadow their minds. When the leading counsel for the defence suggested that hypothesis of suicide, and the figure stood at the learned gentleman's elbow, frightfully sawing at its severed throat, it is undeniable that the counsel faltered in his speech, lost for a few seconds the thread of his ingenious discourse, wiped his forehead with his handkerchief, and turned extremely pale. When the witness to character was confronted by the Appearance, her eyes most certainly did follow the direction of its pointed finger, and rest in great hesitation and trouble upon the prisoner's face. Two additional illustrations will suffice. On the eighth day of the trial, after the pause which was every day made early in the afternoon for a few minutes' rest and refreshment, I came back into Court with the rest of the Jury some little time before the return of the Judges. Standing up in the box and looking about me, I thought the figure was not there, until, chancing to raise my eyes to the gallery, I saw it bending forward, and leaning over a very decent woman, as if to assure itself whether the Judges had resumed their seats or not. Immediately afterwards that woman screamed, fainted, and was carried out. So with the venerable, sagacious, and patient Judge who conducted the trial. When the case was over, and he settled himself and his papers to sum up, the murdered man, entering by the Judges' door, advanced to his Lordship's desk, and looked eagerly over his shoulder at the pages of his notes which he was turning. A change came over his Lordship's face; his hand stopped; the peculiar shiver, that I knew so well, passed over him; he faltered, "Excuse me, gentlemen, for a few moments. I am somewhat oppressed by the vitiated air;" and did not recover until he had drunk a glass of water.

Through all the monotony of six of those interminable ten days,—the same Judges and others on the bench, the same Murderer in the dock, the same lawyers at the table, the same tones of question and answer rising to the roof of the court, the same scratching of the Judge's pen, the same ushers going in and out, the same lights kindled at the same hour when there had been any natural light of day, the same foggy curtain outside the great windows when it was foggy, the same rain pattering and dripping when it was rainy, the same footmarks of turnkeys and prisoner day after day on the same sawdust, the same keys locking and unlocking the same heavy doors,—through all the wearisome monotony which made me feel as if I had been Foreman of the Jury for a vast cried of time, and Piccadilly had flourished coevally with Babylon, the murdered man never lost one trace of his distinctness in my eyes, nor was he at any moment less distinct than anybody else. I must not omit, as a matter of fact, that I never once saw the Appearance which I call by the name of the murdered man look at the Murderer. Again and again I wondered, "Why does he not?" But he never did.

Nor did he look at me, after the production of the miniature, until the last closing minutes of the trial arrived. We retired to consider, at seven minutes before ten at night. The idiotic vestryman and his two parochial parasites gave us so much trouble that we twice returned into Court to beg to have certain extracts from the Judge's notes re-read. Nine of us had not the smallest doubt about those passages, neither, I believe, had any one in the Court; the dunder-headed triumvirate, having no idea but obstruction, disputed them for that very reason. At length we prevailed, and finally the Jury returned into Court at ten minutes past twelve.

The murdered man at that time stood directly opposite the Jury-box, on the other side of the Court. As I took my place, his eyes rested on me with great attention; he seemed satisfied, and slowly shook a great gray veil, which he carried on his arm for the first time, over his head and whole form. As I gave in our verdict, "Guilty," the veil collapsed, all was gone, and his place was empty.

The Murderer, being asked by the Judge, according to usage, whether he had anything to say before sentence of Death should be passed upon him, indistinctly muttered something which was described in the leading newspapers of the following day as "a few rambling, incoherent, and half-audible words, in which he was understood to complain that he had not had a fair trial, because the Foreman of the Jury was prepossessed against him." The remarkable declaration that he really made was this: "MY LORD, I KNEW I WAS A DOOMED MAN, WHEN THE FOREMAN OF MY JURY CAME INTO THE BOX. MY LORD, I KNEW HE WOULD NEVER LET ME OFF, BECAUSE, BEFORE I WAS TAKEN, HE SOMEHOW GOT TO MY BEDSIDE IN THE NIGHT, WOKE ME, AND PUT A ROPE ROUND MY NECK."

THE TWISTING
OF THE ROPE

W. B. Yeats

Poet William Butler Yeats (1865–1939) was the first Irishman to receive
the Nobel Prize in Literature (1923). Yeats was among the founders of the
Abbey Theatre, also known as the National Theatre of Ireland, and was one
of the driving forces behind the Irish Literary Revival. Yeats had a deep love
of folklore, mysticism, and mythology. He was a genuine adept. In March
1890, he joined the metaphysical society, the Order of the Golden Dawn,
resigning in 1905. He was also a member of the Dublin Theosophist Circle.

"The Twisting of the Rope" is one of the stories in Yeats's book *Stories
of Red Hanrahan,* first published in 1897, then rewritten in 1905 with help
from his friend, the folklorist and dramatist Lady Gregory, so as to better
capture local dialect. *Stories of Red Hanrahan* consists of six connected tales that
describe the adventures, as well as the plight, of Owen "Red" Hanrahan,
who is described as a "hedge schoolmaster."

On the eve of Samhain, the Celtic holy day that corresponds in time to
Halloween, Hanrahan falls under an enchantment. He becomes a wandering poet, a bard, who is both welcomed by the people he visits and feared.
The story is peppered with references to Irish myth; for instance, Deirdre
and the sons of Usnach. "Them" refers not to the rock band from Northern
Ireland that once featured Van Morrison, but is a euphemism for the Sidhe,
Ireland's fierce, glamourous, dangerous fairies: it's considered safer not to
refer to them by name, sort of like that old folk warning about not calling
the devil lest he come. Likewise, the story's "Country of the Young" refers
to a fairy paradise.

The Twisting of the Rope

Hanrahan was walking the roads one time near Kinvara at the fall of day, and he heard the sound of a fiddle from a house a little way off the roadside. He turned up the path to it, for he never had the habit of passing by any place where there was music or dancing or good company, without going in. The man of the house was standing at the door, and when Hanrahan came near he knew him and he said: 'A welcome before you, Hanrahan, you have been lost to us this long time.' But the woman of the house came to the door and she said to her husband: 'I would be as well pleased for Hanrahan not to come in to-night, for he has no good name now among the priests, or with women that mind themselves, and I wouldn't wonder from his walk if he has a drop of drink taken.' But the man said, 'I will never turn away Hanrahan of the poets from my door,' and with that he bade him enter.

There were a good many neighbours gathered in the house, and some of them remembered Hanrahan; but some of the little lads that were in the corners had only heard of him, and they stood up to have a view of him, and one of them said: 'Is not that Hanrahan that had the school, and that was brought away by Them?' But his mother put her hand over his mouth and bade him be quiet, and not be saying things like that. 'For Hanrahan is apt to grow wicked,' she said, 'if he hears talk of that story, or if anyone goes questioning him.' One or another called out then, asking him for a song, but the man of the house said it was no time to ask him for a song, before he had rested himself; and he gave him whiskey in a glass, and Hanrahan thanked him and wished him good health and drank it off.

The fiddler was tuning his fiddle for another dance, and the man of the house said to the young men, they would all know what dancing was like when they saw Hanrahan dance, for the like of it had never been seen since he was there before. Hanrahan said he would not dance, he had better use for his feet now, travelling as he was through the five provinces of Ireland. Just as he said that, there came in at the half-door Oona, the daughter of the house, having a few bits of bog deal from Connemara in her arms for the fire. She threw them on the hearth and the flame rose up, and showed her to be very comely and smiling, and two or three of the young men rose up and asked for a dance. But Hanrahan crossed the floor and brushed the others away, and said it was with him she must dance, after the long road he had travelled before he came to her. And it is likely he said some soft word in her ear, for she said nothing against it, and stood out with him, and there were little blushes in her cheeks. Then other couples stood up, but when the dance was going to begin, Hanrahan chanced to look down, and he took notice of his boots that were worn and broken, and the ragged grey socks showing through them; and he said angrily it was a bad floor, and the music no great things, and he sat down in the dark place beside the hearth. But if he did, the girl sat down there with him.

The dancing went on, and when that dance was over another was called for, and no one took much notice of Oona and Red Hanrahan for a while, in the corner where they were. But the mother grew to be uneasy, and she called to Oona to come and help her to set the table in the inner room. But Oona that had never refused her before, said she would come soon, but not yet, for she was listening to whatever he was saying in her ear. The mother grew yet more uneasy then, and she would come nearer them, and let on to be stirring the fire or sweeping the hearth, and she would listen for a minute to hear what the poet was saying to her child. And one time she heard him telling about white-handed Deirdre, and how she brought the sons of Usnach to their death; and how the blush in her cheeks was not so red as the blood of kings' sons that was shed for her, and her sorrows had never gone out of mind; and he said it was maybe the memory of her that made the cry of the plover on the bog as sorrowful in the ear of the poets as the keening of young men for a comrade. And there would never have been that memory of her, he said, if it was not for the poets that had put her beauty in their songs. And the next time she did not well understand what he was saying, but as far as she could hear, it had the sound of poetry though it was not rhymed, and this is what she heard him say: 'The sun and the moon are the man and the girl, they are my life and your life, they are travelling and ever travelling through the skies as if under the one hood. It was God made them for one another. He made your life and my life before the beginning of the world, he made them that they might go through the world, up and down, like the two best dancers that go on with the dance up and down the long floor of the barn, fresh and laughing, when all the rest are tired out and leaning against the wall.'

The old woman went then to where her husband was playing cards, but he would take no notice of her, and then she went to a woman of the neighbours and said: 'Is there no way we can get them from one another?' and without waiting for an answer she said to some young men that were talking together: 'What good are you when you cannot make the best girl in the house come out and dance with you? And go now the whole of you,' she said, 'and see can you bring her away from the poet's talk.' But Oona would not listen to any of them, but only moved her hand as if to send them away. Then they called to Hanrahan and said he had best dance with the girl himself, or let her dance with one of them. When Hanrahan heard what they were saying he said: 'That is so, I will dance with her; there is no man in the house must dance with her but myself.'

He stood up with her then, and led her out by the hand, and some of the young men were vexed, and some began mocking at his ragged coat and his broken boots. But he took no notice, and Oona took no notice, but they looked at one another as if all the world belonged to themselves alone. But another couple that had been sitting together like lovers stood out on the floor at the same time, holding one another's hands and moving their feet to keep time with the music. But Hanrahan turned his back on them as if angry, and in place of dancing he began to sing, and as he sang he held her hand, and his voice grew louder, and the mocking of the young men stopped, and the fiddle stopped, and there was nothing heard but his voice that had in it the sound of the wind. And what he sang was a song he had heard or had made one time in his wanderings on Slieve Echtge, and the words of it as they can be put into English were like this:

> O Death's old bony finger
> Will never find us there
> In the high hollow townland
> Where love's to give and to spare;
> Where boughs have fruit and blossom
> At all times of the year;
> Where rivers are running over
> With red beer and brown beer.
> An old man plays the bagpipes
> In a gold and silver wood;
> Queens, their eyes blue like the ice,
> Are dancing in a crowd.

And while he was singing it Oona moved nearer to him, and the colour had gone from her cheek, and her eyes were not blue now, but grey with the tears that were in them, and anyone that saw her would have thought she was ready to follow him there and then from the west to the east of the world.

But one of the young men called out: 'Where is that country he is singing about? Mind yourself, Oona, it is a long way off, you might be a long time on the road before you would reach to it.' And another said: 'It is not to the Country of the Young you will be going if you go with him, but to Mayo of the bogs.' Oona looked at him then as if she would question him, but he raised her hand in his hand, and called out between singing and shouting: 'It is very near us that country is, it is on every side; it may be on the bare hill behind it is, or it may be in the heart of the wood.' And he said out very loud and clear: 'In the heart of the wood; oh, death will never find us in the heart of the wood. And will you come with me there, Oona?' he said.

But while he was saying this the two old women had gone outside the door, and Oona's mother was crying, and she said: 'He has put an enchantment on Oona. Can we not get the men to put him out of the house?'

'That is a thing you cannot do,' said the other woman, 'for he is a poet of the Gael, and you know well if you would put a poet of the Gael out of the house, he would put a curse on you that would wither the corn in the fields and dry up the milk of the cows, if it had to hang in the air seven years.'

'God help us,' said the mother, 'and why did I ever let him into the house at all, and the wild name he has!'

'It would have been no harm at all to have kept him outside, but there would great harm come upon you if you put him out by force. But listen to the plan I have to get him out of the house by his own doing, without anyone putting him from it at all.'

It was not long after that the two women came in again, each of them having a bundle of hay in her apron. Hanrahan was not singing now, but he was talking to Oona very fast and soft, and he was saying: 'The house is narrow but the world is wide, and there is no true lover that need be afraid of night or morning or sun or stars or shadows of evening, or any earthly thing.' 'Hanrahan,' said the mother then, striking him on the shoulder, 'will you give me a hand here for a minute?' 'Do that, Hanrahan,' said the woman of the neighbours, 'and help us to make this hay into a rope, for you are ready with your hands, and a blast of wind has loosened the thatch on the haystack.'

'I will do that for you,' said he, and he took the little stick in his hands, and the mother began giving out the hay, and he twisting it, but he was hurrying to have done with it, and to be free again. The women went on talking and giving out the hay, and encouraging him, and saying what a good twister of a rope he was, better than their own neighbours or than anyone they had ever seen. And Hanrahan saw that Oona was watching him, and he began to twist very quick and with his head high, and to boast of the readiness of his hands, and the learning he had in his head, and the strength in his arms. And as he was boasting, he went backward, twisting the rope always till he came to the door that was open behind him, and without thinking he passed the threshold and was out on the road. And no sooner was he there than the mother made a sudden rush, and threw out the rope after him, and she shut the door and the half-door and put a bolt upon them.

She was well pleased when she had done that, and laughed out loud, and the neighbours laughed and praised her. But they heard him beating at the door, and saying words of cursing outside it, and the mother had but time to stop Oona that had her hand upon the bolt to open it. She made a sign to the fiddler then, and he began a reel, and one of the young men asked no leave but caught hold of Oona and brought her into the thick of the dance. And when it was over and the fiddle had stopped, there was no sound at all of anything outside, but the road was as quiet as before.

As to Hanrahan, when he knew he was shut out and that there was neither shelter nor drink nor a girl's ear for him that night, the anger and the courage went out of him, and he went on to where the waves were beating on the strand.

He sat down on a big stone, and he began swinging his right arm and singing slowly to himself, the way he did always to hearten himself when every other thing failed him. And whether it was that time or another time he made the song that is called to this day 'The Twisting of the Rope,' and that begins, 'What was the dead cat that put me in this place,' is not known.

But after he had been singing awhile, mist and shadows seemed to gather about him, sometimes coming out of the sea, and sometimes moving upon it. It seemed to him that one of the shadows was the queen-woman he had seen in her sleep at Slieve Echtge; not in her sleep now, but mocking, and calling out to them that were behind her: 'He was weak, he was weak, he had no courage.' And he felt the strands of the rope in his hand yet, and went on twisting it, but it seemed to him as he twisted, that it had all the sorrows of the world in it. And then it seemed to him as if the rope had changed in his dream into a great water-worm that came out of the sea, and that twisted itself about him, and held him closer and closer, and grew from big to bigger till the whole of the earth and skies were wound up in it, and the stars themselves were but the shining of the ridges of its skin. And then he got free of it, and went on, shaking and unsteady, along the edge of the strand, and the grey shapes were flying here and there around him. And this is what they were saying, 'It is a pity for him that refuses the call of the daughters of the Sidhe, for he will find no comfort in the love of the women of the earth to the end of life and time, and the cold of the grave is in his heart for ever. It is death he has chosen; let him die, let him die, let him die.'

THE INMOST LIGHT

Arthur Machen

Arthur Machen (1863–1947), the Welsh author and mystic, is widely considered to be among the greatest writers of supernatural fiction. His many fans include H. P. Lovecraft, who named Machen as one of the four "modern masters" of supernatural horror, alongside Lord Dunsany, M. R. James, and Algernon Blackwood. Stephen King has called Machen's novella, *The Great God Pan*, "Maybe the best in the English language."[5] Aleister Crowley recommended Machen's works to his students. Machen is invoked in *Snakes and Ladders*, Alan Moore's meditation on magic.

Machen is considered among the pioneers of psychogeography, which may be defined as the study of the effects of geographical settings and locales. He was a close friend of the occultist Arthur Waite, cocreator of the Rider-Waite-Smith tarot deck. Through Waite's influence, Machen joined the mystical Order of the Golden Dawn

"The Inmost Light" was first published in 1894, then collected in Machen's 1906 publication, *The House of Souls*. It explores the dangers that may occur when someone completely and blindly dedicated to science above all else ventures into magical and spiritual territories. Although it has supernatural elements, it is a true tale of horror.

---

5 Self-interview by Stephen King, September 4, 2008. *http://stephenking.com/stephens_messages.html*.

The Inmost Light

I

ONE evening in autumn, when the deformities of London were veiled in faint blue mist, and its vistas and far-reaching streets seemed splendid, Mr. Charles Salisbury was slowly pacing down Rupert Street, drawing nearer to his favourite restaurant by slow degrees. His eyes were downcast in study of the pavement, and thus it was that as he passed in at the narrow door a man who had come up from the lower end of the street jostled against him.

'I beg your pardon—wasn't looking where I was going. Why, it's Dyson!'

'Yes, quite so. How are you, Salisbury?'

'Quite well. But where have you been, Dyson? I don't think I can have seen you for the last five years?'

'No; I dare say not. You remember I was getting rather hard up when you came to my place at Charlotte Street?'

'Perfectly. I think I remember your telling me that you owed five weeks' rent, and that you had parted with your watch for a comparatively small sum.'

'My dear Salisbury, your memory is admirable. Yes, I was hard up. But the curious thing is that soon after you saw me I became harder up. My financial state was described by a friend as "stone broke." I don't approve of slang, mind you, but such was my condition. But suppose we go in; there might be other people who would like to dine—it's a human weakness, Salisbury.'

'Certainly; come along. I was wondering as I walked down whether the corner table were taken. It has a velvet back, you know.'

'I know the spot; it's vacant. Yes, as I was saying, I became even harder up.'

'What did you do then?' asked Salisbury, disposing of his hat, and settling down in the corner of the seat, with a glance of fond anticipation at the menu.

'What did I do? Why, I sat down and reflected. I had a good classical education, and a positive distaste for business of any kind: that was the capital with which I faced the world. Do you know, I have heard people describe olives as nasty! What lamentable Philistinism! I have often thought, Salisbury, that I could write genuine poetry under the influence of olives and red wine. Let us have Chianti; it may not be very good, but the flasks are simply charming.'

'It is pretty good here. We may as well have a big flask.'

'Very good. I reflected, then, on my want of prospects, and I determined to embark in literature.'

'Really; that was strange. You seem in pretty comfortable circumstances, though.'

'Though! What a satire upon a noble profession. I am afraid, Salisbury, you haven't a proper idea of the dignity of an artist. You see me sitting at my desk—or at least you can see me if you care to call—with pen and ink, and simple nothingness before me, and if you come again in a few hours you will (in all probability) find a creation!'

'Yes, quite so. I had an idea that literature was not remunerative.'

'You are mistaken; its rewards are great. I may mention, by the way, that shortly after you saw me I succeeded to a small income. An uncle died, and proved unexpectedly generous.'

'Ah, I see. That must have been convenient.'

'It was pleasant—undeniably pleasant. I have always considered it in the light of an endowment of my researches. I told you I was a man of letters; it would, perhaps, be more correct to describe myself as a man of science.'

'Dear me, Dyson, you have really changed very much in the last few years. I had a notion, don't you know, that you were a sort of idler about town, the kind of man one might meet on the north side of Piccadilly every day from May to July.'

'Exactly. I was even then forming myself, though all unconsciously. You know my poor father could not afford to send me to the University. I used to grumble in my ignorance at not having completed my education. That was the folly of youth, Salisbury; my University was

Piccadilly. There I began to study the great science which still occupies me.'

'What science do you mean?'

'The science of the great city; the physiology of London; literally and metaphysically the greatest subject that the mind of man can conceive. What an admirable salmi this is; undoubtedly the final end of the pheasant. Yet I feel sometimes positively overwhelmed with the thought of the vastness and complexity of London. Paris a man may get to understand thoroughly with a reasonable amount of study; but London is always a mystery. In Paris you may say: "Here live the actresses, here the Bohemians, and the Ratés"; but it is different in London. You may point out a street, correctly enough, as the abode of washerwomen; but, in that second floor, a man may be studying Chaldee roots, and in the garret over the way a forgotten artist is dying by inches.'

'I see you are Dyson, unchanged and unchangeable,' said Salisbury, slowly sipping his Chianti. 'I think you are misled by a too fervid imagination; the mystery of London exists only in your fancy. It seems to me a dull place enough. We seldom hear of a really artistic crime in London, whereas I believe Paris abounds in that sort of thing.'

'Give me some more wine. Thanks. You are mistaken, my dear fellow, you are really mistaken. London has nothing to be ashamed of in the way of crime. Where we fail is for want of Homers, not Agamemnons. Carent quia vate sacro, you know.'

'I recall the quotation. But I don't think I quite follow you.'

'Well, in plain language, we have no good writers in London who make a speciality of that kind of thing. Our common reporter is a dull dog; every story that he has to tell is spoilt in the telling. His idea of horror and of what excites horror is so lamentably deficient. Nothing will content the fellow but blood, vulgar red blood, and when he can get it he lays it on thick, and considers that he has produced a telling article. It's a poor notion. And, by some curious fatality, it is the most commonplace and brutal murders which always attract the most attention and get written up the most. For instance, I dare say that you never heard of the Harlesden case?'

'No; no, I don't remember anything about it.'

'Of course not. And yet the story is a curious one. I will tell it you over our coffee. Harlesden, you know, or I expect you don't know, is quite on the out-quarters of London; something curiously different from your fine old crusted suburb like Norwood or Hampstead, different as each of these is from the other. Hampstead, I mean, is where you look for the head of your great China house with his three acres of land and pine-houses, though of late there is the artistic substratum; while Norwood is the home of the prosperous middle-class family who took the house "because it was near the Palace," and sickened of the Palace six months afterwards; but Harlesden is a place of no character. It's too new to have any character as yet. There are the rows of red houses and the rows of white houses and the bright green Venetians, and the blistering doorways, and the little backyards they call gardens, and a few feeble shops, and then, just as you think you're going to grasp the physiognomy of the settlement, it all melts away.'

'How the dickens is that? the houses don't tumble down before one's eyes, I suppose!'

'Well, no, not exactly that. But Harlesden as an entity disappears. Your street turns into a quiet lane, and your staring houses into elm trees, and the back-gardens into green meadows. You pass instantly from town to country; there is no transition as in a small country town, no soft gradations of wider lawns and orchards, with houses gradually becoming less dense, but a dead stop. I believe the people who live there mostly go into the City. I have seen once or twice a laden 'bus bound thitherwards. But however that may be, I can't conceive a greater loneliness in a desert at midnight than there is there at midday. It is like a city of the dead; the streets are glaring and desolate, and as you pass it suddenly strikes you that this too is part of London. Well, a year or two ago there was a doctor living there; he had set up his brass plate and his red lamp at the very end of one of those shining streets, and from the back of the house, the fields stretched away to the north. I don't know what his reason was in settling down in such an out-of-the-way place, perhaps Dr. Black, as we will call him, was a far-seeing man and looked ahead. His relations, so it appeared afterwards, had lost sight of him for many years and didn't even know he was a doctor, much less where he lived. However, there he was settled in Harlesden, with some fragments of a practice, and an uncommonly pretty wife. People used to see them walking out together in the summer evenings soon after they came to Harlesden, and, so far as could be observed, they seemed a very affectionate couple. These walks went on through the autumn, and then ceased; but, of course, as the days grew dark and the weather cold, the lanes near Harlesden might be expected to lose many of their attractions. All through the winter nobody saw anything of Mrs. Black; the doctor used to reply to his patients' inquiries that she was a "little out of sorts, would be better, no doubt, in the spring." But the spring came, and the summer, and no Mrs. Black appeared, and at last people began to rumour and talk amongst themselves, and all sorts of queer things were said at "high teas," which you may possibly have heard are the only form of entertainment known in such suburbs. Dr. Black began to surprise some very odd looks cast in his direction, and the practice, such as it was, fell off before his eyes. In short, when the neighbours whispered about the matter, they whispered that Mrs. Black was dead, and that the doctor had made away with her. But this wasn't the case; Mrs. Black was seen alive in June. It was a Sunday afternoon, one of those few exquisite days that an English climate offers, and half London had strayed out into the fields, north, south, east, and west to smell the scent of the white May, and to see if the wild roses were yet in blossom in the hedges. I had gone out myself early in the morning, and had had a long ramble, and somehow or other as I was steering homeward I found myself in this very Harlesden we have been talking about. To be exact, I had a glass of beer in the "General Gordon," the most flourishing house in the neighbourhood, and as I was wandering rather aimlessly about, I saw an uncommonly tempting gap in a hedgerow, and resolved to explore the meadow beyond. Soft grass is very grateful to the feet after the infernal grit strewn on suburban sidewalks, and after walking about for some time I thought I should like to sit down on a bank and have a smoke. While I was getting out my pouch, I looked up in the direction of the houses, and as I looked I felt my breath caught back, and my teeth began to chatter, and the stick I had in one hand snapped in two with the grip I gave it. It was as if I had had an electric current down my spine, and yet for some moment of time which seemed long, but which must have been very short, I caught myself wondering what on earth was the matter. Then I knew what had made my very heart shudder and my bones grind together in an agony. As I glanced up I had looked straight towards the last house in the row before me, and in an upper window of that house I had seen for some short fraction of a second a face. It was the face of a woman, and yet it was not human. You and I, Salisbury, have heard in our time, as we sat in our seats in church in sober English fashion, of a lust that cannot be satiated and of a fire that is unquenchable, but few of us have any notion what these words mean. I hope you never may, for as I saw that face at the window, with the blue sky above me and the warm air playing in gusts about me, I knew I had looked into another world—looked through the window of a commonplace, brand-new house, and seen hell open before me. When the first shock was over, I thought once or twice that I should have fainted; my face streamed with a cold sweat, and my breath came and went in sobs, as if I had been half drowned. I managed to get up at last, and walked round to the street, and there I saw the name "Dr. Black" on the post by the front gate. As fate or my luck would have it, the door opened and a man came down the steps as I passed by. I had no doubt it was the doctor himself. He was of a type rather common in London; long and thin, with a pasty face and a dull black moustache. He gave me a look as we passed each other on the pavement, and though it was merely the casual glance which one foot-passenger bestows on another, I felt convinced in my mind that here was an ugly customer to deal with. As you may imagine, I went my way a good deal puzzled and horrified too by what I had seen; for I had paid another visit to the "General Gordon," and had got together a good deal of the common gossip of the place about the Blacks. I didn't mention the fact that I had seen a woman's face in the window; but I heard that Mrs. Black had been much admired for her beautiful golden hair, and round what had struck me with such a nameless terror, there was a mist of flowing yellow hair, as it were an aureole of glory round the visage of a satyr. The whole thing bothered me in an indescribable manner; and when I got home I tried my best to think of the impression I had received as an illusion, but it was no use. I knew very well I had seen what I have tried to describe to you, and I was morally certain that I had seen Mrs. Black. And then there was the gossip of the place, the suspicion of foul play, which I knew to be false, and my own conviction that there was some deadly mischief or other going on in that bright red house at the corner of Devon Road: how to construct a theory of a reasonable kind out of these two elements. In short, I found myself in a world of mystery; I puzzled my head over it and filled up my leisure moments by gathering together odd threads of speculation, but I never moved a step towards any real solution, and as the summer days went on the matter seemed to grow misty and indistinct, shadowing some vague terror, like a nightmare of last month. I suppose it would before long have faded into the background of my brain—I should not have forgotten it, for such a thing could never be forgotten—but one morning as I was looking over the paper my eye was caught by a heading over some two dozen lines of small type. The words I had seen were simply, "The Harlesden Case," and I knew what I was going to read. Mrs. Black was dead. Black had called in another medical man to certify as to cause of death, and something or other had aroused the strange doctor's suspicions and there had been an inquest and post-mortem. And the result? That, I will confess, did astonish me considerably; it was the triumph of the unexpected. The two doctors who made the autopsy were obliged to confess that they could not discover the faintest trace of any kind of foul play; their most exquisite tests and reagents failed to detect the presence of poison in the most infinitesimal quantity. Death, they found, had been caused by a somewhat obscure and scientifically interesting form of brain disease. The tissue of the brain and the molecules of the grey matter had undergone a most extraordinary series of changes; and the younger of the two doctors, who has some reputation, I believe, as a specialist in brain trouble, made some remarks in giving his evidence which struck me deeply at the time, though I did not then grasp their full significance. He said: "At the commencement of the examination I was astonished to find appearances of a character entirely new to me, notwithstanding my somewhat large experience. I need not specify these appearances at present, it will be sufficient for me to state that as I proceeded in my task I could scarcely believe that the brain before me was that of a human being at all." There was some surprise at this statement, as you may imagine, and the coroner asked the doctor if he meant to say that the brain resembled that of an animal. "No," he replied, "I should not put it in that way. Some of the appearances I noticed seemed to point in that direction, but others, and these were the more surprising, indicated a nervous organization of a wholly different character from that either of man or the lower animals." It was a curious thing to say, but of course the jury brought in a verdict of death from natural causes, and, so far as the public was concerned, the case came to an end. But after I had read what the doctor said I made up my mind that I should like to know a good deal more, and I set to work on what seemed likely to prove an interesting investigation. I had really a good deal of trouble, but I was successful in a measure. Though why—my dear fellow, I had no notion at the time. Are you aware that we have been here nearly four hours? The waiters are staring at us. Let's have the bill and be gone.'

The two men went out in silence, and stood a moment in the cool air, watching the hurrying traffic of Coventry Street pass before them to the accompaniment of the ringing bells of hansoms and the cries of the newsboys; the deep far murmur of London surging up ever and again from beneath these louder noises.

'It is a strange case, isn't it?' said Dyson at length. 'What do you think of it?'

'My dear fellow, I haven't heard the end, so I will reserve my opinion. When will you give me the sequel?'

'Come to my rooms some evening; say next Thursday. Here's the address. Good-night; I want to get down to the Strand.' Dyson hailed a passing hansom, and Salisbury turned northward to walk home to his lodgings.

II

Mr. Salisbury, as may have been gathered from the few remarks which he had found it possible to introduce in the course of the evening, was a young gentleman of a peculiarly solid form of intellect, coy and retiring before the mysterious and the uncommon, with a constitutional dislike of paradox. During the restaurant dinner he had been forced to listen in almost absolute silence to a strange tissue of improbabilities strung together with the ingenuity of a born meddler in plots and mysteries, and it was with a feeling of weariness that he crossed Shaftesbury Avenue, and dived into the recesses of Soho, for his lodgings were in a modest neighbourhood to the north of Oxford Street. As he walked he speculated on the probable fate of Dyson, relying on literature, unbefriended by a thoughtful relative, and could not help concluding that so much subtlety united to a too vivid imagination would in all likelihood have been rewarded with a pair of sandwich-boards or a super's banner. Absorbed in this train of thought, and admiring the perverse dexterity which could transmute the face of a sickly woman and a case of brain disease into the crude elements of romance, Salisbury strayed on through the dimly-lighted streets, not noticing the gusty wind which drove sharply round corners and whirled the stray rubbish of the pavement into the air in eddies, while black clouds gathered over the sickly yellow moon. Even a stray drop or two of rain blown into his face did not rouse him from his meditations, and it was only when with a sudden rush the storm tore down upon the street that he began to consider the expediency of finding some shelter. The rain, driven by the wind, pelted down with the violence of a thunderstorm, dashing up from the stones and hissing through the air, and soon a perfect torrent of water coursed along the kennels and accumulated in pools over the choked-up drains. The few stray passengers who had been loafing rather than walking about the street had scuttered away, like frightened rabbits, to some invisible places of refuge, and though Salisbury whistled loud and long for a hansom, no hansom appeared. He looked about him, as if to discover how far he might be from the haven of Oxford Street, but strolling carelessly along, he had turned out of his way, and found himself in an unknown region, and one to all appearance devoid even of a public-house where shelter could be bought for the modest sum of twopence. The street lamps were few and at long intervals, and burned behind grimy glasses with the sickly light of oil, and by this wavering glimmer Salisbury could make out the shadowy and vast old houses of which the street was composed. As he passed along, hurrying, and shrinking from the full sweep of the rain, he noticed the innumerable bell-handles, with names that seemed about to vanish of old age graven on brass plates beneath them, and here and there a richly carved penthouse overhung the door, blackening with the grime of fifty years. The storm seemed to grow more and more furious; he was wet through, and a new hat had become a ruin, and still Oxford Street seemed as far off as ever; it was with deep relief that the dripping man caught sight of a dark archway which seemed to promise shelter from the rain if not from the wind. Salisbury took up his position in the driest corner and looked about him; he was standing in a kind of passage contrived under part of a house, and behind him stretched a narrow footway leading between blank walls to regions unknown. He had stood there for some time, vainly endeavouring to rid himself of some of his superfluous moisture, and listening for the passing wheel of a hansom, when his attention was aroused by a loud noise coming from the direction of the passage behind, and growing louder as it drew nearer. In a couple of minutes he could make out the shrill, raucous voice of a woman, threatening and renouncing, and making the very stones echo with her accents, while now and then a man grumbled and expostulated. Though to all appearance devoid of romance, Salisbury had some relish for street rows, and was, indeed, somewhat of an amateur in the more amusing phases of drunkenness; he therefore composed himself to listen and observe with something of the air of a subscriber to grand opera. To his annoyance, however, the tempest seemed suddenly to be composed, and he could hear nothing but the impatient steps of the woman and the slow lurch of the man as they came towards him. Keeping back in the shadow of the wall, he could see the two drawing nearer; the man was evidently drunk, and had much ado to avoid frequent collision with the wall as he tacked across from one side to the other, like some bark beating up against a wind. The woman was looking straight in front of her, with tears streaming from her eyes, but suddenly as they went by the flame blazed up again, and she burst forth into a torrent of abuse, facing round upon her companion.

'You low rascal, you mean, contemptible cur,' she went on, after an incoherent storm of curses, 'you think I'm to work and slave for you always, I suppose, while you're after that Green Street girl and drinking every penny you've got? But you're mistaken, Sam—indeed, I'll bear it no longer. Damn you, you dirty thief, I've done with you and your master too, so you can go your own errands, and I only hope they'll get you into trouble.'

The woman tore at the bosom of her dress, and taking something out that looked like paper, crumpled it up and flung it away. It fell at Salisbury's feet. She ran out and disappeared in the darkness, while the man lurched slowly into the street, grumbling indistinctly to himself in a perplexed tone of voice. Salisbury looked out after him and saw him maundering along the pavement, halting now and then and swaying indecisively, and then starting off at some fresh tangent. The sky had cleared, and white fleecy clouds were fleeting across the moon, high in the heaven. The light came and went by turns, as the clouds passed by, and, turning round as the clear, white rays shone into the passage, Salisbury saw the little ball of crumpled paper which the woman had cast down. Oddly curious to know what it might contain, he picked it up and put it in his pocket, and set out afresh on his journey.

III

Salisbury was a man of habit. When he got home, drenched to the skin, his clothes hanging lank about him, and a ghastly dew besmearing his hat, his only thought was of his health, of which he took studious care. So, after changing his clothes and encasing himself in a warm dressing-gown, he proceeded to prepare a sudorific in the shape of a hot gin and water, warming the latter over one of those spirit-lamps which mitigate the austerities of the modern hermit's life. By the time this preparation had been exhibited, and Salisbury's disturbed feelings had been soothed by a pipe of tobacco, he was able to get into bed in a happy state of vacancy, without a thought of his adventure in the dark archway, or of the weird fancies with which Dyson had seasoned his dinner. It was the same at breakfast the next morning, for Salisbury made a point of not thinking of any thing until that meal was over; but when the cup and saucer were cleared away, and the morning pipe was lit, he remembered the little ball of paper, and began fumbling in the pockets of his wet coat. He did not remember into which pocket he had put it, and as he dived now into one and now into another, he experienced a strange feeling of apprehension lest it should not be there at all, though he could not for the life of him have explained the importance he attached to what was in all probability mere rubbish. But he sighed with relief when his fingers touched the crumpled surface in an inside pocket, and he drew it out gently and laid it on the little desk by his easy-chair with as much care as if it had been some rare jewel. Salisbury sat smoking and staring at his find for a few minutes, an odd temptation to throw the thing in the fire and have done with it struggling with as odd a speculation as to its possible contents, and as to the reason why the infuriated woman should have flung a bit of paper from her with such vehemence. As might be expected, it was the latter feeling that conquered in the end, and yet it was with something like repugnance that he at last took the paper and unrolled it, and laid it out before him. It was a piece of common dirty paper, to all appearance torn out of a cheap exercise-book, and in the middle were a few lines written in a queer cramped hand. Salisbury bent his head and stared eagerly at it for a moment, drawing a long breath, and then fell back in his chair gazing blankly before him, till at last with a sudden revulsion he burst into a peal of laughter, so long and loud and uproarious that the landlady's baby on the floor below awoke from sleep and echoed his mirth with hideous yells. But he laughed again and again, and took the paper up to read a second time what seemed such meaningless nonsense.

'Q. has had to go and see his friends in Paris,' it began. 'Traverse Handle S. "Once around the grass, and twice around the lass, and thrice around the maple tree."'

Salisbury took up the paper and crumpled it as the angry woman had done, and aimed it at the fire. He did not throw it there, however, but tossed it carelessly into the well of the desk, and laughed again. The sheer folly of the thing offended him, and he was ashamed of his own eager speculation, as one who pores over the high-sounding announcements in the agony column of the daily paper, and finds nothing but advertisement and triviality. He walked to the window, and stared out at the languid morning life of his quarter; the maids in slatternly print dresses washing door-steps, the fish-monger and the butcher on their rounds, and the tradesmen standing at the doors of their small shops, drooping for lack of trade and excitement. In the distance a blue haze gave some grandeur to the prospect, but the view as a whole was depressing, and would only have interested a student of the life of London, who finds something rare and choice in its very aspect. Salisbury turned away in disgust, and settled himself in the easy-chair, upholstered in a bright shade of green, and decked with yellow gimp, which was the pride and attraction of the apartments. Here he composed himself to his morning's occupation—the perusal of a novel that dealt with sport and love in a manner that suggested the collaboration of a stud-groom and a ladies' college. In an ordinary way, however, Salisbury would have been carried on by the interest of the story up to lunch-time, but this morning he fidgeted in and out of his chair, took the book up and laid it down again, and swore at last to himself and at himself in mere irritation. In point of fact the jingle of the paper found in the archway had 'got into his head,' and do what he would he could not help muttering over and over, 'Once around the grass, and twice around the lass, and thrice around the maple tree.' It became a positive pain, like the foolish burden of a music-hall song, everlastingly quoted, and sung at all hours of the day and night, and treasured by the street-boys as an unfailing resource for six months together. He went out into the streets, and tried to forget his enemy in the jostling of the crowds and the roar and clatter of the traffic, but presently he would find himself stealing quietly aside, and pacing some deserted byway, vainly puzzling his brains, and trying to fix some meaning to phrases that were meaningless. It was a positive relief when Thursday came, and he remembered that he had made an appointment to go and see Dyson; the flimsy reveries of the self-styled man of letters appeared entertaining when compared with this ceaseless iteration, this maze of thought from which there seemed no possibility of escape. Dyson's abode was in one of the quietest of the quiet streets that led down from the Strand to the river, and when Salisbury passed from the narrow stairway into his friend's room, he saw that the uncle had been beneficent indeed. The floor glowed and flamed with all the colours of the East; it was, as Dyson pompously remarked, 'a sunset in a dream,' and the lamplight, the twilight of London streets, was shut out with strangely worked curtains, glittering here and there with threads of gold. In the shelves of an oak armoire stood jars and plates of old French china, and the black and white of etchings not to be found in the Haymarket or in Bond Street, stood out against the splendour of a Japanese paper. Salisbury sat down on the settle by the hearth, and sniffed the mingled fumes of incense and tobacco, wondering and dumb before all this splendour after the green rep and the oleographs, the gilt-framed mirror, and the lustres of his own apartment.

'I am glad you have come,' said Dyson. 'Comfortable little room, isn't it? But you don't look very well, Salisbury. Nothing disagreed with you, has it?'

'No; but I have been a good deal bothered for the last few days. The fact is I had an odd kind of—of—adventure, I suppose I may call it, that night I saw you, and it has worried me a good deal. And the provoking part of it is that it's the merest nonsense—but, however, I will tell you all about it, by and by. You were going to let me have the rest of that odd story you began at the restaurant.'

'Yes. But I am afraid, Salisbury, you are incorrigible. You are a slave to what you call matter of fact. You know perfectly well that in your heart you think the oddness in that case is of my making, and that it is all really as plain as the police reports. However, as I have begun, I will go on. But first we will have something to drink, and you may as well light your pipe.'

Dyson went up to the oak cupboard, and drew from its depths a rotund bottle and two little glasses, quaintly gilded.

'It's Benedictine,' he said. 'You'll have some, won't you?'

Salisbury assented, and the two men sat sipping and smoking reflectively for some minutes before Dyson began.

'Let me see,' he said at last, 'we were at the inquest, weren't we? No, we had done with that. Ah, I remember. I was telling you that on the whole I had been successful in my inquiries, investigation, or whatever you like to call it, into the matter. Wasn't that where I left off?'

'Yes, that was it. To be precise, I think "though" was the last word you said on the matter.'

'Exactly. I have been thinking it all over since the other night, and I have come to the conclusion that that "though" is a very big "though" indeed. Not to put too fine a point on it, I have had to confess that what I found out, or thought I found out, amounts in reality to nothing. I am as far away from the heart of the case as ever. However, I may as well tell you what I do know. You may remember my saying that I was impressed a good deal by some remarks of one of the doctors who gave evidence at the inquest. Well, I determined

that my first step must be to try if I could get something more definite and intelligible out of that doctor. Somehow or other I managed
to get an introduction to the man, and he gave me an appointment
to come and see him. He turned out to be a pleasant, genial fellow;
rather young and not in the least like the typical medical man, and
he began the conference by offering me whisky and cigars. I didn't
think it worth while to beat about the bush, so I began by saying
that part of his evidence at the Harlesden Inquest struck me as very
peculiar, and I gave him the printed report, with the sentences in
question underlined. He just glanced at the slip, and gave me a queer
look. "It struck you as peculiar, did it?" said he. "Well, you must
remember that the Harlesden case was very peculiar. In fact, I think
I may safely say that in some features it was unique—quite unique."
"Quite so," I replied, "and that's exactly why it interests me, and why
I want to know more about it. And I thought that if anybody could
give me any information it would be you. What is your opinion of
the matter?"

'It was a pretty downright sort of question, and my doctor looked
rather taken aback.

"'Well," he said, "as I fancy your motive in inquiring into the question must be mere curiosity, I think I may tell you my opinion with
tolerable freedom. So, Mr., Mr. Dyson? if you want to know my theory, it is this: I believe that Dr. Black killed his wife."

"'But the verdict," I answered, "the verdict was given from your
own evidence."

"'Quite so; the verdict was given in accordance with the evidence
of my colleague and myself, and, under the circumstances, I think
the jury acted very sensibly. In fact, I don't see what else they could
have done. But I stick to my opinion, mind you, and I say this also. I
don't wonder at Black's doing what I firmly believe he did. I think he
was justified."

"'Justified! How could that be?" I asked. I was astonished, as you
may imagine, at the answer I had got. The doctor wheeled round his
chair and looked steadily at me for a moment before he answered.

"'I suppose you are not a man of science yourself? No; then it would be of no use my going into detail. I have always been firmly opposed myself to any partnership between physiology and psychology. I believe that both are bound to suffer. No one recognizes more decidedly than I do the impassable gulf, the fathomless abyss that separates the world of consciousness from the sphere of matter. We know that every change of consciousness is accompanied by a rearrangement of the molecules in the grey matter; and that is all. What the link between them is, or why they occur together, we do not know, and most authorities believe that we never can know. Yet, I will tell you that as I did my work, the knife in my hand, I felt convinced, in spite of all theories, that what lay before me was not the brain of a dead woman—not the brain of a human being at all. Of course I saw the face; but it was quite placid, devoid of all expression. It must have been a beautiful face, no doubt, but I can honestly say that I would not have looked in that face when there was life behind it for a thousand guineas, no, nor for twice that sum."

"'My dear sir,' I said, "you surprise me extremely. You say that it was not the brain of a human being. What was it then?"

"'The brain of a devil." He spoke quite coolly, and never moved a muscle. "The brain of a devil," he repeated, "and I have no doubt that Black found some way of putting an end to it. I don't blame him if he did. Whatever Mrs. Black was, she was not fit to stay in this world. Will you have anything more? No? Good-night, good-night."

'It was a queer sort of opinion to get from a man of science, wasn't it? When he was saying that he would not have looked on that face when alive for a thousand guineas, or two thousand guineas, I was thinking of the face I had seen, but I said nothing. I went again to Harlesden, and passed from one shop to another, making small purchases, and trying to find out whether there was anything about the Blacks which was not already common property, but there was very little to hear. One of the tradesmen to whom I spoke said he had known the dead woman well; she used to buy of him such quantities of grocery as were required for their small household, for they never kept a servant, but had a charwoman in occasionally, and she had not seen Mrs. Black for months before she died. According to this man Mrs. Black was "a nice lady," always kind and considerate, and so fond of her husband and he of her, as every one thought. And yet, to put the doctor's opinion on one side, I knew what I had seen. And then after thinking it all over, and putting one thing with another, it seemed to me that the only person likely to give me much assistance would be Black himself, and I made up my mind to find him. Of course he wasn't to be found in Harlesden; he had left, I was told, directly after the funeral. Everything in the house had been sold, and one fine day Black got into the train with a small portmanteau, and went, nobody knew where. It was a chance if he were ever heard of again, and it was by a mere chance that I came across him at last. I was walking one day along Gray's Inn Road, not bound for anywhere in particular, but looking about me, as usual, and holding on to my hat, for it was a gusty day in early March, and the wind was making the treetops in the Inn rock and quiver. I had come up from the Holborn end, and I had almost got to Theobald's Road when I noticed a man walking in front of me, leaning on a stick, and to all appearance very feeble. There was something about his look that made me curious, I don't know why, and I began to walk briskly with the idea of overtaking him, when of a sudden his hat blew off and came bounding along the pavement to my feet. Of course I rescued the hat, and gave it a glance as I went towards its owner. It was a biography in itself; a Piccadilly maker's name in the inside, but I don't think a beggar would have picked it out of the gutter. Then I looked up and saw Dr. Black of Harlesden waiting for me. A queer thing, wasn't it? But, Salisbury, what a change! When I saw Dr. Black come down the steps of his house at Harlesden he was an upright man, walking firmly with well-built limbs; a man, I should say, in the prime of his life. And now before me there crouched this wretched creature, bent and feeble, with shrunken cheeks, and hair that was whitening fast, and limbs that trembled and shook together, and misery in his eyes. He thanked me for bringing him his hat, saying, "I don't think I should ever have got it, I can't run much now. A gusty day, sir, isn't it?" and with this he was turning away, but by little and little I contrived to draw him into the current of conversation, and we walked together eastward. I think the man would have been glad to get rid of me; but I didn't intend to let him go, and he stopped at last in front of a miserable house in a miserable street. It was, I verily believe, one of the most wretched quarters I have ever seen: houses that must have been sordid and hideous enough when new, that had gathered foulness with every year, and now seemed to lean and totter to their fall. "I live up there," said Black, pointing to the tiles, "not in the front—in the back. I am very quiet there. I won't ask you to come in now, but perhaps some other day——" I caught him up at that, and told him I should be only too glad to come and see him. He gave me an odd sort of glance, as if he were wondering what on earth I or anybody else could care about him, and I left him fumbling with his latch-key. I think you will say I did pretty well when I tell you that within a few weeks I had made myself an intimate friend of Black's. I shall never forget the first time I went to his room; I hope I shall never see such abject, squalid misery again. The foul paper, from which all pattern or trace of a pattern had long vanished, subdued and penetrated with the grime of the evil street, was hanging in mouldering pennons from the wall. Only at the end of the room was it possible to stand upright, and the sight of the wretched bed and the odour of corruption that pervaded the place made me turn faint and sick. Here I found him munching a piece of bread; he seemed surprised to find that I had kept my promise, but he gave me his chair and sat on the bed while we talked. I used to go to see him often, and we had long conversations together, but he never mentioned Harlesden or his wife. I fancy that he supposed me ignorant of the matter, or thought that if I had heard of it, I should never connect the respectable Dr. Black of Harlesden with a poor garreteer in the backwoods of London. He was a strange man, and as we sat together smoking, I often wondered whether he were mad or sane, for I think the wildest dreams of Paracelsus and the Rosicrucians would appear plain and sober fact compared with the theories I have heard him earnestly advance in that grimy den of his.

I once ventured to hint something of the sort to him. I suggested that something he had said was in flat contradiction to all science and all experience. "No," he answered, "not all experience, for mine counts for something. I am no dealer in unproved theories; what I say I have proved for myself, and at a terrible cost. There is a region of knowledge which you will never know, which wise men seeing from afar off shun like the plague, as well they may, but into that region I have gone. If you knew, if you could even dream of what may be done, of what one or two men have done in this quiet world of ours, your very soul would shudder and faint within you. What you have heard from me has been but the merest husk and outer covering of true science—that science which means death, and that which is more awful than death, to those who gain it. No, when men say that there are strange things in the world, they little know the awe and the terror that dwell always with them and about them." There was a sort of fascination about the man that drew me to him, and I was quite sorry to have to leave London for a month or two; I missed his odd talk. A few days after I came back to town I thought I would look him up, but when I gave the two rings at the bell that used to summon him, there was no answer. I rang and rang again, and was just turning to go away, when the door opened and a dirty woman asked me what I wanted. From her look I fancy she took me for a plain-clothes officer after one of her lodgers, but when I inquired if Mr. Black were in, she gave me a stare of another kind. "There's no Mr. Black lives here," she said. "He's gone. He's dead this six weeks. I always thought he was a bit queer in his head, or else had been and got into some trouble or other. He used to go out every morning from ten till one, and one Monday morning we heard him come in, and go into his room and shut the door, and a few minutes after, just as we was a-sitting down to our dinner, there was such a scream that I thought I should have gone right off. And then we heard a stamping, and down he came, raging and cursing most dreadful, swearing he had been robbed of something that was worth millions. And then he just dropped down in the passage, and we thought he was dead. We got him up to his room, and put him on his bed, and I just sat there and waited, while my 'usband he went for the doctor. And there was the winder wide open, and a little tin box he had lying on the floor open and empty, but of course nobody could possible have got in at the winder, and as for him having anything that was worth anything, it's nonsense, for he was often weeks and weeks behind with his rent, and my 'usband he threatened often and often to turn him into the street, for, as he said, we've got a living to myke like other people—and, of course, that's true; but, somehow, I didn't like to do it, though he was an odd kind of a man, and I fancy had been better off. And then the doctor came and looked at him, and said as he couldn't do nothing, and that night he died as I was a-sitting by his bed; and I can tell you that, with one thing and another, we lost money by him, for the few bits of clothes as he had were worth next to nothing when they came to be sold." I gave the woman half a sovereign for her trouble, and went home thinking of Dr. Black and the epitaph she had made him, and wondering at his strange fancy that he had been robbed. I take it that he had very little to fear on that score, poor fellow; but I suppose that he was really mad, and died in a sudden access of his mania. His landlady said that once or twice when she had had occasion to go into his room (to dun the poor wretch for his rent, most likely), he would keep her at the door for about a minute, and that when she came in she would find him putting away his tin box in the corner by the window; I suppose he had become possessed with the idea of some great treasure, and fancied himself a wealthy man in the midst of all his misery. Explicit, my tale is ended, and you see that though I knew Black, I know nothing of his wife or of the history of her death.—That's the Harlesden case, Salisbury, and I think it interests me all the more deeply because there does not seem the shadow of a possibility that I or any one else will ever know more about it. What do you think of it?'

'Well, Dyson, I must say that I think you have contrived to surround the whole thing with a mystery of your own making. I go for the doctor's solution: Black murdered his wife, being himself in all probability an undeveloped lunatic.'

'What? Do you believe, then, that this woman was something too awful, too terrible to be allowed to remain on the earth? You will remember that the doctor said it was the brain of a devil?'

'Yes, yes, but he was speaking, of course, metaphorically. It's really quite a simple matter if you only look at it like that.'

'Ah, well, you may be right; but yet I am sure you are not. Well, well, it's no good discussing it any more. A little more Benedictine? That's right; try some of this tobacco. Didn't you say that you had been bothered by something—something which happened that night we dined together?'

'Yes, I have been worried, Dyson, worried a great deal. I——But it's such a trivial matter—indeed, such an absurdity—that I feel ashamed to trouble you with it.'

'Never mind, let's have it, absurd or not.'

With many hesitations, and with much inward resentment of the folly of the thing, Salisbury told his tale, and repeated reluctantly the absurd intelligence and the absurder doggerel of the scrap of paper, expecting to hear Dyson burst out into a roar of laughter.

'Isn't it too bad that I should let myself be bothered by such stuff as that?' he asked, when he had stuttered out the jingle of once, and twice, and thrice.

Dyson listened to it all gravely, even to the end, and meditated for a few minutes in silence.

'Yes,' he said at length, 'it was a curious chance, your taking shelter in that archway just as those two went by. But I don't know that I should call what was written on the paper nonsense; it is bizarre certainly, but I expect it has a meaning for somebody. Just repeat it again, will you, and I will write it down. Perhaps we might find a cipher of some sort, though I hardly think we shall.'

Again had the reluctant lips of Salisbury slowly to stammer out the rubbish that he abhorred, while Dyson jotted it down on a slip of paper.

'Look over it, will you?' he said, when it was done; 'it may be important that I should have every word in its place. Is that all right?'

'Yes; that is an accurate copy. But I don't think you will get much out of it. Depend upon it, it is mere nonsense, a wanton scribble. I must be going now, Dyson. No, no more; that stuff of yours is pretty strong. Good-night.'

'I suppose you would like to hear from me, if I did find out anything?'

'No, not I; I don't want to hear about the thing again. You may regard the discovery, if it is one, as your own.'

'Very well. Good-night.'

IV

A good many hours after Salisbury had returned to the company of the green rep chairs, Dyson still sat at his desk, itself a Japanese romance, smoking many pipes, and meditating over his friend's story. The bizarre quality of the inscription which had annoyed Salisbury was to him an attraction, and now and again he took it up and scanned thoughtfully what he had written, especially the quaint jingle at the end. It was a token, a symbol, he decided, and not a cipher, and the woman who had flung it away was in all probability entirely ignorant of its meaning; she was but the agent of the 'Sam' she had abused and discarded, and he too was again the agent of some one unknown, possibly of the individual styled Q, who had been forced to visit his French friends. But what to make of 'Traverse Handle S.' Here was the root and source of the enigma, and not all the tobacco of Virginia seemed likely to suggest any clue here. It seemed almost hopeless, but Dyson regarded himself as the Wellington of mysteries, and went to bed feeling assured that sooner or later he would hit upon the right track For the next few days he was deeply engaged in his literary labours, labours which were a profound mystery even to the most intimate of his friends, who searched the railway bookstalls in vain for the result of so many hours spent at the Japanese bureau in company with strong tobacco and black tea. On this occasion Dyson confined himself to his room for four days, and it was with genuine relief that he laid down his pen and went out into the streets in quest of relaxation and fresh air. The gas-lamps were being lighted, and the fifth edition of the evening papers was being howled through the streets, and Dyson, feeling that he wanted quiet, turned away from the clamorous Strand, and began to trend away to the north-west. Soon he found himself in streets that echoed to his footsteps, and crossing a broad new thoroughfare, and verging still to the west, Dyson discovered that he had penetrated to the depths of Soho. Here again was life; rare vintages of France and Italy, at prices which seemed contemptibly small, allured the passer-by; here were cheeses, vast and rich, here olive oil, and here a grove of Rabelaisian sausages; while in a neighbouring shop the whole Press of Paris appeared to be on sale. In the middle of the roadway a strange miscellany of nations sauntered to and fro, for there cab and hansom rarely ventured; and from window over window the inhabitants looked forth in pleased contemplation of the scene. Dyson made his way slowly along, mingling with the crowd on the cobble-stones, listening to the queer babel of French and German, and Italian and English, glancing now and again at the shop-windows with their levelled batteries of bottles, and had almost gained the end of the street, when his attention was arrested by a small shop at the corner, a vivid contrast to its neighbours. It was the typical shop of the poor quarter; a shop entirely English. Here were vended tobacco and sweets, cheap pipes of clay and cherry-wood; penny exercise-books and penholders jostled for precedence with comic songs, and story papers with appalling cuts showed that romance claimed its place beside the actualities of the evening paper, the bills of which fluttered at the doorway. Dyson glanced up at the name above the door, and stood by the kennel trembling, for a sharp pang, the pang of one who has made a discovery, had for a moment left him incapable of motion. The name over the shop was Travers. Dyson looked up again, this time at the corner of the wall above the lamp-post, and read in white letters on a blue ground the words 'Handel Street, W. C.,' and the legend was repeated in fainter letters just below. He gave a little sigh of satisfaction, and without more ado walked boldly into the shop, and stared full in the face the fat man who was sitting behind the counter. The fellow rose to his feet, and returned the stare a little curiously, and then began in stereotyped phrase—

'What can I do for you, sir?'

Dyson enjoyed the situation and a dawning perplexity on the man's face. He propped his stick carefully against the counter and leaning over it, said slowly and impressively—

'Once around the grass, and twice around the lass, and thrice around the maple-tree.'

Dyson had calculated on his words producing an effect, and he was not disappointed. The vendor of miscellanies gasped, open-mouthed like a fish, and steadied himself against the counter. When he spoke, after a short interval, it was in a hoarse mutter, tremulous and unsteady.

'Would you mind saying that again, sir? I didn't quite catch it.'

'My good man, I shall most certainly do nothing of the kind. You heard what I said perfectly well. You have got a clock in your shop, I see; an admirable timekeeper, I have no doubt. Well, I give you a minute by your own clock.'

The man looked about him in a perplexed indecision, and Dyson felt that it was time to be bold.

'Look here, Travers, the time is nearly up. You have heard of Q, I think. Remember, I hold your life in my hands. Now!'

Dyson was shocked at the result of his own audacity. The man shrank and shrivelled in terror, the sweat poured down a face of ashy white, and he held up his hands before him.

'Mr. Davies, Mr. Davies, don't say that—don't for Heaven's sake. I didn't know you at first, I didn't indeed. Good God! Mr. Davies, you wouldn't ruin me? I'll get it in a moment.'

'You had better not lose any more time.'

The man slunk piteously out of his own shop, and went into a back parlour. Dyson heard his trembling fingers fumbling with a bunch of keys, and the creak of an opening box. He came back presently with a small package neatly tied up in brown paper in his hands, and, still full of terror, handed it to Dyson.

'I'm glad to be rid of it,' he said. 'I'll take no more jobs of this sort.'

Dyson took the parcel and his stick, and walked out of the shop with a nod, turning round as he passed the door. Travers had sunk into his seat, his face still white with terror, with one hand over his eyes, and Dyson speculated a good deal as he walked rapidly away as to what queer chords those could be on which he had played so roughly. He hailed the first hansom he could see and drove home, and when he had lit his hanging lamp, and laid his parcel on the table, he paused for a moment, wondering on what strange thing the lamplight would soon shine. He locked his door, and cut the strings, and unfolded the paper layer after layer, and came at last to a small wooden box, simply but solidly made. There was no lock, and Dyson had simply to raise the lid, and as he did so he drew a long breath and started back. The lamp seemed to glimmer feebly like a single candle, but the whole room blazed with light—and not with light alone, but with a thousand colours, with all the glories of some painted window; and upon the walls of his room and on the familiar furniture, the glow flamed back and seemed to flow again to its source, the little wooden box. For there upon a bed of soft wool lay the most splendid jewel, a jewel such as Dyson had never dreamed of, and within it shone the blue of far skies, and the green of the sea by the shore, and the red of the ruby, and deep violet rays, and in the middle of all it seemed aflame as if a fountain of fire rose up, and fell, and rose again with sparks like stars for drops. Dyson gave a long deep sigh, and dropped into his chair, and put his hands over his eyes to think. The jewel was like an opal, but from a long experience of the shop-windows he knew there was no such thing as an opal one-quarter or one-eighth of its size. He looked at the stone again, with a feeling that was almost awe, and placed it gently on the table under the lamp, and watched the wonderful flame that shone and sparkled in its centre, and then turned to the box, curious to know whether it might contain other marvels. He lifted the bed of wool on which the opal had reclined, and saw beneath, no more jewels, but a little old pocket-book, worn and shabby with use. Dyson opened it at the first leaf, and dropped the book again appalled. He had read the name of the owner, neatly written in blue ink:

Steven Black, M.D.,
Oranmore,
Devon Road,
Harlesden.

It was several minutes before Dyson could bring himself to open the book a second time; he remembered the wretched exile in his garret; and his strange talk, and the memory too of the face he had seen at the window, and of what the specialist had said, surged up in his mind, and as he held his finger on the cover, he shivered, dreading what might be written within. When at last he held it in his hand, and turned the pages, he found that the first two leaves were blank, but the third was covered with clear, minute writing, and Dyson began to read with the light of the opal flaming in his eyes.

V

'Ever since I was a young man'—the record began—'I devoted all my leisure and a good deal of time that ought to have been given to other studies to the investigation of curious and obscure branches of knowledge. What are commonly called the pleasures of life had never any attractions for me, and I lived alone in London, avoiding my fellow-students, and in my turn avoided by them as a man self-absorbed and unsympathetic. So long as I could gratify my desire of knowledge of a peculiar kind, knowledge of which the very existence is a profound secret to most men, I was intensely happy, and I have often spent whole nights sitting in the darkness of my room, and thinking of the strange world on the brink of which I trod. My professional studies, however, and the necessity of obtaining a degree, for some time forced my more obscure employment into the background, and soon after I had qualified I met Agnes, who became my wife. We took a new house in this remote suburb, and I began the regular routine of a sober practice, and for some months lived happily enough, sharing in the life about me, and only thinking at odd intervals of that occult science which had once fascinated my whole being. I had learnt enough of the paths I had begun to tread to know that they were beyond all expression difficult and dangerous, that to persevere meant in all probability the wreck of a life, and that they led to regions so terrible, that the mind of man shrinks appalled at the very thought. Moreover, the quiet and the peace I had enjoyed since my marriage had wiled me away to a great extent from places where I knew no peace could dwell. But suddenly—I think indeed it was the work of a single night, as I lay awake on my bed gazing into the darkness—suddenly, I say, the old desire, the former longing, returned, and returned with a force that had been intensified ten times by its absence; and when the day dawned and I looked out of the window, and saw with haggard eyes the sunrise in the east, I knew that my doom had been pronounced; that as I had gone far, so now I must go farther with unfaltering steps. I turned to the bed where my wife was sleeping peacefully, and lay down again, weeping bitter tears, for the sun had set on our happy life and had risen with a dawn of terror to us both. I will not set down here in minute detail what followed; outwardly I went about the day's labour as before, saying nothing to my wife. But she soon saw that I had changed; I spent my spare time in a room which I had fitted up as a laboratory, and often I crept upstairs in the grey dawn of the morning, when the light of many lamps still glowed over London; and each night I had stolen a step nearer to that great abyss which I was to bridge over, the gulf between the world of consciousness and the world of matter. My experiments were many and complicated in their nature, and it was some months before I realized whither they all pointed, and when this was borne in upon me in a moment's time, I felt my face whiten and my heart still within me. But the power to draw back, the power to stand before the doors that now opened wide before me and not to enter in, had long ago been absent; the way was closed, and I could only pass onward. My position was as utterly hopeless as that of the prisoner in an utter dungeon, whose only light is that of the dungeon above him; the doors were shut and escape was impossible. Experiment after experiment gave the same result, and I knew, and shrank even as the thought passed through my mind, that in the work I had to do there must be elements which no laboratory could furnish, which no scales could ever measure. In that work, from which even I doubted to escape with life, life itself must enter; from some human being there must be drawn that essence which men call the soul, and in its place (for in the scheme of the world there is no vacant chamber)—in its place would enter in what the lips can hardly utter, what the mind cannot conceive without a horror more awful than the horror of death itself. And when I knew this, I knew also on whom this fate would fall; I looked into my wife's eyes. Even at that hour, if I had gone out and taken a rope and hanged myself, I might have escaped, and she also, but in no other way. At last I told her all. She shuddered, and wept, and called on her dead mother for help, and asked me if I had no mercy, and I could only sigh. I concealed nothing from her; I told her what she would become, and what would enter in where her life had been; I told her of all the shame and of all the horror. You who will read this when I am dead—if indeed I allow this record to survive,—you who have opened the box and have seen what lies there, if you could understand what lies hidden in that opal! For one night my wife consented to what I asked of her, consented with the tears running down her beautiful face, and hot shame flushing red over her neck and breast, consented to undergo this for me. I threw open the window, and we looked together at the sky and the dark earth for the last time; it was a fine star-light night, and there was a pleasant breeze blowing, and I kissed her on her lips, and her tears ran down upon my face. That night she came down to my laboratory, and there, with shutters bolted and barred down, with curtains drawn thick and close, so that the very stars might be shut out from the sight of that room, while the crucible hissed and boiled over the lamp, I did what had to be done, and led out what was no longer a woman. But on the table the opal flamed and sparkled with such light as no eyes of man have ever gazed on, and the rays of the flame that was within it flashed and glittered, and shone even to my heart. My wife had only asked one thing of me; that when there came at last what I had told her, I would kill her. I have kept that promise.'

There was nothing more. Dyson let the little pocket-book fall, and turned and looked again at the opal with its flaming inmost light, and then with unutterable irresistible horror surging up in his heart, grasped the jewel, and flung it on the ground, and trampled it beneath his heel. His face was white with terror as he turned away, and for a moment stood sick and trembling, and then with a start he leapt across the room and steadied himself against the door. There was an angry hiss, as of steam escaping under great pressure, and as he gazed, motionless, a volume of heavy yellow smoke was slowly issuing from the very centre of the jewel, and wreathing itself in snake-like coils above it. And then a thin white flame burst forth from the smoke, and shot up into the air and vanished; and on the ground there lay a thing like a cinder, black and crumbling to the touch.

BLOOD LUST

Dion Fortune

Dion Fortune (1890–1946)—mystic, esotericist, psychologist, and, not least, prolific author—was among the most crucial and influential figures of the occult renaissance of the 20th century. Born Violet Mary Firth in Llandudno, Wales, her pen name derives from a family motto, *Deo, Non Fortuna,* meaning "God, not luck." Fortune demonstrated mediumistic aptitude from her early childhood. By the time she was four, she was reputedly experiencing dreams and visions of her prior incarnation in Atlantis.

Pursuing her metaphysical studies, in 1919, Fortune joined the Golden Dawn, but as she became increasingly disillusioned with them, she left to found her own society, which would evolve into the present Society of the Inner Light. Fortune's influence on the metaphysical world remains powerful. She was a prolific author of both fiction and nonfiction. Her beloved magical novels include *The Demon Lover, The Goat Foot God,* and *The Sea Priestess.*

"Blood Lust" is among the stories in Fortune's book *The Secrets of Dr. Taverner,* which was published in 1926. The character of occult detective Dr. Taverner is based on Fortune's teacher Dr. Moriarty, who specialized in astro-etheric psychological conditions.

Blood Lust

I

I have never been able to make up my mind whether Dr. Taverner should be the hero or the villain of these histories. That he was a man of the most selfless ideals could not be questioned, but in his methods of putting these ideals into practice he was absolutely unscrupulous. He did not evade the law, he merely ignored it, and though the exquisite tenderness with which he handled his cases was an education in itself, yet he would use that wonderful psychological method of his to break a soul to pieces, going to work as quietly and methodically and benevolently as if bent upon the cure of his patient. The manner of my meeting with this strange man was quite simple. After being gazetted out of the Royal Army Medical Corps. I went to a medical agency and inquired what posts were available.

I said: 'I have come out of the Army with my nerves shattered. I want some quiet place till I can pull myself together.'

'So does everybody else,' said the clerk.

He looked at me thoughtfully. 'I wonder whether you would care to try a place we have had on our books for some time. We have sent several men down to it but none of them would stop.'

He sent me round to one of the tributaries of Harley Street, and there I made the acquaintance of the man who, whether he was good or bad, I have always regarded as the greatest mind I ever met.

Tall and thin, with a parchment-like countenance, he might have been any age from 35 to 65. I have seen him look both ages within the hour. He lost no time in coming to the point.

'I want a medical superintendent for my nursing home,' he told me. 'I understand that you have specialized, as far as the Army permitted you to, in mental cases. I am afraid you will find my methods very different from the orthodox ones. However, as I sometimes succeed where others fail, I consider I am justified in continuing to experiment, which I think, Dr. Rhodes, is all any of my colleagues can claim to do.'

The man's cynical manner annoyed me, though I could not deny that mental treatment is not an exact science at the present moment. As if in answer to my thought he continued:

'My chief interest lies in those regions of psychology which orthodox science has not as yet ventured to explore. If you will work with me you will see some queer things, but all I ask of you is, that you should keep an open mind and a shut mouth.'

This I undertook to do, for, although I shrank instinctively from the man, yet there was about him such a curious attraction, such a sense of power and adventurous research, that I determined at least to give him the benefit of the doubt and see what it might lead to. His extraordinarily stimulating personality, which seemed to key my brain to concert pitch, made me feel that he might be a good tonic for a man who had lost his grip on life for the time being.

'Unless you have elaborate packing to do,' he said, 'I can motor you down to my place. If you will walk over with me to the garage I will drive you round to your lodgings, pick up your things, and we shall get in before dark.'

We drove at a pretty high speed down the Portsmouth road till we came to Thursley, and, then, to my surprise, my companion turned off to the right and took the big car by a cart track over the heather.

'This is Thor's Ley or field,' he said, as the blighted country unrolled before us. 'The old worship is still kept up about here.'

'The Catholic faith?' I inquired.

'The Catholic faith, my dear sir, is an innovation. I was referring to the pagan worship. The peasants about here still retain bits of the old ritual; they think that it brings them luck, or some such superstition. They have no knowledge of its inner meaning.'

He paused a moment, and then turned to me and said with extraordinary emphasis: 'Have you ever thought what it would mean if a man who had the Knowledge could piece that ritual together?'

I admitted I had not. I was frankly out of my depth, but he had certainly brought me to the most unchristian spot I had ever been in my life.

His nursing home, however, was in delightful contrast to the wild and barren country that surrounded it. The garden was a mass of colour, and the house, old and rambling and covered with creepers, as charming within as without; it reminded me of the East, it reminded me of the Renaissance, and yet it had no style save that of warm rich colouring and comfort.

I soon settled down to my job, which I found exceedingly interesting. As I have already said, Taverner's work began where ordinary medicine ended, and I have under my care cases such as the ordinary doctor would have referred to the safe keeping of an asylum, as being nothing else but mad. Yet Taverner, by his peculiar methods of work, laid bare causes operating both within the soul and in the shadowy realm where the soul has its dwelling, that threw an entirely new light upon the problem, and often enabled him to rescue a man from the dark influences that were closing in upon him. The affair of the sheep-killing was an interesting example of his methods.

II

One showery afternoon at the nursing home we had a call from a neighbor—not a very common occurrence, for Taverner and his ways were regarded somewhat askance. Our visitor shed her dripping mackintosh, but declined to loosen the scarf which, warm as the day was, she had twisted tightly round her neck.

'I believe you specialize in mental cases,' she said to my colleague. 'I should very much like to talk over with you a matter that is troubling me.'

Taverner nodded, his keen eyes watching her for symptoms.

'It concerns a friend of mine—in fact, I think I may call him my *fiancé*, for, although he has asked me to release him from his engagement, I have refused to do so; not because I should wish to hold a man who no longer loved me, but because I am convinced that he still cares for me, and there is something which has come between us that he will not tell me of.

'I have begged him to be frank with me and let us share the trouble together, for the thing that seems an insuperable obstacle to him may not appear in that light to me; but you know what men are when they consider their honour is in question.'

She looked from one to the other of us smiling. No woman ever believes that her men folk are grown up; perhaps she is right. Then she leant forward and clasped her hands eagerly. 'I believe I have found the key to the mystery. I want you to tell me whether it is possible or not.'

'Will you give me particulars?' said Taverner.

Clearly and concisely she gave us what was required.

'We got engaged while Donald was stationed here for his training (that would be nearly five years ago now), and there was always the most perfect harmony between us until he came out of the Army, when we all began to notice a change in him. He came to the house as often as ever, but he always seemed to want to avoid being alone with me. We used to take long walks over the moors together, but he has absolutely refused to do this recently. Then, without any warning, he wrote and told me he could not marry me and did not wish to see me again, and he put a curious thing in his letter. He said: "Even if I should come to you and ask you to see me, I beg you not to do it."

'My people thought he had got entangled with some other girl, and were furious with him for jilting me, but I believe there is something more in it than that. I wrote to him, but could get no answer, and I had come to the conclusion that I must try and put the whole thing out of my life, when he suddenly turned up again. Now, this is where the queer part comes in.

'We heard the fowls shrieking one night, and thought a fox was after them. My brothers turned out armed with golf clubs, and I went too. When we got to the hen-house we found several fowl with their throats torn as if a rat had been at them; but the boys discovered that the hen-house door had been forced open, a thing no rat could do. They said a gipsy must have been trying to steal the birds, and told me to go back to the house. I was returning by way of the shrubberies when someone suddenly stepped out in front of me. It was quite light, for the moon was nearly full, and I recognized Donald. He held out his arms and I went to him, but, instead of kissing me, he suddenly bent his head and—look!'

She drew her scarf from her neck and showed us a semicircle of little blue marks on the skin just under the ear, the unmistakable print of human teeth.

'He was after the jugular,' said Taverner, 'lucky for you he did not break the skin.'

'I said to him: "Donald, what are you doing?" My voice seemed to bring him to himself, and he let me go and tore off through the bushes. The boys chased him but did not catch him, and we have never seen him since.'

'You have informed the police, I suppose?' said Taverner.

'Father told them someone had tried to rob the hen-roost, but they do not know who it was. You see, I did not tell them I had seen Donald.'

'And you walk about the moors by yourself, knowing that he may be lurking in the neighbourhood?'

She nodded.

'I should advise you not to, Miss Wynter; the man is probably exceedingly dangerous, especially to you. We will send you back in the car.'

'You think he has gone mad? That is exactly what I think. I believe he knew he was going mad, and that was why he broke off our engagement. Dr. Taverner, is there nothing that can be done for him? It seems to me that Donald is not mad in the ordinary way. We had a housemaid once who went off her head, and the whole of her seemed to be insane, if you can understand; but with Donald it seems as if only a little bit of him were crazy, as if his insanity were outside himself. Can you grasp what I mean?'

'It seems to me you have given a very clear description of a case of psychic interference—what was known in scriptural days as "being possessed by a devil,"' said Taverner.

'Can you do anything for him?' the girl inquired eagerly.

'I may be able to do a good deal if you can get him to come to me.'

On our next day at the Harley Street consulting-room we found that the butler had booked an appointment for a Captain Donald Craigie. We discovered him to be a personality of singular charm—one of those highly-strung, imaginative men who have the makings of an artist in them. In his normal state he must have been a delightful companion, but as he faced us across the consulting-room desk he was a man under a cloud.

'I may as well make a clean breast of this matter,' he said. 'I suppose Beryl told you about their chickens?'

'She told us that you tried to bite her.'

'Did she tell you I bit the chickens?'

'No.'

'Well, I did.'

Silence fell for a moment. Then Taverner broke it.

'When did this trouble first start?'

'After I got shell shock. I was blown right out of a trench, and it shook me up pretty badly. I thought I had got off lightly, for I was only in hospital about 10 days, but I suppose this is the aftermath.'

'Are you one of those people who have a horror of blood?'

'Not especially so. I didn't like it, but I could put up with it. We had to get used to it in the trenches; someone was always getting wounded, even in the quietest times.'

'And killed,' put in Taverner.

'Yes, and killed,' said our patient.

'So you developed a blood hunger?'

'That's about it.'

'Underdone meat and all the rest of it, I suppose?'

'No, that is no use to me. It seems a horrible thing to say, but it is fresh blood that attracts me, blood as it comes from the veins of my victim.'

'Ah!' said Taverner. 'That puts a different complexion on the case.'

'I shouldn't have thought it could have been much blacker.'

'On the contrary, what you have just told me renders the outlook much more hopeful. You have not so much a blood lust, which might well be an effect of the subconscious mind, as a vitality hunger which is quite a different matter.'

Craigie looked up quickly. 'That's exactly it. I have never been able to put it into words before, but you have hit the nail on the head.'

I saw that my colleague's perspicacity had given him great confidence.

'I should like you to come down to my nursing home for a time and be under my personal observation,' said Taverner.

'I should like to very much, but I think there is something further you ought to know before I do so. This thing has begun to affect my character. At first it seemed something outside myself, but now I am responding to it, almost helping, and trying to find out ways of gratifying it without getting myself into trouble. That is why I went for the hens when I came down to the Wynters' house. I was afraid I should lose my self-control and go for Beryl. I did in the end, as it happened, so it was not much use. In fact I think it did more harm than good, for I seemed to get into much closer touch with "It" after I had yielded to the impulse. I know that the best thing I could do would be to do away with myself, but I daren't. I feel that after I am dead I should have to meet—whatever it is—face to face.'

'You should not be afraid to come down to the nursing home,' said Taverner. 'We will look after you.'

After he had gone Taverner said to me: 'Have you ever heard of vampires, Rhodes?'

'Yes, rather,' I said. 'I used to read myself to sleep with Dracula once when I had a spell of insomnia.'

'That,' nodding his head in the direction of the departing man, 'is a singularly good specimen.'

'Do you mean to say you are going to take a revolting case like that down to Hindhead?'

'Not revolting, Rhodes, a soul in a dungeon. The soul may not be very savoury, but it is a fellow creature. Let it out and it will soon clean itself.'

I often used to marvel at the wonderful tolerance and compassion Taverner had for erring humanity.

'The more you see of human nature,' he said to me once, 'the less you feel inclined to condemn it, for you realize how hard it has struggled. No one does wrong because he likes it, but because it is the lesser of the two evils.'

III

A couple of days later I was called out of the nursing home office to receive a new patient. It was Craigie. He had got as far as the doormat, and there he had stuck. He seemed so thoroughly ashamed of himself that I had not the heart to administer the judicious bullying which is usual under such circumstances.

'I feel as if I were driving a baulking horse,' he said. 'I want to come in, but I can't.'

I called Taverner and the sight of him seemed to relieve our patient.

'Ah,' he said, 'you give me confidence. I feel that I can defy "It,"' and he squared his shoulders and crossed the threshold. Once inside, a weight seemed lifted from his mind, and he settled down quite happily to the routine of the place. Beryl Wynter used to walk over almost every afternoon, unknown to her family, and cheer him up; in fact he seemed on the high road to recovery.

One morning I was strolling round the grounds with the head gardener, planning certain small improvements, when he made a remark to me which I had reason to remember later.

'You would think all the German prisoners should have been returned by now, wouldn't you, sir? But they haven't. I passed one the other night in the lane outside the back door. I never thought that I should see their filthy field-grey again.'

I sympathized with his antipathy; he had been a prisoner in their hands, and the memory was not one to fade. I thought no more of his remarks, but a few days later I was reminded of it when one of our patients came to me and said:

'Dr. Rhodes, I think you are exceedingly unpatriotic to employ German prisoners in the garden when so many discharged soldiers cannot get work.'

I assured her that we did not do so, no German being likely to survive a day's work under the superintendence of our ex-prisoner head gardener.

'But I distinctly saw the man going round the greenhouses at shutting-up time last night,' she declared. 'I recognized him by his flat cap and grey uniform.'

I mentioned this to Taverner.

'Tell Craigie he is on no account to go out after sundown,' he said, 'and tell Miss Wynter she had better keep away for the present.'

A night or two later, as I was strolling round the grounds smoking an after-dinner cigarette, I met Craigie hurrying through the shrubbery.

'You will have Dr. Taverner on your trail,' I called after him.

'I missed the post-bag,' he replied, 'and I am going down to the pillar-box.'

Next evening I again found Craigie in the grounds after dark. I bore down on him.

'Look here, Craigie,' I said, 'if you come to this place you must keep the rules, and Dr. Taverner wants you to stay indoors after sundown.'

Craigie bared his teeth and snarled at me like a dog. I took him by the arm and marched him into the house and reported the incident to Taverner.

'The creature has re-established its influence over him,' he said. 'We cannot evidently starve it out of existence by keeping it away from him; we shall have to use other methods. Where is Craigie at the present moment?'

'Playing the piano in the drawing-room,' I replied.

'Then we will go up to his room and unseal it.'

As I followed Taverner upstairs he said to me: 'Did it ever occur to you to wonder why Craigie jibbed on the doorstep?'

'I paid no attention,' I said. 'Such a thing is common enough with mental cases.'

'There is a sphere of influence, a kind of psychic bell jar, over this house to keep out evil entities, what might in popular language be called a "spell." Craigie's familiar could not come inside, and did not like being left behind. I thought we might be able to tire it out by keeping Craigie away from its influences, but it has got too strong a hold over him, and he deliberately co-operates with it. Evil communications corrupt good manners, and you can't keep company with a thing like that and not be tainted, especially if you are a sensitive Celt like Craigie.'

When we reached the room Taverner went over to the window and passed his hand across the sill, as if sweeping something aside.

'There,' he said. 'It can come in now and fetch him out, and we will see what it does.'

At the doorway he paused again and made a sign on the lintel.

'I don't think it will pass that,' he said.

When I returned to the office I found the village policeman waiting to see me.

'I should be glad if you would keep an eye on your dog, sir,' he said. 'We have been having complaints of sheep-killing lately, and whatever animal is doing it is working in a three mile radius with this as the centre.'

'Our dog is an Airedale,' I said. 'I should not think he is likely to be guilty. It is usually collies that take to sheep-killing.'

At 11 o'clock we turned out the lights and herded our patients off to bed. At Taverner's request I changed into an old suit and rubbersoled tennis shoes and joined him in the smoking-room, which was under Craigie's bedroom. We sat in the darkness awaiting events.

'I don't want you to do anything,' said Taverner, 'but just to follow and see what happens.'

We had not long to wait. In about a quarter-of-an-hour we heard a rustling in the creepers, and down came Craigie hand over fist, swinging himself along by the great ropes of wisteria that clothed the wall. As he disappeared into the shrubbery I slipped after him, keeping in the shadow of the house.

He moved at a stealthy dog-trot over the heather paths towards Frensham.

At first I ran and ducked, taking advantage of every patch of shadow, but presently I saw that this caution was unnecessary. Craigie was absorbed in his own affairs, and thereupon I drew closer to him, following at a distance of some 60 yards. He moved at a swinging pace, a kind of loping trot that put me in mind of a blood-hound. The wide, empty levels of that forsaken country stretched out on either side of us, belts of mist filled the hollows, and the heights of Hindhead stood out against the stars. I felt no nervousness; man for man, I reckoned I was a match for Craigie, and, in addition, I was armed with what is technically known as a 'soother'—two feet of lead gas-piping inserted in a length of rubber hose-pipe. It is not included in the official equipment of the best asylums, but can frequently be found in a keeper's trouser-leg.

If I had known what I had to deal with I should not have put so much reliance on my 'soother.' Ignorance is sometimes an excellent substitute for courage.

Suddenly out of the heather ahead of us a sheep got up, and then the chase began. Away went Craigie in pursuit, and away went the terrified wether. A sheep can move remarkably fast for a short distance, but the poor wool-encumbered beast could not keep pace, and Craigie ran it down, working in gradually lessening circles. It stumbled, went to its knees, and he was on it. He pulled its head back, and whether he used a knife or not I could not see, for a cloud passed over the moon, but dimly luminous in the shadow, I saw something that was semi-transparent pass between me and the dark, struggling mass among the heather. As the moon cleared the clouds I made out the flat-topped cap and field-grey uniform of the German Army.

I cannot possibly convey the sickening horror of that sight— the creature that was not a man assisting the man who, for the moment, was not human.

Gradually the sheep's struggles weakened and ceased. Craigie straightened his back and stood up; then he set off at his steady lope towards the east, his grey familiar at his heels.

How I made the homeward journey I do not know. I dared not look behind lest I should find a Presence at my elbow; every breath of wind that blew across the heather seemed to be cold fingers on my throat; fir trees reached out long arms to clutch me as I passed under them, and heather bushes rose up and assumed human shapes. I moved like a runner in a nightmare, making prodigious efforts after a receding goal.

At last I tore across the moonlit lawns of the house, regardless who might be looking from the windows, burst into the smoking-room and flung myself face downwards on the sofa.

IV

'Tut, tut!' said Taverner. 'Has it been as bad as all that?'

I could not tell him what I had seen, but he seemed to know.

'Which way did Craigie go after he left you?' he asked.

'Towards the moonrise,' I told him.

'And you were on the way to Frensham? He is heading for the Wynters' house. This is very serious, Rhodes. We must go after him; it may be too late as it is. Do you feel equal to coming with me?'

He gave me a stiff glass of brandy, and we went to get the car out of the garage. In Taverner's company I felt secure. I could understand the confidence he inspired in his patients. Whatever that grey shadow might be, I felt he could deal with it and that I would be safe in his hands. We were not long in approaching our destination.

'I think we will leave the car here,' said Taverner, turning into a grass-grown lane. 'We do not want to rouse them if we can help it.'

We moved cautiously over the dew-soaked grass into the paddock that bounded one side of the Wynters' garden. It was separated from the lawn by a sunk fence, and we could command the whole front of the house and easily gain the terrace if we so desired. In the shadow of a rose pergola we paused. The great trusses of bloom, colourless in the moonlight, seemed a ghastly mockery of our business.

For some time we waited, and then a movement caught my eye.

Out in the meadow behind us something was moving at a slow lope; it followed a wide arc, of which the house formed the focus, and disappeared into a little coppice on the left. It might have been imagination, but I thought I saw a wisp of mist at its heels.

We remained where we were, and presently he came round once more, this time moving in a smaller circle—evidently closing in upon the house. The third time he reappeared more quickly, and this time he was between us and the terrace.

'Quick! Head him off,' whispered Taverner. 'He will be up the creepers next round.'

We scrambled up the sunk fence and dashed across the lawn. As we did so a girl's figure appeared at one of the windows; it was Beryl Wynter. Taverner, plainly visible in the moonlight, laid his finger on his lips and beckoned her to come down.

'I am going to do a very risky thing,' he whispered, 'but she is a girl of courage, and if her nerve does not fail we shall be able to pull it off.'

In a few seconds she slipped out of a side door and joined us, a cloak over her night-dress.

'Are you prepared to undertake an exceedingly unpleasant task?' Taverner asked her. 'I can guarantee you will be perfectly safe so long as you keep your head, but if you lose your nerve you will be in grave danger.'

'Is it to do with Donald?' she inquired.

'It is,' said Taverner. 'I hope to be able to rid him of the thing that is overshadowing him and trying to obsess him.'

'I have seen it,' she said; 'it is like a wisp of grey vapour that floats just behind him. It has the most awful face you ever saw. It came up to the window last night, just the face only, while Donald was going round and round the house.'

'What did you do?' asked Taverner.

'I didn't do anything. I was afraid that if someone found him he might be put in an asylum, and then we should have no chance of getting him well.'

Taverner nodded.

'"Perfect love casteth out fear,"' he said. 'You can do the thing that is required of you.'

He placed Miss Wynter on the terrace in full moonlight.

'As soon as Craigie sees you,' he said, 'retreat round the corner of the house into the yard. Rhodes and I will wait for you there.'

A narrow doorway led from the terrace to the back premises, and just inside its arch Taverner bade me take my stand.

'Pinion him as he comes past you and hang on for your life,' he said. 'Only mind he doesn't get his teeth into you; these things are infectious.'

We had hardly taken up our positions when we heard the loping trot come round once more, this time on the terrace itself. Evidently he caught sight of Miss Wynter, for the stealthy padding changed to a wild scurry over the gravel, and the girl slipped quickly through the archway and sought refuge behind Taverner. Right on her heels came Craigie. Another yard and he would have had her, but I caught him by the elbows and pinioned him securely. For a moment we swayed and struggled across the dew-drenched flagstones, but I locked him in an old wrestling grip and held him.

'Now,' said Taverner, 'if you will keep hold of Craigie I will deal with the other. But first of all we must get it away from him, otherwise it will retreat on to him, and he may die of shock. Now, Miss Wynter, are you prepared to play your part?'

'I am prepared to do whatever is necessary,' she replied.

Taverner took a scalpel out of a pocket case and made a small incision in the skin of her neck, just under the ear. A drop of blood slowly gathered, showing black in the moonlight.

'That is the bait,' he said. 'Now go close up to Craigie and entice the creature away; get it to follow you and draw it out into the open.'

As she approached us Craigie plunged and struggled in my arms like a wild beast, and then something grey and shadowy drew out of the gloom of the wall and hovered for a moment at my elbow. Miss Wynter came nearer, walking almost into it.

'Don't go too close,' cried Taverner, and she paused.

Then the grey shape seemed to make up its mind; it drew clear of Craigie and advanced towards her. She retreated towards Taverner, and the Thing came out into the moonlight. We could see it quite clearly from its flat-topped cap to its kneeboots; its high cheek-bones and slit eyes pointed its origin to the south-eastern corner of Europe where strange tribes still defy civilization and keep up their still stranger beliefs.

The shadowy form drifted onwards, following the girl across the yard, and when it was some 20 feet from Craigie, Taverner stepped out quickly behind it, cutting off its retreat. Round it came in a moment, instantly conscious of his presence, and then began a game of 'puss-in-the-corner.' Taverner was trying to drive it into a kind of psychic killing-pen he had made for its reception. Invisible to me, the lines of psychic force which bounded it were evidently plainly perceptible to the creature we were hunting. This way and that way it slid in its efforts to escape, but Taverner all the time herded it towards the apex of the invisible triangle, where he could give it its *coup de grâce*.

Then the end came. Taverner leapt forward. There was a Sign then a Sound. The grey form commenced to spin like a top. Faster and faster it went, its outlines merging into a whirling spiral of mist; then it broke. Out into space went the particles that had composed its form, and with the almost soundless shriek of supreme speed the soul went to its appointed place.

Then something seemed to lift. From a cold hell of limitless horror the flagged space became a normal backyard, the trees ceased to be tentacled menaces, the gloom of the wall was no longer an ambuscade, and I knew that never again would a grey shadow drift out of the darkness upon its horrible hunting.

I released Craigie, who collapsed in a heap at my feet: Miss Wynter went to rouse her father, while Taverner and I got the insensible man into the house.

What masterly lies Taverner told to the family I have never known, but a couple of months later we received instead of the conventional fragment of wedding cake, a really substantial chunk, with a note from the bride to say it was to go in the office cupboard, where she knew we kept provisions for those nocturnal meals that Taverner's peculiar habits imposed upon us.

It was during one of these midnight repasts that I questioned Taverner about the strange matter of Craigie and his familiar. For a long time I had not been able to refer to it; the memory of that horrible sheep-killing was a thing that would not bear recalling.

'You have heard of vampires,' said Taverner. 'That was a typical case. For close on 100 years they have been practically unknown in Europe—Western Europe that is—but the War has caused a renewed outbreak, and quite a number of cases have been reported.

'When they were first observed—that is to say, when some wretched lad was caught attacking the wounded, they took him behind the lines and shot him, which is not a satisfactory way of dealing with a vampire, unless you also go to the trouble of burning his body, according to the good old-fashioned way of dealing with practitioners of black magic. Then our enlightened generation came to the conclusion that they were not dealing with a crime, but with a disease, and put the unfortunate individual afflicted with this horrible obsession into an asylum, where he did not usually live very long, the supply of his peculiar nourishment being cut off. But it never struck anybody that they might be dealing with more than one factor—that what they were really contending with was a gruesome partnership between the dead and the living.'

'What in the world do you mean?' I asked.

'We have two physical bodies, you know,' said Taverner, 'the dense material one, with which we are all familiar, and the subtle etheric one, which inhabits it, and acts as the medium of the life-forces, whose functioning would explain a very great deal if science would only condescend to investigate it. When a man dies, the etheric body, with his soul in it, draws out of the physical form and drifts about in its neighbourhood for about three days, or until decomposition sets in, and then the soul draws out of the etheric body also, which in turn dies, and the man enters upon the first phase of his post mortem existence, the purgatorial one.

'Now, it is possible to keep the etheric body together almost indefinitely if a supply of vitality is available, but, having no stomach which can digest food and turn it into energy, the thing has to batten on someone who has, and develops into a spirit parasite which we call a vampire.

'There is a pretty good working knowledge of black magic in Eastern Europe. Now, supposing some man who has this knowledge gets shot, he knows that in three days time, at the death of the etheric body, he will have to face his reckoning, and with his record he naturally does not want to do it, so he establishes a connection with the subconscious mind of some other soul that still has a body, provided he can find one suitable for his purposes. A very positive type of character is useless; he has to find one of a negative type, such as the lower class of medium affords. Hence one of the many dangers of mediumship to the untrained. Such a negative condition may be temporarily induced by, say, shell-shock, and it is possible then for such a soul as we are considering to obtain an influence over a being of much higher type—Craigie, for instance—and use him as a means of obtaining its gratification.'

'But why did not the creature confine its attentions to Craigie, instead of causing him to attack others?'

'Because Craigie would have been dead in a week if it had done so, and then it would have found itself minus its human feeding bottle. Instead of that it worked through Craigie, getting him to draw extra vitality from others and pass it on to itself; hence it was that Craigie had a vitality hunger rather than a blood hunger, though the fresh blood of a victim was the means of absorbing the vitality.'

'Then that German we all saw—?'

'Was merely a corpse who was insufficiently dead.'

THE WOMAN'S GHOST STORY

Algernon Blackwood

Algernon Blackwood (1869–1951), journalist, broadcaster, and prolific author, is among the masters of the ghost story. Born in Shooter's Hill, now part of London, Blackwood had a varied career, especially in his youth. He worked as a dairy farmer, a bartender, a reporter for the *New York Times,* and a violin teacher. When finances became dire, he occasionally worked as an artist's model, once being painted by Robert W. Chambers, author of *The King in Yellow,* whose story "The Yellow Sign," narrated by an artist, can be found on page 95.

Blackwood immersed himself in studies of the occult and mysticism. He joined the Order of the Golden Dawn in 1900, following Arthur Waite, cocreator of the Rider-Waite-Smith tarot, when the original order split. Blackwood was also a member of the Ghost Club, believed to be the oldest paranormal research and investigation society in the world, having been founded in London in 1862.

"The Woman's Ghost Story" was first published in 1907 in the book *The Listener and Other Stories.* An unusual ghost story, it might serve as reference for many modern ghost hunters.

The Woman's Ghost Story

"Yes," she said, from her seat in the dark corner, "I'll tell you an experience if you care to listen. And, what's more, I'll tell it briefly, without trimmings—I mean without unessentials. That's a thing story-tellers never do, you know," she laughed. "They drag in all the unessentials and leave their listeners to disentangle; but I'll give you just the essentials, and you can make of it what you please. But on one condition: that at the end you ask no questions, because I can't explain it and have no wish to."

We agreed. We were all serious. After listening to a dozen prolix stories from people who merely wished to "talk" but had nothing to tell, we wanted "essentials."

"In those days," she began, feeling from the quality of our silence that we were with her, "in those days I was interested in psychic things, and had arranged to sit up alone in a haunted house in the middle of London. It was a cheap and dingy lodging-house in a mean street, unfurnished. I had already made a preliminary examination in daylight that afternoon, and the keys from the caretaker, who lived next door, were in my pocket. The story was a good one—satisfied me, at any rate, that it was worth investigating; and I won't weary you with details as to the woman's murder and all the tiresome elaboration as to why the place was alive. Enough that it was.

"I was a good deal bored, therefore, to see a man, whom I took to be the talkative old caretaker, waiting for me on the steps when I went in at 11 P.M., for I had sufficiently explained that I wished to be there alone for the night.

"'I wished to show you *the* room,' he mumbled, and of course I couldn't exactly refuse, having tipped him for the temporary loan of a chair and table.

"'Come in, then, and let's be quick,' I said.

"We went in, he shuffling after me through the unlighted hall up to the first floor where the murder had taken place, and I prepared myself to hear his inevitable account before turning him out with the half-crown his persistence had earned. After lighting the gas I sat down in the arm-chair he had provided—a faded, brown plush armchair—and turned for the first time to face him and get through with the performance as quickly as possible. And it was in that instant I got my first shock. The man was *not* the caretaker. It was not the old fool,

Carey, I had interviewed earlier in the day and made my plans with. My heart gave a horrid jump.

"'Now who are *you*, pray?' I said. 'You're not Carey, the man I arranged with this afternoon. Who are you?'

"I felt uncomfortable, as you may imagine. I was a 'psychical researcher,' and a young woman of new tendencies, and proud of my liberty, but I did not care to find myself in an empty house with a stranger. Something of my confidence left me. Confidence with women, you know, is all humbug after a certain point. Or perhaps you don't know, for most of you are men. But anyhow my pluck ebbed in a quick rush, and I felt afraid.

"'Who are you?' I repeated quickly and nervously. The fellow was well dressed, youngish and good-looking, but with a face of great sadness. I myself was barely thirty. I am giving you essentials, or I would not mention it. Out of quite ordinary things comes this story. I think that's why it has value.

"'No,' he said; 'I'm the man who was frightened to death.'

"His voice and his words ran through me like a knife, and I felt ready to drop. In my pocket was the book I had bought to make notes in. I felt the pencil sticking in the socket. I felt, too, the extra warm things I had put on to sit up in, as no bed or sofa was available—a hundred things dashed through my mind, foolishly and without sequence or meaning, as the way is when one is really frightened. Unessentials leaped up and puzzled me, and I thought of what the papers might say if it came out, and what my 'smart' brother-in-law would think, and whether it would be told that I had cigarettes in my pocket, and was a free-thinker.

"'The man who was frightened to death!' I repeated aghast.

"'That's me,' he said stupidly.

"I stared at him just as you would have done—any one of you men now listening to me—and felt my life ebbing and flowing like a sort of hot fluid. You needn't laugh! That's how I felt. Small things, you know, touch the mind with great earnestness when terror is there—*real terror.* But I might have been at a middle-class tea-party, for all the ideas I had: they were so ordinary!

"'But I thought you were the caretaker I tipped this afternoon to let me sleep here!' I gasped. 'Did—did Carey send you to meet me?'

"'No,' he replied in a voice that touched my boots somehow. 'I am the man who was frightened to death. And what is more, I am frightened now!'

"'So am I!' I managed to utter, speaking instinctively. 'I'm simply terrified.'

"'Yes,' he replied in that same odd voice that seemed to sound within me. 'But you are still in the flesh, and I—*am not!*'

"I felt the need for vigorous self-assertion. I stood up in that empty, unfurnished room, digging the nails into my palms and clenching my teeth. I was determined to assert my individuality and my courage as a new woman and a free soul.

"'You mean to say you are not in the flesh!' I gasped. 'What in the world are you talking about?'

"The silence of the night swallowed up my voice. For the first time I realized that darkness was over the city; that dust lay upon the stairs; that the floor above was untenanted and the floor below empty. I was alone in an unoccupied and haunted house, unprotected, and a woman. I chilled. I heard the wind round the house, and knew the stars were hidden. My thoughts rushed to policemen and omnibuses, and everything that was useful and comforting. I suddenly realized what a fool I was to come to such a house alone. I was icily afraid. I thought the end of my life had come. I was an utter fool to go in for psychical research when I had not the necessary nerve.

"'Good God!' I gasped. 'If you're not Carey, the man I arranged with, who are you?'

"I was really stiff with terror. The man moved slowly towards me across the empty room. I held out my arm to stop him, getting up out of my chair at the same moment, and he came to halt just opposite to me, a smile on his worn, sad face.

"'I told you who I am,' he repeated quietly with a sigh, looking at me with the saddest eyes I have ever seen, 'and I am frightened *still*.'

"By this time I was convinced that I was entertaining either a rogue or a madman, and I cursed my stupidity in bringing the man in without having seen his face. My mind was quickly made up, and I knew what to do. Ghosts and psychic phenomena flew to the winds. If I angered the creature my life might pay the price. I must humor him till I got to the door, and then race for the street. I stood bolt upright and faced him. We were about of a height, and I was a strong, athletic woman who played hockey in winter and climbed Alps in summer. My hand itched for a stick, but I had none.

"'Now, of course, I remember,' I said with a sort of stiff smile that was very hard to force. 'Now I remember your case and the wonderful way you behaved. . . .'

"The man stared at me stupidly, turning his head to watch me as I backed more and more quickly to the door. But when his face broke into a smile I could control myself no longer. I reached the door in a run, and shot out on to the landing. Like a fool, I turned the wrong way, and stumbled over the stairs leading to the next story. But it was too late to change. The man was after me, I was sure, though no sound of footsteps came; and I dashed up the next flight, tearing my skirt and banging my ribs in the darkness, and rushed headlong into the first room I came to. Luckily the door stood ajar, and, still more fortunate, there was a key in the lock. In a second I had slammed the door, flung my whole weight against it, and turned the key.

"I was safe, but my heart was beating like a drum. A second later it seemed to stop altogether, for I saw that there was someone else in the room besides myself. A man's figure stood between me and the windows, where the street lamps gave just enough light to outline his shape against the glass. I'm a plucky woman, you know, for even then I didn't give up hope, but I may tell you that I have never felt so vilely frightened in all my born days. I had locked myself in with him!

"The man leaned against the window, watching me where I lay in a collapsed heap upon the floor. So there were two men in the house with me, I reflected. Perhaps other rooms were occupied too! What could it all mean? But, as I stared something changed in the room, or in me—hard to say which—and I realized my mistake, so that my fear, which had so far been physical, at once altered its character and became *psychical*. I became afraid in my soul instead of in my heart, and I knew immediately who this man was.

"'How in the world did you get up here?' I stammered to him across the empty room, amazement momentarily stemming my fear.

"'Now, let me tell you,' he began, in that odd faraway voice of his that went down my spine like a knife. 'I'm in different space, for one thing, and you'd find me in any room you went into; for according to your way of measuring, I'm *all over the house*. Space is a bodily condition, but I am out of the body, and am not affected by space. It's my condition that keeps me here. I want something to change my condition for me, for then I could get away. What I want is sympathy. Or, really, more than sympathy; I want affection—I want *love!*'

"While he was speaking I gathered myself slowly upon my feet. I wanted to scream and cry and laugh all at once, but I only succeeded in sighing, for my emotion was exhausted and a numbness was coming over me. I felt for the matches in my pocket and made a movement towards the gas jet.

"'I should be much happier if you didn't light the gas,' he said at once, 'for the vibrations of your light hurt me a good deal. You need not be afraid that I shall injure you. I can't touch your body to begin with, for there's a great gulf fixed, you know; and really this half-light suits me best. Now, let me continue what I was trying to say before. You know, so many people have come to this house to see me, and most of them have seen me, and one and all have been terrified. If only, oh, if only someone would be *not* terrified, but kind and loving to me! Then, you see, I might be able to change my condition and get away.'

"His voice was so sad that I felt tears start somewhere at the back of my eyes; but fear kept all else in check, and I stood shaking and cold as I listened to him.

"'Who are you then? Of course Carey didn't send you, I know now,' I managed to utter. My thoughts scattered dreadfully and I could think of nothing to say. I was afraid of a stroke.

"'I know nothing about Carey, or who he is,' continued the man quietly, 'and the name my body had I have forgotten, thank God; but I am the man who was frightened to death in this house ten years ago, and I have been frightened ever since, and am frightened still; for the succession of cruel and curious people who come to this house to see the ghost, and thus keep alive its atmosphere of terror, only helps to render my condition worse. If only someone would be kind to me—*laugh*, speak gently and rationally with me, cry if they like, pity, comfort, soothe me—anything but come here in curiosity and tremble as you are now doing in that corner. Now, madam, won't you take pity on me?' His voice rose to a dreadful cry. 'Won't you step out into the middle of the room and try to love me a little?'

"A horrible laughter came gurgling up in my throat as I heard him, but the sense of pity was stronger than the laughter, and I found myself actually leaving the support of the wall and approaching the center of the floor.

"'By God!' he cried, at once straightening up against the window, 'you have done a kind act. That's the first attempt at sympathy that has been shown me since I died, and I feel better already. In life, you know, I was a misanthrope. Everything went wrong with me, and I came to hate my fellow men so much that I couldn't bear to see them even. Of course, like begets like, and this hate was returned. Finally I suffered from horrible delusions, and my room became haunted with demons that laughed and grimaced, and one night I ran into a whole cluster of them near the bed—and the fright stopped my heart and killed me. It's hate and remorse, as much as terror, that clogs me so thickly and keeps me here. If only some one could feel pity, and sympathy, and perhaps a little love for me, I could get away and be happy. When you came this afternoon to see over the house I watched you, and a little hope came to me for the first time. I saw you had courage, originality, resource—*love*. If only I could touch your heart, without frightening you, I knew I could perhaps tap that love you have stored up in your being there, and thus borrow the wings for my escape!'

"Now I must confess my heart began to ache a little, as fear left me and the man's words sank their sad meaning into me. Still, the whole affair was so incredible, and so touched with unholy quality, and the story of a woman's murder I had come to investigate had so obviously nothing to do with this thing, that I felt myself in a kind of wild dream that seemed likely to stop at any moment and leave me somewhere in bed after a nightmare.

"Moreover, his words possessed me to such an extent that I found it impossible to reflect upon anything else at all, or to consider adequately any ways or means of action or escape.

"I moved a little nearer to him in the gloom, horribly frightened, of course, but with the beginnings of a strange determination in my heart.

"'You women,' he continued, his voice plainly thrilling at my approach, 'you wonderful women, to whom life often brings no opportunity of spending your great love, oh, if you only could know how many of *us* simply yearn for it! It would save our souls, if but you knew. Few might find the chance that you now have, but if you only spent your love freely, without definite object, just letting it flow openly for all who need, you would reach hundreds and thousands of souls like me, and *release us!* Oh, madam, I ask you again to feel with me, to be kind and gentle—and if you can to love me a little!'

"My heart did leap within me and this time the tears did come, for I could not restrain them. I laughed too, for the way he called me 'madam' sounded so odd, here in this empty room at midnight in a London street, but my laughter stopped dead and merged in a flood of weeping when I saw how my change of feeling affected him. He had left his place by the window and was kneeling on the floor at my feet, his hands stretched out towards me, and the first signs of a kind of glory about his head.

"'Put your arms round me and kiss me, for the love of God!' he cried. 'Kiss me, oh, kiss me, and I shall be freed! You have done so much already—now do this!'

"I stuck there, hesitating, shaking, my determination on the verge of action, yet not quite able to compass it. But the terror had almost gone.

"'Forget that I'm a man and you're a woman,' he continued in the most beseeching voice I ever heard. 'Forget that I'm a ghost, and come out boldly and press me to you with a great kiss, and let your love flow into me. Forget yourself just for one minute and do a brave thing! Oh, love me, *love me*, LOVE ME! and I shall be free!'

"The words, or the deep force they somehow released in the center of my being, stirred me profoundly, and an emotion infinitely greater than fear surged up over me and carried me with it across the edge of action. Without hesitation I took two steps forward towards him where he knelt, and held out my arms. Pity and love were in my heart at that moment, genuine pity, I swear, and genuine love. I forgot myself and my little tremblings in a great desire to help another soul.

"'I love you! poor, aching, unhappy thing! I love you,' I cried through hot tears; 'and I am not the least bit afraid in the world.'

"The man uttered a curious sound, like laughter, yet not laughter, and turned his face up to me. The light from the street below fell on it, but there was another light, too, shining all round it that seemed to come from the eyes and skin. He rose to his feet and met me, and in that second I folded him to my breast and kissed him full on the lips again and again."

All our pipes had gone out, and not even a skirt rustled in that dark studio as the story-teller paused a moment to steady her voice, and put a hand softly up to her eyes before going on again.

"Now, what can I say, and how can I describe to you, all you skeptical men sitting there with pipes in your mouths, the amazing sensation I experienced of holding an intangible, impalpable thing so closely to my heart that it touched my body with equal pressure all the way down, and then melted away somewhere into my very being? For it was like seizing a rush of cool wind and feeling a touch of burning fire the moment it had struck its swift blow and passed on. A series of shocks ran all over and all through me; a momentary ecstasy of flaming sweetness and wonder thrilled down into me; my heart gave another great leap—and then I was alone.

"The room was empty. I turned on the gas and struck a match to prove it. All fear had left me, and something was singing round me in the air and in my heart like the joy of a spring morning in youth. Not all the devils or shadows or hauntings in the world could then have caused me a single tremor.

"I unlocked the door and went all over the dark house, even into kitchen and cellar and up among the ghostly attics. But the house was empty. Something had left it. I lingered a short hour, analyzing, thinking, wondering—you can guess what and how, perhaps, but I won't detail, for I promised only essentials, remember—and then went out to sleep the remainder of the night in my own flat, locking the door behind me upon a house no longer haunted.

"But my uncle, Sir Henry, the owner of the house, required an account of my adventure, and of course I was in duty bound to give him some kind of a true story. Before I could begin, however, he held up his hand to stop me.

"'First,' he said, 'I wish to tell you a little deception I ventured to practice on you. So many people have been to that house and seen the ghost that I came to think the story acted on their imaginations, and I wished to make a better test. So I invented for their benefit another story, with the idea that if you did see anything I could be sure it was not due merely to an excited imagination.'

"'Then what you told me about a woman having been murdered, and all that, was not the true story of the haunting?'

"'It was not. The true story is that a cousin of mine went mad in that house, and killed himself in a fit of morbid terror following upon years of miserable hypochondriasis. It is his figure that investigators see.'

"'That explains, then,' I gasped——

"'Explains what?'

"I thought of that poor struggling soul, longing all these years for escape, and determined to keep my story for the present to myself.

"'Explains, I mean, why I did not see the ghost of the murdered woman,' I concluded.

"'Precisely,' said Sir Henry, 'and why, if you had seen anything, it would have had value, inasmuch as it could not have been caused by the imagination working upon a story you already knew.'"

THE LADY WITH
THE CARNATIONS

Marie Corelli

It is almost unbelievable that Marie Corelli (1855–1924) could be described as a forgotten author, yet that is now what she is. One cannot overstate Corelli's phenomenal popular success: at the peak of her career, she was England's highest paid and bestselling author. In the 1890s, her novels were devoured by millions of readers throughout the English-speaking world. From the publication of her first novel in 1886 until World War I, Corelli's novels reputedly sold more copies than the combined sales figures of her popular contemporaries, who included Sir Arthur Conan Doyle and H. G. Wells. Her fans included Queen Victoria. Corelli has been described as the queen's favorite writer, but her popularity transcended social boundaries: her work was read by statesmen such as Winston Churchill, as well as clerks and shop girls. She did not, however, receive critical acclaim. Her romantic novels were typically belittled, mocked, or, at best, ignored by critics.

Born in London as Mary Mackay, she was allegedly the illegitimate daughter of Scottish author Charles Mackay and his servant Elizabeth Mills. The facts of her life are mysterious, obfuscated, and sometimes contradictory. By the time her first novel, *A Romance of Two Worlds*, was published in 1886, she had renamed herself Marie Corelli, which, according to her, was a family name. Corelli wrote thirty books; most were bestsellers. Her specialty is a sort of heightened, emotional, spiritual, mystical, highly romantic love story, often infiltrated by Corelli's own strong opinions. In my childhood, I read her Egyptian reincarnation novel *Ziska: The Problem of a Wicked Soul* (1897) and was completely entranced.

"The Lady with the Carnations," an evocative ghost story set in France, was originally published in 1895 in her book, *Cameos: Short Stories*. It contains a self-deprecating reference to Corelli's first novel, *A Romance of Two Worlds*.

The Lady with the Carnations

A DREAM OR A DELUSION?

It was in the Louvre that I first saw her—or rather her picture. Greuze painted her—so I was told; but the name of the artist scarcely affected me—I was absorbed in the woman herself, who looked at me from the dumb canvas with that still smile on her face, and that burning cluster of carnations clasped to her breast. Moreover, there was a strange attraction in her eyes that held mine fascinated. I felt that I knew her. It was as though she said "Stay till I have told thee all!" A faint blush tinged her cheek—one loose tress of fair hair fell carelessly on her half-uncovered bosom. And, surely, was I dreaming?—or did I smell the odour of carnations on the air? I started from my reverie—a slight tremor shook my nerves. I turned to go. An artist carrying a large easel and painting materials just then approached, and placing himself opposite the picture, began to copy it. I watched him at work for a few moments—his strokes were firm, and his eye accurate; but I knew, without waiting to observe his further progress, that there was an indefinable something in that pictured face that he with all his skill would never be able to delineate as Greuze had done—if Greuze were indeed the painter, of which I did not then, and not now, feel sure. I walked slowly away. On the threshold of the room I looked back. Yes! there it was—that fleeting, strange, appearing expression that seemed mutely to call to me; that half-wild yet sweet smile that had a world of unuttered pathos in it. A kind of misgiving troubled me—a presentiment of evil that I could understand—and, vexed with myself for my own foolish imaginings, I hastened down the broad staircase that led from the picture-galleries, and began to make my way out through that noble hall of ancient sculpture in which stands the defiantly beautiful *Apollo Belvedere* and the world-famous *Artemis.* The sun shone brilliantly; numbers of people were passing and repassing. Suddenly my heart gave a violent throb, and I stopped short in my walk, amazed and incredulous. Who was that seated on the bench close to the *Artemis,* reading? Who, if not "the Lady with the Carnations," clad in white, her head slightly bent, and her hand clasping a bunch of her own symbolic flowers! Nervously I approached her. As my steps echoed on the marble pavement she looked up; her grey-green eyes met mine in that slow wistful smile that was so indescribably sad. Confused as my thoughts were, I observed her pallor, and the ethereal delicacy of her face and form—she had no hat on, and her neck and shoulders were uncovered. Struck by this peculiarity, I wondered if the other people who were passing through the hall noticed her *déshabille.* I looked around me enquiringly—not one passer-by turned a glance in our direction! Yet surely the lady's costume was strange enough to attract attention? A chill of horror quivered through me—was I the only one who saw her sitting there? This idea was so alarming that I uttered an involuntary exclamation; the next moment the seat before me was empty, the strange lady had gone, and nothing remained of her but—the strong sweet odour of the carnations she had carried! With a sort of sickness at my heart I hurried out of the Louvre, and was glad when I found myself in the bright Paris streets filled with eager, pressing people, all bent on their different errands of business or pleasure. I entered a carriage and was driven rapidly to the Grand Hotel, where I was staying with a party of friends. I refrained from speaking of the curious sensations that had overcome me—I did not even mention the picture that had exercised so weird an influence upon me. The brilliancy of the life we led, the constant change and activity of our movements, soon dispersed the nervous emotion I had undergone; and though sometimes the remembrance of it returned to me I avoided dwelling on the subject. Ten or twelve days passed, and one night we all went to the Théâtre Français—it was the first evening of my life that I ever was in the strange position of being witness to a play without either knowing its name or understanding its meaning. I could only realise one thing—namely, that "the Lady with the Carnations" sat in the box opposite to me, regarding me fixedly. She was alone; her costume was unchanged. I addressed one of our party in a low voice—

"Do you see that girl opposite, in white, with the shaded crimson carnations in her dress?"

My friend looked, shook her head, and rejoined—

"No; where is she sitting?"

"Right opposite!" I repeated in a more excited tone. "Surely you can see her! She is alone in that large box *en face.*"

My friend turned to me in wonder. "You must be dreaming, my dear! That large box is perfectly empty!"

Empty—I knew better! But I endeavoured to smile; I said I had made a mistake—that the lady I spoke of had moved—and so changed the subject. But throughout the evening, though I feigned to watch the stage, my eyes were continually turning to the place where SHE sat so quietly, with her steadfast, mournful gaze fixed upon me. One addition to her costume she had—a fan—which from the distance at which I beheld it seemed to be made of very old yellow lace, mounted on stick of filigree silver. She used it occasionally, waving it slowly to and fro in a sort of dreamy, meditative fashion; and ever and again she smiled that pained, patient smile which, though it hinted much, betrayed nothing. When we rose to leave the theatre "the Lady with the Carnations" rose also, and drawing a lace wrap about her head, she disappeared. Afterwards I saw her gliding through one of the outer lobbies; she looked so slight and fragile and childlike, alone in the pushing, brilliant crowd that my heart went out to her in a sort of fantastic tenderness.

"Whether she be a disembodied spirit," I mused, "or an illusion called up by some disorder of my own imagination, I do not know; but she seems so sad, that even were she a Dream, I pity her!"

This thought passed through my brain as in company with my friends I reached the outer door of the theatre. A touch on my arm startled me—a little white hand clasping a cluster of carnations rested there for a second—then vanished. I was somewhat overcome by this new experience; but my sensations this time were not those of fear. I became certain that this haunting image followed me for some reason; and I determined not to give way to any foolish terror concerning it, but to calmly await the course of events, that would in time, I felt convinced, explain everything. I stayed a fortnight longer in Paris without seeing anything more of "the Lady with the Carnations," except photographs of her picture in the Louvre, one of which I bought—though it gave but a feeble idea of the original masterpiece—and then I left for Brittany. Some English friends of mine, Mrs. and Mrs. Farleigh, had taken up their abode in a quaint old rambling château near Quimperlé on the coast of Finisterre, and they had pressed me cordially to stay with them for a fortnight—an invitation which I gladly accepted. The house was built on a lofty rock overlooking the sea; the surrounding coast was eminently wild and picturesque; and on the day I arrived, there was a boisterous wind which lifted high the crests of the billows and dashed them against the jutting crags with grand and terrific uproar. Mrs. Farleigh, a bright, practical woman, whose life was entirely absorbed in household management, welcome me with effusion—she and her two handsome boys, Rupert and Frank, were full of enthusiasm for the glories and advantages of their holiday resort.

"Such a beach!" cried Rupert, executing a sort of Indian war-dance beside me on the path.

"And such jolly walks and drives!" chorussed his brother.

"Yes, really!" warbled my hostess in her clear gay voice, "I'm delighted we came here. And the château is such a funny old place, full of odd nooks and corners. The country people, you know, are dreadfully superstitious, and they say it is haunted; but of course that's all nonsense! Though if there *were* a ghost, we should send you to interrogate it, my dear!"

This with a smile of good-natured irony at me. I laughed. Mrs. Farleigh was one of those eminently sensible persons who had seriously lectured me on a book known as "A Romance of Two Words," as inculcating spiritualistic theories, and therefore deserving condemnation.

I turned the subject.

"How long have you been here?" I asked.

"Three weeks—and we haven't explored half the neighborhood yet. There are parts of the house itself we don't know. Once upon a time—so the villagers say—a great painter lived here. Well, his studio runs the whole length of the château, and that and some other rooms are locked up. It seems they are never let to strangers. Not that we want them—the place is too big for us as it is."

"What as the painter's name?" I enquired, pausing as I ascended the terrace to admire the grand sweep of the sea.

"Oh, I forget! His pictures were so like those of Greuze that few can tell the difference between them—and—"

I interrupted her. "Tell me," I said, with a faint smile, "have you any carnations growing here?"

"Carnations! I should think so! The place is full of them. Isn't the odour delicious?" And as we reached the highest terrace in front of the château I saw that the garden was ablaze with these brilliant scented blossoms, of every shade, varying from the palest salmon pink to the deepest, darkest scarlet. This time that subtle fragrance was not my fancy, and I gathered a few of the flowers to wear in my dress at dinner. Mr. Farleigh now came out to receive us, and the conversation became general.

I was delighted with the interior of the house; it was so quaint, and old, and suggestive. There was a dark oaken staircase, with a most curiously carved and twisted balustrade—some ancient tapestry still hung on the walls—and there were faded portraits of stiff ladies in ruffs, and maliciously smiling knights in armour, that depressed rather than decorated the dining-room. The chamber assigned to me upstairs was rather bright than otherwise—it fronted the sea, and was cheerfully and prettily furnished. I noticed, however, that it was next door to the shut-up and long-deserted studio. The garden was, as Mrs. Farleigh had declared, full of carnations. I never saw so many of these flowers growing in one spot. They seemed to spring up everywhere, like weeds, even in the most deserted and shady corners. I had been at the château some three or four days, when one morning I happened to be walking alone in a sort of shrubbery at the back of the house, when I perceived in the long dank grass at my feet a large grey stone, that had evidently once stood upright, but had now fallen flat, burying itself partly in the earth. There was something carved upon it. I stooped down, and clearing away the grass and weeds, made out the words

"MANON

Cœur fidèle!"

Surely this was a strange inscription! I told my discovery to the Farleighs, and we all examined and re-examined the mysterious slab, without being able to arrive at any satisfactory explanation of its pictures. Even enquiries made among the villagers failed to elicit anything save shakes of the head, and such remarks as "Ah, Madame! si on savait! . . ." or "Je crois bien qu'il y a une histoire là!"

One evening we all returned to the château at rather a later hour than usual, after a long and delightful walk on the beach in the mellow radiance of a glorious moon. When I went to my room I had no inclination to go to bed—I was wide awake, and moreover in a sort of expectant frame of mind; expectant, though I knew not what I expected.

I threw my window open, leaning out and looking at the moon-enchanted sea, and inhaling the exquisite fragrance of the carnations wafted to me on every breath of the night wind. I thought of many things—the glory of life; the large benevolence of Nature; the mystery of death; the beauty and certainty of immortality, and then, though my back was turned to the interior of my room, I knew—I felt, I was no longer alone. I forced myself to move round from the window; slowly but determinedly I brought myself to confront whoever it was that had thus entered through my locked door; and I was scarcely surprised when I saw "the Lady with the Carnations" standing at a little distance from me, with a most woebegone, appealing expression on her shadowy lovely face. I looked at her, resolved not to fear her; and then brought all my will to bear on unravelling the mystery of my strange visitant. As I met her gaze unflinchingly she made a sort of timid gesture with her hands, as though she besought something.

"Why are you here?" I asked, in a low, clear tone. "Why do you follow me?"

Again she made that little appealing movement. Her answer, soft as a child's whisper, floated through the room—

"You pitied me!"

"Are you unhappy?"

"Very!" And here she clasped her wan white fingers together in a sort of agony. I was growing nervous, but I continued—

"Tell me, then, what you wish me to do?"

She raised her eyes in passionate supplication.

"Pray for me! No one haws prayed for me ever since I died—no one has pitied me for a hundred years!"

"How did you die?" I asked, trying to control the rapid beating of my heart. The "Lady with the Carnations" smiled most mournfully, and slowly unfasted the cluster of flowers from her breast—there her white robe was darkly stained with blood. She pointed to the stain, and then replaced the flowers. I understood.

"Murdered!" I whispered, more to myself than to my pale visitor—"murdered!"

"No one knows, and no one prays for me!" wailed the faint sweet spirit voice—"and though I am dead I cannot rest. Pray for me—I am tired!"

And her slender head drooped wearily—she seemed about to vanish. I conquered my rising terrors by a strong effort, and said—

"Tell me—you *must* tell me"—here she raised her head, and her large pensive eyes met mine obediently—"who was your murderer?"

"He did not mean it," she answered. "He loved me. It was here"—and she raised one hand and motioned towards the adjacent studio—"here he drew my picture. He thought me false—but I was true. 'Manon, cœur fidèle!'"

She paused and looked at me appealingly. Again she pointed to the studio.

"Go and see!" she sighed. "Then you will pray—and I will never come again. Promise you will pray for me—it was here he killed me—and I died without a prayer."

"Where were you buried?" I asked, in a hushed voice.

"In the waves," she murmured; "thrown into the wild cold waves; and no one knew—no one ever found poor Manon; alone and sad for a hundred years, with no word said to God for her!"

Her face was so full of plaintive pathos that I could have wept. Watching her as she stood, I knelt at the quant old prie-Dieu just within my reach, and prayed as she desired. Slowly, slowly, a rapturous light came into her eyes; she smiled and waved her hands towards me in farewell. She glided backwards towards the door—and her figure grew dim and indistinct. For the last time she turned her now radiant countenance upon me, and said in thrilling accents—

"Write, 'Manon, cœur fidèle!'"

I cannot remember how the rest of the night passed; but I knew that with the very early morning, rousing myself from the stupor of sleep into which I had fallen, I hurried to the door of the closed studio. It was ajar! I pushed it boldly open and entered. The room was long and lofty, but destitute of all furniture save a battered-looking, worm-eaten easel that leaned up against the damp stained wall. I approached this relic of the painter's art, and examining it closely, perceived the name "Manon" cut roughly yet deeply upon it. Looking curiously about, I saw what had nearly escaped my notice—a sort of hanging cupboard, on the left-hand side of the large central bay window. I tried its handle—it was unlocked, and opened easily. Within it lay three things—a palette, on which the blurring marks of long obliterated pigments were still faintly visible; a dagger, unsheathed, with its blade almost black with rust; and—the silver filigree sticks of a fan, to which clung some mouldy shreds of yellow lace. I remembered the fan the "Lady with the Carnations" had carried at the Théâtre Français; and I pieced together her broken story. She had been slain by her artist lover—slain in a sudden fit of jealousy ere the soft colours on his picture of her were yet dry—murdered in this very studio; and no doubt that hidden dagger was the weapon used. Poor Manon! Her frail body had been cast from the high rock on which the château stood "into the cold wild waves," as she or her spirit had said; and her cruel lover had carried his wrath against her so far as to perpetuate a slander against her by writing "Cœur perfide" on that imperishable block of stone! Full of pitying thoughts I shut the cupboard, and slowly left the studio, closing the door noiselessly after me.

That morning as soon as I could get Mrs. Fairleigh alone I told her my adventure, beginning with the very first experience I had had of the picture in the Louvre. Needless to say, she heard me with the utmost incredulity.

"I know you, my dear!" she said, shaking her head at me wisely; "you are full of fancies, and always dreaming about the next world, as if this one wasn't good enough for you. The whole thing is a delusion."

"But," I persisted, "you know the studio was shut and locked; how is it that it is open now?"

"It isn't open!" declared Mrs. Fairleigh—"though I am quite willing to believe you dreamt it was."

"Come and see!" I exclaimed eagerly; and I took her upstairs, though she was somewhat reluctant to follow me. As I had said, the studio was open. I led her in, and showed the name cut on the easel, and the hanging cupboard with its contents. As these convincing proofs of my story met her eyes, she shivered a little, and grew rather pale.

"Come away!" she said nervously—"you are really too horrid! I can't bear this sort of thing! For goodness' sake, keep your ghosts to yourself!" I saw she was vexed and pettish, and I readily followed her out of the barren, forlorn-looking room. Scarcely were we well outside the door when it shut to with a sharp click. I tried it—it was fast locked! This was too much for Mrs. Fairleigh. She rushed downstairs in a perfect paroxysm of terror; and when I found her in the breakfast-room she declared she would stop another day in the house. I managed to calm her fears, however; but she insisted on my remaining with her to brave out whatever else might happen at what she persisted now in calling the "haunted" château, in spite of her practical theories. And so I stayed on. And when we left Brittany, we left all together, without having had our peace disturbed by any more manifestations of an unearthly nature. One thing alone troubled me a little—I should have liked to obliterate the world *"perfide"* from that stone, and to have had *"fidèle"* carved on it instead; but it was too deeply engraved for this. However, I have seen no more of "the Lady with the Carnations." But I know the dead need praying for—and that they often suffer for lack of such prayers—though I cannot pretend to explain the reason why. And I know that the picture in the Louvre is not a Greuze, though it is called one—it is the portrait of a faithful woman deeply wronged and her name is here written as she told me to write it—

"MANON
Cœur fidèle!"

THE GUEST

Lord Dunsany

Irish author and dramatist, Edward John Moreton Drax Plunkett, 18th Baron of Dunsany (1878–1957), is among the foremost masters of the weird tale. His writing had a profound impact on H. P. Lovecraft, but Dunsany is also cited as a major influence on the work of such luminaries of the literary world as J. R. R. Tolkien, Ursula Le Guin, Evangeline Walton, Jack Vance, and Peter S. Beagle. Filmmaker Guillermo Del Toro has described Dunsany as an influence, while author Neil Gaiman has expressed admiration for him, writing an introduction to a collection of Dunsany stories.

Dunsany lived most of his life in Dunsany Castle, his ancestral home, which is considered to be among the longest consistently inhabited dwellings in Ireland, if not the longest. He was a relative of Saint Oliver Plunkett.

"The Guest" was first published in 1915 in Dunsany's collection of stories, *Fifty-One Tales*. It is an extremely short story, the shortest in this book, but, in its brevity and subtlety, perhaps the most terrifying.

The Guest

A young man came into an ornate restaurant at eight o'clock in London.

He was alone, but two places had been laid at the table which was reserved for him. He had chosen the dinner very carefully, by letter a week before.

A waiter asked him about the other guest.

"You probably won't see him till the coffee comes," the young man told him; so he was served alone.

Those at adjacent tables might have noticed the young man continually addressing the empty chair and carrying on a monologue with it throughout his elaborate dinner.

"I think you knew my father," he said to it over the soup.

"I sent for you this evening," he continued, "because I want you to do me a good turn; in fact I must insist on it."

There was nothing eccentric about the man except for this habit of addressing an empty chair, certainly he was eating as good a dinner as any sane man could wish for.

After the Burgundy had been served he became more voluble in his monologue, not that he spoiled his wine by drinking excessively.

"We have several acquaintances in common," he said. "I met King Seti a year ago in Thebes. I think he has altered very little since you knew him. I thought his forehead a little low for a king's. Cheops has left the house that he built for your reception, he must have prepared for you for years and years. I suppose you have seldom been entertained like that. I ordered this dinner over a week ago. I thought then that a lady might have come with me, but as she wouldn't I've asked you. She may not after all be as lovely as Helen of Troy. Was Helen very lovely? Not when you knew her, perhaps. You were lucky in Cleopatra, you must have known her when she was in her prime.

"You never knew the mermaids nor the fairies nor the lovely goddesses of long ago, that's where we have the best of you."

He was silent when the waiters came to his table, but rambled merrily on as soon as they left, still turned to the empty chair.

"You know I saw you here in London only the other day. You were on a motor bus going down Ludgate Hill. It was going much too fast. London is a good place. But I shall be glad enough to leave it. It was in London that I met the lady I that was speaking about. If it hadn't been for London I probably shouldn't have met her, and if it hadn't been for London she probably wouldn't have had so much besides me to amuse her. It cuts both ways."

He paused once to order coffee, gazing earnestly at the waiter and putting a sovereign in his hand. "Don't let it be chicory," said he.

The waiter brought the coffee, and the young man dropped a tabloid of some sort into his cup.

"I don't suppose you come here very often," he went on. "Well, you probably want to be going. I haven't taken you much out of your way, there is plenty for you to do in London."

Then having drunk his coffee he fell on to the floor by a foot of the empty chair, and a doctor who was dining in the room bent over him and announced to the anxious manager the visible presence of the young man's guest.

THE OVAL PORTRAIT

Edgar Allan Poe

What can be said of Edgar Allan Poe (1809–1849) that has not already been said? Poet, editor, critic, Poe is among the most influential and significant authors. He is credited with inventing the entire genre of detective fiction and considered among the leading influences on weird and horror fiction. Over a century after his death, his work, as well as his life and especially his death, continue to fascinate a broad spectrum of the public.

"The Cask of Amontillado," "The Tell-Tale Heart," "The Fall of the House of Usher," "The Murders in the Rue Morgue," "The Raven": Poe's writing resonates worldwide. Charles Baudelaire translated Poe's work into French, while Hanns Heinz Ewers, whose story "The Spider" follows this one, translated Poe into German.

Born in Boston, the second son of two actors, Poe lived in various cities: Baltimore, New York, and Philadelphia. He attempted to earn his living solely by writing, which was as difficult then as now. He was frequently in dire financial straits.

The precise circumstances, not to mention the cause, of Poe's death remain mysterious. On October 3, 1849, Poe, delirious and distressed, was discovered on the streets of Baltimore. The clothes he wore were not his own. He was taken to the hospital, where he died on October 7. He was reputedly never sufficiently coherent to explain what had happened to him, but speculation and theories have raged ever since.

"The Oval Portrait" contains a story within a story. In its present form, it was first published in the April 26, 1845, edition of the *Broadway Journal*. It can be read, if desired, purely as a horror tale; however, it has also been interpreted as a metaphysical or supernatural tale. Is the artist who paints the portrait of the story's title merely a coldhearted, distracted lover, or, in the process of creating the painting, does he vampirize or otherwise capture his subject's soul?

The Oval Portrait

The Chateau into which my valet had ventured to make forcible entrance, rather than permit me, in my desperately wounded condition, to pass a night in the open air, was one of those piles of commingled gloom and grandeur which have so long frowned among the Appennines, not less in fact than in the fancy of Mrs. Radcliffe. To all appearance it had been temporarily and very lately abandoned. We established ourselves in one of the smallest and least sumptuously furnished apartments. It lay in a remote turret of the building. Its decorations were rich, yet tattered and antique. Its walls were hung with tapestry and bedecked with manifold and multiform armorial trophies, together with an unusually great number of very spirited modern paintings in frames of rich golden arabesque. In these paintings, which depended from the walls not only in their main surfaces, but in very many nooks which the bizarre architecture of the chateau rendered necessary—in these paintings my incipient delirium, perhaps, had caused me to take deep interest; so that I bade Pedro to close the heavy shutters of the room—since it was already night—to light the tongues of a tall candelabrum which stood by the head of my bed—and to throw open far and wide the fringed curtains of black velvet which enveloped the bed itself. I wished all this done that I might resign myself, if not to sleep, at least alternately to the contemplation of these pictures, and the perusal of a small volume which had been found upon the pillow, and which purported to criticise and describe them.

Long—long I read—and devoutly, devotedly I gazed. Rapidly and gloriously the hours flew by and the deep midnight came. The position of the candelabrum displeased me, and outreaching my hand with difficulty, rather than disturb my slumbering valet, I placed it so as to throw its rays more fully upon the book.

But the action produced an effect altogether unanticipated. The rays of the numerous candles (for there were many) now fell within a niche of the room which had hitherto been thrown into deep shade by one of the bed-posts. I thus saw in vivid light a picture all unnoticed before. It was the portrait of a young girl just ripening into womanhood. I glanced at the painting hurriedly, and then closed my eyes. Why I did this was not at first apparent even to my own perception. But while my lids remained thus shut, I ran over in my mind my reason for so shutting them. It was an impulsive movement to gain time for thought—to make sure that my vision had not deceived me—to calm and subdue my fancy for a more sober and more certain gaze. In a very few moments I again looked fixedly at the painting.

That I now saw aright I could not and would not doubt; for the first flashing of the candles upon that canvas had seemed to dissipate the dreamy stupor which was stealing over my senses, and to startle me at once into waking life.

The portrait, I have already said, was that of a young girl. It was a mere head and shoulders, done in what is technically termed a vignette manner; much in the style of the favorite heads of Sully. The arms, the bosom, and even the ends of the radiant hair melted imperceptibly into the vague yet deep shadow which formed the back-ground of the whole. The frame was oval, richly gilded and filigreed in Moresque. As a thing of art nothing could be more admirable than the painting itself. But it could have been neither the execution of the work, nor the immortal beauty of the countenance, which had so suddenly and so vehemently moved me. Least of all, could it have been that my fancy, shaken from its half slumber, had mistaken the head for that of a living person. I saw at once that the peculiarities of the design, of the vignetting, and of the frame, must have instantly dispelled such idea— must have prevented even its momentary entertainment. Thinking earnestly upon these points, I remained, for an hour perhaps, half sitting, half reclining, with my vision riveted upon the portrait. At length, satisfied with the true secret of its effect, I fell back within the bed. I had found the spell of the picture in an absolute life-likeliness of expression, which, at first startling, finally confounded, subdued, and appalled me. With deep and reverent awe I replaced the candelabrum in its former position. The cause of my deep agitation being thus shut from view, I sought eagerly the volume which discussed the paintings and their histories. Turning to the number which designated the oval portrait, I there read the vague and quaint words which follow:

"She was a maiden of rarest beauty, and not more lovely than full of glee. And evil was the hour when she saw, and loved, and wedded the painter. He, passionate, studious, austere, and having already a bride in his Art; she a maiden of rarest beauty, and not more lovely than full of glee; all light and smiles, and frolicsome as the young fawn; loving and cherishing all things; hating only the Art which was her rival; dreading only the pallet and brushes and other untoward instruments which deprived her of the countenance of her lover. It was thus a terrible thing for this lady to hear the painter speak of his desire to pourtray even his young bride. But she was humble and obedient, and sat meekly for many weeks in the dark, high turret-chamber where the light dripped upon the pale canvas only from overhead. But he, the painter, took glory in his work, which went on from hour to hour, and from day to day. And be was a passionate, and wild, and moody man, who became lost in reveries; so that he would not see that the light which fell so ghastly in that lone turret withered the health and the spirits of his bride, who pined visibly to all but him. Yet she smiled on and still on, uncomplainingly, because she saw that the painter (who had high renown) took a fervid and burning pleasure in his task, and wrought day and night to depict her who so loved him, yet who grew daily more dispirited and weak. And in sooth some who beheld the portrait spoke of its resemblance in low words, as of a mighty marvel, and a proof not less of the power of the painter than of his deep love for her whom he depicted so surpassingly well. But at length, as the labor drew nearer to its conclusion, there were admitted none into the turret; for the painter had grown wild with the ardor of his work, and turned his eyes from canvas merely, even to regard the countenance of his wife. And he would not see that the tints which he spread upon the canvas were drawn from the cheeks of her who sat beside him. And when many weeks bad passed, and but little remained to do, save one brush upon the mouth and one tint upon the eye, the spirit of the lady again flickered up as the flame within the socket of the lamp. And then the brush was given, and then the tint was placed; and, for one moment, the painter stood entranced before the work which he had wrought; but in the next, while he yet gazed, he grew tremulous and very pallid, and aghast, and crying with a loud voice, 'This is indeed Life itself!' turned suddenly to regard his beloved:—She was dead!

THE SPIDER

Hanns Heinz Ewers

Hanns Heinz Ewers (1871–1943), born in Dusseldorf, Germany, was a prolific and commercially successful author—until he wasn't. Ewers specialized in decadent, supernatural tales of the occult. Lauded as "the German Edgar Allan Poe," Ewers wrote novels, screenplays, radio plays, opera librettos, essays, poems, and stories. His most famous work is his Frank Braun Trilogy—he modeled the hero, Frank Braun, a classic ubermensch, after himself. The trilogy consists of the novels, *The Sorcerer's Apprentice* (1907), *Alraune* (1911), and *Vampyr* (1921). He has been described as an "occult master" and was a friend and correspondent of Aleister Crowley.

Ewers was a victim of his era. Early Nazis initially found him to be glamorously attractive. He was a social acquaintance of Adolf Hitler, although he never joined the Nazi Party. By 1935, however, Ewers had fallen from favor: his works were banned; existing copies were destroyed; he was branded a "nonperson." His assets and property were seized. Completely impoverished, Ewers died of tuberculosis in 1943 in Berlin. The precise reasons for this fall from grace remain controversial: it has been suggested that various Nazi officials, initially impressed by his celebrity alone, eventually actually read his books and found their decadence objectionable, not to mention the major presence of a Jewish heroine, Frank Braun's mistress.

"The Spider" was first published in English in 1915. The narrator's references to Clarimonda allude to French author Théophile Gautier's 1836 story, "La Morte Amoreux," published in English as "Clarimonde," which signal that, at least subliminally, the narrator knows a femme fatale when he sees one.

The Spider

When the student of medicine, Richard Bracquemont, decided to move into room #7 of the small Hotel Stevens, Rue Alfred Stevens (Paris 6), three persons had already hanged themselves from the cross-bar of the window in that room on three successive Fridays.

The first was a Swiss traveling salesman. They found his corpse on Saturday evening. The doctor determined that the death must have occurred between five and six o'clock on Friday afternoon. The corpse hung on a strong hook that had been driven into the window's cross-bar to serve as a hanger for articles of clothing. The window was closed, and the dead man had used the curtain cord as a noose. Since the window was very low, he hung with his knees practically touching the floor—a sign of the great discipline the suicide must have exercised in carrying out his design. Later, it was learned that he was a married man, a father. He had been a man of a continually happy disposition; a man who had achieved a secure place in life. There was not one written word to be found that would have shed light on his suicide . . . not even a will.

Furthermore, none of his acquaintances could recall hearing anything at all from him that would have permitted anyone to predict his end.

The second case was not much different. The artist, Karl Krause, a high wire cyclist in the nearby Medrano Circus, moved into room 7 two days later. When he did not show up at Friday's performance, the director sent an employee to the hotel. There, he found Krause in the unlocked room hanging from the window cross-bar in circumstances exactly like those of the previous suicide. This death was as perplexing as the first. Krause was popular. He earned a very high salary, and had appeared to enjoy life at its fullest. Once again, there was no suicide note; no sinister hints. Krause's sole survivor was his mother to whom the son had regularly sent 300 marks on the first of the month.

For Madame Dubonnet, the owner of the small, cheap guesthouse whose clientele was composed almost completely of employees in a nearby Montmartre vaudeville theater, this second curious death in the same room had very unpleasant consequences. Already several of her guests had moved out, and other regular clients had not come back. She appealed for help to her personal friend, the inspector of police of the ninth precinct, who assured her that he would do everything in his power to help her. He pushed zealously ahead not only with the investigation into the grounds for the suicides of the two guests, but he also placed an officer in the mysterious room.

This man, Charles-Maria Chaumié, actually volunteered for the task. Chaumié was an old "Marsouin," a marine sergeant with eleven years of service, who had lain so many nights at posts in Tonkin and Annam, and had greeted so many stealthily creeping river pirates with a shot from his rifle that he seemed ideally suited to encounter the "ghost" that everyone on Rue Alfred Stevens was talking about.

From then on, each morning and each evening, Chaumié paid a brief visit to the police station to make his report, which, for the first few days, consisted only of his statement that he had not noticed anything unusual. On Wednesday evening, however, he hinted that he had found a clue.

Pressed to say more, he asked to be allowed more time before making any comment, since he was not sure that what he had discovered had any relationship to the two deaths, and he was afraid he might say something that would make him look foolish.

On Thursday, his behavior seemed a bit uncertain, but his mood was noticeably more serious. Still, he had nothing to report. On Friday morning, he came in very excited and spoke, half humorously, half seriously, of the strangely attractive power that his window had. He would not elaborate this notion and said that, in any case, it had nothing to do with the suicides; and that it would be ridiculous of him to say any more. When, on that same Friday, he failed to make his regular evening report, someone went to his room and found him hanging from the cross-bar of the window.

All the circumstances, down to the minutest detail, were the same here as in the previous cases. Chaumié's legs dragged along the ground. The curtain cord had been used for a noose. The window was closed, the door to the room had not been locked and death had occurred at six o'clock. The dead man's mouth was wide open, and his tongue protruded from it.

Chaumié's death, the third in as many weeks in room #7, had the following consequences: all the guests, with the exception of a German high-school teacher in room #16, moved out. The teacher took advantage of the occasion to have his rent reduced by a third. The next day, Mary Garden, the famous Opéra Comique singer, drove up to the Hotel Stevens and paid two hundred francs for the red curtain cord, saying it would bring her luck. The story, small consolation for Madame Dubonnet, got into the papers.

If these events had occurred in summer, in July or August, Madame Dubonnet would have secured three times that price for her cord, but as it was in the middle of a troubled year, with elections, disorders in the Balkans, bank crashes in New York, the visit of the King and Queen of England, the result was that the affaire Rue Alfred Stevens was talked of less than it deserved to be. As for the newspaper accounts, they were brief, being essentially the police reports word for word.

These reports were all that Richard Bracquemont, the medical student, knew of the matter.

There was one detail about which he knew nothing because neither the police inspector nor any of the eyewitnesses had mentioned it to the press. It was only later, after what happened to the medical student, that anyone remembered that when the police removed Sergeant Charles-Maria Chaumié's body from the window cross-bar a large black spider crawled from the dead man's open mouth. A hotel porter flicked it away, exclaiming, "Ugh, another of those damned creatures."

When in later investigations which concerned themselves mostly with Bracquemont the servant was interrogated, he said that he had seen a similar spider crawling on the Swiss traveling salesman's shoulder when his body was removed from the window cross-bar. But Richard Bracquemont knew nothing of all this.

It was more than two weeks after the last suicide that Bracquemont moved into the room. It was a Sunday. Bracquemont conscientiously recorded everything that happened to him in his journal. That journal now follows.

Monday, February 28

I moved in yesterday evening. I unpacked my two wicker suitcases and straightened the room a little. Then I went to bed. I slept so soundly that it was nine o'clock the next morning before a knock at my door woke me. It was my hostess, bringing me breakfast herself. One could read her concern for me in the eggs, the bacon and the superb café au lait she brought me. I washed and dressed, then smoked a pipe as I watched the servant make up the room.

So, here I am. I know well that the situation may prove dangerous, but I think I may just be the one to solve the problem. If, once upon a time, Paris was worth a mass (conquest comes at a dearer rate these days), it is well worth risking my life pour un si bel enjeu. I have at least one chance to win, and I mean to risk it. As it is, I'm not the only one who has had this notion. Twenty-seven people have tried for access to the room. Some went to the police, some went directly to the hotel owner. There were even three women among the candidates. There was plenty of competition. No doubt the others are poor devils like me.

And yet, it was I who was chosen. Why? Because I was the only one who hinted that I had some plan—or the semblance of a plan. Naturally, I was bluffing.

These journal entries are intended for the police. I must say that it amuses me to tell those gentlemen how neatly I fooled them. If the Inspector has any sense, he'll say, "Hm. This Bracquemont is just the man we need." In any case, it doesn't matter what he'll say. The point is I'm here now, and I take it as a good sign that I've begun my task by bamboozling the police.

I had gone first to Madame Dubonnet, and it was she who sent me to the police. They put me off for a whole week—as they put off my rivals as well. Most of them gave up in disgust, having something better to do than hang around the musty squad room. The Inspector was beginning to get irritated at my tenacity. At last, he told me I was wasting my time. That the police had no use for bungling amateurs. "Ah, if only you had a plan. Then . . ."

On the spot, I announced that I had such a plan, though naturally I had no such thing. Still, I hinted that my plan was brilliant, but dangerous, that it might lead to the same end as that which had overtaken the police officer, Chaumié. Still, I promised to describe it to him if he would give me his word that he would personally put it into effect. He made excuses, claiming he was too busy but when he asked me to give him at least a hint of my plan, I saw that I had picqued his interest.

I rattled off some nonsense made up of whole cloth. God alone knows where it all came from.

I told him that six o'clock of a Friday is an occult hour. It is the last hour of the Jewish week; the hour when Christ disappeared from his tomb and descended into hell. That he would do well to remember that the three suicides had taken place at approximately that hour. That was all I could tell him just then, I said, but I pointed him to The Revelations of St. John.

The Inspector assumed the look of a man who understood all that I had been saying, then he asked me to come back that evening.

I returned, precisely on time, and noted a copy of the New Testament on the Inspector's desk. I had, in the meantime, been at the Revelations myself without however having understood a syllable. Perhaps the Inspector was cleverer than I. Very politely—nay—deferentially, he let me know that, despite my extremely vague intimations, he believed he grasped my line of thought and was ready to expedite my plan in every way.

And here, I must acknowledge that he has indeed been tremendously helpful. It was he who made the arrangement with the owner that I was to have anything I needed so long as I stayed in the room. The Inspector gave me a pistol and a police whistle, and he ordered the officers on the beat to pass through the Rue Alfred Stevens as often as possible, and to watch my window for any signal. Most important of all, he had a desk telephone installed which connects directly with the police station. Since the station is only four minutes away, I see no reason to be afraid.

Wednesday, March 1

Nothing has happened. Not yesterday. Not today.

Madame Dubonnet brought a new curtain cord from another room—the rooms are mostly empty, of course. Madame Dubonnet takes every opportunity to visit me, and each time she brings something with her. I have asked her to tell me again everything that happened here, but I have learned nothing new. She has her own opinion of the suicides. Her view is that the music hall artist, Krause, killed himself because of an unhappy love affair. During the last year that Krause lived in the hotel, a young woman had made frequent visits to him. These visits had stopped, just before his death. As for the Swiss gentleman, Madame Dubonnet confessed herself baffled. On the other hand, the death of the policeman was easy to explain. He had killed himself just to annoy her.

These are sad enough explanations, to be sure, but I let her babble on to take the edge off my boredom.

Thursday, March 3

Still nothing. The Inspector calls twice a day. Each time, I tell him that all is well. Apparently, these words do not reassure him.

I have taken out my medical books and I study, so that my self-imposed confinement will have some purpose.

Friday, March 4

I ate uncommonly well at noon. The landlady brought me half a bottle of champagne. It seemed a meal for a condemned man. Madame Dubonnet looked at me as if I were already three-quarters dead. As she was leaving, she begged me tearfully to come with her, fearing no doubt that I would hang myself 'just to annoy her.'

I studied the curtain cord once again. Would I hang myself with it? Certainly, I felt little desire to do so. The cord is stiff and rough—not the sort of cord one makes a noose of. One would need to be truly determined before one could imitate the others.

I am seated now at my table. At my left, the telephone. At my right, the revolver. I'm not frightened; but I am curious.

Six o'clock, the same evening

Nothing has happened. I was about to add, "Unfortunately." The fatal hour has come—and has gone, like any six o'clock on any evening. I won't hide the fact that I occasionally felt a certain impulse to go to the window, but for a quite different reason than one might imagine.

The Inspector called me at least ten times between five and six o'clock. He was as impatient as I was. Madame Dubonnet, on the other hand, is happy. A week has passed without someone in #7 hanging himself. Marvelous.

Monday, March 7

I have a growing conviction that I will learn nothing; that the previous suicides are related to the circumstances surrounding the lives of the three men. I have asked the Inspector to investigate the cases further, convinced that someone will find their motivations. As for me, I hope to stay here as long as possible. I may not conquer Paris here, but I live very well and I'm fattening up nicely. I'm also studying hard, and I am making real progress. There is another reason, too, that keeps me here.

Wednesday, March 9

So! I have taken one step more. Clarimonda.

I haven't yet said anything about Clarimonda. It is she who is my "third" reason for staying here. She is also the reason I was tempted to go to the window during the "fateful" hour last Friday. But of course, not to hang myself.

Clarimonda. Why do I call her that? I have no idea what her name is, but it ought to be Clarimonda. When finally I ask her name, I'm sure it will turn out to be Clarimonda.

I noticed her almost at once . . . in the very first days. She lives across the narrow street; and her window looks right into mine. She sits there, behind her curtains.

I ought to say that she noticed me before I saw her; and that she was obviously interested in me. And no wonder. The whole neighborhood knows I am here, and why. Madame Dubonnet has seen to that.

I am not of a particularly amorous disposition. In fact, my relations with women have been rather meager. When one comes from Verdun to Paris to study medicine, and has hardly money enough for three meals a day, one has something else to think about besides love. I am then not very experienced with women, and I may have begun my adventure with her stupidly. Never mind. It's exciting just the same.

At first, the idea of establishing some relationship with her simply did not occur to me. It was only that, since I was here to make observations, and, since there was nothing in the room to observe, I thought I might as well observe my neighbor—openly, professionally. Anyhow, one can't sit all day long just reading.

Clarimonda, I have concluded, lives alone in the small flat across the way. The flat has three windows, but she sits only before the window that looks into mine. She sits there, spinning on an old-fashioned spindle, such as my grandmother inherited from a great aunt. I had no idea anyone still used such spindles. Clarimonda's spindle is a lovely object. It appears to be made of ivory; and the thread she spins is of an exceptional fineness. She works all day behind her curtains, and stops spinning only as the sun goes down. Since darkness comes abruptly here in this narrow street and in this season of fogs, Clarimonda disappears from her place at five o'clock each evening.

I have never seen a light in her flat.

What does Clarimonda look like? I'm not quite sure. Her hair is black and wavy; her face pale.

Her nose is short and finely shaped with delicate nostrils that seem to quiver. Her lips, too, are pale: and when she smiles, it seems that her small teeth are as keen as those of some beast of prey.

Her eyelashes are long and dark; and her huge dark eyes have an intense glow. I guess all these details more than I know them. It is hard to see clearly through the curtains.

Something else: she always wears a black dress embroidered with a lilac motif; and black gloves, no doubt to protect her hands from the effects of her work. It is a curious sight: her delicate hands moving perpetually, swiftly grasping the thread, pulling it, releasing it, taking it up again; as if one were watching the indefatigable motions of an insect.

Our relationship? For the moment, still very superficial, though it feels deeper. It began with a sudden exchange of glances in which each of us noted the other. I must have pleased her, because one day she studied me a while longer, then smiled tentatively. Naturally, I smiled back. In this fashion, two days went by, each of us smiling more frequently with the passage of time. Yet something kept me from greeting her directly.

Until today.

This afternoon, I did it. And Clarimonda returned my greeting. It was done subtly enough, to be sure, but I saw her nod.

Thursday, March 10

Yesterday, I sat for a long time over my books, though I can't truthfully say that I studied much. I built castles in the air and dreamed of Clarimonda.

I slept fitfully.

This morning, when I approached my window, Clarimonda was already in her place. I waved, and she nodded back. She laughed and studied me for a long time.

I tried to read, but I felt much too uneasy. Instead, I sat down at my window and gazed at Clarimonda. She too had laid her work aside. Her hands were folded in her lap. I drew my curtain wider with the window cord, so that I might see better. At the same moment, Clarimonda did the same with the curtains at her window. We exchanged smiles.

We must have spent a full hour gazing at each other.

Finally, she took up her spinning.

Saturday, March 12

The days pass. I eat and drink. I sit at the desk. I light my pipe; I look down at my book but I don't read a word, though I try again and again. Then I go to the window where I wave to Clarimonda. She nods. We smile. We stare at each other for hours.

Yesterday afternoon, at six o'clock, I grew anxious. The twilight came early, bringing with it something like anguish. I sat at my desk. I waited until I was invaded by an irresistible need to go to the window—not to hang myself; but just to see Clarimonda. I sprang up and stood beside the curtain where it seemed to me I had never been able to see so clearly, though it was already dark.

Clarimonda was spinning, but her eyes looked into mine. I felt myself strangely contented even as I experienced a light sensation of fear.

The telephone rang. It was the Inspector tearing me out of my trance with his idiotic questions.

I was furious.

This morning, the Inspector and Madame Dubonnet visited me. She is enchanted with how things are going. I have now lived for two weeks in room #7. The Inspector, however, does not feel he is getting results. I hinted mysteriously that I was on the trail of something most unusual.

The jackass took me at my word and fulfilled my dearest wish. I've been allowed to stay in the room for another week. God knows it isn't Madame Dubonnet's cooking or wine-cellar that keeps me here. How quickly one can be sated with such things. No. I want to stay because of the window Madame Dubonnet fears and hates. That beloved window that shows me Clarimonda.

I have stared out of my window, trying to discover whether she ever leaves her room, but I've never seen her set foot on the street.

As for me, I have a large, comfortable armchair and a green shade over the lamp whose glow envelopes me in warmth. The Inspector has left me with a huge packet of fine tobacco—and yet I cannot work. I read two or three pages only to discover that I haven't understood a word. My eyes see the letters, but my brain refuses to make any sense of them. Absurd. As if my brain were posted: 'No Trespassing.' It is as if there were no room in my head for any other thought than the one: Clarimonda. I push my books away; I lean back deeply into my chair. I dream.

Sunday, March 13

This morning I watched a tiny drama while the servant was tidying my room. I was strolling in the corridor when I paused before a small window in which a large garden spider had her web.

Madame Dubonnet will not have it removed because she believes spiders bring luck, and she's had enough misfortunes in her house lately. Today, I saw a much smaller spider, a male, moving across the strong threads towards the middle of the web, but when his movements alerted the female, he drew back shyly to the edge of the web from which he made a second attempt to cross it. Finally, the female in the middle appeared attentive to his wooing, and stopped moving. The male tugged at a strand gently, then more strongly till the whole web shook. The female stayed motionless. The male moved quickly forward and the female received him quietly, calmly, giving herself over completely to his embraces. For a long minute, they hung together motionless at the center of the huge web.

Then I saw the male slowly extricating himself, one leg over the other. It was as if he wanted tactfully to leave his companion alone in the dream of love, but as he started away, the female, overwhelmed by a wild life, was after him, hunting him ruthlessly. The male let himself drop from a thread; the female followed, and for a while the lovers hung there, imitating a piece of art. Then they fell to the window-sill where the male, summoning all his strength, tried again to escape. Too late. The female already had him in her powerful grip, and was carrying him back to the center of the web. There, the place that had just served as the couch for their lascivious embraces took on quite another aspect. The lover wriggled, trying to escape from the female's wild embrace, but she was too much for him. It was not long before she had wrapped him completely in her thread, and he was helpless. Then she dug her sharp pincers into his body, and sucked full draughts of her young lover's blood. Finally, she detached herself from the pitiful and unrecognizable shell of his body and threw it out of her web.

So that is what love is like among these creatures. Well for me that I am not a spider.

Monday, March 14

I don't look at my books any longer. I spend my days at the window. When it is dark, Clarimonda is no longer there, but if I close my eyes, I continue to see her.

This journal has become something other than I intended. I've spoken about Madame Dubonnet, about the Inspector; about spiders and about Clarimonda. But I've said nothing about the discoveries I undertook to make. It can't be helped.

Tuesday, March 15

We have invented a strange game, Clarimonda and I. We play it all day long. I greet her; then she greets me. Then I tap my fingers on the windowpanes. The moment she sees me doing that, she too begins tapping. I wave to her; she waves back. I move my lips as if speaking to her; she does the same. I run my hand through my sleep-disheveled hair and instantly her hand is at her forehead. It is a child's game, and we both laugh over it. Actually, she doesn't laugh. She only smiles a gently contained smile. And I smile back in the same way.

The game is not as trivial as it seems. It's not as if we were grossly imitating each other—that would weary us both. Rather, we are communicating with each other. Sometimes, telepathically, it would seem, since Clarimonda follows my movements instantaneously almost before she has had time to see them. I find myself inventing new movements, or new combinations of movements, but each time she repeats them with disconcerting speed. Sometimes. I change the order of the movements to surprise her, making whole series of gestures as rapidly as possible; or I leave out some motions and weave in others, the way children play "Simon Says." What is amazing is that Clarimonda never once makes a mistake, no matter how quickly I change gestures.

That's how I spend my days . . . but never for a moment do I feel that I'm killing time. It seems, on the contrary, that never in my life have I been better occupied.

Wednesday, March 16

Isn't it strange that it hasn't occurred to me to put my relationship with Clarimonda on a more serious basis than these endless games. Last night, I thought about this . . . I can, of course, put on my hat and coat, walk down two flights of stairs, take five steps across the street and mount two flights to her door which is marked with a small sign that says "Clarimonda." Clarimonda what? I don't know. Something. Then I can knock and . . .

Up to this point I imagine everything very clearly, but I cannot see what should happen next. I know that the door opens. But then I stand before it, looking into a dark void. Clarimonda doesn't come. Nothing comes. Nothing is there, only the black, impenetrable dark.

Sometimes, it seems to me that there can be no other Clarimonda but the one I see in the window; the one who plays gesture-games with me. I cannot imagine a Clarimonda wearing a hat, or a dress other than her black dress with the lilac motif. Nor can I imagine a Clarimonda without black gloves. The very notion that I might encounter Clarimonda somewhere in the streets or in a restaurant eating, drinking or chatting is so improbable that it makes me laugh.

Sometimes I ask myself whether I love her. It's impossible to say, since I have never loved before. However, if the feeling that I have for

Clarimonda is really—love, then love is something entirely different from anything I have seen among my friends or read about in novels.

It is hard for me to be sure of my feelings and harder still to think of anything that doesn't relate to Clarimonda or, what is more important, to our game. Undeniably, it is our game that concerns me. Nothing else—and this is what I understand least of all.

There is no doubt that I am drawn to Clarimonda, but with this attraction there is mingled another feeling, fear. No. That's not it either. Say rather a vague apprehension in the presence of the unknown. And this anxiety has a strangely voluptuous quality so that I am at the same time drawn to her even as I am repelled by her. It is as if I were moving in giant circles around her, sometimes coming close, sometimes retreating . . . back and forth, back and forth.

Once, I am sure of it, it will happen, and I will join her.

Clarimonda sits at her window and spins her slender, eternally fine thread, making a strange cloth whose purpose I do not understand. I am amazed that she is able to keep from tangling her delicate thread. Hers is surely a remarkable design, containing mythical beasts and strange masks.

Thursday, March 17

I am curiously excited. I don't talk to people any more. I barely say "hello" to Madame Dubonnet or to the servant. I hardly give myself time to eat. All I can do is sit at the window and play the game with Clarimonda. It is an enthralling game. Overwhelming.

I have the feeling something will happen tomorrow.

Friday, March 18

Yes. Yes. Something will happen today. I tell myself—as loudly as I can—that that's why I am here. And yet, horribly enough, I am afraid. And in the fear that the same thing is going to happen to me as happened to my predecessors, there is strangely mingled another fear: a terror of Clarimonda. And I cannot separate the two fears.

I am frightened. I want to scream.

Six o'clock, evening I have my hat and coat on. Just a couple of words.

At five o'clock, I was at the end of my strength. I'm perfectly aware now that there is a relationship between my despair and the "sixth hour" that was so significant in the previous weeks. I no longer laugh at the trick I played the Inspector.

I was sitting at the window, trying with all my might to stay in my chair, but the window kept drawing me. I had to resume the game with Clarimonda. And yet, the window horrified me. I saw the others hanging there: the Swiss traveling salesman, fat, with a thick neck and a grey stubbly beard; the thin artist; and the powerful police sergeant. I saw them, one after the other, hanging from the same hook, their mouths open, their tongues sticking out. And then, I saw myself among them.

Oh, this unspeakable fear. It was clear to me that it was provoked as much by Clarimonda as by the cross-bar and the horrible hook. May she pardon me . . . but it is the truth. In my terror, I keep seeing the three men hanging there, their legs dragging on the floor.

And yet, the fact is I had not felt the slightest desire to hang myself; nor was I afraid that I would want to do so. No, it was the window I feared; and Clarimonda. I was sure that something horrid was going to happen. Then I was overwhelmed by the need to go to the window—to stand before it. I had to . . .

The telephone rang. I picked up the receiver and before I could hear a word, I screamed, "Come. Come at once."

It was as if my shrill cry had in that instant dissipated the shadows from my soul. I grew calm.

I wiped the sweat from my forehead. I drank a glass of water. Then I considered what I should say to the Inspector when he arrived. Finally, I went to the window. I waved and smiled. And Clarimonda too waved and smiled.

Five minutes later, the Inspector was here. I told him that I was getting to the bottom of the matter, but I begged him not to question me just then. That very soon I would be in a position to make important revelations. Strangely enough, though I was lying to him. I myself had the feeling that I was telling the truth. Even now, against my will, I have that same conviction.

The Inspector could not help noticing my agitated state of mind, especially since I apologized for my anguished cry over the telephone. Naturally, I tried to explain it to him, and yet I could not find a single reason to give for it. He said affectionately that there was no need ever to apologize to him; that he was always at my disposal; that that was his duty. It was better that he should come a dozen times to no effect rather than fail to be here when he was needed. He invited me to go out with him for the evening. It would be a distraction for me. It would do me good not to be alone for a while. I accepted the invitation though I was very reluctant to leave the room.

Saturday, March 19

We went to the Gaieté Rochechouart, La Cigale, and La Lune Rousse. The Inspector was right: It was good for me to get out and breathe the fresh air. At first, I had an uncomfortable feeling, as if I were doing something wrong; as if I were a deserter who had turned his back on the flag. But that soon went away. We drank a lot, laughed and chatted. This morning, when I went to my window, Clarimonda gave me what I thought was a look of reproach, though I may only have imagined it. How could she have known that I had gone out last night? In any case, the look lasted only for an instant, then she smiled again.

We played the game all day long.

Sunday, March 20

Only one thing to record: we played the game.

Monday, March 21

We played the game—all day long.

Tuesday, March 22

Yes, the game. We played it again. And nothing else. Nothing at all.

Sometimes I wonder what is happening to me? What is it I want? Where is all this leading? I know the answer: there is nothing else I want except what is happening. It is what I want . . . what I long for. This only.

Clarimonda and I have spoken with each other in the course of the last few days, but very briefly; scarcely a word. Sometimes we moved our lips, but more often we just looked at each other with deep understanding.

I was right about Clarimonda's reproachful look because I went out with the Inspector last Friday. I asked her to forgive me. I said it was stupid of me, and spiteful to have gone. She forgave me, and I promised never to leave the window again. We kissed, pressing our lips against each of our windowpanes.

Wednesday, March 23

I know now that I love Clarimonda. That she has entered into the very fiber of my being. It may be that the loves of other men are different. But does there exist one head, one ear, one hand that is exactly like hundreds of millions of others? There are always differences, and it must be so with love. My love is strange, I know that, but is it any the less lovely because of that? Besides, my love makes me happy.

If only I were not so frightened. Sometimes my terror slumbers and I forget it for a few moments, then it wakes and does not leave me. The fear is like a poor mouse trying to escape the grip of a powerful serpent. Just wait a bit, poor sad terror. Very soon, the serpent love will devour you.

Thursday, March 24

I have made a discovery: I don't play with Clarimonda. She plays with me.

Last night, thinking as always about our game, I wrote down five new and intricate gesture patterns with which I intended to surprise Clarimonda today. I gave each gesture a number. Then I practiced the series, so I could do the motions as quickly as possible, forwards or backwards. Or sometimes only the even-numbered ones, sometimes the odd. Or the first and the last of the five patterns. It was tiring work, but it made me happy and seemed to bring Clarimonda closer to me. I practiced for hours until I got all the motions down pat, like clockwork.

This morning, I went to the window. Clarimonda and I greeted each other, then our game began. Back and forth! It was incredible how quickly she understood what was to be done; how she kept pace with me.

There was a knock at the door. It was the servant bringing me my shoes. I took them. On my way back to the window, my eye chanced to fall on the slip of paper on which I had noted my gesture patterns. It was then that I understood: in the game just finished, I had not made use of a single one of my patterns.

I reeled back and had to hold on to the chair to keep from falling. It was unbelievable. I read the paper again—and again. It was still true: I had gone through a long series of gestures at the window, and not one of the patterns had been mine.

I had the feeling, once more, that I was standing before Clarimonda's wide open door, through which, though I stared. I could see nothing but a dark void. I knew, too, that if I chose to turn from that door now. I might be saved; and that I still had the power to leave. And yet, I did not leave—because I felt myself at the very edge of the mystery: as if I were holding the secret in my hands.

"Paris! You will conquer Paris," I thought. And in that instant, Paris was more powerful than Clarimonda.

I don't think about that any more. Now, I feel only love. Love, and a delicious terror.

Still, the moment itself endowed me with strength. I read my notes again, engraving the gestures on my mind. Then I went back to the window only to become aware that there was not one of my patterns that I wanted to use. Standing there, it occurred to me to rub the side of my nose; instead I found myself pressing my lips to the windowpane. I tried to drum with my fingers on the window sill;

instead, I brushed my fingers through my hair. And so I understood that it was not that Clarimonda did what I did. Rather, my gestures followed her lead and with such lightning rapidity that we seemed to be moving simultaneously. I, who had been so proud because I thought I had been influencing her, I was in fact being influenced by her. Her influence . . . so gentle . . . so delightful.

I have tried another experiment. I clenched my hands and put them in my pockets firmly intending not to move them one bit. Clarimonda raised her hand and, smiling at me, made a scolding gesture with her finger. I did not budge, and yet I could feel how my right hand wished to leave my pocket. I shoved my fingers against the lining, but against my will, my hand left the pocket; my arm rose into the air. In my turn, I made a scolding gesture with my finger and smiled.

It seemed to me that it was not I who was doing all this. It was a stranger whom I was watching.

But, of course, I was mistaken. It was I making the gesture, and the person watching me was the stranger; that very same stranger who, not long ago, was so sure that he was on the edge of a great discovery. In any case, it was not I.

Of what use to me is this discovery? I am here to do Clarimonda's will. Clarimonda, whom I love with an anguished heart.

Friday, March 25

I have cut the telephone cord. I have no wish to be continually disturbed by the idiotic inspector just as the mysterious hour arrives.

God. Why did I write that? Not a word of it is true. It is as if someone else were directing my pen.

But I want to . . . want to . . . to write the truth here . . . though it is costing me great effort. But I want to . . . once more . . . do what I want.

I have cut the telephone cord . . . ah . . .

Because I had to . . . there it is. Had to . . .

We stood at our windows this morning and played the game, which is now different from what it was yesterday. Clarimonda makes a movement and I resist it for as long as I can. Then I give in and do what she wants without further struggle. I can hardly express what a joy it is to be so conquered; to surrender entirely to her will.

We played. All at once, she stood up and walked back into her room, where I could not see her; she was so engulfed by the dark. Then she came back with a desk telephone, like mine, in her hands. She smiled and set the telephone on the window sill, after which she took a knife and cut the cord. Then I carried my telephone to the window where I cut the cord. After that, I returned my phone to its place.

That's how it happened . . .

I sit at my desk where I have been drinking tea the servant brought me. He has come for the empty teapot, and I ask him for the time, since my watch isn't running properly. He says it is five fifteen. Five fifteen . . .

I know that if I look out of my window, Clarimonda will be there making a gesture that I will have to imitate. I will look just the same. Clarimonda is there, smiling. If only I could turn my eyes away from hers.

Now she parts the curtain. She takes the cord. It is red, just like the cord in my window. She ties a noose and hangs the cord on the hook in the window cross-bar.

She sits down and smiles.

No. Fear is no longer what I feel. Rather, it is a sort of oppressive terror which I would not want to avoid for anything in the world. Its grip is irresistible, profoundly cruel, and voluptuous in its attraction.

I could go to the window, and do what she wants me to do, but I wait. I struggle. I resist though I feel a mounting fascination that becomes more intense each minute.

Here I am once more. Rashly, I went to the window where I did what Clarimonda wanted. I took the cord, tied a noose, and hung it on the hook . . .

Now, I want to see nothing else—except to stare at this paper. Because if I look. I know what she will do . . . now . . . at the sixth hour of the last day of the week. If I see her, I will have to do what she wants. Have to . . .

I won't see her . . .

I laugh. Loudly. No. I'm not laughing. Something is laughing in me, and I know why. It is because of my . . . I won't . . .

I won't, and yet I know very well that I have to . . . have to look at her. I must . . . must . . . and then . . . all that follows.

If I still wait, it is only to prolong this exquisite torture. Yes, that's it. This breathless anguish is my supreme delight. I write quickly, quickly . . . just so I can continue to sit here; so I can attenuate these seconds of pain.

Again, terror. Again. I know that I will look toward her. That I will stand up. That I will hang myself.

That doesn't frighten me. That is beautiful . . . even precious.

There is something else. What will happen afterwards? I don't know, but since my torment is so delicious. I feel . . . feel that something horrible must follow.

Think . . . think . . . Write something. Anything at all . . . to keep from looking toward her . . .

My name . . . Richard Bracquemont. Richard Bracquemont . . . Richard Bracquemont . . .

Richard . . .

I can't . . . go on. I must . . . no . . . no . . . must look at her . . . Richard Bracquemont . . . no . . . no more . . . Richard . . . Richard Bracque— . . .

The inspector of the ninth precinct, after repeated and vain efforts to telephone Richard, arrived at the Hotel Stevens at 6:05. He found the body of the student Richard Bracquemont hanging from the cross-bar of the window in room #7, in the same position as each of his three predecessors.

The expression on the student's face, however, was different, reflecting an appalling fear.

Bracquemont's eyes were wide open and bulging from their sockets. His lips were drawn into a rictus, and his jaws were clamped together. A huge black spider whose body was dotted with purple spots lay crushed and nearly bitten in two between his teeth.

On the table, there lay the student's journal. The inspector read it and went immediately to investigate the house across the street. What he learned was that the second floor of that building had not been lived in for many months.

THE MONKEY'S PAW

W. W. Jacobs

"The Monkey's Paw," a powerful, magical, cautionary tale, ranks among the most famous of all fantastic stories. Adapted for stage, screen, radio, television, and opera, its very title has entered the English language as a byword for a dangerous talisman. "The Monkey's Paw" is likely the most familiar tale in *The Weiser Book of the Fantastic and Forgotten;* yet, paradoxically, it's simultaneously a forgotten story. Virtually everyone knows the basic plotline, but few have actually read the original story. It is truly a tale of horror. Reading it, one understands why "The Monkey's Paw" captured the public imagination, transcending weird fiction to become a cultural touchstone in the same manner as Dracula or Frankenstein's monster. So many adaptations and parodies of "The Monkey's Paw" exist that it's almost impossible to list all of them, although the version in *The Simpsons's* "Treehouse of Horror II" is a special favorite.

William Wymark Jacobs (1863–1943), its author, was not a specialist in weird fiction, although "The Monkey's Paw" is not his only macabre tale. Much of his published work is humorous or thematically related to sailors or both. That said, his entire career would come to be overshadowed by "The Monkey's Paw," first published in 1902 in Jacobs's anthology, *The Lady of the Barge.*

The Monkey's Paw

"Be careful what you wish for, you may receive it."
—Anonymous

Part I

Without, the night was cold and wet, but in the small parlour of Laburnum villa the blinds were drawn and the fire burned brightly. Father and son were at chess; the former, who possessed ideas about the game involving radical chances, putting his king into such sharp and unnecessary perils that it even provoked comment from the white-haired old lady knitting placidly by the fire.

"Hark at the wind," said Mr. White, who, having seen a fatal mistake after it was too late, was amiably desirous of preventing his son from seeing it.

"I'm listening," said the latter grimly surveying the board as he stretched out his hand. "Check."

"I should hardly think that he's come tonight," said his father, with his hand poised over the board.

"Mate," replied the son.

"That's the worst of living so far out," balled Mr. White with sudden and unlooked-for violence; "Of all the beastly, slushy, out of the way places to live in, this is the worst. Path's a bog, and the road's a torrent. I don't know what people are thinking about. I suppose because only two houses in the road are let, they think it doesn't matter."

"Never mind, dear," said his wife soothingly; "perhaps you'll win the next one."

Mr. White looked up sharply, just in time to intercept a knowing glance between mother and son. the words died away on his lips, and he hid a guilty grin in his thin grey beard.

"There he is," said Herbert White as the gate banged to loudly and heavy footsteps came toward the door.

The old man rose with hospitable haste and opening the door, was heard condoling with the new arrival. The new arrival also condoled with himself, so that Mrs. White said, "Tut, tut!" and coughed gently as her husband entered the room followed by a tall, burly man, beady of eye and rubicund of visage.

"Sargeant-Major Morris," he said, introducing him.

The Sargeant-Major took hands and taking the proffered seat by the fire, watched contentedly as his host got out whiskey and tumblers and stood a small copper kettle on the fire.

At the third glass his eyes got brighter, and he began to talk, the little family circle regarding with eager interest this visitor from distant parts, as he squared his broad shoulders in the chair and spoke of wild scenes and doughty deeds; of wars and plagues and strange peoples.

"Twenty-one years of it," said Mr. White, nodding at his wife and son. "When he went away he was a slip of a youth in the warehouse. Now look at him."

"He don't look to have taken much harm." said Mrs. White politely.

"I'd like to go to India myself," said the old man, just to look around a bit, you know."

"Better where you are," said the Sargeant-Major, shaking his head. He put down the empty glass and sighing softly, shook it again.

"I should like to see those old temples and fakirs and jugglers," said the old man. "What was that that you started telling me the other day about a monkey's paw or something, Morris?"

"Nothing." said the soldier hastily. "Leastways, nothing worth hearing."

"Monkey's paw?" said Mrs. White curiously.

"Well, it's just a bit of what you might call magic, perhaps." said the Sargeant-Major off-handedly.

His three listeners leaned forward eagerly. The visitor absent-mindedly put his empty glass to his lips and then set it down again. His host filled it for him again.

"To look at," said the Sargeant-Major, fumbling in his pocket, "it's just an ordinary little paw, dried to a mummy."

He took something out of his pocket and proffered it. Mrs. White drew back with a grimace, but her son, taking it, examined it curiously.

"And what is there special about it?" inquired Mr. White as he took it from his son, and having examined it, placed it upon the table.

"It had a spell put on it by an old Fakir," said the Sargeant-Major, "a very holy man. He wanted to show that fate ruled people's lives, and that those who interfered with it did so to their sorrow. He put a spell on it so that three separate men could each have three wishes from it."

His manners were so impressive that his hearers were conscious that their light laughter had jarred somewhat.

"Well, why don't you have three, sir?" said Herbert White cleverly.

The soldier regarded him the way that middle age is wont to regard presumptuous youth. "I have," he said quietly, and his blotchy face whitened.

"And did you really have the three wishes granted?" asked Mrs. White.

"I did," said the Seargent-Major, and his glass tapped against his strong teeth.

"And has anybody else wished?" persisted the old lady.

"The first man had his three wishes. Yes," was the reply, "I don't know what the first two were, but the third was for death. That's how I got the paw."

His tones were so grave that a hush fell upon the group.

"If you've had your three wishes it's no good to you now then Morris," said the old man at last. "What do you keep it for?"

The soldier shook his head. "Fancy I suppose," he said slowly." I did have some idea of selling it, but I don't think I will. It has caused me enough mischief already. Besides, people won't buy. They think it's a fairy tale, some of them; and those who do think anything of it want to try it first and pay me afterward."

"If you could have another three wishes," said the old man, eyeing him keenly," would you have them?"

"I don't know," said the other. "I don't know."

He took the paw, and dangling it between his forefinger and thumb, suddenly threw it upon the fire. White, with a slight cry, stooped down and snatched it off.

"Better let it burn," said the soldier solemnly.

"If you don't want it Morris," said the other, "give it to me."

"I won't." said his friend doggedly. "I threw it on the fire. If you keep it, don't blame me for what happens. Pitch it on the fire like a sensible man."

The other shook his head and examined his possession closely. "How do you do it?" he inquired.

"Hold it up in your right hand, and wish aloud," said the Sargeant-Major, "But I warn you of the consequences."

"Sounds like the 'Arabian Nights'", said Mrs. White, as she rose and began to set the supper. "Don't you think you might wish for four pairs of hands for me."

Her husband drew the talisman from his pocket, and all three burst into laughter as the Seargent-Major, with a look of alarm on his face, caught him by the arm.

"If you must wish," he said gruffly, "Wish for something sensible."

Mr. White dropped it back in his pocket, and placing chairs, motioned his friend to the table. In the business of supper the talisman was partly forgotten, and afterward the three sat listening in an enthralled fashion to a second installment of the soldier's adventures in India.

"If the tale about the monkey's paw is not more truthful than those he has been telling us," said Herbert, as the door closed behind their guest, just in time to catch the last train, "we shan't make much out of it."

"Did you give anything for it, father?" inquired Mrs. White, regarding her husband closely.

"A trifle," said he, colouring slightly, "He didn't want it, but I made him take it. And he pressed me again to throw it away."

"Likely," said Herbert, with pretended horror. "Why, we're going to be rich, and famous, and happy. Wish to be an emperor, father, to begin with; then you can't be henpecked."

He darted around the table, pursued by the maligned Mrs White armed with an antimacassar.

Mr. White took the paw from his pocket and eyed it dubiously. "I don't know what to wish for, and that's a fact," he said slowly. It seems to me I've got all I want."

"If you only cleared the house, you'd be quite happy, wouldn't you!" said Herbert, with his hand on his shoulder. "Well, wish for two hundred pounds, then; that'll just do it."

His father, smiling shamefacedly at his own credulity, held up the talisman, as his son, with a solemn face, somewhat marred by a wink at his mother, sat down and struck a few impressive chords.

"I wish for two hundred pounds," said the old man distinctly.

A fine crash from the piano greeted his words, interrupted by a shuddering cry from the old man. His wife and son ran toward him.

"It moved," he cried, with a glance of disgust at the object as it lay on the floor. "As I wished, it twisted in my hand like a snake."

"Well, I don't see the money," said his son, as he picked it up and placed it on the table, "and I bet I never shall."

"It must have been your fancy, father," said his wife, regarding him anxiously.

He shook his head. "Never mind, though; there's no harm done, but it gave me a shock all the same."

They sat down by the fire again while the two men finished their pipes. Outside, the wind was higher than ever, and the old man started nervously at the sound of a door banging upstairs. A silence unusual and depressing settled on all three, which lasted until the old couple rose to retire for the rest of the night.

"I expect you'll find the cash tied up in a big bag in the middle of your bed," said Herbert, as he bade them good night, "and something horrible squatting on top of your wardrobe watching you as you pocket your ill-gotten gains."

He sat alone in the darkness, gazing at the dying fire, and seeing faces in it. The last was so horrible and so simian that he gazed at it in amazement. It got so vivid that, with a little uneasy laugh, he felt on the table for a glass containing a little water to throw over it. His hand grasped the monkey's paw, and with a little shiver he wiped his hand on his coat and went up to bed.

Part II

In the brightness of the wintry sun next morning as it streamed over the breakfast table he laughed at his fears. There was an air of prosaic wholesomeness about the room which it had lacked on the previous night, and the dirty, shriveled little paw was pitched on the side-board with a carelessness which betokened no great belief in its virtues.

"I suppose all old soldiers are the same," said Mrs White. "The idea of our listening to such nonsense! How could wishes be granted in these days? And if they could, how could two hundred pounds hurt you, father?"

"Might drop on his head from the sky," said the frivolous Herbert.

"Morris said the things happened so naturally," said his father, "that you might if you so wished attribute it to coincidence."

"Well don't break into the money before I come back," said Herbert as he rose from the table. "I'm afraid it'll turn you into a mean, avaricious man, and we shall have to disown you."

His mother laughed, and following him to the door, watched him down the road; and returning to the breakfast table, was very happy at the expense of her husband's credulity. All of which did not prevent her from scurrying to the door at the postman's knock, nor prevent her from referring somewhat shortly to retired Sargeant-Majors of bibulous habits when she found that the post brought a tailor's bill.

"Herbert will have some more of his funny remarks, I expect, when he comes home," she said as they sat at dinner.

"I dare say," said Mr. White, pouring himself out some beer; "but for all that, the thing moved in my hand; that I'll swear to."

"You thought it did," said the old lady soothingly.

"I say it did," replied the other. "There was no thought about it; I had just—What's the matter?"

His wife made no reply. She was watching the mysterious movements of a man outside, who, peering in an undecided fashion at the house, appeared to be trying to make up his mind to enter. In mental connexion with the two hundred pounds, she noticed that the stranger was well dressed, and wore a silk hat of glossy newness. Three times he paused at the gate, and then walked on again. The fourth time he stood with his hand upon it, and then with sudden resolution flung it open and walked up the path. Mrs White at the same moment placed her hands behind her, and hurriedly unfastening the strings of her apron, put that useful article of apparel beneath the cushion of her chair.

She brought the stranger, who seemed ill at ease, into the room. He gazed at her furtively, and listened in a preoccupied fashion as the old lady apologized for the appearance of the room, and her husband's coat, a garment which he usually reserved for the garden. She then waited as patiently as her sex would permit for him to broach his business, but he was at first strangely silent.

"I—was asked to call," he said at last, and stooped and picked a piece of cotton from his trousers. "I come from 'Maw and Meggins.'"

The old lady started. "Is anything the matter?" she asked breathlessly. "Has anything happened to Herbert? What is it? What is it?"

Her husband interposed. "There there mother," he said hastily. "Sit down, and don't jump to conclusions. You've not brought bad news, I'm sure sir," and eyed the other wistfully.

"I'm sorry—" began the visitor.

"Is he hurt?" demanded the mother wildly.

The visitor bowed in assent. "Badly hurt," he said quietly, "but he is not in any pain."

"Oh thank God!" said the old woman, clasping her hands. "Thank God for that! Thank—"

She broke off as the sinister meaning of the assurance dawned on her and she saw the awful confirmation of her fears in the others averted face. She caught her breath, and turning to her slower-witted husband, laid her trembling hand on his. There was a long silence.

"He was caught in the machinery," said the visitor at length in a low voice.

"Caught in the machinery," repeated Mr. White, in a dazed fashion, "yes."

He sat staring out the window, and taking his wife's hand between his own, pressed it as he had been wont to do in their old courting days nearly forty years before.

"He was the only one left to us," he said, turning gently to the visitor. "It is hard."

The other coughed, and rising, walked slowly to the window. "The firm wishes me to convey their sincere sympathy with you in your great loss," he said, without looking round. "I beg that you will understand I am only their servant and merely obeying orders."

There was no reply; the old woman's face was white, her eyes staring, and her breath inaudible; on the husband's face was a look such as his friend the sargeant might have carried into his first action.

"I was to say that Maw and Meggins disclaim all responsibility," continued the other. "They admit no liability at all, but in consideration of your son's services, they wish to present you with a certain sum as compensation."

Mr. White dropped his wife's hand, and rising to his feet, gazed with a look of horror at his visitor. His dry lips shaped the words, "How much?"

"Two hundred pounds," was the answer.

Unconscious of his wife's shriek, the old man smiled faintly, put out his hands like a sightless man, and dropped, a senseless heap, to the floor.

Part III

In the huge new cemetery, some two miles distant, the old people buried their dead, and came back to the house steeped in shadows and silence. It was all over so quickly that at first they could hardly realize it, and remained in a state of expectation as though of something else to happen—something else which was to lighten this load, too heavy for old hearts to bear.

But the days passed, and expectations gave way to resignation—the hopeless resignation of the old, sometimes mis-called apathy. Sometimes they hardly exchanged a word, for now they had nothing to talk about, and their days were long to weariness.

It was about a week after that the old man, waking suddenly in the night, stretched out his hand and found himself alone. The room was in darkness, and the sound of subdued weeping came from the window. He raised himself in bed and listened.

"Come back," he said tenderly. "You will be cold."

"It is colder for my son," said the old woman, and wept afresh.

The sounds of her sobs died away on his ears. The bed was warm, and his eyes heavy with sleep. He dozed fitfully, and then slept until a sudden wild cry from his wife awoke him with a start.

"THE PAW!" she cried wildly. "THE MONKEY'S PAW!"

He started up in alarm. "Where? Where is it? What's the matter?"

She came stumbling across the room toward him. "I want it," she said quietly. "You've not destroyed it?"

"It's in the parlour, on the bracket," he replied, marveling. "Why?"

She cried and laughed together, and bending over, kissed his cheek.

"I only just thought of it," she said hysterically. "Why didn't I think of it before? Why didn't you think of it?"

"Think of what?" he questioned.

"The other two wishes," she replied rapidly. "We've only had one."

"Was not that enough?" he demanded fiercely.

"No," she cried triumphantly; "We'll have one more. Go down and get it quickly, and wish our boy alive again."

The man sat in bed and flung the bedclothes from his quaking limbs. "Good God, you are mad!" he cried aghast. "Get it," she panted; "get it quickly, and wish—Oh my boy, my boy!"

Her husband struck a match and lit the candle. "Get back to bed," he said unsteadily. "You don't know what you are saying."

"We had the first wish granted," said the old woman, feverishly; "why not the second?"

"A coincidence," stammered the old man.

"Go get it and wish," cried his wife, quivering with excitement.

The old man turned and regarded her, and his voice shook. "He has been dead ten days, and besides he—I would not tell you else, but—I could only recognize him by his clothing. If he was too terrible for you to see then, how now?"

"Bring him back," cried the old woman, and dragged him towards the door. "Do you think I fear the child I have nursed?"

He went down in the darkness, and felt his way to the parlour, and then to the mantlepiece. The talisman was in its place, and a horrible fear that the unspoken wish might bring his mutilated son before him ere he could escape from the room seized up on him, and he caught his breath as he found that he had lost the direction of the door. His brow cold with sweat, he felt his way round the table, and groped along the wall until he found himself in the small passage with the unwholesome thing in his hand.

Even his wife's face seemed changed as he entered the room. It was white and expectant, and to his fears seemed to have an unnatural look upon it. He was afraid of her.

"WISH!" she cried in a strong voice.

"It is foolish and wicked," he faltered.

"WISH!" repeated his wife.

He raised his hand. "I wish my son alive again."

The talisman fell to the floor, and he regarded it fearfully. Then he sank trembling into a chair as the old woman, with burning eyes, walked to the window and raised the blind.

He sat until he was chilled with the cold, glancing occasionally at the figure of the old woman peering through the window. The candle-end, which had burned below the rim of the china candle-stick, was throwing pulsating shadows on the ceiling and walls, until with a flicker larger than the rest, it expired. The old man, with an unspeakable sense of relief at the failure of the talisman, crept back to his bed, and a minute afterward the old woman came silently and apathetically beside him.

Neither spoke, but sat silently listening to the ticking of the clock. A stair creaked, and a squeaky mouse scurried noisily through the wall. The darkness was oppressive, and after lying for some time screwing up his courage, he took the box of matches, and striking one, went downstairs for a candle.

At the foot of the stairs the match went out, and he paused to strike another; and at the same moment a knock came so quiet and stealthy as to be scarcely audible, sounded on the front door.

The matches fell from his hand and spilled in the passage. He stood motionless, his breath suspended until the knock was repeated. Then he turned and fled swiftly back to his room, and closed the door behind him. A third knock sounded through the house.

"WHAT'S THAT?" cried the old woman, starting up.

"A rat," said the old man in shaking tones—"a rat. It passed me on the stairs."

His wife sat up in bed listening. A loud knock resounded through the house.

"It's Herbert!"

She ran to the door, but her husband was before her, and catching her by the arm, held her tightly.

"What are you going to do?" he whispered hoarsely.

"It's my boy; it's Herbert!" she cried, struggling mechanically. "I forgot it was two miles away. What are you holding me for? Let go. I must open the door."

"For God's sake don't let it in," cried the old man, trembling.

"You're afraid of your own son," she cried struggling. "Let me go. I'm coming, Herbert; I'm coming."

There was another knock, and another. The old woman with a sudden wrench broke free and ran from the room. Her husband followed to the landing, and called after her appealingly as she hurried downstairs. He heard the chain rattle back and the bolt drawn slowly and stiffly from the socket. Then the old woman's voice, strained and panting.

"The bolt," she cried loudly. "Come down. I can't reach it."

But her husband was on his hands and knees groping wildly on the floor in search of the paw. If only he could find it before the thing outside got in. A perfect fusillade of knocks reverberated through the house, and he heard the scraping of a chair as his wife as his wife put it down in the passage against the door. He heard the creaking of the bolt as it came slowly back, and at the same moment he found the monkey's paw, and frantically breathed his third and last wish.

The knocking ceased suddenly, although the echoes of it were still in the house. He heard the chair drawn back, and the door opened. A cold wind rushed up the staircase, and a long loud wail of disappointment and misery from his wife gave him the courage to run down to her side, and then to the gate beyond. The street lamp flickering opposite shone on a quiet and deserted road.

ABOUT THE AUTHOR

JUDIKA ILLES fell in love with the magical arts as a child and has been studying them ever since. She is the author of numerous books about traditional spirituality, witchcraft, and the occult including *The Encyclopedia of 5000 Spells*, *The Encyclopedia of Witchcraft*, *Magic When You Need It*, and *The Big Book of Practical Spells*.

To Our Readers

Weiser Books, an imprint of Red Wheel/Weiser, publishes books across the entire spectrum of occult, esoteric, speculative, and New Age subjects. Our mission is to publish quality books that will make a difference in people's lives without advocating any one particular path or field of study. We value the integrity, originality, and depth of knowledge of our authors.

Our readers are our most important resource, and we appreciate your input, suggestions, and ideas about what you would like to see published.

Visit our website at *www.redwheelweiser.com* to learn about our upcoming books and free downloads, and be sure to go to *www.redwheelweiser.com/ newsletter* to sign up for newsletters and exclusive offers.

You can also contact us at *info@rwwbooks.com* or at

Red Wheel/Weiser, LLC
65 Parker Street, Suite 7
Newburyport, MA 01950